In the distance, he could see what had awakened him . . .

He strode toward it, dark boots splashing the water up against his shins. He shouldn't be so interested. And yet, his heart told him this was important. What he found stole the words from his tongue and the air from his lungs.

A woman lay in the water. Dark waves lapped against her cheeks and filled her hollow eyes with tiny pools of glistening ink. Her dark hair floated around her, nearly the same color as the water that surrounded her. A white gown hung from hollow shoulders, torn lace and bloodied fabric clinging to her otherwise pleasing form. A single lock of dark hair lay across her neck, like the delicious parting of flesh after all the blood had drained out, and he wondered what she was doing here. Why would she end up in his realm above all the others? She shouldn't be here.

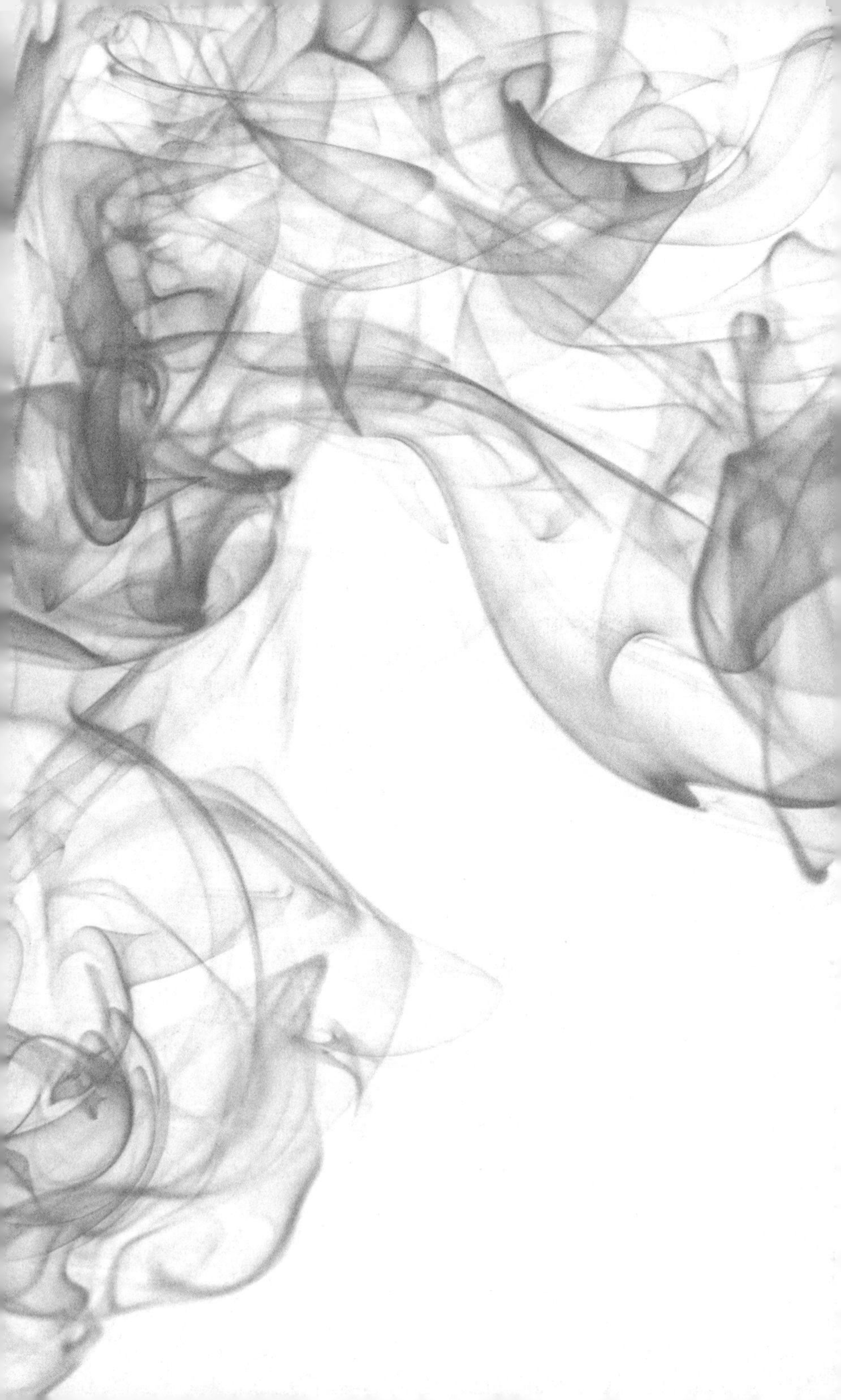

THE DEATHLESS ONE

EMMA HAMM

GALLERY BOOKS

NEW YORK   AMSTERDAM/ANTWERP   LONDON
TORONTO   SYDNEY/MELBOURNE   NEW DELHI

Gallery Books
An Imprint of Simon & Schuster, LLC
1230 Avenue of the Americas
New York, NY 10020

For more than 100 years, Simon & Schuster has championed authors and the stories they create. By respecting the copyright of an author's intellectual property, you enable Simon & Schuster and the author to continue publishing exceptional books for years to come. We thank you for supporting the author's copyright by purchasing an authorized edition of this book.

No amount of this book may be reproduced or stored in any format, nor may it be uploaded to any website, database, language-learning model, or other repository, retrieval, or artificial intelligence system without express permission. All rights reserved. Inquiries may be directed to Simon & Schuster, 1230 Avenue of the Americas, New York, NY 10020 or permissions@simonandschuster.com.

This book is a work of fiction. Any references to historical events, real people, or real places are used fictitiously. Other names, characters, places, and events are products of the author's imagination, and any resemblance to actual events or places or persons, living or dead, is entirely coincidental.

Copyright © 2025 by Emma Hamm

All rights reserved, including the right to reproduce this book or portions thereof in any form whatsoever. For information, address Gallery Books Subsidiary Rights Department, 1230 Avenue of the Americas, New York, NY 10020.

First Gallery Books trade paperback edition August 2025

GALLERY BOOKS and colophon are registered trademarks of Simon & Schuster, LLC

Simon & Schuster strongly believes in freedom of expression and stands against censorship in all its forms. For more information, visit BooksBelong.com.

For information about special discounts for bulk purchases, please contact Simon & Schuster Special Sales at 1-866-506-1949 or business@simonandschuster.com.

The Simon & Schuster Speakers Bureau can bring authors to your live event. For more information or to book an event, contact the Simon & Schuster Speakers Bureau at 1-866-248-3049 or visit our website at www.simonspeakers.com.

Interior design by Kathryn A. Kenney-Peterson

Manufactured in China

10 9 8 7 6 5 4 3 2 1

Library of Congress Cataloging-in-Publication Data has been applied for.

ISBN 978-1-6680-6312-5
ISBN 978-1-6680-6313-2 (ebook)

*For all the women who descended from witches who were burned.
They weren't witches, they were women.
And that rage is something none of us have forgotten.*

THE DEATHLESS ONE

1

"The gods died on a spring morning. All of them; all at once. Everyone could feel it, from the priestesses in the north, to the witches in the south. Those who worshipped the Maiden cried out in anguish. The meager few who still worshipped the God King fell to their knees in horror. . . ."

Her Majesty Jessamine Harmsworth blew out a long breath of frustration, taking the pencil from between her lips that she'd chewed into a ragged end. "I know all this. I know when the gods died, but what I don't know is how the witches caused the plague."

Her eyes ran over the book the vendor had slipped her in secret, his beady eyes looking left and right like he was committing a capital crime. In a way, he was. Books on black magic were forbidden throughout the kingdom. He didn't have to worry about her telling anyone, though. A princess wasn't supposed to have a black magic book at all.

"Really, did he think this would be helpful?" She cast a doleful look at the taxidermied skeleton of a cat on her shelf. Blank, soulless eyes stared back at her. "Well, you're not going to reply."

Poring over the words again, she searched for the origin of the sickness that continued to spread throughout her kingdom. The witches had long been rumored to have cast the spell. Jessamine had a hard time believing anyone would punish her kingdom like that after the gods died, so she searched for answers. What god had given them such power? Did witches still have any power after using all of it to create the plague? She had so many questions about the most powerful creatures that had ever existed in her kingdom.

Perhaps she shouldn't believe there was hope for their goodness, but no one had ever *proven* that the witches had done anything. Even so, all the blame was cast upon their shoulders, and as such, no one had asked the witches to help solve the problem.

Not that there were many of them left. Her great-great-grandfather had destroyed nearly all of them in the days after the gods had died.

Unfortunately, no one else had provided a cure for the plague. Their scholars and healers had slowed the plague's spread, but they were no closer to curing it.

She had just kicked her feet up on her desk to read more when she was interrupted by the awful sound of bones crunching and a wet slosh that could mean only one thing. She winced as the head of her royal guard wiped the gore off the bottom of his boot, scraping the worn leather against her door. The gold buttons of his dark navy uniform gleamed in the light and clinked against the sword strapped to his hip. He'd stomped the poor thing out of existence, but at least it hadn't suffered.

Never mind that it ruined the otherwise peaceful solace she'd found in her laboratory. It was only here, among the quiet bubble and hiss of burner flames, that she felt like herself. All manner of strange findings covered her walls, mostly bugs and beetles in jars, but a few lovelier specimens as well. Like a man's right toe she kept over her workstation.

But today couldn't be saved even by a jaunt through the book of black magic currently resting on her lap, a purchase she'd have hidden from anyone other than the man standing in her doorway.

After all, a bride-to-be in a wedding dress shouldn't be researching witchcraft.

"Is it dead?" she asked.

"What do you think, princess?" The man at least grimaced at his tone. But he was the only person who could get away with talking to her like that.

Callum Quen, after all, had been with her since she was a child. He'd been the one to kiss her bruises after she fell from the horse he'd taught her to ride. He had tucked her in at night when her mother had late meetings with her advisors. And he was the only one who knew how to brush her hair when she was very little, because the long dark locks tangled so easily. She hadn't grown up with a father. She'd grown up with Callum. He'd always been a good substitute.

She could see the disgust on his features. Clearly he hadn't wanted to stomp a rat on this day of all days, but one could never be too careful. The plague didn't care that she was getting married, and no one knew how it spread. Perhaps rats were the cause. Perhaps it was in the very air people breathed. It infected as it went, killing her people by the thousands while mostly staying out of her capital city.

Well, it would not be her capital city much longer. She was getting married, and her mother would abdicate the throne as soon as the ink dried. That would leave only her husband-to-be as the rightful ruler of Inverholm. He'd be the king of both her kingdom and his own now.

"What are you reading, anyway?" Callum asked, still looking at the bottom of his boot.

"A history book I bought from a rather strange peddler who appeared out of the mist. He claimed the history of the plague rested inside these pages."

"And?"

She sighed, fingering the worn edges of the pages. "Just more about the death of the gods."

"May they linger in the halls of the just," Callum murmured. "It would be good to see them again."

"You worshipped when you were younger, didn't you?" Even if the gods were gone, there were still stragglers. Those who believed that if they still paid their respects, perhaps the gods could feel it.

"The Warrior Son. I still do. On the days when things are hard, I like to think he can still hear us." Callum crossed his arms over his broad chest. "From what I've heard, your future husband also worships him—when his people are watching. His sacrifices should have been lavish enough to bring the god back. Perhaps his failure means that they are truly lost to us after all."

She wasn't sure why that made her stomach twist so. Leon Bishop of Orenda was said to be a suitable king, and he had sworn to take care of her kingdom. Even if her mother questioned why the man had propositioned her daughter after twenty-two years of growing up as counterparts in royal courts, he'd offered an answer to any doubts.

Turning to the full-length mirror hanging on the stone wall, she told herself to cast the thoughts out of her mind. No more magic. No more witchcraft. There was only the wedding.

Her reflection looked beautiful. She looked like the princess her people had come to expect.

The white gown fit reasonably well. It pinched in at her waist, creating a waterfall of lace that cascaded down to the floor. The bodice was modest, while still revealing the long, graceful line of her pale neck. Long bell sleeves covered her arms, a small blessing since she was hiding a few bruises, and a strand of diamonds that had been in her family for centuries sat at the base of her throat. The maid had successfully tamed her waist-length dark hair into a crown of braids at the top of her head, where a tiara was nestled among the dark locks.

But her haunted eyes ruined the entire vision. Too large. Too black. Surrounded by dark shadows because she hadn't slept a wink since this deal was signed six months ago. Her life, etched away on a piece of paper, and no one seemed to care that she'd been traded like livestock.

She straightened her shoulders and glared at her reflection. She was the princess of Inverholm. She would do whatever it took to save her kingdom. Jessamine would pull herself together, even if that meant fiddling with the gown until it was just right.

"Princess!" Callum lunged forward, and she froze in fear.

But then he pointed at her hands, and she realized she'd gotten some of the ash from her burners on her fingers. One touch, and she'd leave dark smudges all over her wedding dress.

"Ah," she whispered. Her hands shook as she wiped them off on a cloth nearby. "Thank you."

He nodded before clasping his hands behind his back. "I'll watch the wedding from the balcony. Good luck."

The knock she dreaded soon came, and she followed the train of royal attendants waiting for her down the dark halls. Much of their castle had to be reopened for the visiting neighbors. This wing hadn't even been furnished with the whale-oil lamps that illuminated the rest of her home. The new lighting made her normal chambers much more welcoming than the guttering torches of this unfriendly wing. Black soot seeped down from the ceilings, dripping through the stories above her head to meld with the years of candle smoke that stained the walls.

Her mother waited for her at the end of the hall. Queen Rhiannon of Inverholm was stunning, no matter what day it was. But on the day of her daughter's wedding, her mother was exquisite.

Gray hair curled carefully around her face, braided in intricate knots all the way down her back. Her azure gown was the same color as the depths of the sea that surrounded their peninsula kingdom. Gemstones decorated every limb, from neck, to wrist, to fingers. Her ears glimmered with more diamonds, but the stony expression on her face did not match her sparkling attire.

Jessamine bowed low. "Mother."

"You do not have to do this." The queen's voice echoed through the hall, bouncing back a hundred times before it faded. "We could yet save this kingdom."

They both knew it was a lie. The plague had cut them off at the knees. No one could work, and those who did got sick. The kingdom didn't have the money or the means to cure the plague, and if it were left unchecked, soon there would be no one in Inverholm at all.

"I wish to marry him." She stood strong and tall, her shoulders broad as they held the weight of her lie. "I wish to save my home."

Her mother's eyes saw straight through her, and Jessamine's heart ached, knowing the lie now stood between them. But one of them had to do something. And her mother had already tried and failed to fix this problem.

This was their last and only choice.

The queen nodded and held out her arm for Jessamine to take. Together, they descended through the darkness and stepped out into the brilliant sunlight illuminating the courtyard, where a crowd awaited.

Leon Bishop had brought a small entourage. A few dukes and duchesses all wore the customary black garb of his kingdom. All the others—guards, maids, and footmen—were in dark shades as well, though they stood out with their pressed white collars. They looked like guests at her funeral, and she'd never hated the color black more.

Her people intermingled with his, wearing navy and other shades of blue. Most of them were nobility, hoping to get a good word in before the merger of the kingdoms. All were running like rats from a sinking ship toward what they hoped might save them.

The image of them all wavered in front of her as her gaze turned inward. Her vision blurred and the crowd became a bruise that spread throughout her kingdom, smudges of black and blue, just like the ones hidden underneath the sleeves of her wedding dress.

Leon waited at the altar, all handsome golden man dripping in rich colors. In contrast to the shadowy shades he made his courtiers wear, he was clad in a pale cream suit edged in golden threads, the picture of conquering wealth, framed by the sea behind him. The entrance gates were now closed, the seal of her family crest ensuring they were locked—their giant raven spread its wings over the entire doorway. The courtyard became a balcony that extended out over the water, the only part of the castle without walls. A sheer cliff dropped down to the channel that led into the city.

She ignored everyone around her and instead stared out at her kingdom. Her home towered over the sea, and everything spread out from there. The Water District was tucked against the coastline, with its tall, five-story homes packed tightly against each other. All the city's water was first pumped through the sewers and then into the manufacturing plants for filtering. The Factory District lay to its left, belching out pillars of smoke. The Merchant District that spread thin beside the border so tradesmen didn't have to travel deep into Inverholm. Both the Pleasure District and the homes of the nobility were tucked up against the massive stairwell that led to the castle gates.

Leon had supplied his own priest, of course, and that left her mother to walk with her all the way to the front of the crowd. The onlookers took their seats as the priest intoned some nonsense about matrimony and gods.

She heard a whisper from the book of witchcraft. No god would bless their union. They'd all died years ago, and the echoing cries of her people in mourning trailed like ghosts through her mind.

Leon grabbed her hands in his, icy fingers lacing through her own. When he squeezed, she looked into his eyes and wondered if she'd ever find him handsome. Oh, he was fine enough. Everyone said so when the nobles from Orenda visited, which they did every year for the harvest festival. Golden locks often flopped in front of his eyes, and she'd seen many noblewomen brush that lovely hair back for him. His blue eyes were so pale they were nearly white in some lights. Angular features, broad shoulders: he was a handsome man by every regard.

She just didn't want him. Never had. Not when they were younger, and certainly not now.

They'd known each other since they were children, and she'd always seen the cruel edge to him. And now, after they'd sacrificed her to him, she could see it even more clearly. He'd arrived two nights ago with the rest of the Orenda guards. It had taken only a few hours for her to see that harsh nature again.

"Are you excited?" he asked quietly, his voice barely audible over the priest's droning.

Jessamine had no idea how to respond. No, she wasn't excited. She loathed the idea of getting into bed with him tonight, especially considering that she knew what he would expect. Kissing. Touching. Lingering underneath the covers, where so few men had ever touched her, and she didn't really want them to. Men were too . . . boring. She found far more excitement in researching witchcraft than in clumsy kisses and fumbling hands.

"I am," she replied. Her voice was a breathy whisper. A lovely sound that only a princess could make. She'd spent her entire life developing that exact sound.

"And you've given up all that . . . nonsense?" He stared at her a little too hard.

"I don't know what you're talking about."

His fingers squeezed hers almost to the point of pain. "I have friends in high places, remember? A little rumor reached my ears that you've been dabbling in magic."

"Magic? I'm researching ways to stop the plague." Jessamine wanted to rip her hands from his, but she didn't want to spark gossip in the crowd.

But who did he think he was? She was the crown princess of Inverholm! If she wanted to resort to witchcraft or black magic, then she would. If that was what it took to save her people . . .

A commotion erupted at the front gates. Loud voices, shouting, angry words thrown about too readily for a day of celebration. What was going on?

Leon's gaze only flicked in that direction before he squeezed even harder. The bones in her fingers flared white-hot with pain, and she let out a little gasp before she clenched her teeth to silence it.

"Jessamine," he hissed. "Are you still researching black magic?"

She could lie. She could tell him that she'd been a good little princess who would never touch a grimoire or spell book. Not in her life. Never.

But he planned to move into the castle, and he'd eventually find her workroom. He'd see all the glass jars full of specimens and items that no princess should touch. Bloody hearts. Black ooze. Scrapings from the infected and even a few fingers from the dead. All items used in dark magic. Not that she'd tried the spells herself, but she was researching.

Just in case. What if it helped?

What if no one else saw the answer, but she did? Her advisors were too afraid of what the covens might still do. They never tried to talk with the witches. They refused to do anything other than sit in their stupid prejudices and refuse to even consider other views.

So she straightened her shoulders and looked him dead in the eyes. "I am."

The front gates burst open. People surged through them, angry and rioting and . . . oh.

Oh no.

They were infected. Twenty men and women, their eyes swollen in their sockets, black pustules dotting down their exposed arms and up their necks. Even from this distance, she could see that the boils had broken open on many of them. They would infect anyone they touched, or whoever got near enough for that fluid to spread. At this stage, they moved in packs. Sticking together with other infected, sometimes quite literally, as they wandered through the streets of her kingdom.

Guards raced in after them, muskets at the ready and pikes held out to keep the infected at bay.

"Kill them all!" Leon shouted, and he half turned toward the intruders.

"Corral them as usual!" she shouted, turning already and lifting her skirts to run into the brawl. They had been herding the infected into groups and keeping them separate from others, just in case there was still a chance to save them. "Those are my people, Leon. You do not get to make that call."

"Oh, but I do." He reached for her, grabbing her arm and yanking her back. The bruises there, the ones he'd placed in the same way a few nights ago, screamed again. "Come here, princess."

"Let go of me!"

She struggled, but he wouldn't let her go. He hauled her to the front of the altar, shaking her hard enough to knock the tiara from the top of her head. It clanked against the ground, rolling down the steps and onto the stones as he shouted, "The princess admits to practicing dark magic! We all know the truth—the witches spread this plague! And your would-be queen sympathizes with these people who try to kill your loved ones. For the sake of both our kingdoms, I lay claim to this castle and to the people of Inverholm, *without* the guidance of the Harmsworth family."

The nobles in front of her froze. Her mother stared at her, wide eyes filled with fear. And Jessamine realized this was so much worse than she had ever dreamed.

This wasn't marrying a man for her people. It was fighting for her life as he threw her to her knees on the altar. It all happened so fast. His guards moved closer, swords raised, muskets held high, the sunlight gleaming off the edges of metal pointed at the nobility. She couldn't hear over the sound of thunder, but then realized it was her own heartbeat in her ears.

His people had let the infected in. A distraction so they could line up behind her people, preparing to take the lives of all those she loved so dearly. Already the infected were dead, killed by Leon's men, but so were most of her family's guards. Bodies littered the ground, their blood a shocking red against the pristine green-and-white marble cobblestones.

One of Leon's men stepped forward, the black of his uniform so dark it looked like ink. He beat a hand against his chest and shouted, "Long live the king!"

Others echoed the words, and Leon stood above her like a conqueror, as though he'd done this single-handedly when she knew he wasn't intelligent enough to do it on his own. Someone else was behind this. The thought burned so clearly through her heart it was like a brand, a premonition of truth that seared her very soul.

A few of her own nobles repeated the words, their eyes downcast, refusing to even look at her. Those who didn't echo the phrase were the first to fall.

Her mouth hung open as the sharp points of swords and blades atop muskets dug into flesh. They pierced through lace and velvet and silk, erupting from chests and bellies. Glistening bright red.

She couldn't hear their cries or their pleas. She couldn't hear anything but the insistent beat of her heart telling her, *Jessamine, get up. Get up. Do not let them die while staring at you on your knees.*

Breath shuddering in her lungs, she forced herself to stand. The fancy lace at the bottom of her gown ripped, tearing a hole all the way to her knee. The tattered white edge hung like a funeral shroud as she met her mother's gaze.

Her beautiful mother. Her darling, fearless, tenacious mother who had ruled this kingdom alone for twenty-two years after her father's death. Jessamine had never known him, but she hadn't had to. Her mother had been enough. Now a sneering, black-clad swordsman grabbed her, his blade clutched in his other hand.

"Thank you," Leon said, stepping up behind Jessamine and wrapping an arm around her shoulders. He held her back tight to his chest, his arm a prison that forced her to freeze as the guard wrestled her mother to standing. "Your kingdom will be the perfect way to save mine. Your nightmarish plague is spilling into other kingdoms, you see. So I will throw everyone who is infected here, and you can kill each other for all I care. This place will become a dumping ground for the dead and the dying."

"This is my home," Jessamine replied, her voice thick. "You cannot take it from me."

He inhaled deeply in her ear, and then sighed long and slow. "Oh, princess. I already have."

One of the guards slid his blade across her mother's throat. A gush of bright red erupted from the wound, spilling out and sinking into the deep blue sea of her dress. The hard set of her mother's eyes never changed. Her jaw clenched, her fingers fisted the fabric of her skirts, but she barely reacted. Through it all, the queen of Inverholm never flinched. She greeted death as an old friend and died with grace and beauty.

Any of the old guard, the still-living noblemen and noblewomen who had renounced them, would remember the moment when their queen had died for no reason. Their eyes turned as one to Jessamine.

She held herself stiffly, refusing to look afraid or even feel an ounce of that fear. Leon still held her, his arm around her shoulders, the prison he created with his body still strong.

"Should I let the infected have you?" he asked, his voice rumbling behind her. "Should I feed you to our mutual problem?"

She trembled in his arms but did not reply.

Leon tsked. "No, I think I'd best fix this permanently, rather than have you wandering around. After all, if I'm going to sit on the throne, I cannot have anyone threatening my claim."

The cold press of a blade against her throat should have frightened her. But she accepted her death with the glint of steel in her own gaze as she memorized every face of every traitor who had touched one of her people.

"Goodbye, Lady Jessamine," Leon murmured in her ear. He wrenched the knife across her throat, sending a kaleidoscope of pain through her entire body. And with a twist of his arms, he sent her tumbling over the edge of the cliff and into the sea.

2

His existence was only ice and pain.

Centuries of it.

Memories flickered through his mind. Bitter iron biting through his wrists after a hundred years of being chained to a wall. The hot sting of blades against his skin as they cut through his flesh for a single drop of ichor. The hissing laughter of a hundred witches as they used him, destroyed him, purged their hatred of the world by ripping out his organs and masticating what was left behind.

He was inevitable. The end for all things. And still they had destroyed him, bit by ever-darkening bit.

He couldn't remember much of the living realm. Only that the scent of green grass had once made his mind calm. He remembered the feather-light touch of yarrow as he ran his fingers through the fine white petals, like lace. And he remembered the shimmering darkness of a raven as it looked into his eyes and reminded him that all the gods were dead.

All but him.

That was right. The humans called him the Deathless One. He who escaped the end of all things. The end of magic and life itself.

All the gods were dead, they claimed. But one was still alive. One who lingered in the darkness, in the shadows, waiting . . . *waiting* . . .

For what, he could not remember.

He drifted through this endless night, his body floating on a lake as inky dark as the starless sky, his eyes staring unseeing into the mass of nothing above his head. Hadn't there used to be stars? He thought he remembered the little pinpricks of light that had always captivated him. He could have lain in a field and watched them for months if the sun hadn't come and washed them all away. Even then, he wouldn't mind staring into the sun just to savor the bright spots left in his gaze.

That was right. There had been stars. And a sun. And grass that tickled the back of his head, and little grasshoppers that bounced up and down his arms.

Until someone had come with a knife, reminding him that there was only one good end for a deathless god like him.

Sacrifice.

Pain.

Darker memories threatened to swallow him up again, sinking him into the muck. Dark hands rose out of the inky liquid, pressing against his face and digging into his jaw. They tried to turn his head toward the bitter memories, the ones that turned acidic and rotten in his mind.

But he wanted just a few more moments in that field. With the sun moving across dappled leaves, and the feeling of a breeze cooling the sweat on his skin. Oh, it had been wondrous, and the world had been so kind, until witches had found him and turned it all to shit.

Baring his teeth in a snarl, he ripped at the ink. The hands tried to pull him back, to make him wallow in the memories that seared through his very soul. He would not allow them to. Not this time. Not when he was so close to remembering the softer moments they always stole from his mind.

No, he would not linger in darkness today.

Pulling his way out of the inky darkness, he got onto his hands and knees. The darkness that bound him turned sharp-edged, plunging into his back and breathing all his memories back into him.

Years of being a god. An unending life of learning and living and taking whatever he wanted. Until the witches had claimed him as their own, until he'd claimed them in return. He had raised a city for them, a realm of power and magic. All of that would have been fine if it hadn't been for . . .

The ink turned into feet that stood before him. Delicate ankles that led up to shapely calves and curved thighs.

If it hadn't been for her.

Leaning back on his heels, the Deathless One stared up at the one witch who had changed it all. The one who had seen into his heart and saw him as a person, not a god.

She leaned down, the shapeless mass of her face rolling with black sludge, the long locks of her dark hair sliding over her shoulder. Her hand cupped his jaw, trying to force him back into the dark memories.

"You wanted us to worship you," she whispered. "And I did. Oh, Deathless One, I worshipped at your feet until you fell in love with me. And then what did you do?"

"I killed you," he whispered.

Perhaps not in practice, but in meaning. He had turned his back on them, and the witches had done what they must to fix what was broken.

He did not remember what had been broken all those years ago. But he did remember the last time they sacrificed him. When this witch had drawn him into her arms, kissed him into oblivion, and then laid him out on an altar.

The memories made him shake. "No," he whispered. "*You* killed *me*."

"I did." The darkness leaned down and pressed icy-cold lips to his cheek. "You were supposed to stay dead, godling. We took your power, all of it. We banished you here, and you were supposed to stay dead."

Yes, that was what had happened. The witches had taken all his power, and then he had felt them blinking out of existence. One by one. And then had died the lovely gravesingers, more than worshippers, vital to a god like him. A gift. An anchor to the real world, where he had never been able to create a strong tie. Every gravesinger sacrificed themselves along with him, and thus his ability to be resurrected had died with them. He'd been trapped here ever since.

They had all blinked out, until there was no connection but the shattered remains of a coven that hardly existed. And then they had left him alone to suffer for centuries. Banishment was not a strong enough word.

But though this realm in between life and death was created for his punishment, it was still his.

With a surge of power, he stood. The shape of the woman he had once loved tumbled out of existence, falling back into the darkness that threatened to drown him.

He turned away from the nebulous pool, ignoring how the hands clung to his boots, and remembered that this was a place he could control. How long had he been lost this time? So stuck in the bottom of that inky pit that he had forgotten who he was?

It wasn't the first time. It wouldn't even be the last. But something had awakened him.

He wandered for a while. But walking in darkness was difficult. So he lifted his hands above his head and twisted his fingers, rotating his wrist until a faint light illuminated the endless eddies of ankle-deep dark water.

"Yes," he murmured. "This will do."

In the distance, he could see what had awakened him. A lump. Too small to be a god visiting his realm. There were no other gods left, he reminded himself. And none had ever come to his realm, even when they were alive.

He strode toward it, dark boots splashing the water up against his shins. He shouldn't be so interested. It was too small to be of note, likely just another trick to pull him back into that slumber. To control him, as so many wished to. And yet, his heart told him this was important. So he went.

What he found stole the words from his tongue and the air from his lungs.

A woman lay in the water. Dark waves lapped against her cheeks and filled her hollow eyes with tiny pools of glistening ink. Her dark hair floated around her, nearly the same color as the water that surrounded her. A white gown hung from hollow shoulders, torn lace and bloodied fabric clinging to her otherwise pleasing form.

A single lock of dark hair lay across her neck, like the delicious parting of flesh after all the blood had drained out, and he wondered what she was doing here. Why would she end up in his realm above all the others?

Crouching beside her, he let his hands dangle off his knees as he looked her over. It wasn't right. Something about this wriggled in the back of his brain, like worms in a jar. She shouldn't be here. There was a realm for the dead, and she was supposed to go there. Why would she end up—

A memory hit him like a sledgehammer to the skull. And he remembered.

Oh, he remembered everything

He fell onto his knees, black water soaking through his pants. He was in a memory, kneeling with his arms tied above his head, twisted with rope and then dipped in molten silver that burned to the bone. He was surrounded by etchings marked on the ground and black candles already guttering. He'd been there awhile.

Footsteps clicked around him, too light to be those of a man. Then the woman rounded in front of him, all angular shadows and dark hair that made her look like a spectral figure. Perhaps she was. Perhaps she was all that remained of this memory.

"Deathless One," she murmured, her voice cast through the centuries and dulled by time. "There will be another who comes. The oracle has seen it. Another who can summon you back from the dead. One who can return all your stolen powers, and then it is up to you. You will either destroy this world, or rule it."

He remembered the sadness. The ache in his chest as he knew the woman made of ink had prevented him from doing . . . something. Something great.

"You have betrayed me," he found himself saying through swollen lips.

"I have to save my sisters and my coven. I have to give you up," she replied. Her mouth split open before she started to bleed. From her eyes, her lips, her nose. Even her ears gushed red liquid.

"Witch," he snarled.

The woman he had thought he loved, the one who was supposed to place him above all others, lifted a blade above her head. "Deathless One."

She brought the blade down, and the memory cast him back into this moment. With this woman. This figure who lay before him with her delicate hands resting in the ink, which twisted through her fingers like an old friend holding her hand.

This was madness. A gravesinger hadn't been born in over two hundred years, more than that if time had slipped away from him. And if she was one, she would never summon him willingly. He would be a plague upon her world and all others. Her kind had tried to kill him. Then they had trapped him.

He would destroy them all with a single breath, a single wave of his hand. Why was she here?

But his thoughts were scattered. It was hard to think past the rose-red bow of her lips and the strange dark slashes of brows that were a little too thick. She was so serious in her slumber.

He ghosted his fingers over the lock of hair across her throat and discovered it was not slumber but death, after all. The deep cut of a sword through her pale flesh had been made with violence, and he could easily see the threads of red that vibrated around it. She'd been murdered.

If he wanted salvation, then first he would need to save her.

"But saving a soul like yours isn't so easy, little nightmare," he muttered. "You cannot be so willing to die."

Pressing his hand down on the center of her chest, he drew out her soul. He expected to find a light, ephemeral thing, and was surprised to be greeted instead by darkness.

"A delicate casing for a much harder soul," he said. "How intriguing. Now let's see what kind of monster you are willing to become."

Rolling her soul up into a ball, he tossed it into the darkness and watched as it splintered into hundreds of pieces, memories she held dear to her heart. He walked among them, peering into the pieces like the shattered edges of a mirror. Her mother. Her laboratory. A book of magic. A dog that wagged its tail so fast, it frequently hit the appendage on walls and doorframes. Silly memories of a girl who had not seen enough of the world to know evil.

So how had this soul become so blackened?

Then he came to her wedding to a man who left bruises on her skin long before she'd agreed to the marriage. The loss of a kingdom. The loss of a mother.

"Curious," he mused as he stepped through the shards of her memories to peer into the futures that might be. Some of them were blank, revealing nothing at all. Her death, perhaps, or an afterlife that rejected her.

But then he saw the futures he'd been searching for. A woman with a dark crown made of black glass. A throne splattered with blood. Men and women afflicted by a plague that turned mortals into weeping husks of what they had once been. It was a tragic future, full of pain. But there was another. A similar crown, a similar throne, and two hands upon the armrests. Two hands from two different people.

Plucking that shard out of the air, he stared into it a little harder. Her delicate, pale fingers were covered in rings and clasped a man's hand. It was difficult to tell, but he recognized it as his own. They were seated upon a throne slowly sinking into a sea of blood.

It was perfect.

"Ah," he said. "So you are a gravesinger, after all."

He carried this future back to her, then stood over her limp body and pondered his choices. He could let her go. He could easily piece her soul back together and let it sink into her body. She'd drift through the beyond, out of his realm and into another, where she would join the dead. Perhaps she would never even know that she could have once been great.

Or he could use her, free himself from this place, manipulate her so she had no idea what his real plan was. When he was finished, when he was finally home, he would make sure she could not send him back. And so he kept the piece of her future that she would never know could become a possibility, and the rest of her soul he allowed to sink into the depths of his realm. Hands reached out of the inky darkness, each one clasping a piece of her and disappearing into the murk. Perhaps someday she would want those pieces back. Perhaps someday he would let her fight for them.

But not until he got what he wanted.

Crouching above her again, he gently ushered the water away from her eyes. The liquid poured down her temples like black tears. Though he should have felt pity for this poor creature, all he could feel was a sudden sense of relief. She had made it to his side. The witch who had betrayed him was not lying. There would come a day, very soon, when he would finally be free.

He placed her future in his pocket, then pressed his thumbs against her eyes and breathed out an ancient word, unknown in her language or any yet spoken.

It meant "life."

She arched into his hands like he'd struck her with lightning. Wide, horrified eyes stared up at him, eyes so dark he could almost see the lack of a soul in them. She opened her mouth, perhaps to scream, but he placed a single finger over those bloodred lips.

"No screaming," he said. "You will listen."

She nodded, clearly too terrified to speak.

"You are dead. And you will not remember this in a few moments. But I am who you think I am. Your soul has traveled to me, the Deathless One, and I will feast upon it if you wish. Or I can give you back your life so that you may fight another day."

He drew his finger away from her mouth, trailing the scarred tip over her plump lower lip.

She met his gaze without fear this time, a hardness settling inside her. "I want to fight. I want my kingdom back."

"Revenge is a dangerous game, little nightmare."

Still, she glared at him. No fear in her eyes any longer. Not even hope. Just anger and rage. "I want him to suffer for what he did to me. I want him to know how it feels to watch everyone he loves die, and then to see me standing above him with a knife."

"I will give you that." What a feral creature he'd found. He drew his hand along her jaw. "But you will give yourself to me. There will come a time when I have need of you, and you will not be able to say no. You will not like what I ask of you."

"Anything," she spat with surprising heat in her voice. "I will do anything."

"And so you will have a chance." He had never met a soul filled with such rage. He could hardly wait to understand what had given her such power. "But I want to see you burn your kingdom down and rebuild it in my name."

Without hesitation, she ground her teeth together and replied, "I will."

3

She tumbled through the darkness, rolling through the depths of death and some in-between place for which she had no name. It was cold. Bitter cold and biting against whatever she had left to feel.

Her mother, dead. Her family, gone. Her kingdom ripped from her hands without giving her even a chance to fight for it. She wanted to fight! She wanted to destroy everyone who had dared to take it from her.

Jessamine wanted a chance. That was all she was asking for.

In that darkness, she heard a voice. The black shifted underneath her eyes, and a figure stood above her, shadowy and obscured. She couldn't make out anything other than the silhouette of a trim waist, wide shoulders, and shaggy hair. A hand reached for her, thick and broad-fingered, scarred tips dancing above her face.

"And so you will have a chance," the voice murmured, low and rumbling. "But I want to see you burn your kingdom down and rebuild it in my name."

In her desperation, rage, and fear, she heard herself reply, "I will."

What madness had overtaken her? She did not know what monster visited her in this dark place. Nor did she have any clue what this deal might bring. But she felt . . . *him*.

Pulling. Tugging. Not letting her go when everything inside her screamed she needed to leave, to go deeper into the darkness and rest. But he wouldn't let her. And with one final, hard pull, suddenly she felt it all. The cold. The bitter aching. The pain.

Oh, the pain.

It felt like ages, but she slowly became aware of her body again. Of how much everything hurt. Every inch of her burned with the heat of a thousand suns, and her throat . . .

"Is it . . . alive?" someone asked, the voice heavily accented.

"Och, aye, I think it's alive. Did you see it twitch?"

Something hard nudged her side. A shoe? No, it would be too dangerous to touch someone who might have the plague with even a shoe. They'd prodded her with a stick, most likely.

With a low moan, she rolled away from the jabbing pain that made her ribs spasm. She ached, and the last thing she needed was yet another injury to add to the thousands that prickled over her entire body.

The first voice harrumphed. "Oh, it's alive, all right. Sorry sap prolly got dumped over the cliff after they found out she was infected. Wot a shame. Pretty body and all that."

"I'm not—" Her voice didn't sound like her own. Rusty and rough, like she'd been screaming for hours on end. "I'm not infected."

"It can speak!" the second voice said, decidedly more high-pitched than the first. She didn't think it was female, more likely that of a child. "I didn't know the infected could speak."

"You 'aven't 'eard 'em before? Mumbling about, constantly making those awful moaning noises?"

"I never really stopped that long when I saw 'em." The child, and it had to be a child, made a spitting noise.

Jessamine reared away from the two when she felt the wet wad hit the back of her head. Her entire body cracked as she stood, or maybe it wasn't her body, but whatever covered her. Black mud had hardened all over her skin and clothes, like a prison of darkness that left stains in its wake. The mud crumbled, shattering into dusty patterns as she moved. She scraped at her eyes, ripping the pieces away until she could finally open them and cast a dark-eyed glare at the two figures.

She was right: a boy and his father, presumably. They looked enough alike, their skin leathery from too many years in the sun. Their clothes were ripped and moth-eaten, patched with different colors. The boy had a smudge of black on his cheek. The same substance that covered her, she thought.

They both jerked back at her movement, and the man dropped the stick he was holding. He made a gesture with a circle of his pointer finger and thumb, flicked the rest of his fingers upright, and held his hand to his eye to ward off evil. "I've never seen black eyes like that."

She tried to look around, but it was so dark she couldn't see very far. Small green lights flickered on the walls. They were in a tunnel of some sort. A shallow channel of water cut through it, with walkways on either side. She was in the muck, covered in who knew what, along with brackish seawater. Thigh-high in muck and refuse, she could only be in one place in her kingdom. The sewers funneled into the sea, and likewise, the sea belched back into the sewers. The two people were standing on the grated walkway above her, which had already rusted through in a few places.

Jessamine reached for the metal grate but paused when the father's hand snuck into his pocket. A weapon? Surely the man wouldn't draw a weapon on her!

The boy gasped and made the same gesture. "The Deathless One has touched her."

"No one has touched me," she snarled, shakily trying to get her balance. They needed to get out of her way. She had to get back to the castle. Her people needed her, and they had no idea what Leon was planning. She had to—

No, that would be too dangerous. Leon likely had all his men already there.

Who could she trust?

None of the nobles had stood beside her mother, at least none that were still alive. The guard had likely changed over. Not that she really knew too many of the key players there, but there had to be someone left still loyal to the queen, and therefore loyal to her.

Where could she go? Nowhere was safe any longer.

Eyeing the two figures, who had already moved away from her, clearly uncomfortable, she decided they weren't an option. They wouldn't help her. They thought she was infected or cursed.

"Wot?" the boy asked, and she couldn't remember what they'd been talking about. "You never 'eard of the Deathless One?"

Ah, right.

"I have." She tried not to list left or right, her body shuddering with exhaustion. "He's not real. And if he ever was, he died with the rest of the gods."

The two looked at each other and burst out laughing. The sound wasn't happy, though. It was mirthless and cruel, and they didn't stop until she glared ever harder at them.

At least the man had the manners to cough into his hand, but it was his son who made a slashing motion over his own throat. "You've already been touched, lady. You might not believe in 'im, but 'e sure does believe in you."

Her hand flew to her throat, and there it was. Not a scabbed wound as she expected, but the thick rope of a scar. That wasn't possible. How long had she been out? For that matter, how had she survived the throat cutting? The fall? The mad tumble into the sea and the funneling of her body into the sewers of her kingdom?

"A mirror," she croaked, snapping her fingers at the man. "Surely one of you has a pocket mirror?"

"Ye'll get me infected," he grumbled.

"Again, do I look infected?"

"'Ow would one be able to tell? You're covered in muck."

"And many other things, I'm sure." She shook her arms out at her sides, trying once again to dislodge the mud. "I'm not infected. I'm covered in mud and somehow survived a murder attempt, and all I want is a shower and a comfortable bed."

The older man scratched his head, and she swore she saw two bugs tumble onto his shoulder. "Well, if ye ain't infected, I suppose we can 'elp get ye out of 'ere. It's a long walk, though."

At this point, she'd walk miles on end if she got to fall asleep in something that wasn't a sewer. "I really don't care."

"Ye say that now, but you'll be complainin' in just a few. Mark my words." He crossed his arms over his chest and nodded at his boy. The child held out a hand, as though he was . . . expecting something?

Payment? Really?

She stared up at them in shock. "You find a woman who clearly needs your help, alone in a sewer, and you expect me to pay you?"

"Aye," the older man said.

"Wha—" Jessamine shoved her pride down. If that was what it took, then that was what it took. She would not look at this as anything other than the gift it was. She did not know where she had landed. She had no idea how to get home, and she was alone. She would be grateful, and she would be kind. That was the only thing she could do.

If she gritted her teeth while moving mud away from the engagement ring on her finger, then it was only in frustration. She supposed it would only be a good thing for Leon to find out his ring had been peddled in a market somewhere. Let him think someone had taken it from her dead body.

"This is all I have." She deposited it in the boy's hand. "It's worth a fortune. Sell it. I don't care."

He turned it this way and that, letting the meager green light filter through the shiny diamond. "Looks real."

"It is."

He put it in his mouth and bit down hard. At his yelp, his father smacked him upside the head. "Not so 'ard."

"Feels real, too," the boy grumbled, rubbing his head as he slid the ring into his pocket.

His father stared at her a little too hard. A woman with a diamond ring of that size wasn't likely to end up in the sewer system. She braced her shoulders and stared right back at him. He could look all he wanted, but he would never guess who she really was.

"Now, what are we calling ye, then?" the man asked.

Those eyes never moved from her, dancing over what was likely a very dingy gray gown, if he could see the small bits of it revealed through the mud. Her hair had frozen in place, but she could feel sore spots on her scalp where the tiara had ripped strands out. She looked terrible, and she knew it. That, fortunately, would work in her favor.

"Alyssa," she muttered, reaching out her hand for their help. The name had belonged to her first governess, an elderly woman who had passed away years ago. "My name is Alyssa."

"Anders and Pike." The old man pointed to himself and then his son. "We're only getting ye out, lass. That's it."

"That's all I need."

He took her offered hand, and he hauled her out of the muck like she weighed nothing at all. She landed on her hands and knees on the walkway, staring through the grate at the dim murk below her. Neither of them offered to help her stand.

They turned from her, walking into the darkness as though the dim green light was plenty for them to see by. She could barely see her own hand held up in front of her eyes. But she tried to follow them, with her hand on the wall and her breath shuddering in her lungs.

She'd lied to them—and to herself. Jessamine needed so much more than help getting out of the sewers. She needed a safe place to stay, someone to listen to her who wouldn't sell her out to Leon's men. What if she'd been asleep for a few days? Her knees were shaky enough to make her think something strange was happening here. She shouldn't have been able to survive the fall, let alone live through the water filtration system.

Swallowing hard, she recognized she couldn't say any of this to these people. She didn't even know if they were leading her out of the sewers or deeper into the darkness. What if they weren't trustworthy?

Suddenly she noticed the twitchy way Anders kept looking back over his shoulder. Pike kept touching her ring in his pocket, rolling it between his fingers as he looked back at her as well. For some reason, the constantly rippling fabric made her nauseous.

What were they thinking? That she would be easy to rob? Were they going to betray her?

Like everyone else.

The air in her lungs froze as her heart rate sped up. She couldn't think beyond the utter terror that she'd trusted the wrong people again. But who could she trust? It seemed everyone in this damned kingdom would give her up to Leon in a heartbeat. Someone had introduced that man into the castle. Someone had to have been working with him, because there wasn't a chance that he'd flipped her court so easily on his own.

Killing the queen should have made the guards rise up. Someone should have fought against Leon. There were plans in place in case someone tried to take the life of a royal. Her mother wouldn't have let that happen without *reason*.

There was no air left. She was suffocating in the sewers, and these people would do whatever they wanted and then they would toss her body back into the sea.

A dark voice whispered in her mind. A voice like the sound of rustling velvet and slithering snakes. *I want to see you burn your kingdom down and rebuild it in my name.*

She'd made a deal.

She intended to keep it.

The first ladder they passed by was her opportunity. Neither man looked at it. In fact, they'd crossed the channel long before the ladder came into view, slogging through the muck to get to the other side. Hiding the ladder from her? Perhaps. She swore she could hear the moaning sounds of the infected echoing down the tunnel, and she refused to allow yet another person to trick her.

"'Ey!" Anders shouted the moment he noticed her bolt in the opposite direction.

The water was up to her waist this time, harder to get through. But adrenaline rushed through her veins, strengthening her, urging her forward. Jessamine hauled herself up onto the other side and lunged for the ladder.

She clambered up so quickly she thought the others might not have even gotten across yet. All that was left of her was a faint smattering of black sludge as she grabbed the ring of the vent above her head, twisted it in a circle, and shoved hard. The opening flooded with light, burning her eyes and sending the world into sparkles, but she didn't care. She was free.

Jessamine tumbled out onto the street, turning at the last second to close the vent behind her. Instead of the two people she expected to see, all she saw was a dark figure standing at the base of the ladder.

The frightened, fluttering heart in her chest recognized him before her mind did. She knew that dark shadow, the broad shoulders and thick fingers that held on to the rungs. But this time, she could see his eyes. Nothing else. Just those black, soulless eyes that stared so deeply into her own.

Looking at him was like looking into oblivion.

Then she heard it again. The thunder of her own heart, beating in her ears and casting out all other sounds, warning that she stared at a predator. She was looking at death itself, and she needed to go. *Jessamine, why aren't you moving?*

With a gasp, she shut the heavy cover and locked it so hard she felt her bones grind together. Scuttling back from the entrance, she didn't stop until her back slammed into the stone wall of a building behind her.

She realized that she was in an alleyway. To her left was the sea, the waves lapping at the stone that angled beneath them. To her right, men and women were setting up stalls filled with fish. The scents overwhelmed her. Ocean, fish, blood. There was so much blood.

Jessamine lifted her hands and realized she was sitting in a river of it. Red fluid, all coming down from the fish stalls in streams on either side of the street. Her palms were stained crimson like her mother's dress after blood had fountained out of her wound. Red like her palms when she'd tried so hard to stanch the bleeding around her own neck, praying that she wouldn't die before she hit the waves so hard they felt like stone.

Cold water poured over her head, dousing her entire body with icy seawater. Spluttering, she stood, shaking off the droplets and blinking through the stinging ache.

A round woman stood in front of her, a now-empty bucket clutched in her hands. "You're filthy, love. Just helping you out."

Helping her out? By dumping a bucket of dirty water over her head?

Jessamine couldn't breathe. She couldn't think. The tall buildings loomed over her head, drawing closer, sinking tighter, until she could barely see the faint strip of sunlight through the gap between the stones. They'd bury her alive. She'd die again, and she'd *made a deal*.

Stumbling away from the woman and the laughter of the fishermen, she found the next alleyway and disappeared into it. Frantically turning left, right, straight, whatever way led her farther and farther from people.

Until she found a small nook between two empty crates and tucked herself there. Shivering, terrified, and utterly alone.

4

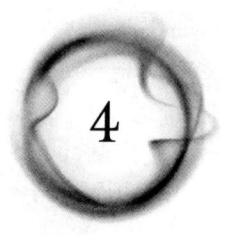

He couldn't get her future out of his head. Because her future was his future, and they were inextricably linked. She was a witch who could raise him. A witch who could finally bring him back into the land of the living, which he had missed so much.

When?

He did not know.

A gravesinger hadn't been born in hundreds of years. Her kind had made certain that they would not be born again, not wanting to give him the opportunity to raise himself and seek his vengeance. Witches like her were rare, and witches of any sect had been nearly wiped out. But before she could free him, she would have to learn.

The Deathless One had control only in his realm of darkness and sleep. The living realm remained just out of his reach without the witches to anchor him. But he and this girl were not anchored together. He had no way of knowing when she would seek him out—but gravesingers always did. They were lost without their connection to a god, and he was all that remained.

The gravesingers had sacrificed themselves many years ago, but there were still plenty of people who remembered what it was to worship a god and know the blessing of that god's favor. Witches remained, even some still connected to him. Though they were in hiding, he could find them. There were ways to see into their realm, to reach out to those who still walked the ancient path.

Conjuring a mirror in front of him, made out of inky oil that dripped onto his toes, was far easier than he had thought it would be. The Deathless One had spent so many years in this sad place, he had forgotten his innate power. A god did not have to wait for the witches. His magic came from deep within his bones. Yes, these old memories threatened to swallow him up, but they did not control him. Not entirely. Not yet.

Clutching the edges of the cold mirror in his hand, he peered into her realm. He sought out his little nightmare. The woman who had been born for him, to whom he'd given new life to fulfill her purpose and satisfy his revenge. But what he found disappointed him. She had not stormed back to her castle and rained havoc down upon the head of her murderer. No, she had gone to the streets, slithering about in the shadows like a snake cringing from the slightest movement.

Why? She was powerful. Capable of anchoring him to the living realm and tying him to reality. Soon, she would be linked to him. Surely she felt it. She must have seen that her gaze now mirrored his, haunted and black as night. Instead, she scuttled from shadow to shadow, hiding behind barrels with haunted wide eyes.

That . . . disturbed him.

He didn't remember why until after a few days of watching her movements. He saw her steal food from a vendor, who chased her off with a knife in his hand. She tripped over her skirt and fell into a mud puddle, and the man had snatched the bread back with a sneer and left her there. She lay shivering in the water, her head bleeding from where she'd hit it against the cobblestones.

She was filthy. Ragged around the edges. Clearly in need of help, and yet no one reached out to her. This was not the city he had helped his witches build.

In his time, the witches were powerful. They had been scorned like this in his early days of godhood, until he had reached out a hand to them. He'd made them powerful. Dangerous. Terrifying to all who looked upon them.

No one would dare treat a witch the way this human refuse treated her. They wouldn't dare look at a witch with pity or refuse her entry to their home.

His little nightmare flinched again, freezing in fear before darting away to hide. Then he saw them. Figures standing at the end of the alleyway she'd walked into. He needed to see more. Stretching his awareness, he sent his mind down that street through the darkness on windowpanes and the inky black of puddles underneath their feet. Then he remembered.

A plague. A sickness unlike anything this realm had seen. These people stood frozen in the streets, their arms bent awkwardly at their sides like they didn't remember how to hold them. Pustules burst all over their bodies, revealed through the tears in their clothing. Slack-jawed, they remained still as if listening for their next prey. They had but one urge: to find the next person to infect.

So, his last witches had failed. Even though they had murdered their own god, forsaking all their future power, they had not saved the kingdom that had hunted and feared them for centuries. Self-sacrifice, in the end, had earned them nothing.

The coven.

There were few alive who still worshipped the dead god they had killed and thereby condemned their world to utter madness. But he could feel them, living, breathing, practicing. All he had to do was reach out.

Casting one last glance back to his frightened, frozen deer in that alleyway, he turned his attention away from the witch who could awaken him. She would find her own path, he was confident of that. Though she was terrified and surely felt as though everyone had abandoned her, he knew the truth.

Lady Jessamine Harmsworth would soon have the most powerful patron she had ever dreamed of. And together, they would lay waste to all who stood in her way.

He let his powers stretch, reaching for any who still had a tie with him. When he followed that meager, thin thread, he was surprised to find its end in the same place his last coven had made their home.

From what he recalled, the witches lived in a luxurious manor at the edge of the sea. He remembered beautiful rooms filled with carvings of deities from times long past. Every statue of a dead god was decorated with flowers, filling the ancient cracks and wounds of battle with beauty and life that burst into bright colors whenever they bloomed. He'd thought it poetic in the grand home made of marble and luxurious stone.

That home no longer stood.

While the gravesinger might not yet worship him, she had given him a gift. Flexing his power, he could feel the connection to the living realm become stronger. More real. No longer was he tied entirely to this place of darkness. Peeling his own shadow off and sending it into the living realm, he lingered in the shade of a tree and saw a home abandoned. The manor had been consumed by time. One side of the building was exposed to the elements, blasted open in some battle the witches had lost without his help. Crows wheeled overhead, vultures joining them in a haunting call that grated on his nerves. Slipping through every dark and dim corner he could find, he moved inside.

Moss covered the broken tiles of the once-stunning marble floor. Grass grew on the rotting windowsills, twigs and branches spilled in through shattered glass. Chandeliers still hung cockeyed overhead in almost every room, but now they were covered in dust and cobwebs. The drapes had long since rotted into small piles by every window. Shards of mirror on the floor reflected the darkness that barely looked like his shape as he moved through rooms that had not seen the sun in years.

How long had it been since he last died? How long had it been since he'd tended to his coven?

One of the piles under a window moved, shifting into focus as a woman suddenly appeared before him. She stood tall and confident, although she was a mere specter of what a witch should be.

"What demon disturbs the home of a witch?" she asked, her voice raspy with disuse. "You are not welcome here, dark spirit."

"Do not attempt to banish a god," he snarled. The anger at her response felt unusual. He hadn't felt emotions in such a long time. He hadn't even realized he still could. "Whom do you serve?"

"I serve no one."

He lunged forward, a hand made of ink and oil gripping her throat. Oh, he could touch her. Interesting. He hadn't touched anyone in the living realm in centuries, and without his body, without being summoned, he was so limited in his power. In this form he could touch only one of his own witches—and this seemed a paltry one indeed.

Dragging her closer to his featureless face, he tilted his head as he growled, "There is but one god you serve, witch."

She croaked, "All the gods are dead."

"I am not dead."

He released her, letting her fall to the floor, gasping to fill her weakened lungs. His black handprint remained on her neck. She served him still.

He surveyed the last of his coven, kneeling before him. She was a dark-skinned woman, her hair pinned back in neat braids. She looked... healthy. And that simply was not possible considering how long he had been gone.

"What year is it?" he asked.

"It has been two hundred and seventy-five years since the last god died," she replied, before looking up at him with wide eyes filled with determination. "After you were last sacrificed."

He crouched before her, looking into those dark eyes that he knew had seen so much. "Prove it."

She knew he didn't mean the year. She lifted her hands, poking them out of her sleeves to reveal how the centuries had twisted them. Crumpled, curled in on themselves, wrinkled beyond belief, they looked more like the hands of a mummy than those of a living creature. But that was not what he wanted to see. All witches paid a price for their magic.

She grasped the collar of her dress, shakily unbuttoning it before she pulled the halves to the sides and revealed the skin beneath. From her collarbone to just below her left breast was a crack in her skin, a tear as if two pieces of a stone had split apart and revealed a void beneath. Darkness shimmered there, shadows reaching out for him. It was the last well of her magic, held together by a spell that bound her to him.

It was so lovely to see again. Reaching out, he gently coiled one of those shadows around his finger and pulled it out of her chest. She hissed out an angry sound, watching him with no small amount of hatred in her gaze.

"There is not much left," she grumbled. "If you take it all, there will be nothing left for me."

"I gave it to you in the first place," he replied, lifting the shadow so he could see the tendril reaching for his face. Strangely, he could feel the darkness of his features splitting open like a black maw, jagged teeth salivating at the thought of devouring his old magic. "I can take it back whenever I wish."

"You are here for a reason, Deathless One."

"I'm certainly not here to see you." He dropped the tendril into his open mouth, feeling it wriggle deep inside his body and join the rest of his power. It had been so long since he'd tasted his own power flavored with the taint of witch, but instead of nectar, this magic was but ashes on his tongue. There was no flavor in this form, no kindness without resurrection. "I am to be reborn."

"There was a prophecy, but no one has been born with your mark. Perhaps the oracle spoke false."

"What is your name, witch?" He stood, motioning for her to do the same.

"Sybil, sire."

"You will find the gravesinger for me and bring her here." He turned his attention to the statue in this room. He knew this figure well. An altar stood before it, one upon which many witches had sacrificed to his sister. They would cut open a chicken for her every month during their bleeds, allowing the black cock's blood to seep onto the stone.

The hollow eyes of her statue mocked him. She was a triple-faced goddess in her time, being maiden, mother, and crone. Combined, she had been a deadly creature who knew how to both nurture and destroy. She had never once flinched away from her nature, born in gruesome gore and violence. What he wouldn't give to see her one last time.

He touched his fingers to his forehead, then flicked them at her. "Sister. The Many-Faced Mother. Our world is worse without you in it."

The world needed women who were willing to put aside their kind or nurturing natures. It needed women who could fight and scream and bleed until the very earth understood the burden of their pain.

He turned his attention to the witch standing beside him. She gestured to the altar, still faintly darkened. "I keep the old ways alive."

"I can see that."

"How am I supposed to find this woman? For all I know, she has not even been born yet."

"She has. I saw her." He turned his head to look up at the moss hanging from the ceiling, then ground his teeth together in anger. "You live in squalor."

"I live." Sybil shrugged when he looked at her. "There are so few witches left, Deathless One. If I remain here in secret, then I remain alive. That is all I wish to do."

"You fear joining the others." It was not a question.

She nodded, the motion nearly knocking her over. The rags hanging off her rippled with her movement. "I was not always loyal to the coven. And I was not here at your last sacrifice, so I did not absorb the magic your death provided. I was the weakest."

He surveyed her, running his tongue over his teeth. "No, not the weakest. You were the only one brave enough to survive."

He strode past her, toward the inner depths of his manor, where he knew there was still an altar for him. Pausing, he pulled off some of the inky darkness that made up his body. It was painful, but he was used to pain. In the realm where his soul actually lingered, he could feel his flesh splitting apart as it always did when he tore himself. Like the magic ripped back at him.

But then those dark tendrils, far more than he'd taken from her, sank into the crack of her chest. They burrowed deep inside her, and for a moment, she arched into his touch, sucking in a deep breath of pain before relaxing in ease.

"There," he murmured. "You have your payment from me, for your many years of loyalty."

"Deathless One, I cannot—"

He reached into the cavern of her chest, silencing her immediately. "It was not a gift," he growled. "You will find this woman for me, this dark-haired, sunken-eyed nightmare of a person, and you will bring her here. I need her to make the sacrifice to summon me back to this realm, and then I will gift you all the power you could ever desire. If you do not do this, I will rip you apart."

Shuddering, she reached up her hands to grasp his wrist. But his body was no longer easy to grab, and her hands groped at shadow and smoke. Instead, Sybil wheezed out a long breath of pain and nodded.

He released his hold on her magic, the only thing still keeping this ancient crone alive, but paused when he saw her hands. They made it too easy to tell what she was, dangerously easy considering all that she would have to do for him. So he took them in his own and slowly allowed his magic to seep into the wrinkled skin.

When he pulled away, they were smooth as black glass. Though they were still curled with centuries of arthritis and pain, they at least looked young again.

Sybil let out a breathless sound of surprise. "Sire, I cannot . . . You did not have to . . ."

He waved a hand in the air and started out of the room. "Find her, Sybil. Or you will not like what happens next."

He heard the witch scramble to gather her things, likely her scrying bowl and all manner of creatures and blood to sacrifice. Perhaps she would find this woman who lingered in the shadows and who had forgotten her importance. Soon, he would remind his nightmare exactly how powerful she was. But for now, he wandered through the remaining pieces of his old home until he found the altar at which all witches worshipped.

A stone carving of a man on a throne. His hands on the arms, his legs spread wide in confidence. He had forgotten that he was once handsome. That he had once been more than just shadows and darkness.

He did not know how long he stayed there, staring at himself, before his realm took him back into black memories.

5

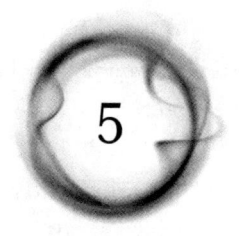

She wandered for a long time.

Jessamine wasn't sure how many days passed as she slipped through the streets. She stole whatever food she could find, usually from trash bins outside people's homes. The food wasn't good. It made her sick a few times. But it was better than starvation.

She stole clothes out of one of those bins as well. A pair of black pants that hung off her hips, baggy and smelling like fish. But everyone in the Water District smelled like fish, and people gave her fewer looks than they had when she'd been wearing the wedding dress. She'd torn the skirt off and left it in a limp pile on the ground, the fine fabric a lingering specter of who she had once been.

But now, the ripped pieces of her bodice were falling apart, and the smell of the pants added to her nausea. Her hair had knotted beyond anything she could fix, and she felt . . . like a monster. Stripped of her humanity. She skittered through the shadows, avoiding those who might recognize her. But she couldn't stay anywhere for too long. Hands reached out of the darkness, thick-fingered hands along with whispers that asked her to burn down her kingdom and didn't she remember that he'd given her life?

The Deathless One wasn't real. The gods were all dead. They'd been murdered a long time ago, and none of them were coming back. They weren't.

He wasn't real. She was just losing her mind.

Arms wrapped around her waist, she moved through the Water District like a wraith. Sodden, dirty, she was not the person she had once been.

Until she heard a group of people talking, laughing. "Been a month since the queen died, did you hear the news? Someone else already took her place. Long live the king and all that."

"He gonna give us a raise?"

"Probably not. They all forget we live down here in the Water District. Just filtering seawater into drinkable liquid for 'em, not like we're necessary or nothin'." The speaker was a big man, whose beer belly shook as he laughed. "Such a shame, though. Rumor is he killed the princess, too, and she was a lovely little thing. Always smiling when she came to visit with her mother. Remember the last time we saw her? The princess and her mother brought all that produce from the kingdom they'd visited. She didn't marry that one, but she should have. The strawberries were so sweet."

Lovely.

Always smiling.

She felt a whine pressing against the back of her throat as she fled from those men. She'd apparently been dead a month. She had no idea what Leon had done since he'd stolen her kingdom. And her people remembered her as the pretty one. The smiling one. The princess who was supposed to give them hope. It was all too much.

Her feet took her to the sea long before her mind realized what she was doing. There she stood, the sunlight blinding as it danced upon the rippling waves that clung to her feet. No one was here. It was too early, and this was the last place anyone would bathe. The runoff from the fish market tinged the water red just a few steps to her right.

But this water was clean. It was blue and shining, like her mother's eyes. And suddenly, she couldn't stand this anymore. She couldn't stand herself.

Jessamine stripped, yanking her clothing off and tossing it into the waves ahead of herself as she waded into the water. She submerged herself, not caring that the icy chill stole her breath, that the waves slapped at her face, or that the salt stung all the scrapes and cuts that marred her once-pretty flesh. It was all *hers*. The pain, the ice, the desperation to breathe. All of it.

When she came out of the waves, she was more herself. Everything was clearer in her mind. Clean, even if the salt was already hardening on her skin.

This was her kingdom, and no man would push her off her throne without a fight. She'd been a shadow of herself for too long. But first, she had to figure out who she could trust to help. Her mother would have wanted that. Her mother would have been brave and resilient.

She set her clothes on a nearby rock to dry and kept only a few strips of fabric on as she sat down in the sand. The band around her breasts that she'd ripped from her wedding dress, and her thin briefs that had been worn too many days in a row, but they'd have to do for a little while longer.

A stick. She needed a stick.

Muttering to herself, she found something that would help her draw in the sand and started on a diagram before her.

First she put herself and her mother, drawing a line through the symbols she'd drawn for the two of them to mark their deaths. She drew a set of horns to represent Leon, and the rest she'd figure out more symbols for. The last thing she needed was anyone to look over her shoulder and realize she was drawing rather confidential names in the sand.

First, what were their ties? Most of the nobility knew Leon, of course, but Baron Edgerton had family in Orenda. He visited them every year, and Leon had been rather chummy with the baron the last time she'd seen them together. Of course, then there was her cousin Lady Fortuna. A noblewoman by day and a theater owner by night, she regularly welcomed the realm's most wealthy—Leon included—to her shows. Not to mention Lord and Lady Prescott, both of whom must have taken significant bribes from Leon for the wedding. They'd provided the food, though neither of them had ever catered in their life.

She snorted. Any food they'd made was probably poisoned. In case the infected hadn't distracted everyone at the wedding, Leon likely had another plan. Too bad no one stayed alive long enough to eat it.

When she finished sketching, it all looked rather . . . dismal. So she turned to other names of people she might be able to trust. Her mother's head of the guard, Callum Quen. The head gardener at the castle, although she'd forgotten the woman's name. Two maids who had been with her since childhood, and a single pageboy, Benji, who had always brought her mother a sweet treat in the afternoon.

Slim pickings, really.

The gardener was likely dead. So was Callum, if she was being honest. If she had any inkling at all that he might be alive, she'd run right to him. Unless he was still at the castle. She'd get her head cut off for that kind of recklessness.

The head of the military had done nothing during the coup, so she could only assume he, too, had been working against her family. Any of the royal advisors would be a risk. She had no one who was even remotely higher up in the entire kingdom who would help her. After what had happened to any who stood against Leon at her wedding? No one would take the risk.

Jessamine swatted a fly that landed on her arm, likely licking at the salt that had already stiffened there. Her pale skin looked even worse, flaking sand and salt and whatever mud she hadn't scrubbed off. It was . . . hopeless.

This felt impossible. She'd never wanted to marry Leon, and even if she had, she would still have been queen eventually. The throne was supposed to be hers after her mother's death, which shouldn't have happened for years to come. She shouldn't be sitting here, with nothing to her name, wondering if everyone thought she was dead.

What was the right answer? Something had to be the correct choice, but instead, all she could feel was . . . lost.

Staring at the waves helped. It made the rolling ache of hunger in her stomach subside, but her near-constant thirst whispered that the sea hadn't tasted that bad. Maybe just a few mouthfuls. If she got sick, then everything would end just a little quicker. Wouldn't that be nice?

She saw the shadows moving in the waves long before she saw him.

He stood there, below the surface, watching her. As if he didn't need to breathe. As if his soulless gaze saw right through her, into the darkest parts of herself that she didn't want anyone to see.

"Jessamine," his voice whispered, floating through the darkness. "Ask me for more."

Ask him for more? He had already given her life. He'd saved her when she should have rotted in the waters he now stood in. A wave crested and broke over his face, the white foam obscuring him from her vision once again.

A part of her soul whispered that she knew who he was, that they were tied together, woven into a tapestry of blood and sacrifice. He'd saved her, but he was still dead. She hadn't summoned him, nor had she left a sacrifice at a carefully laid altar. Black magic had a price, of course, and his help had more of a price than most.

But she hadn't asked for this.

He'd given her a second chance, and now he hoped she'd pay for it of her own accord. He wanted a price that he wasn't owed.

Strengthened by the thought, she rose, dusting sand from the backs of her thighs. "I am not indebted to you. I don't have to do anything you tell me to do."

A wave rolled higher than the others, licking at her toes with foam that hardened into shards of ice. "I saved you." His voice rippled through her mind. "I took your cold, lifeless body from the depths and I delivered you here. To your kingdom that was stolen from you."

"I did not ask for your help," she replied, her voice maybe a little triumphant. "I didn't ask for this."

"But you did." And ah, that velvet voice smoothed over her ears like the finest of symphonies. "Don't you remember?"

"No," she started, but then she did. In a flash, she remembered all the moments in that terrifying realm made of ink and darkness. She remembered that deep, velvety voice telling her that she wouldn't remember what he had to say.

He'd *told* her to ask for his help, though! That had to break the rules?

He had forced her into making this decision, and she'd only . . . she'd done . . .

Exactly what he wanted.

Her knees turned to jelly, and she almost sat right back down into the sand. He wasn't playing fair, but why would he? The Deathless One had never been a just god, and it was shocking that he'd outlived all the others.

Or was it? After all, his name explained why he was still here. And why he had decided to torment her.

She pointed at him and the sea and all the nonsense that her life had devolved into. "I will not do what you want me to do."

She wouldn't destroy her kingdom. And she damn well wouldn't rebuild it in his name.

Another wave rose, higher than she was tall. The image of him loomed, larger than life, a pillar of darkness that consumed all living things within it. He was the night, and she did not have enough sunlight to beat him back.

"No," she whispered again, taking another step back. "I won't do it."

"I gave you your life," he hissed, the wave holding impossibly still. "I can take it back."

It rolled toward her, all the strength of the sea mashed into one terrible wave that surely would drag her into the depths. She braced herself, certain that he would make good on his threat and throw her out to feed the sharks.

But the wave didn't crash over her head. Instead, it merely lapped at her toes. Just like all the others.

Blinking, she opened her eyes to see that the sea had evened out. It was calm and still, with sparkling diamonds of sunlight in the tiny ripples. Smooth. No deathless god trying to convince her to do his bidding.

"Excuse me?"

The voice interrupted her thoughts like a blade through her ribs. Awkwardly raising her fists, she stumbled into the waves before leaping out again for fear of what that god would do to her. It left her dancing back and forth between the person who had startled her and the person she actually feared.

A woman stood there, one arm hooked through a lovely wicker basket full of seaweed and shells. Her dark hair was pulled back from her equally dark face, but her dark eyes watched Jessamine with amusement. "No need to be startled. I won't hurt you."

Jessamine lowered her hands, her face flaming with embarrassment. She'd never hit someone in her life. What did she think she was going to do with her fists?

This newcomer didn't seem to mind overmuch, though. She just shifted the basket to her other hip and watched as Jessamine gathered herself. It took a while to remind herself that she was the princess of this land, the rightful heir to the throne, and . . . Well. She knew how to treat someone with respect.

"My apologies." Jessamine cleared her throat, trying to straighten her shoulders and regain a decent posture. "It's been a trying few days. Weeks, if I'm being honest."

"It looks like." The woman hooked her thumb over her shoulder. "My house is just over there if you'd like to clean up. I don't have much room, but I have enough for a spare cot and a good bowl of broth."

Was this woman going to be like the men in the sewers? Would she have to run for her life yet again?

Jessamine looked over her shoulder at the cold, bitter sea, and a wave of exhaustion crashed over her. She was so tired. Tired of running, of hiding, of fearing whatever shadow lurked over the corner.

For once, she just wanted to trust someone.

Swallowing hard, she nodded. "Alyssa. My name is Alyssa."

"Sybil," the dark woman replied, and then started down the beach. "Care to share what trouble you've found yourself in?"

She didn't. Jessamine trailed along behind her until they reached a small hut by the shore. The exterior wood had gone gray with age, urchins moving along the sides and dead barnacles all over the planks. The door hung off one hinge, but Sybil didn't seem all that concerned. She opened the door, ignoring the folded metal roof as it groaned, and gestured for Jessamine to go ahead.

Into the shadows. Into the darkness. Where she'd already gotten into more trouble than she could abide.

Gritting her teeth, she walked into the single room before her.

It was rather . . . cozy, she supposed. Herbs hung in neat little bundles above her head. A single cot in the corner was covered with a patchwork quilt, clearly loved and well taken care of. A small table on the side was covered with more seaweed and jars filled with what looked like sea creatures, although none that Jessamine recognized.

"Thank you again," she said, peering through the shadows for where she was meant to clean up. She'd assumed she would find a bath, or at least a bucket of fresh rainwater. But there wasn't much in here at all.

Sybil walked in behind her and deposited her findings on the table. "You're welcome. Anyone touched by the Deathless One deserves favor among witches."

It felt like the floor dropped out from beneath her. Jessamine suddenly couldn't breathe again. She wanted to claw at her throat, but when she touched the long length of it, all she could feel was that damn scar. It was a rope around her neck that tightened with every breath.

"Sit," Sybil said, taking her arm and forcing her down onto the cot. "You look like you've seen a ghost."

"Isn't he?" she whispered. Jessamine stared up at the witch with pleading eyes, for surely this woman knew the ancient magic. "I don't know what I made a bargain with. There was a book in my library that spoke of him, but in language that made him sound like he was dead. All the gods are dead. Aren't they?"

"His name speaks volumes. The Deathless One. Did you really believe he was dead, too?" Sybil somehow manifested a stool—had that been hiding underneath the table?—and sat in front of her. Folded over her knees, the woman looked more like a crone than she had mere moments ago.

Fingers laced together, the witch surveyed her, watching her every twitch and move. But Sybil's eyes always landed back on the scar around her throat.

"What?" Jessamine asked. "What is it?"

"Have you not seen it yet?"

"Where would I have found a mirror? The Water District isn't kind to people who . . ." People who had nothing. People she should have protected but hadn't even realized were alive while she luxuriated in her castle above them all.

The witch reached into her pocket and pulled out a small mirror. She pressed the button on the front, which clicked it open, then turned it toward Jessamine.

And there it was. The thick, terrible scar that was banded around her neck. Impossible, considering she'd been murdered only a few weeks ago. Yet the scar around her neck wasn't like any other she'd ever seen. The wound was silvery, and as she stared, it seemed to writhe, moving underneath her skin as though there was something embedded within.

Gasping, she pushed the mirror away, trying to catch the breath that refused to fill her lungs. "What is that? Why does it look like that?"

"You've been touched."

"Touched?" Jessamine stared at the other woman, wondering why she wasn't panicking as well. The scar around her neck *was moving*. "Touched by what?"

"By whom." Sybil gathered Jessamine's hands in hers and squeezed. "You know the Deathless One. You have met him, have you not? You've stared into those soulless eyes and have seen oblivion beyond them. He is the beginning and the end. The only god who cannot die, and he has been gone for far too long."

The words echoed what she'd read. *Fanatics*, her mind whispered. She feared his followers would stop at nothing to raise him from the dead. They wished to bring him back to his full power, and if she did that . . . if she gave them that power . . .

Again, Sybil squeezed her fingers. "Would you like to see him?"

"Who?" Jessamine whispered, but she already knew the answer.

"The Deathless One. He's been dying to see you."

6

He'd been waiting for days. And he hated waiting. Lingering in the wreckage of the witches' manor, skulking in shadows like he didn't belong here. As if he hadn't built the entire monolith for his own followers.

Instead, he was the god no one wanted, the unwelcome visitor forced to remain behind while he trusted an ancient witch to do his bidding. Witches congregated with each other first and foremost. If he wanted to win Jessamine's trust, he had to give her someone else to spin the web of lies that would lead to his resurrection. Sybil was supposed to bring the other to his home. She would walk into this manor with the gravesinger and convince the woman to raise him from the dead. It was a simple plan.

But he didn't trust witches. Perhaps it had been too long since he'd had to trust anyone. The longer he remained alone in his dark realm, the more the silence was a stark reminder that they could not be trusted.

Even now, he stood in the very bowels of the manor, staring at a flat altar ten feet long that had seen more of his blood in the past millennia than any other place. He couldn't move his gaze from the blackened and stained stone, memories flashing through his mind. Too many to count. All those times when he had died in pain, alone, and no one had cared.

Not even the witch who had claimed her bond with him was different from all the others. The witch who, all those years ago, had given him hope that someone might love *him* for the first time in all his ancient years. The witch who, after everything, had promised so much.

His heart hardened and his hands curled into fists. Not this time. He would not be soft again, for a witch would always choose herself.

Something stirred above his head—not the sound of footsteps yet, but the energy of witches approaching. He stared up through the floor and willed himself to believe this was the moment things would change. He would not allow anyone to wriggle their way into his good graces. He was darkness. He was the end.

And so, when he moved through the shadows into what used to be the drawing room, he only watched as the two women staggered into his home.

His little gravesinger held on to the other witch like a lifeline. Perhaps she was so weak that she could not walk on her own, but he suspected it was merely exhaustion. She had had a trying day, after all, considering he'd threatened to drown her.

Not that he could—yet. They needed a connection before he could touch her body instead of just her mind. She didn't worship him now, but eventually she would. If not spiritual devotion, an emotional one would do, but he had lost all ability to cajole anyone into liking him. Two hundred years of isolation would do that to a person.

She'd been terrified of him every time she saw him, and he had so enjoyed it. Seeing her dark eyes widen with fear and the tremble in her bottom lip when she'd thought it was the end.

But he'd equally enjoyed her rebellion. Something in him had coiled with glee at the triumph in her gaze when she'd thought she'd bested him. As though he hadn't thought of every way she could try to trick him. The little thing clearly had never dealt with a god before.

They staggered past his shadowy corner, neither noticing the dark shape lingering behind a pillar.

Sybil was already tutting, her voice carrying through the rafters as she scolded the other woman. "You cannot be so weak, Alyssa. If he catches you like this, he'll only take advantage."

"I know that," his gravesinger wheezed. "I just need a night. I just need a warm bed."

"I don't have one of those. The royal guards burned all of them the last time they were here." Sybil heaved her toward a pile of rags but was gentle as she laid the other woman down to rest. "They come in every now and then to make sure no witches have taken refuge here like the old days. Unfortunately, the last time they did so, they burned whatever they could find while they got drunk in what used to be a functioning parlor."

"I'm sorry," his gravesinger whispered. "I'm so sorry for that."

Sybil patted her shoulder and eased her down on the rags. "It's not your fault, dear."

His mind fractured at the pitying words. It was her fault, wasn't it? From her memories, he knew that his little gravesinger was the princess. She was one of the few who could have stopped the raids, and she was just as responsible for the destruction they caused as the powers that had ordered them in the first place.

As his little nightmare drifted off into sleep, he trailed the other witch through the manor. Sybil ended up in a room full of rotting furniture and piles of dirt from which bright blue flowers grew in riotous blooms. She rummaged through the shambles of an old trunk, muttering under her breath until she turned around and almost ran right into him.

A low gasp echoed from her lips before she steadied herself. "What are you doing here?"

"I never left."

"Oh." Her breathing was ragged as she pulled herself together enough to ask, "Why did you stay?"

Because he didn't trust her. He didn't trust anyone. Especially a witch who would do dangerous things to keep him away from her life and under her thumb.

But he couldn't say any of that. Not only because it made him seem weak, but because she would realize she had a lot more power than she thought.

He leaned a little closer to Sybil, the darkness in him expanding around them both until they stood in a black bubble of silence. "Alyssa is the name she gave you?"

"I—I was just gathering my things to see if she's even the grave . . . gravesinger," Sybil stammered.

"Oh, she is. You did a good job of finding her." His eyes closed, his mind returning to that darkened lake until he could filter through the soul he still held captured inside of himself. There was more to her than what she'd told the witch.

"She shouldn't be left alone," Sybil replied. They were nervous words, bit out through chattering teeth. "I don't entirely trust her."

"No, you shouldn't. She's been lying." There it was, he'd forgotten it for a few moments. The memory of her mother and her talking. "Jessamine."

"Excuse me?"

"Her name is Jessamine, not Alyssa. She is not what she seems." The magic vibrated around him with his anger, rolling through his form as he realized this princess had tried to control both of them. Him and his witch. "She is the princess who died."

Sybil's body was framed by a window behind her. The frame was covered in grime and ivy hung outside, leaving diamond shadows to play across her dark skin. Her eyes widened in shock, shadows forming underneath. "She's the princess? The one that died?"

"Is that not what I just said?"

"That's not possible. You said we were looking for a gravesinger, and that little shipwrecked soul is just another witch. I've seen your mark on her neck."

He remained silent, staring down at her until she realized what it meant.

"She was dead?" Sybil whispered, her face somehow paling. "You brought her back? Do you have any idea what that could have done to her? A soul isn't meant to die multiple times. You could have ripped her spirit apart, torn her into pieces of herself, and . . . and . . . A gravesinger? Deathless One, if she is truly a gravesinger, then bringing her back was defying life itself."

Remaining silent, he allowed all the shadows to be sucked back into his body as he lifted a hand to his own throat. That was all he had to do for Sybil to understand that the girl sleeping on a pile of rags was more his than any witch had ever been before. He knew the dangers of bringing her back, but the mark on Jessamine's neck was his mark. He'd done what he had to do to be resurrected, and now he would take what he wanted from her.

"Right," Sybil said as she staggered out of the room. "I'll wake her."

"Let her sleep."

"What?" She spun. "You were the one who told me—"

"So you would not walk into this without knowing the truth." And because he wanted to see what chaos he could sow. This witch should know that she was dealing with a princess. The bundle of mud and salt and tears that she had so carefully guided into her home was responsible for the life that Sybil had led. "She is no innocent, and you should not grow attached."

A frown creased Sybil's face, and for the first time, she looked him in the eye without flinching. "What if you're wrong?"

His witch disappeared down the hall, her arms laden with the tools it would take to confirm that Jessamine was the witch he sought. He already knew what the answer would be.

There was no way he was wrong. He would wait for her to summon him, because Sybil wouldn't rush through it now. His witch had a good reason to use Lady Jessamine now. Let it simmer in Sybil's mind. Soon enough, that witch would want more power, and this was the perfect way to get it. A gravesinger in their pocket would give both him and his coven significantly more power.

So he would wait.

He watched from the shadows as Jessamine slept. Fitfully. She didn't rest easily, and he wasn't surprised to find that nightmares plagued her just as they plagued him. Eventually, though, she sat up from her rags and rubbed her eyes.

The first thing she did was seek out Sybil. She stood and didn't even try to look at the items scattered around her. Piles of ancient curtains, bins filled with bones, even a pile of mushrooms in the corner that were notoriously used in spells, but Jessamine looked at nothing. He had thought there would at least be a moment where she picked through a few of the things, trying to discern where she was. But she didn't.

She wandered through the halls, calling out Sybil's name until the other witch appeared from a doorway.

"You're awake," Sybil said. "And you've been lying to me."

Jessamine turned bright red. "I thought I'd have more time to explain myself before you figured that out."

"The Deathless One sees all." He had thought perhaps Sybil would be gentle with her, but instead, the witch's tone turned hard. "Now it is time to summon him."

"What if I don't want to?" Jessamine's pale face turned comically white.

"If you wanted me on your side, then you shouldn't have lied." Sybil gestured with her hand. "Come now. I have set everything up for you. All you have to do is perform the spell."

"I'm not a witch."

"You were born a witch," Sybil corrected as Jessamine made her way through the door. "Besides, spell casting is as easy as baking."

He wanted to snort but feared one of them would hear him. He'd never in his life heard a witch claim that spell casting was easy. It wasn't. There were rules that had to be followed meticulously. The worst thing that could happen in baking was burnt bread. In spells, it was burnt flesh.

He followed them into a quiet room where peace radiated through his form. A calming spell, it seemed, etched into the wall by a hundred witches who had come before. Even Sybil paused to trace her finger over a worn stone with a sigil marked by a thousand touches.

This was a lesser-known altar room, likely used for training. There was no god statue here. Only a small altar with a pillow in front of it for kneeling. Sybil had set up four candles, all black. There was salt, a small bowl of water, a match, and a bell. How quaint. An old spell that used to summon him easily, and now he couldn't care less if someone used it.

But he supposed he should uphold the formality of things. In summoning, the magic didn't matter so much as the intent.

He could almost taste his liberation. He could feel it strengthening in his body, stretching into his fingertips and pushing through his form. Soon he would be free. He wouldn't be chained to any witch after that, because he was going to wring this pretty little gravesinger's neck.

"What do I do?" Jessamine asked. She walked into the room like a wraith. All the bones in her body stood out in stark relief, the shadows creating lovely hollows around her throat and collarbone. That pale skin seemed kissed by moonlight until he saw all the bruises forming beneath it. A mottled expression of hardship.

"Read the book," Sybil said in a clipped tone. "I put it on the altar for you. Just don't do anything other than what it says, and you're finished."

"You aren't staying?"

"Oh, gods no." Sybil had already backed out of the door, holding the doorknob in one hand as she shook her head. "He's terrible enough without having a physical form. I have no interest in meeting him in the flesh. Good luck, Lady Jessamine. You're going to need it."

And with that, the witch slammed the door hard enough to rain dust from the ceiling. Then came the distinctive sound of a lock turning.

Jessamine was shaking when she turned to the altar. It didn't escape his notice that she touched her hand to her throat often when she was nervous. Like she was feeling the disgusting length of his mark wriggling underneath her flesh. He hoped it made her uncomfortable.

But then she surprised him, as she often did. She walked up to the altar, slowly fell onto her knees on the pillow, and then bowed her head and started whispering. The image of her reflected in the single window of the room, a supplicant kneeling in prayer while uttering hymns of need.

He had to take a few steps closer to hear what she was saying, looming over her like the darkest night sky.

"—if you have ever listened to me, please. I need to know if this is the right thing to do."

She was praying? To whom?

He almost laughed in her ear, just to see how she would respond, but then he saw there was a shadow cast across the altar and stretching up onto it in the candlelight. He could use that. All it would take was a single flex of his power and then . . . yes. Now he was seated on the altar right in front of her. Legs spread wide, staring at those deep furrows underneath her eyes that spoke of a woman who hadn't slept in ages.

She didn't hold her hands together in prayer, instead pressing them against the ground as she bent over, braced on her dirty palms.

Who was she talking to?

He couldn't stand not knowing. So the Deathless One reached through the shadows, his pitch-black hand formless as he tried his best to scare her. He couldn't touch her, not without her being in his coven. But he could show her something out of her worst dreams.

But she didn't frighten easily, not his nightmare. She stiffened and then looked up at him, hollow eyes staring straight into his darkness. "I don't know if I want you to have a physical form."

Like she'd known he was here the entire time. Like she had felt him as he felt her.

A stirring rustled in his chest. The scraping of dry leaves pushed by a breeze that threatened to knock him ever closer to her. "All you have to do is summon me, and I will take control."

"I don't want you to take control. I just want what is mine."

"I cannot even be before you without you giving me a form. You need my power, Jessamine."

She reached for the book in front of her and flipped through its pages. He heard each one, like scissors snipping away at his opportunity. "What are you doing?" he snarled.

"There has to be another way. I know this book. I've seen it before, when I bought it from a peddler." She found the page she wanted and then started moving the spell ingredients around.

She got rid of the match entirely, then licked her dirty fingers to stick the salt onto them. She coated one of the candles with that salt and her own spit before he realized he had to stop her. He had to. This wasn't right. She was meant to summon him, not to make him wait even longer.

"I told you there was a debt—"

"And I will repay it," she hissed before crawling on her hands and knees to find that match she'd discarded. "But first I want answers from you, Deathless One, and I will not go another step further in this plan until I get them."

7

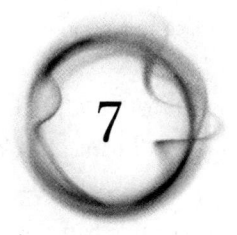

All her life, she had been told what to do. She should do what someone else said, because they knew best. She should trust that everyone was going to take care of her, because she was beloved by all in the kingdom, including the people who worked for her. She should be polite, poised, and kind, because that was what princesses were.

What a load of bullshit.

Where had trusting people led her? To a knife at her throat, a debt to a god, and nothing to her name.

So excuse the god in front of her, who was clearly sulking as she figured out what she wanted to do. She had read this spell book before, and she knew which spell she wanted to cast. No one was going to tell her what to do. Not anymore. This was her kingdom, her responsibility, and she definitely did not trust the god who sat on the altar.

Because Sybil had called her Jessamine. And only this asshole in front of her knew her real name.

"Obviously you told her who I am," she muttered as she placed the book on the floor and smoothed out the pages. "I don't appreciate that."

He had receded back into the shadows, either no longer capable of responding to her or deciding that he didn't want to play this game. Whichever it was, his silence was enough of an answer.

Salt-covered black candle. Match in hand. All she had to do was set the black candle at the base of an altar, and she assumed this one would suffice. Then she had to light the candle while clearing her mind. This spell was very different from the one Sybil had laid out for her. The other had words to say, a ritual to complete, and a list of rules before starting the incantation.

But this one? It said to clear her mind of all intent other than speaking with the deity, and then to say their name. Invoking the spirit through will alone would summon them.

Of course, that was easier said than done. Jessamine lit the candle, closed her eyes, and forced her mind to reach out. She wanted to talk to him. She wanted him to answer her questions, and he *would* answer her questions.

There was no other option.

On a long exhale, she breathed, "Deathless One."

She poured every ounce of her need into it, and she had plenty. So much that she was fairly bursting with it, and then . . .

Holding her breath, she watched for what felt like forever. Then she peeled one of her eyes open, looking around before she sealed it shut again. Maybe she needed to will it a little harder. Focusing on her breathing, she tried one more time. "Deathless One."

"This is almost sad to watch."

Ah, there he was.

Frowning, she looked up at the altar to realize he was still seated upon it. Or at least, what little she could see of him was. As always, he appeared to be nothing more than the silhouette of a man, a shadow that had detached itself from a body and left the meat somewhere else.

"You were the one who wanted me to summon you," she muttered, folding her hands carefully in her lap. "I am merely doing what you asked."

"This is not summoning me, witch," he hissed, and the shadows undulated around him. The more she stared, the more she realized it wasn't just shadows. It looked like someone had used charcoal to sketch a shadow. There were marks around him, jagged edges and crude smudges that made him look almost like a painting.

"Is it not?" she asked, then smiled as though this wasn't bothering her in the slightest. "You're here. You're talking to me."

His voice changed into a mocking tone, mimicking her. "I was here. I was talking to you."

Her jaw snapped shut with an audible click. Through gritted teeth she muttered, "I intended to control the conversation a little more than you insulting me."

"The only reason for this spell is to commune with gods. It's used to speak with a patron, not to give the wielder any sort of power." He sighed. "A patron, my dear gravesinger, is a god that you worship directly for power. In case you didn't know."

"I know what a patron is," she snapped. "That was the point. I'm trying to talk to you without you lying to me."

All the hairs on her arms stood up at his low snarl. Some part of her mind whispered that she was a tiny little mouse, and he was a massive cat. If she said something wrong, moved in the wrong direction, he'd snap his jaws around her and that would be it. But then she reminded herself those fears weren't true. According to this spell, she was in control of this encounter. That gave her a little more power than she had before.

Narrowing her eyes on him, she refused to flinch or show any fear. "Why do you want me to summon you?"

"I have been dead for centuries, witch. Do I need a reason other than that? I desire to be real again. I desire life."

It made enough sense, she supposed. "Why do you keep calling me 'witch'?"

"Because you are one."

"I'm not a witch," she replied. Jessamine clutched her hands together in her lap, trying not to let him see how hard they were shaking. "I've read a lot of books on witchcraft, and I've studied the nature of the beast for most of my life. It's a fascinating fairy tale, but I am not a witch."

"You are a gravesinger, to be more accurate." He hopped off the altar and began to circle her slowly. "Do you know what a gravesinger is?"

"No."

"It's a particular kind of witch. The kind I've been looking for. There used to be countless of your kind, natural-born witches who could connect directly with a patron. In the old days, I had twenty gravesingers at my beck and call." His cold breath fanned over the sweat at the base of her neck. "Now I have only you."

"How disappointing."

"You have no idea."

It made little sense, though. Jessamine had never practiced magic in her life. And didn't witches show signs? Magical . . . happenings started around them when they were very young, didn't they? Either way, she couldn't be who he wanted her to be. She wasn't sure she wanted to be his gravesinger even if she could.

The Deathless One circled behind her, the dark shape of him undulating and changing forms in the window's reflection. "You are certainly a disappointing witch, but you can be shaped. Molded into what I wish."

Everything in her clenched at his words and then darted out of her lips. "No!"

The word echoed. If he had a face, she supposed she might see surprise on his features as he stared down at her on her knees. "No?" he repeated, his tone utterly shocked. "What do you mean, no?"

"I mean you will not shape me. I cast the spell to speak with you, not the other way around. No one will ever shape me into what they want again." She glared up at him, her hands curled into fists. "No one will tell me who or what I am. Not even a god."

"Ah, there's the feral creature who bartered for her life. A life that I gave back to you as the benevolent god that I am." He continued circling, then crouched in front of her, a hulking beast prickling with thorns. "Now, tell me again why you think I will not control every action you take from here on out."

Confidence surged through her veins. She tilted her chin up, watching as he stood again and meandered behind her. Circling again like some great bird of prey. "Because I summoned you only to speak, Deathless One. You cannot touch me, just as you cannot control me until I give you physical form."

Again she felt his cold presence leaning over her, the whisper of his words chilling her ear. "Are you so sure about that?"

She froze as a ghostly hand wrapped around her throat from behind.

No, not ghostly. It was an actual hand. Long, thick fingers, scarred tips brushing against her pulse as he tightened his grip. By the gods, he could nearly encircle her entire throat and his fingers would touch. How big was this man?

"You aren't supposed to be able to touch me," she whispered, her voice trembling.

"Gravesingers are connected to their gods. Any god, really. All you need is a deep feeling. One that sometimes you cannot control." Again his voice whispered in her ear, sending waves of ice through her veins. That deep growl seemed to hum with desire. "Hate is a strong enough emotion. I can work with hate. Even though I would entertain you if it was something more . . . pleasurable for the both of us."

"This isn't real," she croaked.

His hand tightened. There was no real threat, just the feeling of his fingers around her neck and the slightest pressure as he lifted her. Her spine bumped against a strong figure, the sensation of muscles and heat pressed against her in a decidedly sinful way.

She should have been afraid. She should have wriggled in his grasp and told him to unhand her because he would leave bruises like Leon. But that wasn't how she felt.

All she could focus on was the hand around her throat, how those fingers so carefully held her. Then she could only hold her breath as his other hand slid across her belly, lingering where her stomach had hollowed at his touch. His words inspired ice, but his touch made her burn.

His hand suddenly tightened around her throat as his gravelly voice ground out, "Tell me this doesn't feel real to you. If you want, I could seduce you. I could reach into your thoughts and play out all your deepest desires. If you wish for me to service you when I return to life, I will do so. Have you ever wanted a god to worship you, Jessamine?"

Images of what that might look like flickered in her mind. She almost wanted him to get on his knees for her. What would it feel like to have that much power over someone brimming with magic?

This wasn't real, she told herself. It was an illusion. Because he wasn't here. She had to have faith in the spell she had cast, so no matter how hard he squeezed, no matter how much it felt like she had to hold her breath, it wasn't actually happening.

"You're not here," she wheezed. "This is . . . all in my head."

"Is it?" Every muscle in her body clenched, and that strange heat seared through her as his lips brushed against the seashell of her ear and his voice rumbled. "Then perhaps we should see how far I can go before this dream turns into a nightmare."

Should she let him? That hand on her stomach flexed, his fingers brushing down until they touched one of her hips, his pinky hovering over the other. He was so much *larger* than her. She hadn't realized it until this moment, when he'd almost consumed her. Enveloped her. Dragged her deeper into this darkness that whispered, *You want this*.

She'd wanted to feel powerful, hadn't she? Bending a god to her will would do that. Making a god service her, telling him exactly what she wanted and where she wanted him to touch.

All it would take was a single nod. She just had to let him know, and she knew those wicked fingers would slide between her legs. He would touch her, finding her wet and waiting for him to bring her to that pleasure that no man had managed before. But surely a god . . .

He'd inspired madness—a seed of insanity in her mind—because this was not her. She'd never had thoughts like this before. Gasping, she wrenched herself free of his grip. She had to get away from him, from what he would do . . .

From how he made her feel.

Rioting emotions turned her head upside down and inside out. She didn't know what he wanted from her, or what she wanted from him. The strange heat wouldn't let her go, not even when she knocked over the candle and scrambled away from him.

Her back hit the altar hard enough that the slab groaned, shifting on its base even as he strode toward her. "You're not real. All of this is an illusion you've cast," she muttered.

The Deathless One paused in front of her, waiting for her eyes to trail up his impossibly tall form before he growled, "You and I are bound, Jessamine. Have you forgotten that? I gave you life. No spell can keep me away from you. Not even you can control that."

But then a gust of wind blew through the shattered window, and his form disappeared on the tail of it.

She was left alone in the dark room with a guttering candle lying on its side and the scattered remains of a spell that hadn't worked. Or maybe it had worked too well.

She stood, shook herself off, and closed the spell book like its pages were the cause of all this. Feeling stripped and hollow, she ran her shaking fingers through her hair. What had that been? How had he made her feel like that?

Carefully gathering the spell book, she clutched it to her chest and made her way to the door. She knocked on it, hesitant in her hope that she wouldn't have to spend the night in here until she finally decided to free the Deathless One.

"Sybil?" she called out. "Can I please come out now?"

Silence from the other side made her stomach twist with nausea. Was this the plan? Were they going to lock her in here, starving her in the hopes that she would eventually give in?

Torture wasn't something she thought she could survive. Though she was strong, she'd never really suffered in her life until recently, and . . . ending that suffering was all too tempting. Look at how easily she'd trusted a kind stranger just because Sybil had promised her a safe place to sleep.

Maybe she was alone here. This would be her prison and her tomb until she did what they wanted her to do.

Sighing, she thudded her forehead against the door. "I don't know what I'm doing," she whispered, sending the words out to anything that might help her. "I'm no longer a princess. No longer a daughter. I'm not a witch. I am nothing and no one, and I do not know what to do."

The lock clicked and the door eased open slowly, drawing her head with it until she had to stagger forward into the hall beyond. Her eyes caught first on the moss at the edges of the floor where it met the walls, emerald green and dotted with tiny white flowers. Then she dragged her gaze to the woman on the other side of the door, her dark features creased with worry.

Sybil held out her arm, gesturing that Jessamine should walk ahead of her. "A witch is never alone."

With a snort of disbelief, Jessamine staggered down the hall. "I find that hard to believe. Why is she never alone? Because other witches are always going to be with her?"

"No. Because any witch worth her salt has a patron, and that patron is always with them. Strengthening them. It is a gift as much as it is a . . . burden."

She heard the weight in that last word. Turning, she made eye contact with Sybil and watched as the other woman's eyes drifted down to her throat.

"What?" Jessamine found herself asking. "Did he make the scar worse?"

"No," Sybil muttered. "But I did not think what he left behind was possible, considering you aren't part of our coven."

What could possibly happen now? She lifted a hand and touched her throat, gently stroking the scar there as though it might hurt to touch. But when she drew her fingers away, she was surprised to find them smudged with black.

Like charcoal. She rubbed her fingers together, letting the darkness smear from finger to finger. So it had been real. He hadn't been lying to her.

He'd been in the room with her. The Deathless One had touched her, pulled her against his warm muscles and held her throat like he owned her. Like he had a right to touch her however he wanted, and she . . .

Hadn't minded?

No, that definitely wasn't how she felt. She minded very much. She didn't like that he'd touched her at all, and that was the story she was sticking to. Even if it gave her a certain thrill to know that she must have a black handprint around her neck.

Sybil caught her hand, holding Jessamine's fingers out to look at the substance still clinging to her. "Magic," she muttered. "He left a magical residue on you."

"What does that mean?"

"I don't know." The witch looked perplexed before she narrowed her eyes on Jessamine. "What happened in there?"

Jessamine quickly ran through what she had done, stammering her explanation for why, as though it made a difference. "I don't want anyone to tell me what to do anymore. I have lived that way my entire life, and for once I just want to make my own decisions."

The troubled expression never left Sybil's face. "We need to teach you more spells. If he's going to be like this as your patron, then you need to learn how to protect yourself. The gravesingers I knew centuries ago could connect with multiple patrons if they wished, but he is a dangerous one to choose. The longer you are with him, the tighter your bond will tie you. Do you understand?"

"Like a noose?"

Sybil flinched, but then gave her the smallest of nods. "You will want to avoid that fate."

"Isn't he your patron as well?"

The stiff silence was enough of an answer.

Jessamine turned her hand in Sybil's grip, holding on to the witch now with what she hoped was surprising strength. "How can you stand to serve a god like that?"

With a wince, Sybil pulled herself free. "We all do foolish things for a taste of power, do we not?"

Jessamine found herself unsettled by the truth of that statement. As they walked away, she cast one more glance back toward that room of power and knew she would do more foolish things. Likely soon.

Because the mark of his power on her skin had only created more questions. And Jessamine wanted answers.

8

Her dreams were twisted, warped, and wrong as she wandered through a black landscape full of nothing. Just ink. All she could see were writhing figures, creatures of muck and mire.

"Jessamine," they called out, reaching for her with hands whose fingers ended in clawed tips. "Jessamine, come to us."

"No," she whispered as she shied away from them. But her skirts stuck in the mud. She was sinking deeper into it. "Leave me alone."

"Jessamine, you cannot trust him."

Who? Who was she not supposed to trust? She was asleep, wasn't she? She vaguely remembered falling onto another one of those piles that Sybil had given her, and it wasn't comfortable, but at least she could sleep.

She missed her bed at home. She missed her castle, where there was always sound. Maids moving through the halls as they finished up their last rounds of the night. Guards passing by on patrol. Soft voices of people meandering past her doorway. There was always someone or something that she could hear.

But in this manor full of shadows and villainous gods, she was alone in the silence. Except for the darkness pursuing her. Voices that whispered they could help her, hands that trailed along her sides, leaving inky smears in their wake.

They wanted her to listen, but she did not know how to interpret their words.

"Jessamine!" they called out again, growing angry with her. "Listen to us."

"No!" she shouted as she finally yanked one of her legs out of the mud. It clung to her, so sticky and thick that it was almost impossible to move. "I don't want to listen to you."

A wall of darkness suddenly drew up in front of her, converging into the figure of a woman who towered over her. The open maw of her mouth shone with a white light, but everything else was black as night.

"Gravesinger," the woman said, freezing Jessamine in place. "You will hear what we have to say."

"I am not a gravesinger." But she trembled as she said the words. "You have the wrong person."

"A gravesinger follows in the path of those who came before her. A gravesinger finds a patron and bends them to her will." The darkness bent a little closer, and drops of ink fell from the woman's dripping hair onto Jessamine's cheeks. "You will control him. You are the last of our kind. You will rip him apart, and when it is time, you will take from him as all of us have before. We are waiting for your power, sister."

Take from him? What she was going to take from him? She didn't want anything to do with the Deathless One; it would be foolish to tie herself to him even more. Hadn't Sybil warned her?

"Jessamine." The voice filtered through the dream, through the darkness. She could smell smoke in the air, and it seemed that the other creatures who lingered in front of her did not want her to smell that.

Hands reached up out of the darkness, black hands dripping in ink that gripped her face and forced her to look at the woman in front of her.

"Take from him," the creature made of oil said again, her voice deepening with meaning. "Destroy him. And you will become all that you have ever desired."

She didn't understand what they wanted from her! She wasn't a gravesinger or a witch. She could only follow the spell books, and even then, look at how that went! That moment was proof, laid out before them. The Deathless One had done what he wanted with her, even though that should have been impossible. Either that spell book had lied or she wasn't a witch at all.

She wasn't what they all thought she was. Maybe her mother had been. Maybe there was someone else out there who looked like her, some urchin who should have been a princess.

More smoke poured into her senses, making her eyes and nose burn. She couldn't even think because it was so hot. She thought maybe she was burning somewhere else. Why could she smell this? Why was everything hurting?

"Remember," the ink said before it started to disappear. A blinding white light suddenly erupted from the woman's mouth and then radiated out of all the other feminine images, blasting away the darkness and leaving only brightness behind.

The smoke became overwhelming, and Jessamine suddenly lurched upright. Coughing, she cupped a hand around her mouth and tried very hard not to vomit. What was that smell? Where was she?

"Oh, good." Sybil's voice broke through her coughing, but only for a few moments before she went into another fit again. "You're back."

"Back?" she croaked out through coughs.

"You were gone for a little while. It's a good thing I walked by and noticed your spirit was missing. Otherwise you might not have returned at all."

The room was filled with smoke. Sybil crouched next to her, the coiled locks of her hair falling in front of her face. Those dark eyes saw straight into her soul and the fear that still lingered there. With a nod, Sybil stood and made her way to the window of Jessamine's room. She opened it wide, even though some of the glass panes were already shattered.

She left behind a tangle of herbs and a smoking bundle of dried greenery that Jessamine couldn't identify.

"What were you doing to me?" Jessamine asked, her voice sounding like it came from another person.

"That is eucalyptus and juniper, both hard to come by and very expensive. You're welcome." Sybil tsked. "Don't encourage the ancestors if you don't want them to speak with you! It's like you know nothing about witchcraft."

"I didn't encourage anyone or anything. They were talking to me about . . . gravesingers, and I don't . . . I'm not one of them."

Sybil chuckled as though Jessamine had made a joke until she looked back at Jessamine and froze. "You really believe that, don't you? That you aren't a gravesinger?"

"I know that witches show themselves early in life. Nothing unexpected has ever happened around me. I have never levitated a candle. I have never spoken with animals or created a spell through cooking." Jessamine's hands shook as she curled them in her lap, trying her best to control the fear that suddenly made her heart race and sweat trail down her temples. "I know about witches. I have researched your kind my entire life, and I have prayed that I would find the answer to my kingdom's sickness in your books, but I am not one of you."

Perhaps it was the loss in her voice that had Sybil's shoulders curving in on themselves. Jessamine liked to think maybe there was some ounce of pity in the witch, who had so far been nothing but a hard-edged fanatic disappointed in what she had found on the beach.

Sighing, Sybil settled on the pile of rags with her. "Not all witches are the same."

"That's not what the books say."

"I'm not listening to anything from books written about our kind. Witches have been here for centuries, longer than anyone who has read or written books. Trust me, any book worth its salt was burned by your ancestors years ago. Or even longer before that."

At least that settled some of her churning stomach. Sybil was right. No one would leave books like that lying around. No one wanted the witches to become powerful again.

"No one talks about what happened to you all," she murmured. "Just that it was necessary for the good of the kingdom and that it happened right after all the gods died. Do you know the truth of it?"

"Ach, it's a sad story. You just woke up from talking with the ancestors and you want to know that? You're going to go right back into a nightmare."

She didn't want to think about those ink-covered creatures who had begged her to steal from a god. She didn't want to even consider that they really had been in her mind, so yes, she wanted the distraction.

"Please?" she asked. "I have read so much about witches and witchcraft, and I know your people could help the kingdom if you wanted to. And I don't believe you caused the plague, no matter what my ancestors claimed. I suppose that's always been something that has confused me. Why won't any of you help the kingdom now with this plague?"

Sybil took a deep breath. Her dark eyes searched Jessamine's, and there was a moment of recognition there. A moment where the witch saw straight through her and into what she had seen in that dream.

Or maybe it wasn't a dream, and that terrified Jessamine more than a nightmare ever could.

Sybil grunted. "Fine. You know the gods died?"

"On a spring day, according to the legends."

"They didn't want to die, according to legend. The gods used to be like us. Just people. But eventually they discovered that our worship turned them into something more, and they were so powerful compared to mere mortals, if we were foolhardy enough to give them that power. It was a family of them, or perhaps people who just called themselves family. The Warrior Son. The Heartless Maiden. The Deathless One. The God King. The names go on and on, for creatures more powerful than our minds could ever dream of.

"They eventually gained their own followings. The Heartless Maiden and her huntresses. The Warrior Son and his band of reckless soldiers, who prayed for strength and turned berserker. The Deathless One and his witches." Sybil tapped a finger to her chin, her brows furrowing. "There was also the Wizened Crone. Priestesses worshipped her. Glorified witches, but they always held themselves to a higher standard. All the gods gave power in return for sacrifice. It was a loop, you see. We sacrificed to them, they grew stronger, and they shared an increment of that power with us."

Jessamine snorted at the sarcasm in Sybil's tone. "You speak of them like you were there."

"I was."

She blinked at the witch for a few moments, her jaw dropping open in shock. "What do you mean, you were?"

"Magic gives more than just power." A soft movement, one of Sybil tucking her hands into her sleeves, before she continued. "Anyway, it was hard to worship so many gods without some people thinking theirs was more powerful than the others. Every faction seemed to hate another. Every sect of powerful magic users claimed to be more useful than the next. Magic boiled over from so many people using it and so many gods giving it, and then the plague appeared. We didn't know where it came from, only that it was spreading rapidly. Everyone had their own opinions on how to fix it. Scholars, healers, none of them could touch the disaster that followed.

"The witches were the ones with the most power. The Deathless One has always been the most powerful conduit. He gave us more of himself than any of the others."

Words whispered through Jessamine's mind, a ghost of those dark creatures. *Take from him. Rip from him.* Tear her future out of his flesh and become something she had never dreamed of being.

Jessamine shook off those thoughts. "So the followers attacked each other because they wanted to be the ones to fix the plague? We've always been told that the plague happened after the gods died."

"It is the lie we created. The plague happened first, and still no one knows where it came from. Everyone wanted to be the hero, and they focused more on each other than actually fixing the problem. My coven saw what was coming. The witches did what we had to do, what we had always done. We sacrificed our god and all our gravesingers combined to be given the most amount of magic this realm has ever seen, and the Deathless One has been trapped ever since." Her frown deepened. "After we couldn't cure the plague, everyone wanted someone to blame. They called our arts black magic, darkness incarnate. They claimed we were the reason for all the evils in the kingdom, and they hunted us. We were destroyed as so many other powerful sects banded together. A few of us survived, hiding as we always did."

"What happened to the others?"

Sybil shrugged. "The gods died. No one knows how or when that happened, perhaps only the Deathless One knows the truth. Their followers used up all the magic that their patrons had given them, and then there was nothing left. The berserkers became mere men. Priestesses lost their value when blessings no longer came true. Scholars lost the knowledge gifted them by the God King. Without the gods, we are nothing. What remained of those who worshipped attacked each other, and then almost all magic disappeared. We were left with what you see now."

"A shell of what once was," she whispered. "I'm so sorry to hear that."

"It is like living in the skeleton of a leviathan you once knew well. There is still fear of its jaws and teeth that I walk through every day." Sybil patted her knee and then stood. "But it is just a skeleton, my dear. All the things for you to fear are dead."

An icy touch traveled her spine. "I think I might be dead, too. Should I fear myself?"

The words made Sybil shiver. Jessamine noticed the flick of Sybil's fingers, the start of the same motion those men in the sewers had made. A motion that was meant to summon the Deathless One's favor in times of need.

"I do not know whether to tell you to be afraid of yourself, Jessamine. Your path is yours to walk. Do you *want* people to fear you?"

Yes, a voice whispered in her mind. *I do.*

But she shook her head. "You said those were ancestors in my dreams?"

"They are usually the ones who summon our spirits out of our bodies to speak with us, yes." Sybil turned to leave, pausing in the doorway to look back at her. "You shouldn't be afraid of them either."

"Why were they covered in ink?"

Jessamine didn't imagine the way those curled hands suddenly clutched at the wooden frame of the door. The inhalation of breath, and the way Sybil's eyes widened not with surprise, but fear. "Covered in ink?"

"They were dripping with it. Just like the Deathless One." She wrapped her arms around herself, shuddering in the brisk wind that came in through the open window. "They told me not to trust him and to rip him apart. I don't know what that means."

Sybil sagged against the door, her spine rounding and her hunched figure looking more like the ancient crone she was. "The gravesingers spoke with you."

"You said there weren't any gravesingers left."

"They all sacrificed themselves," she muttered. "The last of their kind, to keep him locked away. To take his magic and save our world. Along with the coven, the gravesingers sacrificed the last living god, stripped his power, and tried to use it to cure the plague. We knew what we were doing. We knew that by sacrificing all who could bring him back at the same time, that it was the only magic this realm would ever see again. At least, so we thought, until you. But the spell failed, and then there was no one left to get magic from."

"Then they're all dead?"

"Except you."

Jessamine shook her head. "Who was talking to me, then?"

Haunted eyes stared back at her. "What remains of a great dynasty of women. They are the last vestiges of magic that linger in the realm between, where the Deathless One is bound. They wished to give you a warning, and perhaps a prophecy of their own."

"So they want me to hurt him?"

"No, Jessamine. They want to you follow in their footsteps."

Sybil slipped out the door and left Jessamine with only lingering questions and a continued icy feeling that trailed down her spine. If the people who had come before her wanted her to follow in their footsteps, did that mean they wanted her to sacrifice herself?

She lay down on the rags that covered the floor and couldn't help but feel like that wasn't at all what they were asking.

They wanted her to take from the Deathless One and use his power. To do what? She had no idea. She wasn't a witch. She didn't know how to cure the plague, and if that was what they wanted . . . they would be sorely disappointed.

9

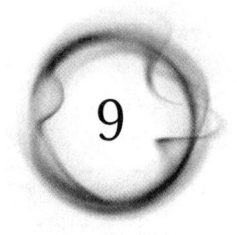

The Deathless One sat in the corner of her room, his fingers steepled and pressed against his lips. Every time he visited her in the living realm, it drained some of his magic. But he was learning.

He had to gather up his magic from that realm of endless power that was his to control. He had to bring it with him, because he had no connection to that realm here. If he had a body, he would be connected to both living and dead. But for now, he was limited by his spectral form, which could only store so much power. His strength would ebb, and he would find himself sucked back into the same shadow realm where he had existed before.

It was infuriating.

And it was more infuriating that he even wanted to see her. He had things to do in that realm of darkness. Plans to make for the moment he was released from his confines. Now that he had a reason to be awake and aware, he remembered almost everything that he'd lost.

Jessamine had made that happen, even if unwillingly. She had awakened the demon deep inside him, and now he wanted to seize the world again. He would punish the witches for what they had done to him, even if that meant that he had to scour the earth for the few living ones remaining.

This one would bring him into an age of ruin when he would finally get his revenge, and she didn't know how much it would eventually hurt her. Although, considering the past few nights he'd been watching over her, he suspected she might know something.

She lay on that pile of rags like a lost soul he'd found in the rubble of a fallen empire. Legs splayed, her skirt had ridden up those pale thighs. Though he couldn't see that much of her, the sight of her skin made a fire rage in his chest.

He wanted her, and that was a problem. The last time he'd wanted a gravesinger, it had ended poorly for him. No one could blame him for thinking she would be the same.

If she was like the others, then she would soon try to seduce him. She would wriggle her way underneath his guard and then be angry when he didn't give her everything that she wanted. The pouting and the tears would get under his shell even more. Pathetic creatures like her had always been his weakness.

So he had to beat her to it. He had to seduce her first. Get her under his thumb until she couldn't think of a life without him. Then, and only then, would he have complete and utter control over her.

"What are you doing here?" Sybil's quiet voice interrupted his staring at the little woman currently curled in the bundle of rags.

"You know what I'm doing," he grunted.

Sybil stood in the doorway, lingering in those shadows like she feared coming into the room. "But you're . . ."

"Patrons can summon me at will. Gravesingers I can find without needing a summons. You know how this works, witch." He looked over at her, certain that she couldn't tell where he was looking unless he turned his head and she saw the movement. "I wouldn't need a summons at all if I had my body back. As you were supposed to convince her to do."

"I'm not asking for the how. I'm asking the why." Sybil stepped into the room quietly, her hands wringing the skirts around her waist. "Why are you here with her?"

He didn't have an answer for that. Only that she was here, and so was he. Sitting in the corner of her room like some bird of prey, just waiting for the twitches she made in her sleep that made him want to leap on top of her.

Sybil blew out a long breath, casting her eyes up to the ceiling, and he could see the caution running through her head. She was telling herself not to say anything, and yet, she opened her mouth anyway. "She dreams of the other gravesingers."

"Nightmares are normal in her situation."

"She dreams of *your* gravesingers. They tell her things that are dangerous for her to learn this early." At his sudden jerk in her direction, she took a step away from him and added, "They tell her to take from you. To rip from you."

This was a problem. He didn't want her to think that there was another end to this story. Why Sybil didn't want her to hear it, he wasn't sure. Perhaps this witch thought she would take his power from him before Jessamine did.

She was wrong, but he did not care what reasoning she had. He nodded and turned his attention back to the sleeping woman. "I will take care of them."

"Can you?"

"They exist in my realm, witch. I cannot destroy the energy they have left behind, but I can and will control them."

At least he thought so. They were bound to him just as he was to them. They were the lingering remnants of those witches who had sacrificed their lives so the one remaining gravesinger could use that power in whatever way she saw fit; they were the ones who had dragged him down into the muck. Their curse was a thorn in his side, but not one he couldn't control.

Chains would do. Once he got back into that realm, he would loop the chains over their forms. Over and over again until they were trapped in a small section of his realm that Jessamine would never find.

And if they still bothered her, then he would cut out their tongues.

A shudder rippled through his body at the feral thoughts. He wasn't... like that. Not with witches. Not with anyone, although he had very little experience in any of these matters, he supposed.

The Deathless One was a god who was used and then discarded. That was his function in life, and always had been.

Sybil still hesitated, standing in that doorway with more thoughts on her mind.

"What is it?" he growled.

"Isn't there something you can do for her? For now? She's just... She's awfully frightened. It's hard to teach someone who is so afraid of what she might turn into."

He sighed. "I do not know anything about comforting witches. That is why you are here."

"You've been around us for centuries on end, and you still don't know how to make us feel better?" She clearly had not intended to blurt the words, because the moment she said them, her eyes went round and her jaw hung open. "I'm sorry, Your Holiness. I should never have thought—"

He lifted a shadow hand, pausing her apologetic rant. "You do not have to be fearful, witch. I have use for you yet."

Sybil nodded but was already backing away. "I will do my best."

"I tire of the bowing supplicant. Think of me as your . . ." He didn't know what to call himself. He was her god, and she *should* be afraid of him. "I am your patron, witch. You may speak your mind without fear."

She'd already ducked out of the room, though. Leaving him with a unconscious gravesinger and a hundred questions running through his mind.

Though it might have been smarter to think about the opinionated witch with some semblance of power, he couldn't focus on Sybil. His gaze continually returned to Jessamine's trembling figure. Over and over again, no matter how many times he told himself to stop.

What was going on with this little nightmare who had walked into his life? He had all her memories. He knew every step of her past and all the decisions she'd made. Nothing was hidden from him. Not the number of times she'd snuck into her room to pleasure herself, not the trysts she'd had with neighboring dignitaries, nor the disgust she felt when they did not satisfy her.

And why was he even thinking about those memories? He didn't care about her sexual history, just like he didn't care about Sybil's. They were both witches. Both creatures who would stab him in the back the moment they were given the opportunity to do so.

Still, every time she shivered in her sleep, something coiled tighter inside him. A knot that he could not loosen, no matter how much he tugged at it.

Dropping his head into his hands, he ran those scarred fingers through the strands. "Comfort the witch," he breathed.

There wasn't much that he knew comforted their kind, other than power. They didn't call him to ask for anything along those lines, anyway. All they cared about was his magic and what he could offer them. That was the nature of his patronage, unlike his brother the Warrior Son, who fucked anything with legs. Some that didn't have legs, too, if he remembered right. Although his memory of his family was still rather hazy.

Blowing out a breath, he sat up again to look at her. She was such a tiny thing. Nightmares were apparently terrifying to her, and he had no way of knowing what would ease that fear.

A low rumble rolled through his chest, the growl deep and echoing in the room. Strangely, she seemed to hear it. Jessamine relaxed in her sleep for a moment, and then went right back to twitching.

Warmth. Rumbling sounds. What else had she liked when she was a child?

It seemed he could still sift through her memories even when he wasn't in his realm. Interesting. A small part of him wanted to explore her current thoughts just a bit more—was she thinking of him?—but he had all of her past to go through whenever he wished. Perhaps it wasn't fair of him to want to know more.

He flipped through the memories of her soul until he found the perfect thing. And it was so easy to conjure.

Sinking onto his knees beside her, he hovered his hands over her. Words poured from his mouth, the ancient tongue flowing with power and pulling at all the meager remains of magic he had to keep him in this realm. But he needed to do this.

Shadows ripped from his hands, wispy things, delicate as smoke but strong as steel. They coiled around each other, drawing in until they had almost a physical manifestation. Baring his teeth, he forced them into a tighter swirl, giving them life where there had been none before. Just as he had for her.

With one last spark of power, nearly dragging the air out of him until he could no longer breathe with it, he severed the spell. Gasping, he braced himself with a fist on the floor. He had to stay here. Just to see what he had conjured—or, if he was being honest, to see her reaction.

Jessamine stirred, her eyes blearily blinking open to see the small bundle of shadows that had curled in the vacant space near her belly. She was wrapped around his gift, her knees drawn up to cradle it against her heartbeat.

"What?" she whispered, her hands coming down to comb through the fur that he was certain was soft as velvet. "Where did you come from?"

The tiny void pressed against her skin yawned, revealing a bright pink tongue and a set of teeth that were razor sharp. Its tail was maybe a little too long for its form, and it was certainly the largest kitten he'd ever seen in this realm, but it was a cat nonetheless. Pointed ears flicked at the sound of her voice.

It stood, stretching its front paws out and flexing long nails in the rags. Tail in the air, it flattened its chest against the floor while pinning its ears back in a long stretch of its spine. But then it sauntered up to Jessamine's face, rubbing that soft fur against her chin before curling up again next to her chest.

The heavy sigh that followed clearly said the kitten was exhausted, and what was all the fuss about?

Her eyes flicked up to find him crouched there, his hand still braced against the floor, looming above the two of them.

"Was this you?" she whispered, as though she was afraid to disturb the kitten now purring very loudly.

He didn't know what to say. The way her eyes filled with tears, and all that hope in her gaze, it did something to him.

The Deathless One decided then and there that he preferred her angry. The feisty witch with a scornful mouth was infinitely easier to deal with than the woman before him. He didn't want to see her so pliant from sleep, warm and snuggling with one of his creations. He didn't want to see that small smile at the corners of her lips, or the way she looked at him like maybe he wasn't so terrible. Maybe, just maybe, he wasn't the nightmarish god that she'd always heard about.

This soft version of her was too tempting, and it hurt too much to look at her and know it was all a lie.

Grunting, he stood so he didn't have to look at her. "Every witch needs a familiar, nightmare. Make good use of it."

"What am I supposed to do with a familiar?"

He shrugged, already feeling that ever-present tug of his realm. He'd used too much power, and now he could hardly keep himself here with her. "Care for it. Get rid of it. I don't care what you do with the beastie."

But the lie fizzled on his tongue even as he said the words, because she drew the kitten closer to her face and breathed in the scent of his magic still lingering on its fur. "Thank you."

He disappeared before he could do something foolish. Before he could decide to stay a little while longer and crawl onto those rags with her. A kitten would keep her nightmares at bay for now.

He would banish them forever.

The cold breeze of his realm covered him, sinking into his skin as ink immediately grabbed at his legs. The remains of those gravesingers wanted to keep him here. They had given their lives to lock him away for good, to steal his power in one final attempt to save a dying kingdom. And they had failed. Instead, they were stuck with him here. Knowing what they had done.

He turned toward their spirits, dark claws pushing through his fingers even as he summoned chains out of the dark waters. He would think about these complicated and unwelcome thoughts later. For now, he had witches to bind.

10

He knew it wouldn't take long for Jessamine to summon him after that. She was a naturally curious little thing. That was what had brought her to this abandoned manor and what had led her to trust a rotting figure of a witch.

Soon enough, she would call upon him again. All he had to do was wait.

Thankfully, he had entertainment waiting for him. It took him a long time to find every remaining soul of previous gravesingers. They were particularly good at hiding in the ink, but he was particularly good at finding them.

Looping the chains around their necks had barely satisfied his need to see them punished. These souls were so weak, merely a hint of what they used to be. What he wanted was to punish the one who remained out there. The one who should have summoned him by now.

He'd waited, and then he'd succumbed to the darkness of his realm. The ink claimed him, grabbing him by the shoulders and pulling him into the shadows of his own power. This was where he would replenish himself. This was how he would gather his power, if only it didn't drown him while he did so.

Then he heard her. The whispering need flowing through his realm and through that tiny thread of hatred that connected them.

For a moment, he forgot that he'd vowed to remain separate from this new gravesinger. He forgot that years of manipulation and pain should make his mind scream when he heard Jessamine's voice. Instead, all he heard was the softness there. The begging.

"Deathless One." Her voice filtered through all the memories.

He turned his face toward the sound of it, as though he was turning his face toward the moonlight. A cool breeze. A frigid kiss that burned away the fever in his body. The whispered promise of trust and perhaps a connection that would lead him out of this place.

Such dreams were fairy tales that would never come true. She was like all the others, he reminded himself. She was a witch, and a witch only knew power. Even if she had no interest in it now, she would use him eventually. There would come a time when power was more important than connection. It always ended up like that.

But he still wanted. He still dreamed.

Even the magic of this place could not hold him when a witch summoned him. It was why he found his body dragged out of the black muck, coughing up obsidian blood that dripped down his chin and splattered upon the equally dark ground. His ribs ached. His stomach rebelled at the pain as hands tried to drag him back into the abyss, leaving dark bruises behind.

He couldn't stay away even if he wanted to. Jessamine's voice pulled at him. Tugging deep in his body, forcing him to return to the realm of waking. Like a drop of ink in clear water, he manifested in the shadows of the altar room.

She'd chosen the same place to meet him. Though he ached and exhaustion crept into his vision, he knew this was by design.

Jessamine was far too intelligent. She knew how to choose a battlefield of wits, and for some reason, she had chosen this one again. To conquer him? To bury a memory?

No, he decided, looking at her as she knelt prim and proper before the altar. She had summoned him here to defeat a nightmare. The dark circles under her eyes betrayed her.

"Sleeping better?" he asked, trying to keep his voice unaffected. But even he could hear the hoarse crackle in the words.

Her head snapped in his direction, a disapproving scowl already on her face. "I could ask you the same."

"I don't sleep."

"Hmm." She crossed her arms over her chest and looked him up and down. "You sound awful."

"Being dead does that to a person."

"Thank you for the cat," she said. And there it was again. That softness that made her long lashes flicker against her cheeks as her gaze dropped. "It . . . helped. Even if I'm not certain it actually is a cat."

No. He couldn't suffer through this again. Jessamine had bared that swanlike neck to him, and it made him *need*. He wanted to bite down on it, to leave his mark even more than that scar that wrapped around her throat. He wanted to mar that pretty skin until it was covered with bruises made not by his hands, but by his mouth.

The Deathless One needed to control this situation. He sat down on top of the altar before he fell down, staring down at her kneeling between his legs. "Pretty picture," he murmured.

Her face turned bright red. "You're trying to distract me."

"Is it working?"

"No."

Tsking, he leaned back on his hands. The altar felt a little more real today. He could almost feel the texture of the stone and how cold it was against his palms. That was strange. He usually couldn't feel anything at all in this form.

Except her.

He curled his fingers around the stone so he didn't touch her again. It was hard to ignore the memory of her soft skin in his hands. Or the way she'd swallowed against his palm, her heart beating rapidly against his scarred fingertips. She'd been so fragile in his arms and yet didn't struggle to free herself. Stupid girl. But brave, he'd admit.

She glared up at him, all regal indignation, as if he owed her something.

"What?" he finally asked, exasperated with her already. "What do you want now?"

"I'm the one controlling this meeting, not you." She tilted her nose up, looking all the more like the princess she was. It made him want to ruffle her again, if only to see this mask break.

He had thought this would be easier. The Deathless One had spent a long time dreaming about what the next gravesinger would be like. In his experience, witches were easy to control. They all wanted the same thing: power. They enjoyed toying with him, but in the end, he always won until it was time for them to sacrifice him.

This one didn't seem to be all that interested in power. In fact, he had yet to figure out what she did want. Other than her throne back, of course. But that would not happen anytime soon.

The girl had been betrayed by everyone she'd held dear. Soon enough, she would realize that in the worst way possible.

"Then control the meeting." He waved a hand in the air. "So far, all I've heard is bickering and childish snipes. You do remember I am a god? I am busy."

"You're a dead god. What could you possibly have to do?"

"Stare into the everlasting eternal darkness and dream about a time when I wasn't dead," he snarled, leaning forward as anger flashed through him. "And I'm late for that appointment, witch."

"Stop calling me that." Jessamine glared at him with obvious hatred. "I am not a witch."

"Do you prefer 'princess'?"

"Not when you say it like that!" She almost shouted the words, so angry with him that all her years of decorum flew out the window.

Oh, that was satisfying. He liked the way her cheeks flushed with anger, and how she tried to keep her tiny hands fisted so he wouldn't know how badly they trembled.

Tempting. She really was a pretty little thing, and even in her anger, he wanted to prod her. Make her even angrier. He wanted to see what it would take to make her explode, and just how glorious she would be when she did.

Jessamine lurched away from him, perhaps so she didn't have to look at him. If she couldn't see him, maybe there was less for her to be infuriated with.

"How's that working for you?" he asked, leaning forward even more to watch what happened next.

"What are you talking about?"

"You're clearly not looking at me to get your emotions under control. I want to know how that is working for you."

Tilting her head up to the ceiling, she muttered a short prayer. He wondered what god she still prayed to before she turned around to glare at him.

She raised a finger and jabbed it in his direction. "Is this your plan? Annoy me to no end and eventually I'll forget why I summoned you in the first place?"

He shrugged. "Perhaps."

"Well, it's not going to work." She visibly pulled herself back together before sinking into the same position before the altar. Between his legs. Her hands folded in her lap. So pretty, yet a few erratic strands of hair now stood out, freed by her wild pacing before she'd returned to him.

Ah, he had gotten to her. Now all he wanted to do was loosen a few more of those strands, to see what she looked like completely wild.

He was unable to stop himself. He'd never had the ability to deny himself soft things. The Deathless One leaned forward and snagged a strand of her hair between his fingers. He marveled at the texture. It caught on the calluses and scars on his fingertips, still somehow silken even when it snapped in his grip. So fragile.

Just like her.

"I want to know my future," she said, her voice a low rasp. "And you're the only one who can help me. I've talked with Sybil. Both of us agree that if I am to continue forward and get my throne back, the only person who can help me is you."

"You've already gotten my help. I gave you life, and now you will do with it as you wish."

"We both know that's a lie." She tugged her hair from his grip, forcing his attention back to her. "You know something that you aren't telling me."

"What could I possibly know?"

"I have researched you and the other gods for years. I've read countless books that cover your powers, the people who worshipped you, everything I should need to know." Crossing her arms over her chest, she bit her lip before begrudgingly adding, "And I still know nothing, clearly. That book claimed you can sneak into someone's mind. You can see what they saw at any point. You can break into their memories and find details in there that tell you everything you need to know about them. Is that true?"

Again, he shrugged, just because he knew it annoyed her. "Perhaps."

What could she want from him? He would not give her the easy answer. If she wanted to know more, she would need to beg. He wouldn't make anything easy for her—she hadn't earned that.

Not yet at least.

"You could give me a straight answer for once," she growled. "Just tell me, yes or no? Is it possible for you to see into my past?"

"I can see into your memories," he corrected. "I can see whatever you saw. That is all. Will that give you any more answers? I doubt it. Already you have realized that there is much you ignored or did not see, and that has nothing to do with me. You were unobservant. Your entire kingdom was ripped out from under you without you realizing why or who did it. None of that is my fault."

"Yes, but you can help."

"Why should I help you?" He hopped off the altar and crouched in front of her. He couldn't stop himself from stealing another touch of her skin, gliding his finger underneath her chin as he lifted her face to look at him. "Convince me, nightmare."

She hesitated for a few moments. Perhaps because she speculated about what he wanted her to do, perhaps she was wondering what she could offer a god like himself.

Eventually, she looked him straight in the eye. "I have nothing to offer that you want. That's the trick in this, isn't it? You want me to think that there's something I can trade. But there isn't."

"There is one thing you can do for me."

"I'm not bringing you into this world. Not without knowing why you want to be here so much."

Tossing her head to the side, he strode away from her in anger. The spiking emotion pushed into his heart like she'd shoved a dagger into that empty cavity. The girl asked too much. She wanted him to give her something freely, without a bargain. He didn't do that. He wasn't a benevolent god anymore. Not to witches, and not to her.

"Is it not enough for me to say that I miss being alive?" He paused in front of the cracked windowpane, covered in grime from years of neglect. "I miss what it feels like to stand in the sun. To see the dappled shadows of leaves on the ground. To taste wine on my tongue and feel the heat of a fire."

"You don't miss the touch of a woman?" she asked, her voice dry and unexpectedly cruel. "Or a man, if that's your interest."

"Why would I miss that?" The words were bitter, and she was lucky he didn't whirl on her in anger. "Touch is cruel to someone like me. Who touches a deathless god with tenderness when the intent behind those touches is to sacrifice me in the end? Why would I miss the touch of those who see me as nothing more than a bargaining chip? A bid for power that they can control? No, I do not miss the touch of anyone."

Phantom pains danced down his arms, his chest, his back. All the spots where he had been maimed, tortured, tormented.

Sacrificed.

He heard the sound of her rising before he knew she had moved. One moment she was kneeling before the altar, and the next she stood beside him, though he noted she left a sizable distance between them. Out of respect or fear, he would not guess.

"I don't know what memory plagues you, but I do know what it is like to be manipulated." She swallowed, her throat working, before she took a deep breath and plunged ahead. "I'm not asking you to give me anything. I just want you to help me walk through my memories so that I can notice what I didn't before. I need to know what I did not see before I continue forward."

"You do not need me for that."

"But it will be a lot faster if you help me." She wrapped her arms around her chest before turning to him. "I cannot and will not bring you back to life without fully understanding this world that I am now part of. You want me to be a witch? Fine. I'll be a witch. I will learn everything there is to know about being a witch, and then I will make my choice. Satisfied?"

"I don't want you to be a witch," he hissed. "I want you to be a gravesinger."

"Then I will be a gravesinger."

It was a shitty bargain, and he knew it. But it was likely the only bargain he'd give her.

He looked her over, watching her squirm under his gaze the longer he stayed quiet. If she truly dedicated herself to becoming a gravesinger, to learning spells and investing her time here with Sybil, there was a chance she would realize its benefit. All witches had a patron.

All witches made deals.

It kept her closer to him, closer than she was aware. His little nightmare likely thought this just meant she got his help for longer, but that was not at all what she was agreeing to. Every spell she used drew upon his power, tying them closer and closer together.

So he nodded. "Fine. You have a deal, Jessamine."

She held out her hand, as if that made all of this more official. Rolling his eyes, he ignored her offered hand and reached out for her face instead. Placing his hands over her eyes, he let the power roll from between his fingers and attach to the orbs there. He muttered a word in the old language, a word that would force her back into her memories, then drew his hands back.

Her dark pupils spread into the whites, spiderweb patterns breaking through her skin and stretching across her cheeks and forehead. She blew out a shaky breath. "I can't feel your hand anymore."

"That's because I'm not touching you, nightmare."

She lifted shaking hands to touch her eyes, skating over her forehead before she let out a little sound of distress. "My eyes. I can't see, Deathless One. What did you do to my eyes?"

He leaned closer, breathing out a low growl in her ear before replying, "I took them so you *could* see. Did you think magic would come without a price?"

The whimper almost made him feel a little bad for not preparing her. Almost.

As it was, he cupped his hands around her shoulders and squeezed. "Now, remember."

"I can't . . . I can't see . . ."

"Jessamine." He gave her a little shake, her head snapping back and forth before she focused on him again. "Remember."

Then he dove into her memories with her at his side.

11

She couldn't *see*! What had that monster done to her?

She knew better than to make deals with creatures like him. She knew he would trick her, try to control her, do something that would ruin all this. And when he whispered in her ear that all magic had a price, she realized she had known that, too. Though he had tricked her, all of this was her fault. If she had known he would take her eyes in return for seeing the past, she would have figured something else out.

But then she felt him touch her shoulders, and all the world fell away. Suddenly she tumbled through her past, seeing the long days she'd been on the streets trying to pull herself together. The sewer. The fall. The wedding, the moment she stood in her laboratory and wondered if she was making a horrible mistake.

"Stop," she croaked, realizing that at least in her memories she could still see. "Stop, right there."

There it was, the image of herself in the lab and Callum standing in the doorway. She stood to the side of herself, as though she'd just stepped out of her own body and could waltz around the room.

Eerily, everything else remained frozen. She could see Callum's foot halfway lifted to stomp on the rat. The bubbles in the glass beakers stayed halfway up the necks, and if she squinted hard, she could even see smoke rising from the candles and the flames that no longer flickered.

It was equally strange and exhilarating. She had gone back in time, with everything else frozen around her. She walked to the door, then peered around Callum into a black hallway. Like someone had set up a diorama of what she could remember, and nothing else existed beyond it.

"How . . . strange," she muttered, walking back into the room. "This is my memory?"

She didn't know who she was asking. Certainly not the shadowy figure standing in front of her books. She couldn't even tell if he was looking at her, although she realized he wasn't when a dark chuckle filled the room, followed by the soft scrape of his boots as he turned.

"So it's true you were already researching witchcraft long before you came to me?" His featureless face turned, as if looking at her, before he pointed out her books. "Some of these are quite wicked."

She lunged forward as he pulled down a particularly devious spell book on sex magic. Grabbing it out of his hands, she glowered at him while putting it back in its place. "Keep your sticky fingers to yourself."

"Why should I do that? Some of these books you don't remember at all." His dark finger trailed over a few of the titles that had only the vague impression of a name. "But you remember this one all too clearly."

Cheeks flaming bright red, she ground her teeth together before replying, "Can we please get back to my memories?"

"We are in your memories. If you were interested in carnal magic, you should have told me." He leaned closer, and she suddenly had the distinct realization that he smelled strongly of citrus and mint. "I would be most interested in teaching you that kind of magic."

Planting her hands hard on his chest, and trying to ignore the muscles that flexed underneath his palm, she gave him a quick shove. At least that created a little more space between them, even if she couldn't take her eyes off him.

He wasn't quite the rough charcoal sketch that she was used to. At least not here. There was more of a form to him, a shape that wasn't what she had expected. Tall, yes. But so very lean.

"I can see you better in this space," she murmured, furrowing her brows in confusion. "You're smaller than I thought you'd be."

He reared back from her. "Not words men usually like to hear."

"Not... It's just your hands. You have really big hands. I thought..." She shrugged. "I thought you'd be larger, that's all."

"I don't know whether to be insulted or flattered."

"That you're smaller than I thought?" She started toward the door. "Take that however you will, Deathless One."

"I don't appreciate the sass, nightmare."

Trying hard to smother her smile, she stood in front of the door and waved at him. "It needs to go further. To the wedding."

She could feel his gaze on the back of her head. But time started moving again, shifting and pushing them through the halls, and suddenly she was at the altar, standing in front of Leon as he glared down at her.

"Stop," she said, her heart in her throat.

She knew this moment. She knew without having to hear what he was saying that Leon was asking about her witchcraft. He only asked if she was still researching black magic, but she knew that he was really asking if there were still grotesque things in her lab and if she... she...

A different memory suddenly flashed in front of this one. Leon gripped her biceps so tightly that she'd had a ring of dark bruises around it. He'd asked her about the magic then, too. He'd wanted to know the answer, and when she refused to tell him, he'd grabbed her so hard she'd cried out.

That was when she'd seen the passion in his eyes. He'd never looked at her with anything other than apathy, but in that moment, her pain had made desire burn through his core.

"Jessamine." The voice merged with Leon's. But that voice was more terrifying than Leon's, wasn't it?

There was the fear she'd felt when she had seen the desire in Leon's eyes, but then there was another kind of fear entirely. One that crawled up from inside her very being and whispered that she stood before a predator and that she needed to run... run... run...

"Jessamine," the voice said again, and this time she blinked to see a dark figure before her. A figure who, if she squinted hard enough, was wearing her eyes.

"What?" she croaked.

"Oh, good, I didn't break you." He stepped back from her, shaking his head with what was clearly disapproval. "Memories are a delicate business, nightmare. You can't go wandering around without me."

"I'm sorry." Jessamine staggered away from him, trying to put some space between herself and Leon. "I didn't mean to."

"Don't waste your apologies on me. I don't care for them." He took one step after her, almost as though he was . . . worried?

"I'm—"

"Don't, nightmare." He looked like he wanted to touch her. His hands flexed at his sides, opening and closing before he turned from her.

"Right," she muttered, squeezing her own hands into fists. "No more apologies."

Jessamine gathered the tattered edges of her courage and held them close to her. Nothing could happen here. Leon couldn't kill her again; he was frozen in memory. Standing in front of her with that stupid lock of hair flopped down on his forehead. He looked so docile. So safe.

But he was not a safe person to be around, and she hated that her kingdom was at his feet.

She hated even more the expression frozen on her face. The anxiety that pinched her mouth and the resolve that wrinkled her brow. She'd be married to this man, this monster who would soon kill her, and there was nothing she could do to stop it.

"Why were you going to marry him, anyway?" the Deathless One asked as he wandered behind the image of Leon.

"It's what the kingdom needed."

"Was it? How do you know?"

She shrugged. "I didn't. But the plague is getting out of control. All of our people are either ill or risk getting sick if they stay outside for too long. They risk their lives working, so we had to do something. We had to convince them that we were going to bring money and a solution into the kingdom."

"From what I saw, plenty of people still wander the streets."

The words made her mind stutter. He was right. The streets were thronged with townsfolk, even if there were sick people as well. Why had that been?

Frowning, she shook her head. "No, all the reports were that the city wasn't functioning at all. That's why my mother made the deal with the kingdom of Orenda in the first place."

"And you trusted those reports?" The Deathless One leaned around Leon's shoulder, his darkness looming tall above the other man. "Or were you just told that things were bad, and you believed them?"

Oh, she had no idea. As she might have if this was real, she looked down the aisle to where her mother sat. The queen always knew what to do. Always.

But this time, her mother wasn't going to respond. Her mother was dead, and this image of her was so perfect that she could almost pretend for a few moments that she was still here. That she hadn't faded away out of existence. Because nothing had happened yet. Not in this memory.

She took a step down the stairs, then froze in place. A single tear dripped down her cheek as she felt like her entire soul was ripped open. "She'd know what to do."

"Who?" The Deathless One didn't follow her down the stairs, but he looked where she was staring. "The queen?"

"She always made the right decision."

"Not this time, it seems. After all, she died. Her daughter died. Her entire kingdom was thrown into turmoil, and it took me to save everything." He snorted. "Of all people."

"I'm not taking advice from a dead man."

"Dead god," he corrected. "And are you really done with this one?"

She glanced over her shoulder to see him pointing at Leon. "Not yet. But this is just a memory, and there's nothing I can do about it. I can't go back in time and change the fact that he killed me."

"But—" He drew out the word.

"But I intend to see him dead, eventually."

"So why not now? It's your memory. If you want him gone, I can make him gone." He turned toward Leon, and she swore she saw his entire shape darken even further. Suddenly, it was like she stared into utter darkness without a single spark of light. "I wouldn't mind the order if you asked me to kill him, witch."

A thrill of power echoed through her chest. Jessamine touched the sudden ache between her ribs, only to realize it wasn't she who had the reaction. No, it was him. The Deathless One wanted to hurt Leon. He wanted to do whatever he could, even in this memory.

And she found herself more than a little intrigued. "All right," she found herself saying. "Get rid of him."

"Gladly." The feral sound of a snarl echoed throughout the courtyard before the Deathless One raised a suddenly clawed hand and plunged it into Leon's chest.

To her shock, the memory staggered at the sudden attack. Leon's eyes bulged out of his head; he stared down at his torso before looking up at the massive outline of darkness that stood before him. A black hand, inky with blood, withdrew from his chest to hover in front of Leon's horrified gaze.

"You reek of murder," the Deathless One snarled. "What survived your attack will not be so easy to kill a second time."

Cracks formed all up and down Leon's memory, like she'd dropped a glass from a great height. With the barest touch of the Deathless One's claw, he shattered. All that remained was the faintest gray dust on the ground.

Her mouth was open, she realized. But really, he had just turned a memory to dust.

"Could . . ."

"Could he feel that in the real world?" the Deathless One grumbled, wiping his hand on his leg before turning to her. "Probably. He likely saw the image of me as well, though he'll ignore it as a nightmare or a passing panic attack. It was a good warning for him, though. He shouldn't get too comfortable on that stolen throne."

He'd . . . sent a warning? For her?

Warmth bloomed in her chest. "Thank you."

"For what?" he growled.

"For looking out for me."

He didn't respond to that, but she had a feeling she'd made him very uncomfortable. Something about that was so satisfying.

Pleased with herself, she turned her attention once again to her mother. The queen was perfect. But Jessamine hadn't remembered her brow being wrinkled with concern, or the way her mother had clutched the skirts in her lap so hard that she'd crumpled them.

Had she thought this might happen? Was there some worry in her mother's mind that maybe this hadn't been the right choice?

Perhaps she'd realized the same thing the Deathless One had realized. They'd been fooled, and they were all about to suffer for it.

"Move the memory forward," she whispered. "Just by a few moments."

Jessamine stood there in the center of chaos as the gates burst open, as Leon yelled at her, as her mother sat there in the middle of all that madness and never moved a muscle. As though her memory was frozen while everything else moved.

"I'm afraid I'll forget," she whispered as the Deathless One paused the memories once again. "I'm afraid that one day, I will try to remember her and I won't know what her smile looks like. I won't know the sound of her laughter, or the way she used to make this little noise whenever she disapproved of my outfit. Someday I won't be able to recall if her gray streak was on the right or the left side of her head. Maybe I won't even remember the exact shade of her eyes. Were they an icy blue? Or were they the color of the sky?"

She felt his presence behind her, lurking just out of reach. "Well?" he asked. "What color are they?"

She stared into her mother's eyes, feeling twin tears drip down her cheeks as she answered. "Sapphire. Like a calm lake on the clearest of days. I thought I had years to learn and remember all this. To commit every detail to memory. If only I had known there were mere seconds left."

There was the strange sensation of a hand hovering over her shoulder before it drifted away.

"I am uncomfortable with emotion," he grumbled before clearing his throat. "But I am sorry for your loss."

Wiping away her tears, she nodded. "I am, too."

Jessamine stood in the silence, feeling the ache of her heart still beating in her chest. She was supposed to be with them. All of them. Her mother, the nobles who had died loyal to their queen. They were all waiting for her, and instead she was here, fighting for a kingdom that might not even want her.

"You missed him," the Deathless One said, breaking through her thoughts. "There's your answer, nightmare."

She blinked, then followed his pointing arm to the gates, where the infected were just making their way into her home. "Who . . . Benji?"

A young man with a pageboy hat and a stick in his mouth stood holding the gate open. He always had some kind of pick between his teeth, gnawing on the wood like it was his job. He was easy to miss.

"No," she whispered, taking a step closer to the memory, even though it was hazy around the edges. "He's just a pageboy. Mother used to send him to fetch her peach pie from the market."

"Peach pie?" the Deathless One repeated. "That sounds terrible."

"It's delicious," she corrected absentmindedly. "Why would Benji open the gates? We gave him a place to sleep, a home, food, and money. There was no reason for him to turn against us."

"Then that sounds like what you have to find out, nightmare. Why did he betray you, and just how far was he willing to go to do so?"

"And who made him betray us?"

The memory shivered, warped, and then splintered apart like a cracked glass mirror. She could feel herself falling long before the memories disappeared and Jessamine was weightless. Floating between reality and her own mind. But this time, she wasn't so afraid as she felt her body coming alive beneath her.

She blinked once, twice, three times, and the room came back into view.

This time, she was alone. No god to crouch by her side or make her feel questionable things.

But as she sat up, wiping her eyes with the heels of her palms, she stared down at the black charcoal that came from where he'd stolen her sight. And she couldn't help but wonder if he felt as bereft as she did.

12

He didn't know what was happening, but the longer he was around her, the more real he felt.

Perhaps it was part of the magic that came with siphoning off some of his power to her. She was absorbing that, which in turn meant that he could steal some of it back from her. It allowed him to stay in the living realm longer, feel more alive. As long as she called him, at least. And she called him often, if his understanding of time was correct.

Time was so difficult to keep track of, especially when he spent so many days in his dark realm. The ink and the memories were always so convincing that it felt like ages, not days. It made him long to be around her, closer to her, and the other gravesingers whispered to give in to her allure.

A witch had made him trust her once before. He'd forgiven her every fault, because he'd thought himself in love. Countless times he'd ignored the warning signs as he played the fool who had hoped that to her, he wasn't just a monster. That he could actually find someone who saw . . . him.

But those gravesingers whispered that he didn't even know who he was. How could he? The only time he'd spent trying to discover himself had been under the watchful eyes of a witch who had guided him toward what she wanted. An end for both of them, filled with blood and power.

Shaking himself free from the dark thoughts yet again, he searched the void around him. He had come to realize that he now waited to hear Jessamine's voice. He would stand still, for days on end, he feared, listening.

Sometimes it was just her voice bleeding into this realm as she took lessons from Sybil. Or maybe it was her dreams. She called out for him in that dreamscape, and it took everything in him not to place himself in her mind during those moments. Did she think she was dead again? Or did she cry out for him for other reasons?

Dangerous thoughts for a creature like him. Especially when he knew how this ended.

Now, though, he didn't hear her at all. There was a strange stillness in this place. Like even the inky darkness held its breath, waiting for the moment when he would sense a change. Because there had to be a change, otherwise he wouldn't be listening so hard. He wouldn't feel all the hairs on his arms rising as he . . .

Waited.

"You're a godsdamned fool," he muttered to himself. "Waiting for her to call on you like she's already turned you into her pet, just like the cat you made her. You could just go yourself."

But he couldn't do that either. He didn't want to be her puppet, waiting with bated breath for the first order she would give him. The other gravesinger, the other witches, they had all tried to wield him like a weapon, and he had let them. For an ounce of their attention, for a drop of genuine affection, he would have ended the world.

These feelings had nothing to do with her, he told himself, and everything to do with his desperation to feel something other than pain or abandonment.

In her memories, when she said he appeared to have more of a shape, he'd realized that was dangerously true. Even when he'd watched her from the shadows as she scrubbed her eyes afterward, there was more definition to his body, a sensation of weightiness that he hadn't experienced before.

His mind and time were all scrambled. When had he shown her the memory? It felt like years, but in truth was only a few days ago. The memory of the boy she'd called Benji.

The timeline straightened out, and that was when he saw a reflection in the inky blackness at his feet. Not his reflection at all, but a dark-haired woman with haunted eyes, leaning against the side of a building.

Frowning, he stared down at his feet as Jessamine bolted forward and was gone.

"Wait," he muttered, following her through the watery pools.

Puddles, he realized as his foot matched hers and stomped through the water so hard it splashed up in his realm as well. She was running, racing, flying through the streets, and he had no choice but to follow her.

Bitterly, he felt his body move without his permission. The darkness took on form around him, stretching into the vague shapes of buildings with darkened windows as he ran with her. Sprinting through the black streets, watching as she turned a corner and his realm mimicked hers, conjuring reality out of nothing.

For a while they ran, their feet matching in the puddles. But then he could see her to his right, just below his shoulder. She truly was a slip of a thing.

"Why are you running?" he asked, his voice a low murmur.

She startled, looking through a mirror at him. "What are you doing here?"

"Following you."

"I don't need you to follow me right now."

"Tell me why you're running." He didn't understand why she was acting like this. There were far too many reasons for her to run, and nearly all of them required that he get involved.

"You can't see them?" Her cheeks were bright red with exertion, and her breathing was ragged. "You seem to know everything else, so I assumed you could see the damn infected trailing me."

He looked behind them and watched as muddy creatures appeared in the darkness. They trailed ink drops, plopping down from their fingers in long tendrils of madness.

"Ah," he muttered. "That is a problem."

"You're telling me. I've been trying to lose them for a while." She leaned to the right, out of his sight, before returning into view. "Can you do something about them?"

"I am dead, nightmare. Did you forget?"

"Right." She cursed, surprisingly raunchy for a princess. "Time to keep running, then."

"I don't believe they can climb." He had no idea where that memory came from, but there was the faintest flash of another life. A life when he had tried to prevent these creatures from spreading. "Perhaps try to find a way higher."

"Right. Worth a try." Jessamine seemed to scan her surroundings before she caught a glimpse of something. "That might work."

A ladder appeared beside him, dripping more of that liquid that coated everything in his home. But he found himself climbing it, rung by rung, all the way to the very top of a building. Once on top, he felt like he could see the end of forever.

His realm stretched so far beyond his reach. There was nothing there. Just a horizon with the vague sense of light to show him just how far away from everything he really was. So far. So beyond what he could ever dream or hope to find.

Between him and forever stood nothing at all.

"How far does it go?" he murmured.

"The city?" Jessamine seemed to still be with him, at least. "I don't know. Seems to stretch as far as the eye can see."

"It ends." He wasn't talking about her city. "Everything does. So there must be an end to this as well."

"I wouldn't be so sure about that."

The Deathless One looked down at the puddle he stood in, seeing her reflection instead. She wasn't looking at her city anymore. She was looking at him and the darkness beyond. "What makes you say that?"

"Just a hunch." She crouched, and his body was forced to mimic hers, as though he was *her* shadow. Her hand was so close to the water, they were almost touching.

"What are you doing out here, Jessamine?"

"I can't go anywhere looking like this. Clothes that don't fit, trousers falling off, a bodice that's clearly the top half of a wedding dress. It's not like Sybil had anything to give me. She only has the clothes on her back." She touched a hand to her snarled hair, then winced. "A hairbrush wouldn't be halfway bad either. My fingers aren't cutting it anymore."

"Sybil has all that."

"Actually, she doesn't." Jessamine looked troubled by the thought before she sucked in a breath through her teeth. "So I'm going to get myself something better."

"You plan on stealing? Princess, I didn't know you had it in you."

"I have money," she hissed. "And whenever you call me that, it sounds like an insult."

He grinned and wished she could see that grin. She certainly shivered like she could. "It's never meant as a compliment, I'll admit."

She stood, forcing him upright as well. Perhaps he'd insulted her. She didn't say another word for a while as she walked across construction planks, stretching from rooftop to rooftop, sometimes backtracking to find a plank and drag it with her. Anyone living on the top floor would know what she was doing, but perhaps the people of this city were so used to danger that they ignored someone scurrying around on their roof like a rat.

Eventually, she reached a roof where she could climb down a fire escape. The stairs on the side of the building must have been ancient. Even in his realm, he could feel them swaying under his weight.

But then she opened up a window and slipped inside, and he lost her.

With no puddles to show him her surroundings, his illusory building just . . . dissolved. He placed his hands in his pockets and rode the dark ink as it flattened back to the ground, where it eventually conjured a floor-length mirror. Oval in shape, it revealed her image on the other side and matched a mirror in the living realm where she stood.

She was desperately trying to remove her bodice, her arms straining as she reached behind herself to yank viciously at the ties. They were so soiled and knotted, however, they might as well have been one sewn thread.

And he stood there, tongue-tied, watching the lovely line of her neck and the hollows of her collarbones. She was . . . beautiful. He could see a small cluster of freckles on her right shoulder, and a little scar underneath her chin. Small imperfections of a princess who had always striven to be perfect. No matter how many times he looked at her, he knew that was the intention. Every memory he'd pawed through said the same thing. She was a paragon, a vision of perfection, a goddess come to life.

And yet, here she was. With freckles and a scar.

"Need help?" he asked through the mirror, his voice perhaps a little too hoarse.

"I can't get the damn thing off," she whispered. "Keep your voice down. Someone might wake."

"They'll definitely wake up if you don't stop stomping around in their dress shop." He peered around her, trying to see more details of the room. "If that's what you're standing in."

"*Can* you even help? It's not like I summoned you." She looked around and then growled in frustration. "There's not even a black candle in here."

Flexing his hands, he tested the boundaries of his own magic. Stepping forward, he found he could reach through the glass. He could almost feel the warmth of the store. Someone had recently left. Surely the heat would have already leaked out the drafty windows if they hadn't. A fire might still be in the hearth, if the shopkeeper was a risk-taker.

"Oh," she said, then turned away from him and backed into his hand.

He could feel the ties. The silken threads that even now were still so soft to the touch. Letting his eyes drift shut, he traced his fingers along the boning of the corset. When was the last time he'd felt texture? Anything other than damp and cold?

The cloth was warm from her skin, and he wanted to linger there. The scars on the tips of his fingers caught on the delicate fabric, and he could hear the scrape of his rough flesh against the thin weaving.

She shivered. He knew he was playing with fire, because eventually she'd tell him to stop. She'd take away the sensation that he hadn't felt in hundreds of years. He told himself to rush, but then the soft tail of her straight, dark hair brushed the back of his hand. Danced over the scars there, too, and oh . . . It was lovely.

Curling his fingers into claws, he used a surge of magic to slice through every single thread that held her corset onto her body in one clean swipe.

He heard her sharp gasp, and then there it was. Against his scarred, swollen fingertips, the warmth of her back. Like velvet. He could feel the delicate ridges of her spine. Then, as she bent, his fingers trailed down the piano keys of her ribs.

Her body sang a symphony of texture and warmth and sensation in just the briefest touch.

He blinked, opening his eyes to admire the delicate sway of her back before him. So pale he could see the spiderweb network of veins underneath it. If he looked hard enough, he swore he could see the beat of her heart through her ribs. A fragile little bird in front of him, all painted in ivory and silk.

"Thanks," she muttered, her voice a little wobbly. "Can you not look for a second?"

The Deathless One tried to swallow and found it almost impossible to speak yet again. Clearing his throat, he took a step away and turned his gaze from the mirror. "Of course."

She slipped out of view, and he berated himself again. He had told her that he did not miss the touch of a woman, and he didn't. He knew where that touch led, no matter how tempting or lovely it was. Yes, she was so delicate, and of course, it made his entire body clench with need. But if he gave in, she would use him and take whatever she wanted from him. He refused to fall to a witch ever again.

Pulling his mantle of darkness around him like a well-worn cloak, he returned to the mirror after he heard the rustle of fabric. This time, he wore the same face she must have come to expect. A god who had nothing in this world. A creature who was made to tease and test and perhaps even annoy.

She stepped in front of the mirror in a woolen white shirt that was far too big for her, draped over worn leather pants that actually fit. Fiddling with the sleeves, she looked up at him, and a wave of her dark hair fell in front of her eyes. Staring into that obscured, he reminded himself yet again that he was not here for her.

He was here for himself.

"Would you move?" she asked, clearly annoyed.

"No."

"I can't see past you."

"Then allow me to be your mirror." He looked her up and down, then tsked. "The shirt is terrible. It doesn't even remotely fit. The pants, however, are good enough."

"The pants are too tight, but the shirt is comfortable and practical."

"Try on something else." He enjoyed nothing more than watching her bare her teeth in a fake smile. "Something a little more feminine, if I might suggest such a thing."

"A man who hasn't changed his appearance in centuries is not one I would trust for fashion advice. Besides, shouldn't you want me to be in clothing that's a little easier to move in? Taking advice from a man with scarred hands and only historical knowledge about fashion seems like a bad idea." She disappeared from sight again, though, returning in a much nicer shirt that was better fitted for her shape. This one even had the barest hint of blue color to it.

Forcing his eyes not to linger on the gentle swells of her breasts or the way her waist nipped in over her hips, he shook his head. "Magic always has a price. Didn't you learn that the last time we saw each other?"

"What are you talking about?"

"My hands."

She froze, her fingers still pressing down on the fabric over her belly. "Your hands? You mean your scars?"

"I pay my price all the time. I don't even notice the scars anymore, and so I forget that my hands are rather grisly to look at." His shoulders stiffened so tight they ached. "And I'm sure it is not a pleasant sensation to be touched by them."

"Oh, I . . . No," she stammered before finding her words. "I didn't mind it. They aren't that bad."

He shouldn't be so pleased with those words. Trying to control the situation, and his reaction to her, his eyes darted around the room before he focused on the situation in front of them. "Turn around, then. Let's see what other clothes we can find."

"Why are you helping?"

"Because I want you powerful, and to do that you must feel like yourself. We have a lot of work to do, and I won't have you out there looking and feeling like a street rat."

Her eyes widened. She bit her lip, clearly trying to hold the words in before she blurted out, "Someone's always picked my clothes for me. I was dressed by someone else my entire life."

The Deathless One conjured a chair behind him, then sat down and crossed his ankle over his knee. With an imperious wave and a long-suffering sigh, he said, "There's a first time for everything, nightmare. Try the whole store on. We've got all night. Let's see what you like and I will hold my tongue."

The flash of her grin shouldn't have eased something in his tormented soul, but it did.

13

Coming back to the manor felt a little strange. She'd had a moment in that closed shop with the Deathless One. She swore there was more of him that she could see in that reflection. There was the hint of a pant leg, the creased fabric so starched it almost didn't look real. Maybe the hint of his hands on his knees as he held himself still, lifting a finger only to tell her to turn so he could see how she looked in the outfits.

His commanding voice made shivers dance up and down her spine. Jessamine did whatever he told her to do, as though he'd wrapped her up in a spell. And he didn't tell her to do anything that she didn't want to do.

Instead, he was hyper-focused on making her choose what she liked. So . . . she did.

Her arms were laden with the clothing that had made her feel good. Not because someone else told her she looked nice, but because she felt like herself in them. No painful dresses with so much beading it was difficult to breathe. Just comfortable shirts that she could tie at the waist, worn cotton trousers that actually fit, and a single brown dress that ended right at the knee. She still felt like a princess in the soft, buttery material, but also felt like she could move.

She'd expected to have to run on the way back. There were so many infected on her journey to the shop, she'd anticipated having to sprint for her life. But there was no one on the streets on her way home, as though a dark magic trailed in front of her, ushering her away from everything and anything that would threaten her.

This wasn't how it was supposed to be, was it? She paused with her hand on the manor door. She'd read that witches had patrons, but they weren't like this, were they?

Thudding her head hard against the door, she tried to jolt the thoughts out of her mind. She wasn't a witch, first of all, and second, he was trying to manipulate her. Or maybe he had just been bored.

That shadowy kingdom she could see beyond him in the reflection certainly seemed like a boring place. There didn't appear to be much other than him. And . . . well, she supposed that made her a little sad.

"Pity for a devil," she muttered as she finally opened the door and made herself stride into the castle. "You've lost your mind, Jessamine."

"Is that so?" The voice cut through the air like a knife, severing any good feelings attached to Jessamine's person.

Wincing, she froze in the doorway. "Sybil?"

"You've been gone for a while." The witch slid into the meager sunlight that just barely sliced through the window. "And I see you've been out . . . shopping?"

Right. This conversation was going to happen, no matter what. She had known that Sybil would eventually find out that she'd stolen from the other woman, and money like that wasn't easy to come by. And she was also very aware that there weren't a lot of places that gave any support to a woman who was clearly a witch.

Sighing, she hunched her shoulders as she prepared herself for the scolding of a lifetime. "If I am going to find out why my mother died and how to get the throne back, then I need to dress the part. No one is going to take me seriously in rags."

"So you stole them?"

Another wince. "No," Jessamine replied before straightening her shoulders and forcing herself to look the other woman in the eye. "I paid for them."

"With whose money?"

"Yours."

Sybil didn't respond. She just arched her brow and crossed her arms over her chest.

This was just like when her mother scolded her. The stinging in her chest only made her realize just how deeply she'd forgotten herself. Wallowing in the reality of her own pain didn't bring her mother any closer. In this moment, it felt like the soul of her mother was staring down at her in disappointment.

So Jessamine did the only thing she knew how to do in moments like this. Confess.

"I snuck into your room to see if there was anything I could steal from you to get the clothing. I didn't want to leave someone else with a lack of materials, and I know that means I likely chose their well-being over your own. But it does seem like you make life easier for yourself without ever leaving this place. What money you have, I don't know what your plan was for it. And I do realize it was the wrong thing to do. I am sorry. I will try my best to replace it, but know that once I am back on my throne, I will do everything I can to make up for it."

Still, silence. Sybil looked her over, calculating and clearly disappointed, but then she . . . shrugged?

"All right," Sybil finally said. "I was wondering when you'd start acting like a witch, anyway."

"I—" More apologies stuck in Jessamine's throat. What did she mean by that?

"Come on." Sybil turned and started down the hall. "I figured you'd be getting hungry by now. Yes?"

"I suppose." Her stomach rumbled. "I'm very hungry, yes. There were quite a few infected on my way into the city."

"But not on your way out?"

The witch really didn't miss much. "No, on the way back they all seemed to have moved on. It's not like they're hard to get away from, it's just . . . Well, I was led to believe there were a lot more, too."

Come to think of it, she didn't know how there weren't any infected bothering Sybil's home. Everyone had always made it seem like the infected were crawling around every part of her city. Her mother hadn't let Jessamine even leave their castle grounds for a good while before everything had fallen apart.

A tiny mew broke through her thoughts, then the thunder of paws as the kitten came careening around the corner. Like a little black hurricane, it zinged from wall to wall before stopping right in front of her.

Jessamine watched with wide eyes, but the little beastie just arched its back and rubbed against her legs.

"Miss me?" she asked, stooping and picking the little one up. Immediately it pressed against her neck. An impressive rumble started up, sounding much less like a cat and far more like a tiger.

As they wandered through the moss-covered halls toward the kitchen, Sybil snorted. "A stray you found?"

"A familiar," she corrected. The kitten wound itself around her neck, balancing on her shoulder before stretching over both like some kind of living stole. "The Deathless One claimed all witches have them."

"I . . ." Sybil shook her head, a faint smile crossing her features. "Some do, yes. They are exceedingly rare gifts from a patron, however. You are lucky to have one."

Jessamine tried very hard not to think about what that meant. All she knew was that she had one, and the warm kitten helped ease all her fears as it kneaded tiny claws into her shoulder with every step.

Clearing her throat, Sybil gestured for Jessamine to step into the kitchen ahead of her. "About the infected. I'm sure your advisors wanted you to believe this city is crawling with them. The infected are a problem, don't get me wrong. But they're easily confused, and they really don't bother anyone too much unless they're in a pack. Then it's a much larger issue."

"A pack?"

"That's what I call them. A group of them, wandering around. Makes it hard to get away." Sybil winked as she stepped over to the central island. "It's part of the reason why magic is so useful. Here we are, certain that the only way to fix things is to what? Gather them all up and ship them somewhere else? Magic could solve a lot of these problems, but no one wants to admit that we should use it."

Setting her new clothes down on a fairly clean spot on the floor, Jessamine peered around the ancient kitchen. It was the cleanest part of the entire building that she'd seen so far. Fresh herbs hung from the ceiling in neatly tied bundles. The counters were now filled with flowering plants that spilled down to the floor in vibrant colors. The island was clean, mostly, and held a few freshly picked fruits and vegetables. The ancient cast-iron stove in the back had seen better days, but it was free from rust or the effects of time.

Everything smelled warm and herby, and with the faintest hint of freshly baked bread. This was clearly a room well loved, and often used.

Sybil chuckled at the look on her face. "What? Did you think every room in the manor was falling apart?"

"Yes."

"A hearth witch wouldn't be caught dead with her kitchen in disarray." Sybil walked around the island and started putting a plate together. She unwrapped a wax-covered cheese from the cloth, pulled down a small slice of cured meat, and . . . Was that jam in a jar? "Have a seat. I can see you've been talking with the Deathless One again. You've been doing that a lot lately."

"How did you know?" Jessamine sat down carefully on the stool in front of the island, just in case the rickety old wood decided to collapse.

"Flushed cheeks, bright eyes." Sybil set the plate down in front of her, then reached under the counter and somehow procured a small fish she tossed to the kitten. "No charcoal on your neck this time, though. You must have pleased him."

She didn't want to think about the last two times Sybil had found her after talking with that god. The charcoal took forever to wash off. Something about it just clung to her skin.

Maybe it had something to do with the part of her that was connected to him. The fact that he'd given her life had certainly made it hard to get away from him, that was for sure. She supposed it was as good a guess as any.

Shrugging, she tucked into the food. Her feline companion leapt off her shoulders, lying down with its big paws on either side of the bowl while it gnawed on the hunk of flesh. Sybil was an exceptional cook, and Jessamine thought that as a woman who had grown up with personal chefs. After a few weeks here, she'd learned to just eat and devour whatever Sybil gave her. And even though she'd choked down rotten food during her weeks in the street, she could still recognize the skill of a master. Even this simple meal of homemade bread, a small amount of homemade cheese, and bites of fresh fruit was ridiculously flavorful.

Mouth full, she glanced up to see Sybil watching her with a soft expression. One that she hadn't seen on the witch's face before.

"What?" Jessamine asked.

"It's been a long time since I've seen someone enjoy food like you do."

"Oh, sorry." Quickly wiping her mouth on her sleeve, Jessamine tried to sit up straight and stop shoving the food into her mouth. "It's hard to imagine I was a princess seated at many important functions, I'm sure. I do know how to be polite and eat the correct way."

"Is there a correct way to eat?"

"Yes. I know what utensil is correct to use depending on the situation, and I know how slowly to eat the food. Women are to take only small bites and never have so much food in their mouth that they couldn't respond to anyone at the drop of a hat." She parroted the words that she'd been taught her entire life. "Decorum is important. It is what makes us stand out from the animals."

Said animal had gorged itself on milk and was now pawing at Jessamine's plate. She let the little one steal a piece of cheese, which it messily ate. Scales covered its paws, fur, and face.

Sighing, she speared the appropriate square of cheese with her fork and gently placed the small amount on her tongue. Chewing slowly and deliberately, she swallowed before looking at Sybil and saying, "See? A perfect lady." But as she stared longingly at the food, she wanted to just shovel it into her mouth and fill her belly. She was starving after a night spent running around, and it really was tasty.

"I didn't realize a lady had to eat slowly when she was hungry."

"We're supposed to know what we're eating, too. It's not necessarily just for our figures, but also to make sure that we are healthy." She paused, taking the correct amount of time between bites, even if it made her stomach rumble painfully.

Sybil reached across the island and placed her hand on top of Jessamine's. "Maybe while you're here, you just eat, love. Forget all the rules.

You aren't sitting at a table with officials or nobles or politicians. You're in my kitchen, and you're hungry. So eat however you'd like."

The permission made tears burn in her eyes before she nodded and began eating to her heart's content. She barely stopped, even to breathe, as she chewed and swallowed and rushed through every delicious bite until she didn't feel like she was about to pass out. When she was done, her belly was distended and she'd never cared less in her life.

With a heaving breath of relief, she even put her elbows on the table as she leaned over the plate of food. "I don't think I've ever eaten so much in one sitting."

"Good. You deserve that."

It was so warm in here. So cozy and so . . . everything that she'd ever wanted. The kitchens were off-limits where she came from, and it wasn't like she was going to break those rules. Not when she knew just how much trouble she'd be in.

But she had read books about warm hearths like this. A friend on the other side, food and stories that made people laugh.

She just . . . didn't know how to have that. Not yet, at least. But this moment made her dream that maybe, someday, she could. She would know how to laugh with friends and to tell stories they would enjoy. Someday, she wouldn't feel like a princess pretending to be a peasant to experience what life might be like.

What was she supposed to do now? Thank Sybil and slink off back to the altar room, where she would read more spell books that she didn't understand? She didn't want to do that.

She wanted to talk. She wanted to have a conversation with this woman who very much intimidated her. And Sybil was standing there like she was expecting Jessamine to say something, or ask something, or do something rather than sit like a lump at the island, floundering because she didn't know how to talk to someone who didn't have some kind of expectation of her.

Opening her mouth, she blurted out the first thing that she could think of. "Why do you like magic so much?"

Sybil blinked. "Because it gives me power."

"I had power as a princess. It wasn't all that great." She touched a hand to her neck. "It got me killed."

"We're women. We all need whatever power we can eke out of this universe."

Power had gotten Jessamine nothing in her life, but the more she thought about it, the more she wondered if she'd ever really had any to begin with. "I guess I don't know what you mean."

"How many women have you met who are convinced they're on the brink of madness? They've been told countless times to bury everything they are. Their emotions. Their hopes and dreams. Their anger. All of it shoved so deep down that they cannot even think or breathe through the pain of hiding it. But not us. Not a witch. A witch is everything they tell us not to be. We are chaos and blood. Wetness and rage. Howling at the moon that we will not be silenced or forgotten. We are everything that they fear and covet."

With every word, Jessamine felt something unlock inside of her. She stared down at her plate, realizing there were chains wrapped around her from generations of locks that had long ago lost their keys. Just like knowing there was a particular way she was allowed to eat. Just like not knowing what she wanted to wear.

And being uncomfortable sitting at a table with someone she wanted to call a friend, because she didn't know how to talk to someone who wasn't of the same station.

"You're right," she whispered. "I just don't know how to be what everyone wants me to be."

"Then don't." Sybil pushed herself away from the island, casting a sad smile in her direction before she gathered up the kitten in her arms. "Be who you want to be, Lady Jessamine. Even if that takes a lifetime to figure out. I'll put the little one to bed in your room. It's been wreaking havoc on the house all day. By the way, do you have any plans to name it?"

"Nyx," Jessamine said, something deep inside of her nearly screaming the name. "Her name is Nyx."

14

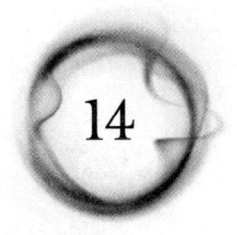

"Cast the damn spell, Jessamine," he snarled. He'd been gathering his magic to leave his realm for longer, and teaching her shouldn't have taken so much effort. Yet here he was, trying to teach her without physically being around her. And failing.

Sybil's teachings were getting her nowhere. She could barely cast a single spell, and he'd finally decided to take matters into his own hands. If the witch couldn't teach her, then Jessamine needed a patron to push her over the edge.

"I can't. It's not working, and we both know why. I'm not a witch! I can follow the spells that are formulas, the ones that literally anyone could do. But the ones that come from actual magic? You know I can't do them."

"You're not trying hard enough."

"I'm trying plenty hard! Every time I try to do it, my mind just . . ." She lifted a shaking hand to run it over her mouth, before gently tipping the bowl in front of her. The liquid spilled out, certainly ruining the spell now. "You're expecting the impossible."

"Focus." He paced in his realm, watching her through a mirror she'd placed on the altar. "Magic is not easy, Jessamine. It shouldn't come to you naturally. It's work and dedication and hours of pain."

"I've been doing this for hours and I am tired."

"Not tired enough," he snapped.

Maybe he was pushing her too hard. She had been working on this for the better part of a day, but it was the most basic of spells! She should be able to light a fire, and they'd tried every other easy spell he could think of. This one was a ridiculously simple spell meant to spin her mind in the right direction for the magic to take flight. Even the least talented of witches could cast it.

He tried to ease his voice a little, so maybe it wouldn't sound like a whip cracking above her head. "This is a very easy spell, Jessamine. You should be able to do this."

"I have told you time and time again, I am not a witch."

"You *are* a witch," he ground through his teeth. "Just not a very good one."

She stiffened, gave him a scathing glare, before snapping back, "Then find yourself a better one."

"Jessamine—"

She didn't stop to listen to him. If anything, she stomped out of the room faster before slamming the door so hard the mirror rocked back and slipped onto the floor.

Bracing himself on the mirror's frame, he bared his teeth in frustration. Why did she have to be so difficult? He was teaching her magic, just as he'd promised. This was the bare minimum for any witch.

He'd trained countless witches. Hundreds of them, all of whom had grown in power every day under his guidance. He had never trained a witch who did not become a powerful creature, who then sacrificed him for even more influence. It was his place in their world. He taught them, they killed him, the cycle continued.

Why did she have to break the mold?

She questioned herself too much. She had no confidence in the magic that brewed inside her. Every ounce of her ability to create magic was squandered because some inner voice in her head said she wasn't good enough.

Or maybe she was afraid of it. There was meaning behind becoming a witch, and it used to mean something good. Perhaps all her weeks spent in this forgotten, forbidden, cursed place had changed her opinion.

Shoving himself away from the mirror's frame, and away from the limited view of the ceiling, he stalked away into the darkness. Power boiled underneath his skin, more and more the longer he stayed with her. It was only a matter of time before he had to expel that energy.

It was boiling over. Already he could see it in this realm. The dark ink reached for him, arms outstretched with electric shocks running down them. It would hurt if they caught him, so perhaps it was time to see if his chains had loosened more as he and Jessamine grew even closer.

Bursting free from the realm that bound him, he slunk through the shadows of hers. Without her, he felt nothing. No breeze, no frigid touch, no warmth either. He could only make out a small portion of what was around him. It was like living in constant shadows, darkness blanketing his eyes so that he could only see what was important—and most of everything was not.

His gravesinger was wasting his time. He needed to get her back on that throne so she could awaken him. That was the only purpose that mattered to the Deathless One, because he was losing his mind in his realm of ink and obsidian stone.

It had been far too long. He feared if he suffered much longer, then every part of him would splinter into a thousand pieces. Pieces that would funnel into those who still worshipped him, and then there would be nothing left of him at all.

All the gods would finally be dead. And then the world would end.

With the weight of expectation and responsibility on his shoulders, he focused his magic and power on the young man he hadn't been able to stop thinking about. The boy who had held the gates open, and who he had a gut feeling was the key to the beginning of their journey.

"Benji," he whispered, his thread of connection to Jessamine tightening as he siphoned magic from her.

He hadn't realized he could connect with her so easily. Her power tasted like ashes on his tongue, but he swore there was a floral aftertaste when he used her as his anchor in this realm. He could stay here just a bit longer with that connection, and he intended to use every minute to haunt the pageboy.

He could abuse this power. Maybe even summon her to his side, puppet her to do whatever he wished. But their connection was still blooming, and it felt more like a violation than a fun game.

So instead, he used her mind only to find out more about this "Benji."

Her thoughts were rather scattered around the young man. He had been a pageboy, just like she'd said. Someone who inhabited mostly the lowest parts of the castle, but when he was on the more opulent levels, he'd been quite dedicated to his job.

Jessamine had regularly seen the young man, and when she had, he'd always been polite. He took his time to do every job right, and he always loved the coins she pressed into his hands when he'd done something special for her. But of course he had. The boy was little more than a street urchin who had found himself a safe place to rest.

Flicking through her memories, he found the one he was looking for. Benji had claimed to have been from the Factory District, a rather rough-and-tumble area of the kingdom. The Deathless One turned his attention to that part of the city, expecting to waste a considerable amount of time aimlessly wandering until he stumbled upon the young man.

Leon Bishop of Orenda wouldn't keep the boy working at the castle, that much was certain. The new king would want a clean sweep, making sure there were no surprises lingering in the shadows to stab him, just as he had stabbed everyone else. So why had the boy been allowed to go home?

Surprisingly, as he glided through the moonlit streets, barely moving his feet as he stepped from shadow to shadow, he realized there was a magical signature in this part of the city. At first, he thought perhaps he was sensing another power source. Impossible, though, considering none of his other siblings were alive to give their supplicants gifts. Was it possible someone had been smart about their magic and still had some measure of power, even this long after the death of the gods?

But no, the closer he got, the more he recognized the magic. It was *his* magic. It was his magical signature still lingering somewhere in this part of the city.

Which made no sense. As someone opened a storefront, light spilled out into the street, and his form fractured into spectral shards. Every single one of them wondered the same thing. There had never been a sector of his coven in the Factory District, so what felt like his own magic?

All the shadows came together in one undulating mass of rage. He did not know who dared to steal magic from him, but they would not survive the night.

At least, that was what he intended. He still didn't have his body, so the most he could do was an illusion that made him seem very real. Unless it was a witch from his own coven, which he was almost certain was not the case. It would be easier if it were some defector from his coven who thought to use his magic without summoning the god himself. Perhaps Sybil would know.

She had been a good witch thus far. He hated it when they did that. He didn't want her to be good. He wanted her to be manipulative and to try to sway his attention from Jessamine to herself. She should covet the power he offered, because she certainly could do more with it than a cast-off princess who couldn't even cast a simple flame spell. Maybe she was just lying in wait until he was reborn. Then she would ask him for his sacrifice.

And who was he to deny her?

Hating the way his thoughts had turned, he focused instead on tracking down the magical signature. Strangely enough, it wasn't in some patched-together shack or even in a dark hovel where the witches might be hiding. It came from above.

Frowning, he peered up through the buildings and spotted a very old sign. It hung from only one hinge, so he had to turn his head to the side to read the words "Owl's Nest."

An abandoned tavern? That was what it seemed like—a haunt for people who wished to forget themselves for a little while. He could see the downstairs had been somewhat of a bar and meeting place, while the upstairs windows revealed what might have once been rooms to rent for the night. It was starting to look more and more like one of his old coven members had fled their home and remained unaware that he had returned. But why would they end up here?

Flexing his power, he slithered up the building on the side in darkness and approached a window. Unlike his coven's home, this building still had all its glass panes still intact. Whoever lived within wasn't very careful about thieves, however, and that certainly worked in his favor as he nudged the sash open and poured himself inside.

Once within, his power failed him. There were many shadows to hide in, but almost too many. It was so dark that he couldn't make out anything other than hands stretching forward, reaching for him, trying to pull him back into the realm where he was bound. But he wasn't ready to return to that madness just yet.

First, he would find out who had stolen from him.

Batting the hands away, he plunged into the darkness, unseeing and staggering. One step forward, then another, as a tugging sensation pulled at his belly.

His damned gravesinger was summoning him.

He was loath to ignore her. It took a lot of his power to deny someone that right, especially a gravesinger, and if he wasn't careful, it would deplete all the new power that she'd given him.

Baring his teeth in a snarl, he spun in the direction of that tug, but he stopped as he realized a man stood beside him.

Or perhaps not quite a man. He was young, barely an adult. His hair was lank, dark, a little too greasy. His eyes were sunken into his skull, dark circles gathered underneath them as he staggered past the Deathless One, making his way to what appeared to be a cot in the corner. The young man tossed himself down on it, laying an arm across his eyes, with one leg dangling onto the floor.

His entire body went suddenly limp, and the Deathless One wondered for a moment if he had died. But no, his chest was still rising and falling.

Then he had the horrified fear that this young man had somehow stolen magic from him. This fool of a creature wasn't good enough to even clean a god's boots, let alone wield immortal magic.

No, it wasn't this pageboy. There wasn't an ounce of power in him, a pathetic little amount even to suggest that he was alive. But as he leaned over him and stared down into the features slowly revealed by a limp arm falling to his side, he realized this was the idiot Jessamine was looking for.

"Benji," he said, his voice reaching out through the ether, stern enough that the boy snorted in his sleep. "We've been looking for you, Benji."

The young man's eyes flew open, and he sat up so fast that he actually passed through the shadowy figure looming over him. Wincing, the Deathless One gathered the scattered pieces of himself together before moving in front of Benji again.

Benji breathed hard, his eyes wild and wide as he stared into the darkness around himself. "Who's there?"

"No one," the Deathless One breathed into his ear. "Just your nightmares."

Again, somehow, his voice crossed into the living realm. Benji bolted out of his bed, stumbled away from the cot, and then tripped over something that was so encased in darkness that the Deathless One couldn't make out what it was. But as the young man landed on the floor, gulping in lungfuls of air, the Deathless One wondered just how much he could push.

Jessamine had given him more power than she realized, and he wasn't even reborn yet. Soon, he would remember what it was like to have that much power. Soon he would recall exactly what it was like to be a god among men.

"No one's here," Benji muttered. "No one is here, you big idiot. You shouldn't have taken those mushrooms."

"Probably not," the Deathless One replied, although this time he made sure the young man couldn't hear him. "Mushrooms rarely give a man a vision into the future, and most of the time just confuse more than they clarify. What else did you expect?"

But then Benji climbed shakily to his feet and moved to the end of the bed. He opened a trunk there and stared down at something in it. "And I never should have taken you. Nothing but bad luck has followed me since."

Curious now, the Deathless One wandered behind the young man and peered over his shoulder. What he saw in that trunk turned his blood ice cold and sent fire surging through his heart, threatening to burn him alive. The magical signature hadn't been coming from a person after all.

"That is my book," he snarled. "Why does a wretch like you have *my grimoire?*"

He thundered the words so loudly that they rang into the living realm again, filled with fury and frustration at this form's inability to seize the grimoire and bring it with him. Benji let the lid drop with a thud that sent dust billowing around him. Coughing, the young man whirled again.

The Deathless One lunged at him, all shadow and magic that passed through the young man but also ripped through his mind. He could taste every single memory for a brief moment, every fear, every nightmare, every single thing that this door holder had felt. And details. Oh, the Deathless One had gathered so many details from that brush against this rotting mind.

"Who's there?" Benji called out as the Deathless One faded from the room, answering the tugging call in his belly. "Who are you?"

"Death," he replied. "And I am coming for you, Benji Broadback."

15

He arrived already talking. "We have to go to this Benji."

Jessamine knew this. She was more interested in the fact that she couldn't light a damn candle, but apparently could summon him whenever she wished. "Why is it that I can make this spell work, but I struggle to do even the most basic spells for anything else?"

"Benji, witch."

"Yes, I realize he's a problem and that we should be working toward that common goal. I'm more interested in why this magic is fighting against me, since you seem to think I am actually a witch."

She looked up from her perch on the island stool, waiting for him to realize that she hadn't summoned him in the same spot she usually did. The altar room was nice, but she thought the kitchen was nicer. She felt more powerful here, perhaps because of her conversation with Sybil. She could be wherever she wanted now that she wasn't in the castle. She was allowed to be whoever she felt like she was in the moment, and right now, she wanted to be a woman who sat in the kitchen.

He strode into the room like he owned the place, and she realized that he was more corporeal than she had ever seen before. Those were definitely pants that he was wearing. Black as night and dark as sin, but they were pants. And the shadows had coiled a little tighter around his shoulders. She could see that he really was an abnormally tall man, lean and strong, with broad shoulders and a tapered waist that were pleasing to the eye.

If only she could see his face. There was still nothing there but a dark mass surrounded by the beginnings of a sketch, as if she'd conjured him out of her dreams.

Bracing her chin on her closed fist, she stared at him a little harder before asking, "Do you only have a shape because I'm giving you a shape?"

"Jessamine, we don't have time for these theoreticals."

"I just want to know the answer."

"I think it's much more likely that I'm slowly regaining my form as I remember what I used to be," he replied offhandedly. "The longer I spend time in this realm, the more I remember myself."

"There's a statue of you in the parlor."

"A statue that was a version of me, not the same one that will eventually be resurrected. I never know who I will be or what I will look like." He sounded cross as he stopped on the other side of the island and slammed his hands down onto the surface.

She jumped at the loud bang, and even he seemed to look down at his hands in surprise. A thick clay vase toppled over, fell off the table, and rolled onto the floor. "How did you do that?" she asked.

"I don't know." He shook his head before looking back at her. "You are trying to distract me."

"I'm the one who summoned you!"

Senseless, arrogant god. She'd had a reason for summoning him, and now she had no idea why she'd done it. Her mind had been so scattered today as she tried to get all the pieces together to move forward. She had clothing, she could figure out what to do with herself now. And he was right. They had to find Benji and force him to tell them who'd convinced him to betray her family, who was behind the plot to seize the castle.

"I need to learn more magic before I feel comfortable finding Benji," she finally said. "I called you here because I found another spell book that I think might be useful in our research. It said that sometimes a grave-singer's magic can be blocked, and if you can figure out where the block—"

"Why are you preventing us from going to this boy? Are you afraid of what we might find?"

A spike of anxiety coiled through her chest. "No."

"I can see that in both your magic and in this, you are trying to slow down the process. Why is that, princess?"

"I won't run blind into a situation that feels a bit like you're manipulating me. I know nothing about you, only that at this moment, you can only touch me and Sybil." She took a deep breath. "And the table, it seems. Everything is so far out of my realm of understanding, I don't want to make the wrong choice."

He stared at her, and she stared at him, and she wondered just how wrong she was to hold him back. He seemed so confident in everything he did. She wished she had an ounce of that confidence. Especially when he cocked his head to the side and she swore she could feel his eyes on her like a physical touch.

Curling her fingers in the hem of her cream-colored skirt, she told herself not to try to decipher if he was looking at what she wore. It wasn't one of the skirts they had bought. Mostly she'd gotten pants in that store. But this was one of Sybil's, and it was rather pretty, even if there were a few colorful patches over her knees and one large one over the thigh where the fabric had torn.

The Deathless One rounded the island, turned her to face him, and took a seat on the stool right in front of her. He sat with his knees on either side of hers, trapping her legs between his and making it so she couldn't look anywhere but at him. Suddenly, he was everywhere. The smell of him filled her nose with the sharp shock of mint and citrus as her gaze filled with black.

But it wasn't entirely darkness anymore, was it? She could see that his pants were made of the finest cotton she'd ever seen. They weren't leather as she'd imagined. They looked comfortable, even with the fine starched lines in them. If she squinted her eyes and tried to see through him, she swore she could also see the toe of a leather boot.

"Jessamine."

His sharp tone didn't make her stop looking at him. It was easier to focus on his shape than it was to focus on the tumultuous thoughts rumbling around in her head. Like, she should touch him. She could drag her finger down the pants to see if they felt real. No, she would just look at him instead. At the way his thighs bunched when he leaned forward and how there was the faint outline of a hand resting on his right leg.

"Nightmare." He said the word so softly it made her squeeze her eyes shut. "Benji is the key to everything."

"He's the key to nothing. All he did was hold the gate open. What makes you think he knows more than a when and where?"

"Intuition. And he has something of mine that I need you to take back."

"He has something of yours?"

At his silence, fear bloomed.

His honeyed words were so pretty, and she wanted to believe he was here to help her. But he was the Deathless One, a god with no love or ability to think about anyone other than himself. He was a dangerous creature who made deals with witches and consumed them in return.

So she whispered behind the safety of her closed eyes. "I'm afraid you're trying to control me."

"I'm trying to *save* you."

Two warm hands landed on her knees. She could feel the heat of them through the fabric of her skirt, and quickly realized one of the patches wasn't stitched closed. Once again, she could feel his calloused fingertips against her skin. But this time, she swore the scars felt like symbols etched into the pads when he touched her.

The heavy weight of his grip was more comforting than any words he could have said. He squeezed her knees, and he and Jessamine both let out matching gasps. She could feel him. Not just the sensation of him, or the strange warmth when he'd undone her laces in the shop.

He was really here. Holding on to her like she was a lifeline, and he didn't know how to let go.

"I shouldn't—" His guttural words cut off as she interrupted him.

"It's fine."

"It's not fine, I shouldn't—"

"Just . . . Stay still. For a moment." Eyes shut, she tried to memorize the feeling of him.

His hands were broad and strong, though swollen. She could feel how painful they must be for him. There was a give to them that skin shouldn't have, especially not fingers. And as he shifted his grip, she felt the creak of his joints. But even through all that, there was a sense of strength in his touch. She knew without a doubt that these hands would have been beautiful if he had not sacrificed so much for power.

His fingers were long. His palms were not necessarily broad, but graceful. In another world, these would have been the hands of a pianist, or an artist. A man who had hands that made people look at them and think of devilish things.

"If I keep my eyes shut, you feel almost real," she whispered. "Can you feel me, too?"

"I can." Though he admitted it, he sounded like he was in pain.

"Why?"

"Why what?"

"Why can I feel you like this? I'm not . . . I don't worship you. Not like Sybil. I've seen her leaving offerings at your altar, grisly dead things that she finds out in the sand. I don't do that."

Swallowing hard, she waited to understand. She knew perhaps some of it was because of what he claimed she was. A gravesinger. A witch who had no spell book, because apparently none of them wrote down how they did things.

Oral tradition, Sybil had said. Gravesingers weren't allowed to keep anything in any kind of tome or grimoire. They were supposed to tell others how to summon the Deathless One, and therein lay a large problem. But the Deathless One knew the spell required to resurrect himself.

"Nightmare," he rasped. "If I knew the answer to that, I wouldn't be so surprised, now would I? Gravesingers are a direct line to their patron, but I have never stayed dead for this long."

Jessamine was afraid to open her eyes. Because what if she did and he disappeared? What if she opened her eyes and realized that she had imagined all this? She wasn't even sure what that would mean if she suddenly woke up on her pile of rags and realized her mind had conjured this entire thing.

"I just don't understand why you can touch me."

"Neither do I." She heard the sound of a click, almost as though he'd swallowed a little too hard. "Do you want me to stop?"

She should. The idea of this villainous god touching her should make her want to sprint out of the room. But instead, all she could focus on was that scarred thumb gently moving against the inside of her knee. The delicate skin there felt like it was on fire.

And a wayward thought whispered through her mind that she wanted him to slide his hands higher. To know what it felt like for those calluses to touch even softer, slicker skin.

"No," she whispered. "And that frightens me."

His hands disappeared, and the stool he sat upon suddenly fell and slammed into the floor. Flinching, she opened her eyes to see him standing so far on the other side of the room she almost didn't notice he was there.

All the details of his body had disappeared again. He was an undulating mass of dark shadows that twisted and warped the more she looked at him. Almost as though he'd lost all control over his body—or perhaps he didn't want her to see him.

Gripping the bottom of her stool, she stayed right where she was. She couldn't take the words back, nor did she want to. Jessamine had spent her entire life simpering and pretending to be something that she wasn't.

She knew how to flirt. She knew how to quirk her eyebrow and have a man on his knees before her. It was the sign of a good princess if she could manipulate men. Her mother had trained her to capture their attention. Plenty of visiting politicians and neighboring countries thought it was luck to get a few moments with a royal princess, and she would perform dutifully.

But this was the first time she'd said something like this and really meant it. She hadn't minded the feeling of his hands on her knees. Every time he touched her, it felt like some wild and wicked thing unfurled its wings inside her body. It stretched underneath her skin, awakening for the very first time in her life, and she was deathly afraid to admit she liked it.

Eyeing him, she wondered why that answer created such a visceral response in him. And she feared it was perhaps not a good thing.

"Why did you come here to talk about Benji?" she asked.

His voice was a low rumble of emotion as he responded. "I found the boy myself. He's staying in a place called the Owl's Nest. I don't know where it is in the Factory District, but I suspect it's on the outskirts, considering how shabby it was."

"Thank you for finding him."

"For all that you think I'm untrustworthy, I am bound to see you back on your throne, Jessamine." His shape warped, melting into the shadows as they usually did when he was about to disappear, but then she saw him hesitate.

His shadows lingered in the room. And she didn't think that was because he wanted to watch what she did next.

"Do you have something else to say?"

"He has a book in his possession that is very important to me. When we go to see him, we need to take it back."

A book? Frowning, she hopped off the stool and took a step closer to him. "A spell book?"

"Something much worse than that."

"You won't give me a clearer answer, will you?"

"No." The shadows drifted apart a little again before sticking back together. "You'll know it when you see it, nightmare. And then I need you to take it back for me."

Frustrated, she tossed her hands in the air and spat, "You won't give me a reason why?"

"Because I said so." The growled words were sharper than before, all edged in anger and madness. "I may be your patron, Jessamine Harmsworth, but you so easily forget that you do not control me."

"You're the one who insists I summon you—or do you no longer want that?"

A cry of rage blasted toward her like a swarm of bats. She raised her arms to protect herself from his anger, only to feel the shadows pass over her like a cool wind as he disappeared.

It took her a long time to drop her arms. Even longer to take a step on shaking knees that threatened to send her tumbling onto the floor. But she managed to stagger back to the island and sink down onto the stool again.

"The Owl's Nest," she muttered, before glancing down at her skirt.

There were two charcoal handprints there. Black stains through the very fabric, and she should have been frightened at the sight of them. She should have quaked with the fear that there were lingering marks every time he touched her, but instead . . .

That wicked thing inside her rejoiced. She enjoyed wearing his mark. She enjoyed knowing where he had touched her and that she had felt him.

But oh, she was afraid of the thing inside her. Because now that it had awakened, she wouldn't easily cajole it back to sleep.

16

The witches and their god all prepared to journey together to the Owl's Nest. Unfortunately, that meant that the Deathless One was relegated to a small hand mirror perched over Jessamine's shoulder, the better to preserve his power for when it was most needed. When he looked through the mirror, its handle strapped to her pack, his view swayed with her as she walked, and he found himself nauseous almost immediately.

Why wouldn't Jessamine just summon him? It was an argument they'd had for hours before the two women finally persuaded him that they weren't going to do it. Neither of them trusted him in any sort of physical form.

He supposed he couldn't blame them, but he'd forgotten what it felt like to be disappointed. He wasn't sure what to do with the feeling. It made him uncomfortable, and a little itchy. Of course, he blamed them for this feeling.

Witches.

"Ready?" Jessamine asked for the last time. Her hand came into view as she straightened her pack.

A thread of nerves coiled through her voice, as though she wasn't all that ready herself. She had been more than prepared only a few hours ago to go on her own, and yet, this required all three of them.

He'd needed to spend time convincing Sybil. The usually stoic woman had nearly crumpled into a panic attack at the thought of leaving the manor. The last time he'd sent her on an errand, he hadn't stayed to see how she had reacted.

The Deathless One had thought to push her until she pointed a gnarled finger in the direction of the blooming statues, a reminder of how witches worshipped the dead. Her meaning was clear. Even the gods had died in this realm, and she feared what that meant for a mortal like her. He had so easily forgotten that mortals feared death.

So he'd threatened to kill her if she stayed in the manor. That had gotten her moving.

"If we'd left hours ago, we would have already been there," he grumbled.

Apparently, it was the wrong thing to say.

Jessamine tapped the mirror hard enough that he felt the impact echo through his realm, and Sybil stepped in front of the mirror to give him a long stare.

At least it was the practiced witch who responded, "Times have changed since you last died, Deathless One. It is not safe for us to wander the streets whenever we wish."

"Yes, yes. You are connected to the only god left alive. Surely that gives you some sort of protection."

Though even he knew that was currently weak protection at best. Too bad the only woman who could summon him into a physical form had decided she didn't want to do that. Because she needed to trust him before she resurrected an ancient god and allowed him to rampage across her kingdom.

Smart, probably. But that didn't mean he had to like it.

Relaxing back in his conjured chair, he watched through his own version of her tiny mirror as they started up a path that led them away from the sea. This hadn't changed much since the last time he'd been here. The light yellow grass still waved in a breeze he could not feel. But he could hear the crunching of stones underneath their feet, and he could see the ocean every time Jessamine turned to see how far they had come.

The sound of her ragged breath filled his lungs with the same sensation, as though he remembered what it felt like to actually exert himself. It had been hundreds of years since he'd felt that way, though. His body remembered, perhaps. If he let it.

Sybil walked ahead of them, her strong back never once hesitating, though they clambered over more stone than he had expected. When was the last time he'd traveled this way from the manor? He was quite certain it had been right before he died, but the memories just weren't there. At least, not like they used to be.

Eventually, the sparse grass gave way to mud pits the closer they got to the city. And it was right on the outskirts of the Factory District where they stopped. Sybil hesitated in front of them as she held her coat a little tighter to her form.

"Jessamine," she said very quietly. "Take a few steps to your right slowly. We'll have to go the other way."

Now what? What could possibly delay these ladies even further?

As he leaned forward to have a closer look, Jessamine did the same, giving him a very clear view of exactly what was the problem.

A man stood in the center of the road. His shoulders heaved up and down with gulps, as though he'd been running for miles. Except . . . he wasn't covered in sweat, but instead fluid oozed from the pustules riddling his body. Lank, greasy hair stuck to his neck and face, and his clothing was torn from misuse.

A small bundle huddled on the ground in front of the man, shivering so slightly it was almost impossible to tell it was a child. Fear, he expected. Fear that had frozen the little beast right in the worst place.

"Is this your infected?" he asked, amused. "The man looks like he can hardly walk."

At the sound of his voice, the infected's head jerked toward them. His face was so covered in bumps that it must have been unrecognizable to anyone who had known him before. His eyes were nearly swollen shut, and his lips were permanently forced open, so drool spilled down his chin in a long strand.

It was a horrible sight to behold, especially when the man took a step toward them. His muscles bunched, his legs suddenly appearing far more powerful than they had moments before.

"Run!" Sybil said, before she threw up her arms.

Dark magic coiled around her wrists and spread up into her hands. He knew where it came from. That well of magic that split through her chest, the same well he'd replenished the first time he'd been at the manor. Only desperate witches pulled from that place. It was the source of all their magic, the source of who they were.

"Sybil," he warned just moments before she let her spell fly free.

Jessamine should have run in the opposite direction when Sybil told her to. But she didn't. His foolish princess bolted toward the child in front of the infected man. Slavering and moaning, the man pounded against the opaque shield that Sybil had conjured mere inches from the child on the ground.

He didn't look at the man. He didn't look at the child now huddled in Jessamine's arms. No, he stared at the witch holding on to the power with her fingers spread wide and her face creased in an impressive snarl. Here he was, thinking Sybil was just as weak as she had claimed to be. The weakest of her coven, she'd said.

And yet, she wielded his power easily. She twisted it with her hands, slowly wrapping that shield around the infected man as she warped her spell into a cage.

"Sybil," he said again, his voice a sharp crack in the air. "Summon your patron."

"I don't need to," she said, her voice strained with effort. "I can do this."

"Summon me, witch."

Jessamine's voice fractured through the conversation, quiet as a summer breeze. "I thought you couldn't do anything if you were dead."

"Illusion has its uses, nightmare. But she has to call upon me first. As her patron, I can protect her."

This was what he had been created for. It was what he was good at. The witches used to bring him here for protection. He knew how to fight for them. It was all he'd ever done.

Until they decided they would rather protect themselves.

The child whimpered in Jessamine's arms, its arms and legs pinwheeling until it tore out of Jessamine's grip and bolted away. Small and ragged like a mouse, the child disappeared faster than he could blink.

"Wait!" Jessamine shouted, only to freeze as she realized she was right in front of the infected man now.

"I can do this," Sybil grunted, forming her hands into a circle as the black magic closed. "I can . . . I can . . ."

There was a strange thud from inside her chest, the knocking of a fist against a door and the echo of something empty beneath it. With an enraged cry, she threw out her hands, and suddenly the dark cage around the infected contracted.

Jessamine whirled away from the sight, so he couldn't see what happened to the man, but he knew the sound of an implosion. Sybil had destroyed the man, completely and utterly, as though he were a bug to be squashed. When Jessamine finally turned back to the grisly sight, he was glad to see Sybil had the wherewithal to keep the magic blanketing the infected body in a dark shroud.

Breathing hard, Sybil gestured to the wet pile. "See? No problem at all. I don't know what I was so worried about."

"Other than the dead man currently trapped in a spell?" he asked sarcastically.

"Oh, no one will notice. If they do, they won't know it was either of us. There's no easy way to track magical signatures anymore, not without a witch at their side. And there's so few of us left!"

He didn't think there was any confidence in her voice at all. He'd known Sybil to be proud, but this . . . she almost sounded nervous. Or exhausted.

With a narrowed gaze, he watched the witch attempt to straighten before she nearly tripped over her own feet. Breathing hard, she pressed a hand to her chest, and that was when he knew. She was weakened from just that attack? What little power did she have left?

"What kind of spell was that?" Jessamine breathed.

"Old magic," the other witch replied, but it wasn't entirely the truth.

He knew why Sybil didn't want Jessamine to have the answer.

Apparently, they were still keeping secrets from each other. But he wanted his gravesinger to know what kind of magic that was. It would only entice her to his side even more.

"That was the magic only a patron can give a witch," he rasped. "The kind of magic that is stolen or gifted from the gods themselves, and can be tapped only in small amounts. The spells you have cast thus far are magic any witch can cast. But the power she just used comes only from true worship of a god."

Jessamine glanced over her shoulder into the mirror. "Then why haven't you asked me to worship—"

"I'm fine," Sybil said, holding up a hand before he could answer that question. "I can see your disapproval through the mirror, Deathless One. I will get her to the Owl's Nest safe enough."

"You're hardly a witch anymore, with the meager coffers of magic you have left."

"I am well enough," she hissed in response.

But when they both turned toward the road again, they froze. Three more infected stood there. Two men and a woman this time, all of them hovering in the middle of the road as though they were waiting for something. A noise, a smell, anything that would send them sprinting after their prey, just like the man Sybil had killed.

Three against two weren't fantastic odds, especially considering that Sybil had already depleted her rather meager source of magic. He needed to be summoned, or lose his opportunity to come back for good. He could not use an infected witch.

Growling, he slammed his fist onto the mirror. "Summon me, damn it!"

He heard the words at the same time he felt the tug at his navel. Not the summoning spell that Jessamine had used, but the magic that only a worshipping witch could use. Not a resurrection, but at least it brought him into the realm of the living for a few moments before his magic depleted. It was a cry for help in the darkest of times, as only a witch could do.

It wasn't bringing him fully back into being, but it was a call he could answer.

The tugging yanked him out through the mirror, a black mist gathering in front of Sybil like the shield he was. Still nowhere near as powerful as he should be, but it was a power he was a little more used to. He could feel his direct tie to Sybil, and the intent behind the summons. He would linger no longer than the amount of time it took to save them. Nothing more. Nothing less.

Apparently, even his own disciple didn't trust him. He'd never been more proud.

Turning, he faced the infected, who were already sprinting down the street toward them. They were nasty beasts, dripping with all manner of disgusting liquids that no person should ever leak. But they were human, nonetheless.

Crouching to the ground, he pressed his palms to the sparse grass that he could not feel and let his magic sink into the shadows that surrounded him. Summoned, the shadows came to him like puppies ready to please their master. They pulled from where they were attached: trees, buildings, even Sybil's and Jessamine's shadows—they all came to his call.

Then he sent them down the road, all coiling together to create something so much worse. First, he tried to give it the shape of a bear. Most humans knew better than to toy with a creature such as that. But he could feel the excitement rolling through the infected. They were pleased with the image of a bear. They wished to feast upon its flesh, and that simply wouldn't do.

He wanted them afraid, not more bloodthirsty than they already were. Flexing his power again, he created paths around them. Buildings like he'd seen in his own realm when he had followed Jessamine. When he had given her permission to just be a woman for that night.

There it was. Confusion settled into the creatures as they looked down the sudden alleyways that appeared in front of their eyes.

"Go," he ground through gritted teeth. "Stay to the right. That way is blocked off from their view."

"But where will you—" Jessamine stopped talking the moment he snapped at her.

"I will find you. Get moving. Now!"

They didn't stop to ask more questions. Both of the witches raced away from him, moving quietly but quickly. They were efficient, even if Sybil trailed behind Jessamine now. He kept his eyes on them, watching as they progressed through the false city he had conjured until they reached the real one.

He couldn't know if there were even more infected waiting for them there. Right now, he had to deal with the problem in front of him.

Yanking all the shadows down upon the heads of the three infected, he let dark magic seep into every pore of their bodies. It wriggled through their eyes, their ears, their noses, jamming their mouths open even further so it could pour down their throats. They tore at their faces, trying to stop him from sneaking inside their forms, but he had to know what they were. How they were so sick.

Strangely enough, he found no illness in their bodies. No bacteria or virus, no strangeness that grew throughout their body as though they had been overtaken by another creature. All he found was magic. Not quite the same as his own, but familiar. It had the taste of another god . . . but that was impossible.

He let the shadows slowly dissipate, returning to their hosts. The infected each dropped, their bodies deflating as his magic left them, until they were nothing more than dark smudges on the ground. Straightening, he cracked his neck as he muttered, "A magical malady."

Strange. He hadn't seen one of those since long before this kingdom was even built. Witches accidentally created such things, sometimes, when a spell got out of hand. But there were no more witches powerful enough to do this. He knew that without a doubt. There was no flavor of a particular spell caster or even a single person who had caused this.

So what had infected these people? Or, he supposed, the correct question was *who*?

17

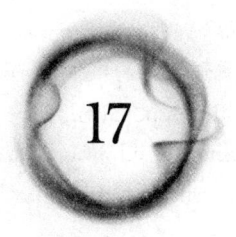

Staring up at the Owl's Nest, Jessamine realized she'd never been quite so afraid. Even when she was wandering the streets and scrounging for scraps. Even when she had tumbled down the cliff's edge toward the ocean.

Because if she believed what she herself had seen, then all this was real, not some lengthy fever dream, and the people closest to her really had betrayed her in a murderous coup. The only thing standing between her and the truth was the young man at the top of this building, who had been part of her life since he was a boy.

What could have turned his loyalty away from the royal family? They had fed him, clothed him, given him every opportunity to better himself.

And instead, he had chosen to hide here, in this building that leaned drastically to the left, crowned with a strange hat of random sticks poking out in all directions. At one point those had probably formed a dome; it might even have been elegant. But time and neglect had eventually ruined the building. Beams rotted, and the original beauty of this place had faded beyond recognition.

The Owl's Nest sign still hung, even if precariously. She wondered if it would fall on someone someday, and if anyone would care.

"I'm going to stay down here," Sybil murmured; her face was drawn, and dark hollows shadowed beneath her eyes. "I'm not sure I can . . . can . . ."

Jessamine really looked at the witch, then. The pallid sheen on Sybil's face was one Jessamine had only seen when someone was very sick. The shaking of her fingers was concerning, as was the way she leaned against the wall. Sybil's shoulder barely held her up against the building, which looked like it might topple over on her at any second.

"Stay down here," Jessamine replied. "I can do this on my own."

A dark mass gathered behind Sybil, the shape now very familiar to Jessamine's trained eye. She turned away as the Deathless One pulled a wriggling shadow off his form and brought it to Sybil as the witch fumbled to open her gown.

Her stomach twisted, knowing what they were doing. She wanted Sybil to feel better, but she hated the relieved sigh that echoed in the small alleyway. The strange feeling felt almost like jealousy, which was silly. She wasn't a witch, nor did she worship the Deathless One. Not like Sybil did. She wanted nothing from him but answers.

Scuffing her shoes in the dirt, she tried to remain silent as they finished . . . whatever it was they were doing.

This was part of being a witch, she reminded herself. It didn't matter that she could hear the sound of rustling clothing or the faint sigh of a witch being fed. She didn't want to know that part of the ritual because she herself would never have to endure it.

She had not given herself to the Deathless One. They were bound for reasons beyond the mere transfer of magic.

Finally, Sybil groaned and said, "I'll cast a few spells down here. A containment spell to keep him in, and a silencing spell. That should be enough for you to get what you need."

Would it? Jessamine wasn't so sure. There were so many risks, and she didn't think Benji was just going to tell her what happened. In the best-case scenario, he'd prove he had nothing to do with it at all, that he was still the same boy who'd brought her mother sweets.

But Jessamine knew better than to hope for that.

"Thank you," she said as she started into the building.

The front door nearly fell off its hinges as she opened it. Immediately she was hit with the rank smell of mildew and rotting wood. There wasn't even a reception hall any longer, or much of anything left. Just piles of what might have once been curtains and a mound in the back that she suspected was once a desk. It had the general shape of what might have been a tavern, but certainly was not any longer.

The stairs, if one could call them that, were just as terrifying as the rest of the building. Missing wooden planks made every step precarious as she clung to an iron bar screwed into the wall, though it felt as though it could rip off at any moment. Every creak and shudder of the building made her wince.

But there were only three floors. She was brave enough to manage three floors.

Jessamine held her breath the entire time until she got to the top, which opened onto what had once been a dining hall. Or, considering where she was, a place where the unscrupulous held their parties. Though there was hardly a roof, and water dripped onto the floor made of old and shattered tiles, she could see this used to be a welcoming room.

Stepping over the cracked shards, she covered her nose as she was assaulted with the smell of refuse. Whatever was up here had died a long time ago.

"Benji?" she whispered, her heart squeezing in fear.

Then she kicked something thick and . . . wet.

Wincing, she stared up at the sky while trying to steel herself for what she was about to find. Casting her eyes downward, she breathed out a sigh of relief at the sight of what might have once been a boar. Even if it made her stomach roll to see it, at least it wasn't human. The rib bones stuck out from where someone had been cleaning pieces of it off. Whoever was carving this shouldn't be eating it any longer. The meat was long past spoiled.

Still holding her nose, she moved deeper into the room, where the light from the moon didn't quite reach. Her sight was different now, though. She felt power flowing through her body, burning behind her eyes so she could see through the darkness like a cat.

And that was when she found him.

Benji lay on top of a pile of silks and velvets, colors she recognized. A deep blue, a vivid azure, the signature colors of her court, and he lay on top of them like they were rags.

Then a twinkle of moonlight hit more of the items surrounding him. Jewels and gemstone-crusted necklaces. Goblets made of pure gold that glimmered and winked in the pale light. He snorted and rolled, a ring falling out of his hand and thudding onto the floor. A familiar one, with a face carved into a sapphire and surrounded by priceless diamonds.

Bending down, she quietly scooped up her mother's signet ring and put it into her pocket.

Tears burned in her eyes. Benji was lying here, completely unaffected, surrounded by her things. Her *stolen* things. The precious items that had been passed down through her family for generations, and he lay on top of them like they were trash.

She sank a vicious kick into his side. He rolled off the pile of silks and velvets, flailing as he struck the floor with a startled shout before sitting up and glaring at the person who had dared to wake him.

It shouldn't have been so satisfying to see the blood drain out of his features. Pale lips, tired eyes, and shaking hands that clutched something beside him as he stared up at her.

"Are you a ghost?" he asked, his voice wavering.

"Worse," she replied. "I died and came back, Benji."

He lashed out at her with the thing in his hand. She didn't have time to gasp as he stabbed a knife into her shoulder, but strangely, she couldn't feel the pain. And when he ripped it out of her skin, there was no blood. Only a smooth black shadow that wrapped around the wound and then warped into a smooth silver line.

Paper white and trembling, he scrambled away and bolted for the window. Jessamine wasn't sure what he planned to do, perhaps throw himself out of it and hope the ground was less hard than his own guilt. But instead of open air, he struck the barrier that Sybil must have built. Invisible but hard as stone, it threw him back into the room. He landed on his behind, skidding to a halt against the opposite wall.

Dust plumed down on him, mold spores and mildew flakes frosting his hair like snow.

He coughed a few times, trying hard to hack up a lung and gain sympathy from her before he sighed and stopped acting. "So you somehow survived all that?"

Oh, how quickly the pretenses dropped.

She clutched her mother's ring in her pocket so hard it bit through the skin of her palm. "Who paid you?"

"For what?"

"Don't be cute, Benji. I know you wouldn't have betrayed us like that unless a significant amount of money was involved. What I don't understand is why, and who."

"I didn't do nothing, Miss Jessamine." She could see him piecing his mask back together bit by bit. He gathered up the person she recognized and laid those pieces over his own face.

It was disturbing to watch, and even more heart-wrenching than she could have guessed.

"Don't do this to me," she whispered. "We gave you a home, a safe place to rest your head. We fed you, gave you new clothing. You said you thought of me like a sister. Now you *have* to tell me who wanted me dead."

"Your husband. He was the one who threw you off the cliff. We all thought you were dead." He got onto his knees, looking up at her with big eyes just the same as he had the first time she'd met him. "Please, Miss Jessamine, you have to understand. I would never do nothing to harm you or your mother."

A dark shadow descended around her. She could feel his cold arms wrapping around her shoulders, drawing her into a deep, inky mire. "You don't believe him, do you?" the Deathless One asked. "Surely you don't believe these lies."

"Are you lying to me?" she asked. Even Jessamine could hear the sorrow in her words.

Another puzzle piece clicked back into place over his features, and she could see he planned to use her own emotions against her. "Why would I want to hurt you? You said it yourself. You gave me everything."

"He's still lying." Again the Deathless One whispered. "He knows what happened. You saw him open the gate."

Dark fingers closed around her arms, which should have been intimidating. But she could feel him vibrating with anger, not at her, but at the man in front of her. When was the last time someone had been angry on her behalf? She couldn't remember the last time someone had been protective of her and not the kingdom or the princess who would rule them. Just her.

The Deathless One cared that this young man had taken part in harming her. And that made her trust the god at her back far more than this pageboy on his knees.

"Don't make me do this," she said, her voice warbling with emotion. "I don't want to do something I regret."

Jessamine didn't know if she was talking to the god or the man. Perhaps both of them.

But Benji looked up at her, and the mask slipped. "You don't have to do anything you don't want to do, Miss Jessamine. You're a princess." His voice dripped with sarcasm and deep disdain.

She could hear the judgment in those words. Like she had asked some higher power to be reborn into the body of a princess. Like she had gotten some leg up over everyone else without having to work for it.

"Please, just tell me what happened."

The Deathless One growled in her ear. "Stop stalling."

His dark hand passed over her eyes, and she saw the image of her mother. The memory of what she had looked like sitting in the aisle. She could see with such certainty the glistening tears in the queen's eyes as she watched her daughter marry a man who would take pleasure in her pain. And she remembered standing in this memory with him, so afraid that she would forget a single detail of what her mother looked like, or how she'd lived.

The ring in her hand grew slippery with her own blood. She'd clasped it too hard, and the stone had bitten into her palm.

Benji chuckled, and the sound was like a knife to her heart. "You're no good at interrogation, princess."

Another pulsing memory took the place of the first. This time, a ruby necklace rested right above her mother's heart. And then it started to bleed. Her mother was dying right in front of her, and in the background stood Benji, holding open the gate with a gleeful smile on his face. She couldn't take it anymore.

Lunging forward, she wrapped both of her hands around his neck and gave him a shake. "You useless bastard. You know something and you will tell me!"

It was like something shattered in front of her. Those innocent eyes narrowed into a fox's gaze. His brows drew down, and his quivering lips curved into a sinister smile. "You and your mother could never understand this kingdom like I do. I did what was right for *my* people. Neither of you spoiled brats could do that, living in a castle above all our heads. You can threaten me all you want, princess. But you don't scare me."

The darkness behind her pressed against her spine, bolstering her courage and giving her strength. "He means 'princess' as an insult," the Deathless One murmured. "Is it an insult, Jessamine?"

No.

She could feel the power flowing between the two of them. Like she was an extension of the Deathless One. Like he was inside her, using her body to puppet his grand plan, and still it didn't frighten her. Because she wanted what he wanted. Revenge. Fear. She wanted to taste it on her tongue because she wanted this young man to know what real terror felt like.

Magic poured out of her hands, ink wriggling around his throat and up his cheeks. His eyes widened in horror as those tendrils ripped open his mouth and she stared down at his tongue, which tried desperately not to swallow the darkness pouring into his throat.

Shaking, she hissed, "Then I will rip out your memories, Benji. This kingdom is *mine*. And I will decide what it needs."

With a jerk of her arm, she ripped. She tore the memories straight out of him, and they erupted from his mouth like the smog that hung over the Factory District. She ignored the whimpers that came with it.

She had to know.

She had to know who had put him up to this horrible thing that had changed all their lives. And she had to know *why*.

"Consume it," the Deathless One said. "Breathe it into your body. Claim his memories."

She didn't even hesitate. Later, perhaps, she would wonder why she'd listened to someone she knew to be so dangerous. But she trusted him now, and that was a problem all on its own.

Breathing in Benji's memory, she could see everything he saw, from his earliest time in the castle to the day of her death. His images melded with her own memories, connecting with still other pieces, until she was certain who had paid him. She had found the architect of her destruction.

A man who had known her for her entire life. A man who had been so important to her mother that it was like he also was family. A betrayal. A heartbreak.

"No," she gasped, wrenching away from Benji and dropping him back onto the treasure trove he'd stolen from her family. "No, he could not have . . ."

She looked back at Benji, hoping to see remorse. But all she saw was a pool of blood leaking out of his mouth and a vacant stare that was now frozen on his face for all eternity. Her heart stuttered, thudded hard against her ribs, and all she could hear was the haunting wail of an organ that had once thought everyone was honorable.

"This was what you wanted, wasn't it?" the Deathless One said.

"I don't know anymore." Goose bumps rose on her arms and her teeth chattered. She staggered away from the body, unable to look at what she had done. "I didn't want to hurt anybody."

"You're taking back a kingdom, Jessamine. People are going to get hurt."

"I didn't think it would feel like . . . this." Her hands were shaking, too, now. She couldn't quite think right, other than to stare at them and realize she had done that. With her magic.

No, not her magic. His. The magic he had given her because she'd made a deal with a horrible god who had resurrected her for his own purposes. She wasn't in her right mind. If she had been, she never would have hurt Benji. She wouldn't have.

"Jessamine." The dark voice had softened. So quiet that she almost didn't hear her name as he whispered it. "Pick up the book in the trunk at the foot of his bed and go find Sybil."

"I don't know if I can walk."

"You can walk because you must. Get going, Jessamine."

She found her body moving of its own accord. She continued forward, her knees weak and wobbling. The book was exactly where he'd said it would be. A black leather-bound grimoire with etchings all over the cover. She held it to her heart, tucking it against her chest as she made her way down the rickety stairs.

Some part of her heard the creaking noises and the warning sounds of a building that was far too close to collapse, but she didn't feel the spike of fear this time. All she could feel was a sense of numbness that should have made her nervous.

Sybil waited for her at the bottom of the stairs. The witch took one look at her, and her face crumpled into pity. "Oh, sweet thing. Come here."

Safe beneath the arm of a witch, Jessamine was ashamed to admit she felt much better. Even as her heart turned brittle and thin as the first winter ice.

18

He worried that perhaps he had broken her. A tie between them had knotted a little tighter, though, and he no longer needed to wait to be summoned. Wherever she was, he could follow.

The first time he'd tried to find her after what happened with Benji, she'd slammed a door in his face. Which, considering the crumbling nature of their current home, only resulted in the door falling onto the floor straight through the shadow of his body. She'd glared at him before pointing to the exit.

The second time, she had ignored him, purposefully looking straight through him like he wasn't there at all.

It was at this point that he realized perhaps he had pushed her too far. Which was silly, really. He hadn't made her do anything that she hadn't wanted to do.

The boy was venal, heartless, dangerous. This Benji had taken royal lives into his own hands and then crushed them in that weak, sweat-slicked grip. It wasn't even an indirect attack. That young man had allowed infected people to walk into the castle and kill everyone who stood in their way. He was the reason Jessamine's mother was dead.

She should *want* to hurt him. Revenge tasted sweeter when your hands got dirty—how did she not see that?

By all the dead gods, *he* was the consequence of her actions.

And it annoyed him that he was so upset about why she wouldn't talk to him. He'd never wondered if the witches who served him actually *liked* him. Liking him wasn't required to perform magic, nor was it required for him to exist.

But he wanted this one to like him. He couldn't explain why or how or what it was about her that made him care, but he did.

Maybe he was just getting too soft in his old age.

Blowing out a breath, he stood in front of her room again. Because the door was broken, she'd hung a sheet over the space and remained aloof. Even Sybil hadn't gotten through to the young woman, who wandered the halls like a wraith.

The only living creature who walked in and out with impunity was the kitten he had conjured. He'd half a mind to tell the creature to do his bidding, but the one time he'd poked his head in, he had seen it resting on her chest, purring so loud he could see its entire body rattle.

But she'd been sleeping. And she hadn't slept in days.

"Jessamine?" he called out, standing in front of her door like an awkward suitor, hoping for her attention. "Are you ready to talk?"

Nothing stirred on the other side of the curtain.

"It's been nearly a week. I understand you're feeling a certain amount of remorse after Benji, but you do realize we're running out of time? The people who killed your mother are slipping through your fingers while you're—"

He didn't get a chance to finish that sentence.

The curtain whipped open and sunlight speared through him. It shattered his strange corporeal form for a few seconds before his magic realized she was there. He could feel his body solidifying, all that darkness pooling together and dragging into one body that felt . . . solid.

Actually solid.

He had a weight to him that pulled him toward the earth. And there was a sensation of clothing on his body, shoes on his feet.

Gods, the texture of clothing distracted him. That there was a heaviness against his skin when he wore it and that the boots on his feet made his toes jam against the tips uncomfortably.

She gripped the sheet in both fists, so hard he worried she might rip it from the wall. "I'm not talking to you."

He looked left, then right, assuring himself that there was no one else in the hallway before replying, "You're talking to me right now."

"Well, I don't want to." She brought the sheet closed with another snap.

But that wouldn't do. He hadn't felt sensations like these in centuries, and the moment he lost sight of her was the moment he lost all those sensations again. He was back to the cold, unfeeling, bitter existence that had led him to this point, and how dare she try to take that away from him.

Storming into her room, decorum be damned, he followed her to the cot where she had set up a strange-looking nest. The blankets were piled a little too high, and there were quite a few plates lying beside the bed, as though that was acceptable or clean. Her cat sat on top of that pile, a little royal in a crumbling kingdom. It blinked at him before curling up into a tiny ball. Evidently, it also did not want to get involved with him.

She even looked a little dirty and wild. Her hair hadn't been brushed in days, it seemed, and it billowed around her head like a rat's nest. There were dark rings around her eyes, but then there were always dark rings around her eyes. He found them rather pretty. A pale purple that made her gaze look bottomless.

She spun on him, those dark eyes flaring with an inner anger that seared him to his bones. "You did this!"

"I did what, nightmare?"

"You made me do this. I felt your magic inside me, and I couldn't stop you."

He blinked a few times. "Stop me from what, exactly? I'm not saying I didn't do it, but I certainly don't want to take credit for your creativity."

"You made me kill him." She snapped out the words, the sound of them cracking from her lips like a whip. "You took control of my body and you made me kill someone who meant something to me."

He wasn't following, and she wasn't making any sense. Shaking his head, he tried to reason with her. "A pageboy meant something to you?

Wasn't he only good for fetching your pretty baubles and supper when you didn't want to dine with the others?"

"He was a person, and he didn't deserve to die like that."

Ah, he saw where the real problem was. Tsking, he approached until she was backed against the wall. Her chest rose and fell with angry huffs of air, her glare searing in its intensity.

He reached forward and wrapped a curl of her hair around his finger. So pretty, glimmering like an oil slick. "Did you really think you were going to take your kingdom back without spilling a single drop of blood? That just because you snap your fingers, your would-be husband will suddenly have to see the madness of his ways? No, Jessamine. You're going to get your hands bloody, because that is what war is."

"They're my people," she growled, that anger still flashing in her eyes. "I don't want to hurt any of them!"

"Even the boy who was the reason your mother died? I'll take credit for his death if that is what you wish. A rat stomped beneath my heel certainly won't prevent me from sleeping at night, but Jessamine, I don't control the power you take from me. A part of you wanted him dead for what he did, and so he is dead. That is all. You need to understand that your desires have consequences. Especially when you use magic to fulfill them."

Her eyes widened as he spoke, and she fought to disagree. He could see the tiny wrinkles gathering between her brows and the sudden frown that formed lines around her mouth. "No," she whispered. "You did this. You had to have done this, because if you didn't, then I have to live with the knowledge that I . . . I . . ."

"Killed someone?" He braced his forearm over her head, leaning ever closer to the shock and horror in her gaze. "Yes, all humans do. Perhaps they do not realize that a choice they make one morning leads to the death of another, but your little lives are a hand of cards traded for another. You scrabble with tooth and claw to live, and you trade other people's lives to do so."

Her long, pretty throat worked in a swallow. "I am not a monster."

"No. *But I am.*"

He leaned down, swearing he could smell her. The scent of lilies left on a grave. Faintly clove-like, the barest hint of space and the scent of freshly turned earth. It was a scent he remembered well and loved dearly, if it was possible for him to love anything in this existence.

She planted her hands against his chest and shoved. She wasn't very strong, though. A mere slip of a woman couldn't force him to move. Not when she barely came up to his shoulder and was so waif thin that he could see her collarbones protruding and the shadows of her cheeks.

She wasn't taking care of herself. The thought appeared belatedly in his mind. She shouldn't look like this. He wasn't certain if it was her death that had done it, or if perhaps she had always looked like this. A hollow woman, just waiting to be filled.

Fire erupted in his chest, coursing through his entire body. Suddenly, he wanted her to touch him again. He wanted to feel her hands sliding up the flat planes of his chest. Perhaps her fingers would dig into his shoulders, still angry but seeking some other way to release such emotion. He had never felt like this about any witch. He needed to know what she tasted like.

If she smelled like the grave, would she taste just as bitter?

When he didn't move, apparently Jessamine took that as the opportunity to vent her fury. Amused, he watched as she struck him with her fists. Over and over again, growing more angry with each strike even though he'd have thought this would make her feel better.

Perhaps it was not helpful that he wasn't reacting. So he flinched just slightly every time her fists hit him.

"*You* did this," she hissed with each strike. Tears sparkled in her eyes as she repeated the words. "You had to have done this, because if you didn't, then I was the one who killed him. And then I'd have to live with the knowledge that I killed him and he's not coming back."

He let her hit him. Though he would never admit it, it felt good to have someone touch him, even in anger. He hadn't been touched in centuries and even then, it was usually in violence. But he took whatever touch he could get.

As her strikes slowed, she seemed to deflate just slightly, those bony shoulders curving and her angry breaths calming, until at last her forehead dropped against his chest.

"I don't know how to deal with this," she whispered. "I feel so guilty. And I'm also so happy that he's gone. How can I be happy that someone is no longer alive?"

He shrugged, feeling her head rock against his chest. "I think it's best not to look into those emotions too much. Diving deeper into that darkness is rarely good for anyone, my nightmare."

Then she surprised him again. She always surprised him. With a heavy sigh, Jessamine wrapped her arms around his waist and tucked herself in close.

His arms hung awkwardly at his sides. What was he supposed to do in this situation? She'd just been hitting him, and now she was . . . holding on to him. Should he put his arms around her? He'd seen humans do that before, but they never wanted to touch him like this. He had thought that in this circumstance he'd know what to do, but he certainly did not.

"Don't think about it so much," she muttered. "Just hold me, please."

Carefully, he lifted his hands. Setting one on her shoulder felt right, the other he slowly slid across her back until his thumb rested on her ribs and the rest of his hand lay on top of her hip. Yes, this was right. They fit together rather like two puzzle pieces. She sighed, and he felt her go boneless in his arms.

Something clicked inside him. Something that he wasn't quite comfortable with. But it was there now, a small beacon of light glowing in his chest. Licking his lips, he turned his head and gently bent down to rest his cheek on top of her head. He was enveloped by her death-lily smell, and some of the tension leaked out of his shoulders and spine as he eased himself into the hug.

She was . . .

Right, he thought. That was the only word he could think of. This was right. This moment had been destined from the first time he'd seen her.

"I'm sorry for yelling," she said against his chest. "It's not fair for me to blame you for all my own struggles. I just thought if it was your magic, then at least it wasn't my fault."

"You can blame me for whatever you wish, nightmare." His grip tightened around her, hauling her just a little closer, and he hoped she didn't feel how desperately he clutched her to him.

This meant nothing. He was touch starved, and he'd never been hugged so sweetly before. He was merely using her to experience something new, not that he enjoyed the feeling of her in his arms.

"No, I can't blame you for everything. I just am so angry about all of this, and I worry that anger is going to take over."

"May I ask you a question?" He lifted his head, looking down at her until she stared up at him. Those big eyes were so fearful of what he might ask. "Do you even want this throne?"

She blinked, the bruises around her eyes darkening. "Of course I do."

That wasn't the answer he was looking for, though. "Why? Why do you want the throne?"

"Because it is my birthright."

He hummed low underneath his breath. "That is the answer of a child who has been given everything in her life. You can do better than that."

"Because I wish to honor the memory of my mother, who is now dead and gave everything for me to have that throne." Her eyes flicked to the side, as they always did when she lied.

"Now you sound naïve. Come on, nightmare, there's a real reason in there, and I want to hear it."

He released her, even if it felt like bending metal just to let her go. But this was important. He needed her to hear this. He needed her to say it.

Her arms hung in the shape of him for a few moments. Glistening tracks of tears marred her cheeks as anger flashed in her eyes again. "Because in the months since I was killed, I have seen the true state of my kingdom. I have seen the best and worst of its citizens, and I know now that we failed our people. My mother and I were not given the whole story. Without knowing the whole truth, we were bound to fail. I will not fail again. I have put in too much work and effort to lose it all to some idiot who thought he could kill me on our wedding day. I fucking deserve that crown."

"There it is," he murmured. "Now you sound like a queen."

He could see the realization fill her body. She would do anything to keep this kingdom, her throne, and everything in between—because it was hers.

And he would do whatever it took to help her get it back.

19

In the days to come, Jessamine would try not to think about that moment. She staggered out of her room, got herself clean for the first time in what must have been a week. She had to scrub so hard that her skin turned bright red, but once she was done, she felt a little more like herself.

Sybil had been helpful. The moment she saw Jessamine walk into the kitchen, the other witch went into full damage control. Food appeared wherever Jessamine was, and they continued with their magical lessons, although they were becoming much easier.

For the most part, Sybil just handed Jessamine a book in the morning to read about the magical properties of plants or what particular spells were supposed to do.

No magic was cast for the week that passed after Jessamine had hugged a god.

What the hells had she been thinking?

Even now, sitting with her back against the crumbled statue that had once been the Wizened Crone, an ancient goddess known for gifting knowledge to her priestesses, she could think about the memory. What had possessed her to hug the man who held her life in his hands? He was a dangerous god who wanted nothing more than to unleash chaos on her entire kingdom, and she had hugged him!

Shaking her head, she tried to focus on the book in her lap and not the one that she had taken to carrying around with her. The black book that the Deathless One had her grab from Benji was a curiosity that she wasn't sure she wanted to explore just yet. It was a book that didn't open.

That much she knew. She had tried repeatedly when they returned from the Owl's Nest, hoping to make the Deathless One as angry as she was. But the book refused to open. It wasn't locked. There was no clasp that held it closed.

It just . . . didn't open.

She wasn't sure if that was by mechanical or magical design. All she knew was that a thrum of dark power emanating from between the covers made her want to open it, and thus it was very frustrating not to be able to open it at all.

Grumbling under her breath, she sighed dramatically and closed the book that *did* open in her lap.

"Jessamine, you have to focus," she muttered to herself. "You cannot be thinking about these things."

"And just what things are bothering you?" The voice came from behind her.

She was so used to him appearing out of nowhere that she no longer even flinched when she heard his voice. It came from all manner of places, and she supposed she expected him to always be around now.

It was exhausting.

She looked behind her to see a dark shadow leaning against the side of the Crone's statue. He had his hands in his pockets, his ankles crossed over each other, and she felt her cheeks blush.

"I can see more of you today," she said.

"Can you now?"

"You're not so much a charcoal sketch. You even have pockets."

He hopped down from the statue and strode around to face her. The Deathless One looked very much like a man trying hard to seem nonchalant. He looked at her expectantly.

"Well?" he said, impatience sharpening his words.

"Well what?"

"How much can you see?"

She blinked. It was like parts of him had shifted back into place. "A sharp jaw," she murmured, her eyes tracing these new features as though they were her fingertips. "You have the faintest hint of stubble on your cheeks and chin. I can't see anything else, though, just the outer edges of your face."

Should she continue?

Some part of her whispered that she was playing with fire right now. Dangerous to keep going when all she wanted to do was touch him and see if that stubble had texture.

He swallowed, and she could see his throat working. "How interesting that I keep changing the longer I am around you."

"Why is that?"

"I do not know, nightmare. Perhaps it is because you are the one who can resurrect me."

She licked her lips, and it felt as though he was staring at them, but she wished she could see his features to know for certain that he was. "But I haven't yet."

"No, and that's even more curious, isn't it? I'm becoming more and more real, and here you are, defying me every step of the way."

He took a step closer to her, standing in between her parted legs. Her borrowed trousers suddenly felt a little too tight. Or maybe that was her entire body, too hot because he was right in front of her again. Just like he had been when she wound her arms around him and clung to him like the only rock in the middle of a hurricane.

She'd been able to feel how strong he was. How every breath expanded those wide ribs and how much power was barely leashed inside a body that was so much larger than her own.

He stepped a little closer again, and a beam of light played along his strong jaw and the muscle ticking inside it. But for the first time, his form didn't shatter in the brightness. "Jessamine," he rasped.

"Yes?" Did that word sound as breathless as it had felt?

"You still have the book I told you to gather. Don't you?"

She blinked, the words settling in before she realized what he was asking.

"Oh." Bursting into movement, she awkwardly pulled the book out of the bag next to her. "Yes, yes, of course. I still have it. I don't know why you wanted it. It won't open."

"It will open for me." He stared down at it, and she could almost feel the intensity coming out of his gaze. It was like a warm touch spilling over her hands and pooling in her lap where the book rested. "It is mine, after all."

She looked down at the book, and it all made sense. Of course it was his. The black pages and black binding would only be for the Deathless One himself. It was a book dedicated to him, or perhaps written by him? She had no way of guessing what was inside the pages, but she suddenly saw them flutter against her fingertips.

The book unlocked. That easily. It stopped being so stubborn simply because he was glaring at it.

She opened the first page, feathering a light touch over the illuminated pages, which were meticulously designed. Demons ran along every page, twisting creatures with horns and tails that merged into dark shadows. Borders of ink stains were clearly intentional, as though trying to mimic the power he possessed. The writing was in a language she couldn't understand, but the loops and swirls were hypnotic. And then, at her touch, all the ink disappeared.

She flipped through the pages, watching as words continued to disappear until it was entirely empty. A journal now, no longer a grimoire. With a small gasp, she closed it and opened it again, hoping the words would come back. But they didn't. They were gone, like it was intended for them to disappear the moment her eyes started reading the words.

Closing it, she turned the book over and traced her fingers over the sigil on the back that had captivated her attention since the start. Its strange markings and harsh lines were not a sigil she recognized—Sybil had given her countless books on witch marks, but none of them looked like this.

It felt important. "This mark on the back. What is it?"

He leaned even closer, and she swore there was almost a hint of a lock of hair that fell in front of the shadowy visage of his face. "It's a sigil. It depicts my name."

"You have a name?" she asked, her voice incredulous. "What is it?"

"I have a name, Jessamine Harmsworth. There are many interpretations of it, many meanings. But in this realm and this time, I suppose it would be . . . Elric Hellebore."

He moved away from her then, rounding the statue until he appeared again. He'd picked something up from the dirt at the foot of the statue, and tossed it back and forth between his hands.

Almost as though he was now ignoring her.

"Why haven't you told me before?"

"I forgot I had one."

"That seems unlikely. You're a person, so of course you have a name. I just . . ." She shook her head again, stunned at this realization. "I didn't think gods had names. I thought you were the Deathless One, and that was the end of it."

He opened his hand and revealed an emerald-green gemstone in his palm. It had cracked in half at some point, ruined by time or perhaps a careless bootheel. But he gently placed both pieces in the eyes of the Crone. "We were all people once. A hard lesson for humans to learn, because to you we have always been gods. But there was a time when we weren't."

"What were you?" she asked.

"I'm not sure there's a name for what we were. Not entirely human, if that's what you're asking. I don't think any mortal could survive what we did to become what we are now. But not a god either."

"Oh." She hadn't ever thought about what they were before they were gods. "Even the Crone?"

"Even her. We were close once. But power, greed, and madness can tear a family apart."

That hadn't been her experience. Her mother had always been the only person there for her. But then she remembered what she had seen in Benji's memories, and she realized that perhaps she was wrong. Maybe her family had been torn apart from the inside out.

There was a darkness in this world. A darkness that she couldn't fix, and the only person who had ever honestly seen it was this dangerous god in front of her.

She made up her mind and stood. The base of the statue was uneven, with cracks down almost every side. But she stood in front of him, gazing up into the shadows of his face, and she wanted to touch him. She wanted him to feel real.

So she didn't think about it. She just reached out and cupped his jaw in her hand.

Bristles scratched her palm, and she swore she felt the faintest hint of a scar around his neck. One that matched hers, if she could look closely enough. She felt the ripple of another scar on his jaw under her fingers as he ground his teeth together at her touch.

"What are you doing?" he asked.

"It's nice to meet you, Elric Hellebore." She didn't know why saying it felt so important; she just knew she wanted someone to say his name. She wanted him to know that his name existed beyond the strange markings on a book that the world had long forgotten.

And then it was like a fog lifted. She watched the shadows obscuring his face slowly peel away from the bottom. Without a thought, she ghosted her thumb over his revealed lips. Almost too full for a man, but now she could see the way they twisted with a sneer that was strangely attractive. A scar bisected his top lip, and then the shadows revealed a long, hawkish nose that had been broken many times and dark eyes with slashes of black brows, each one with a scar on either side. Bone-white scars that nearly glowed on his face.

He was devastatingly handsome. His eyes saw straight into her soul, like some kind of bird of prey. A single curl escaped his tamed hair, just as she thought it would.

And she stood there, staring into those harsh features with her breath caught in her lungs. Because her thumb was still pressed against his lips. Because he stared at her with eyes that saw too much. And because his tongue gently licked her finger, and suddenly she could think of nothing else but that warm, slick touch.

Those lips.

Those eyes that flashed with something more than just a deep power inside him, but a power that she suddenly wanted to feel inside . . . her.

The front door opened and closed, the slam shuddering through her body even though she was stuck in this position. She couldn't move. She wanted to see what he would do if she pushed her thumb through those plush lips.

It was a wicked thought. A thought that never would have occurred to her before she met this man, this monster who made her want to be something wild and free.

His lips shifted, and that tongue flicked against her thumb one more time before she felt his hand move around her waist. He dragged her closer, and she knew she should stop him. She should end all this madness before the two of them did something they couldn't come back from.

But she didn't want to stop him. She didn't even struggle when his scarred hand scooped beneath her hair to clasp the back of her neck. Her hand trembled against his lips and jaw as he dragged her so close she could feel his breath play across her cheek.

"Elric," she whispered.

And oh, it felt like she'd uttered a curse into the world. Like she'd summoned a demon and released him out into the wild. She knew this wasn't how to free him, but to her, it felt like he was suddenly real.

So much more real than he had been moments before.

The hard planes of his chest pressed against her. He slid his thigh between her legs and something—someone—woke deep inside her. A woman she didn't recognize, but who knew exactly what she wanted and screamed that she would claim it.

Just an inch. That was all that separated her from the knowledge of what a god tasted like.

But then the door to this room opened, the statues of dead gods suddenly felt like nosy onlookers, and she felt him fade from her grasp.

Gone was the god in her embrace, and all she was left with was a sense of emptiness in her arms.

"Jessamine?" Sybil asked, a laugh at the end of the word. "Are you practicing for some prince who's coming to sweep you off your feet, darling?"

She let out a breath, her arms falling to her sides. "No, no, I suppose I was just . . . daydreaming. That's all."

"Daydreaming. Right." Sybil clearly didn't believe her. "Do you mind helping me bring all this in? I was lucky enough to come across a few chickens that had gotten out of a garden. I don't think the farmer will mind all that much if they're missing, but it is a rather suspicious amount of blood on our doorstep. I had forgotten how much I adore having a coven, even if it's just you."

"Of course, I'm happy to help." She barely even registered the words that she was saying.

Her mind was still lingering on moments ago, when she'd almost kissed a deathless god.

20

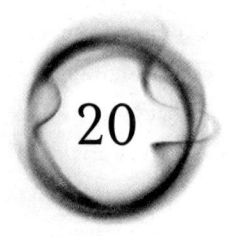

"She knows something," Elric muttered, standing in the shadows as Sybil worshipped with an ancient spell. "I don't like that she's keeping it to herself."

"You seem very invested in this girl for reasons that are far more to do with the personal than the necessary." Sybil kept her eyes closed, her hands moving over the altar where a dead chicken bled out. Her bloodied fingers traced runes on the stone. "I don't understand why you're so interested in what she's hiding, and why you aren't focusing on training her to resurrect you."

"She's not interested in summoning me to this realm for good. I have to earn her trust."

"Is that so?"

"She's said as much." He huffed out an angry breath. "Why are you arguing with me about this? You should want me to have my full powers back. That's the only way you will get all your powers back as well."

Sybil cracked one eye open to look into his gaze, and then shrugged. "I've lived this long without the full extent of my powers. And as I said, I was the weakest of the coven. I do not know what true power feels like."

A lie.

He could sense it in the air, hovering between them. She even held her breath for a few moments, waiting for him to call her out on that very lie. After all, he had seen what she did with that infected man. She had more power in her than she wanted him to know, but he wasn't sure how, when he had given her so little.

Let her keep her little secrets if she wanted. He had more important problems than figuring out what had happened to his coven.

"She's hiding what she saw in Benji's memories. If I do not restore this woman to the throne, then she will not summon me. She's made it very clear those are her terms, and I am not going to lose this opportunity because I didn't win her a measly little throne."

"A throne for an entire kingdom."

"I have changed the tides of war before, and I have placed kings on thrones who were less worthy than Jessamine. It will be easy enough to do." He prowled around the altar, pacing behind her as his witch pretended he didn't exist. "But I need to know what she saw."

"Deathless One." Sybil sighed. "Perhaps you should just ask her."

He startled at the sound of his title. How strange it was now that he'd remembered his name. He didn't actually enjoy the title. He wanted to hear other people say his name, just like Jessamine had done.

Because his name had sounded so pretty coming from her lips.

He'd forgotten that he even had a name. He'd forgotten that he was a person before all of this. Before the first knife, the first sacrifice, the first time someone saw him as a tool rather than a being. She'd given that back to him.

So perhaps he had reason to help her. If only because she had returned to him that little piece of humanity.

Sybil sighed and dropped her hands onto the altar, effectively ending the spell, which likely had taken hours to set up. "Just talk to her."

"I have no interest in pleading for information that she should freely give."

"Then I will ask her for you." Sybil stood, her hands on her hips as she glared at him. "You're how old and you cannot ask a woman to give you the information you want?"

"I'm not going to beg!" he repeated, although even he could hear the petulance in his voice. "I am her patron. I should know everything that she knows. If she's unwilling to give me the information, that is her own fault. Not mine."

Sybil looked up at the ceiling and expelled a long sigh. "I am exhausted by the both of you. Things were so much simpler when it was only me in this house."

"You had very little power," he pointed out as she started out of the room.

"I had enough!"

The sound of her voice trailed through the halls, and then he could hear the quiet murmuring from another room. Fading through the shadows, he followed her to a room where the two witches stood.

Jessamine had been working on restoring this room. In its time, it had been a gallery. Artwork from many of the talented witches in his coven had graced the walls, depicting gods and goddesses as they performed their most heroic deeds.

He'd forgotten that he used to be so well known. Standing in this room, however, surrounded by empty canvases that had long since rotted, he remembered that he had once helped people readily and often. There were so many paintings of him before his sacrifices.

How he had fed an entire town as he hunted for days on end in the middle of winter. The cold hadn't affected him, and he'd been bloodthirsty during that reincarnation. Another painting showed him swimming through the sea for hours, seeking a witch's child who had been lost at sea. He'd found the boy miraculously alive.

But then, as he turned to the opposite wall, he realized there was one painting still more or less intact. A depiction of a dark room deep in the heart of the earth, its walls shiny with constantly dripping water. The soft plinks had echoed in his ears for hours as he bled out from a hundred tiny cuts dotting across his chest, thighs, and arms. He had been in so much pain, and that pain had brought the coven a massive amount of power.

Swallowing, he turned his attention to the witches in the room, who hadn't yet thought to sacrifice him.

"Jessamine, you have to tell him whatever you saw. Otherwise, neither of us can help you." Sybil patted her shoulder. "No matter how hard it is to face."

"I don't know if I can say it." Jessamine stood in the corner of the room, her hands clutching his book like a lifeline.

"Then don't say it. Just show him." Sybil turned to leave, jolting at the sight of the block of his shadows before she pressed a hand to her chest. "I hate it when you do that. It's even worse now that you have a face."

The witch left them together, awkwardly standing at opposite ends of the room, with Jessamine barely even looking at him. She stared at his feet, her hands white against the leather book, her fingers twitching every now and then.

Finally, he couldn't stand it. "I can just take a look at your memories."

"I'm not sure why you need to."

"We have to keep going. You already killed a man, Jessamine. What could possibly make you want to stray from the path now?"

It wasn't the right thing to say. He had always known he was a cold and callous creature, but he had forgotten how fragile humans could be.

She closed her eyes as if in pain, and then whispered, "I suppose it's best if you just look."

He wasn't sure how to take that. Looking into her mind the last time had been rather . . . traumatic for her. She had lost her sight, something he should have at least warned her about. And even then, it had been difficult for her to watch the death of her mother. He wasn't sure why he should make her relive this memory as well.

But why did he care? Elric hadn't thought about another person's feelings in such a long time. It shouldn't matter what she had to see.

Swallowing hard, he tried to slip back into that version of himself who cared less about mortal problems, and stepped closer to her. "I will have to—"

"I know," she interrupted. "My eyesight."

"Just for a few moments."

He raised his hand and slowly shifted a small lock of her hair behind her ear. The slick strands glided through his fingers, as fine as a spiderweb. The small seashell of her ear captivated him as his hand slid behind it.

Gods, she was so fragile. He could snap her in a moment, and that terrified him as much as it intrigued him.

"I'll make it painless," he rasped. "And then we'll figure out what to do from here."

"I trust you."

The whispered words made him freeze. He stared down at those big black eyes, looking up at him with the truth in that gaze. She trusted him.

The heaviness of that settled on his shoulders. He had wanted this, he knew, but it was also . . . daunting to live up to her expectations. Squaring his shoulders, he moved his hand to cover her eyes. "I will try to be gentle."

Then he dove into her mind.

She was thinking about him, he realized. A faint burn of a blush traveled through both of them as he found himself back beside the statue of the Crone. He watched himself with his hands tangled in her hair, their lips only an inch apart as he breathed in her death-lily scent.

"This is not what we're here for," he murmured, his voice a low grumble.

"I know." Was that a whimper?

His hand spasmed on her face, and suddenly he realized how close they were even now. He could feel his power drawing out of her mind, away from her memories and closer to this moment. To the way her body shuddered beside his and how he wanted nothing more than to lay her beneath him. He wanted to worship this witch underneath the painting of his own death.

But she shuddered again, and he felt her memories shifting. He was standing in front of Benji. The boy's body arched uncomfortably as black magic poured into his mouth. The power beckoned to him. Both he and Jessamine tumbled through the open maw of the body and into the memories of the young man.

The stolen memories were hazy at best, but clear enough for him to realize they were standing in an opulent room. Warm wooden walls, a massive desk at one end, with dark smoke swirling around their legs. Benji sat in a chair in front of the desk, glee turning his eyes to sparkling gemstones.

"So all I got to do is open the gate?"

"That's it." A large man stood beside the desk, bent over with his silver hair hiding most of his features. "It's a simple task, Benji. Can you do it or not?"

"I can do it. Easy enough. And then I get whatever I want from the castle?"

"Within reason. All you're doing is opening a gate, boy."

"I'll take whatever I want from the dead. That's good enough for me."

The man looked up, and Elric froze the memory. He felt the darkness of his own power swirling around his legs as he paused in front of the stranger.

This was a strong man. His features were square, almost startlingly so. A square face, a slash for a mouth, bright blue eyes cold as the sea in winter. A man who saw much, this one. He wore a uniform of the deepest blue, gold buttons dotting down either side of his chest.

"Who's this?" he asked.

Jessamine appeared beside him. He'd forced her to physically appear in her memories, he thought, because her eyes were glassy with tears as she hugged both of her arms around her waist. "I can't."

"We're already in the memory, Jessamine. You might as well tell me who he is."

She swallowed hard. "Callum Quen. He's the head of the guard at the castle. He was the person responsible for our safety at all times. I've known him my entire life."

Elric felt the moment she lost grip on the memory. And then suddenly they were hurtling through her own memories, crystal clear and bright, as though they were happening right in front of him.

He saw a little girl on a horse, her unbound dark hair wild as she thundered bareback across a field, her laughter bubbling through the air. The man rode behind her, his expression murderous until he realized the little girl wasn't going to fall. Then he rode beside her, both of them allowing the horses to run as quickly as they wished.

Another memory. A scrape on a knee and a dark head ducking down to press a kiss just below the wound.

An older Jessamine standing in front of a door, her face creased with anxiety. And the guard standing there, this Callum Quen, who gave her a wink and opened the door while whispering, "You're going to do just fine."

Countless memories, each one supportive and kind. It was likely impossible for her to fathom that this was the man behind all of it. Callum Quen was not someone who would betray the royal family.

It all ended on a memory where he could see little Jessamine peeking around the corner of a hallway. There was a woman there, tall and powerful, with the faintest hint of purple around her eyes. The same as Jessamine always had. Her mother? The closer he looked, the more he saw the similarities. This had to be a younger version of her mother.

And she was clasped in the arms of Callum Quen. They were locked in an embrace before the queen pulled away. She held on to his biceps, her eyes perhaps a little wild and her lips berry red. "We can't. You know we can't, Callum."

In the wake of those words, everything fell away. The power leaked out of Elric's body, and soon he found himself kneeling in the gallery with Jessamine before him. His hand slid away from her eyes, and she slowly parted her lips on a long sigh.

"They loved each other," she said. "I knew every time I saw them in a room together. They could barely keep their eyes off each other, no matter how many times they tried. But she was the queen, and she couldn't marry anyone other than my father. Even after his death, the queen remains symbolically with the king. If it had ever gotten out that she was with the head of the guard, the entire kingdom would have rioted."

"So she kept him a secret, and he became bitter?"

She shook her head. "I never saw him angry with her. He looked at her with longing. Of course, how could he not? He was never a violent man. Not with us. He had a tendency for it, but he was always so kind to both me and my mother. He wouldn't . . . I can't imagine what would bring him to a place where he would do this."

Elric could feel the pain radiating through her body. Suddenly, he realized she hadn't just been suffering because she'd killed Benji. She'd been suffering because her entire childhood had been ripped out from under her. She didn't know what to do with this truth.

He smoothed her hair back from her face and gently cupped her cheeks in his palms. "We're going to figure this out, Jessamine. But we cannot find this man while we hide away in this manor."

"I know." She looked up at him with those wide, emotional dark eyes. "I have to go."

"Not alone." The words burned, falling from his tongue. "I'm going with you."

21

Leaving the safety of the manor was surprisingly difficult. Jessamine had assumed this family she'd built around herself would come with her. Obviously Elric would remain at her side, but surely Sybil would as well?

She'd sensed the first stirrings of hesitancy a few nights after they'd decided to leave. Jessamine had walked through the halls for a glass of water and heard Elric and Sybil speaking. The quiet words had haunted her mind for the rest of the night.

"I can't go," Sybil had whispered.

"Because you don't wish to?"

"I've not left this manor for more than a few hours in many years. Going to the Owl's Nest with you was the farthest I've gone in nearly a century, and that almost killed me. I can't . . . I can't go. I can't do it."

"If I bid you to be brave? If I ordered you to come with us as the last remaining survivor of my coven?"

Jessamine had peeked through the doorway at his harsh tone. She was ready to leap to the defense of the other witch, who had always treated her kindly.

But they sat in front of a warm fire, and Elric had Sybil's hands in his. Their silhouettes were soft and quiet in the room, where the only sound was the crackling of wood.

Sybil shook her head. "I don't think I could do it."

"Then you shall stay," Elric had replied. "And if we should have need of you, I hope that you will find the bravery in your heart to save us. If not, then I hope you have the strength to return to your loneliness."

"I'll keep Nyx with me. She's far too young, and far too important to let loose on the streets. It's barely formed in this realm as it is. Familiars take time to . . . become, as we both well know. I'll take care of it for you, and for her."

Jessamine hadn't been able to forget their conversation. She'd always known that Sybil had been here alone for a long time, but she'd thought the witch was excited to have them there. They'd certainly struck up an odd sort of friendship, and she liked cooking with Sybil in the kitchen.

Still. This was Sybil's home, and Jessamine knew how hard it was to leave a place she loved and felt safe in. They were all warm. Dry. Fed.

But she was the princess of this kingdom, and she was going to take it back. No matter how hard that was.

Anxiety churned in her belly as she situated the backpack on her shoulders one last time. It wasn't overly heavy, filled with only enough food to get her through the day, a bag of coins, useful items for spells, Elric's black book, and a ward that should keep her safe for a few days at least.

Sybil had pressed the small sachet that smelled like herbs into her hand as she left. "A talisman for guidance and good luck," she'd said.

But then the witch's eyes had flicked to the hulking shadow that was so close to her at all times. They'd both known that the guidance portion wasn't really necessary when the Deathless God had stitched himself to her shadow.

Literally.

She'd woken up this morning with him at her feet, weaving a needle made of bone through her actual shadow. When she asked what he was doing, he'd told her to be quiet and not ask questions. Apparently, he wasn't a morning person. She'd pestered him until he admitted this way she didn't have to continue summoning him to her side. He could follow her for longer without returning to his realm to replenish his energy.

They had a long journey ahead of them, and she supposed if he was stitched to her, then he was preparing himself to walk just as much as she was.

With one last wave to Sybil, Jessamine turned her gaze to the road.

"Where are we going again?" he grumbled, already the most annoying companion she'd ever had to travel with.

"Callum said he grew up in the Factory District, and so did Benji. I can only assume that is the direction we should go."

"I don't understand how no one knows this man exists. Sybil sent out more than enough messages to whatever covens still survive, and not a single witch has ever heard of a Callum Quen."

That anxiety churned a little more in her belly, shoving her hearty breakfast up her throat. "That's why I'm a little concerned."

"You don't think he's a real person?"

"Oh, he's real." She shaded her eyes with her hands, glancing down to the area of the road where they had murdered that infected man. There was still a black smudge on the ground where he'd died.

A shiver traveled down her spine. Hopefully, they wouldn't run into another creature like that on this journey. Or if they did, at the very least, there would be other people to help. Or distract the monster.

It took half a day for her to get through the Water District. They couldn't travel the same route as before, not without risking people recognizing her after seeing her so often. But thankfully, it was a rather uneventful journey. People were out already, cleaning fish in the streets until they ran bright red with blood. Carts with massive ice blocks waited to load the fishermen's catch, and then those carts moved off to wherever people had money to buy. It reeked to the high heavens, and she pulled her shirt up over her nose so she didn't smell the pungent scent of fish so strongly.

At one point, they passed a blockade that a group of men were putting up. She read the words on the sign they hammered into it. "Sick beyond."

Then another home with all its windows bordered up. Each one was splashed with yellow paint in the same color as the warning sign they'd put on the blockade.

Glancing over at the Deathless One—Elric, she corrected herself—she grumbled, "You're lucky you can't smell this place."

A flash of something darkened his gaze. "You'd be surprised how much I wish to smell it, nightmare."

They didn't talk for a while after that. Not even when she reached the border of the Factory District. It was like someone had drawn a line through the city. One moment, she was surrounded by leaning buildings decorated with fishing nets and streets running red with blood, and the next she was surrounded by smog.

She stood in line with all the other people entering the district. There were walls separating the two areas, ones with barbed wire wrapped around them. She had to open her mouth and let a woman with dirty hands look her all over before she grunted and said, "Healthy enough. She'll be a hard worker."

And then she was let through.

The buildings in the Factory District were shorter, squatter, but much more sturdy. A layer of smoke hung over the district, and every ten houses seemed to be framed by factory buildings that had tall stacks belching more smoke out into the air.

The streets were much flatter here. No grooves for blood to run through, although the ground was oily and dark, leaving everything a little slippery and shiny. Then she walked by one of the factories and noticed that slick shine was coming from the buildings.

Oil, she realized. A lot of it.

Soot smeared the faces of most people who walked by, but no one made eye contact or even looked at her. Their clothing was equally dirty, and they wore hoods and hats and helmets that covered their features from any prying eyes.

"I wouldn't even know if one of them was infected," she murmured, stepping to the side of the street to get her bearings. "How can they tell?"

"They can't," Elric replied. She didn't think anyone could see him other than her, so she was the only one who noticed the wrinkles of worry between his eyes. "That is something we'll have to figure out along our path."

"What?"

"I could feel the infected when we got rid of the one on the path. They aren't... sick."

"Of course they're sick. Haven't you seen them? The boils, the pus, the drooling." She shuddered. "I just don't know how to fix them."

He was quiet. Way, way too quiet.

Glancing over at him, she saw him frowning at a young man who was standing in the center of an alley. The man had just walked by her. She'd seen the vacant expression on his eyes and his dirt-smudged cheeks, but other than that, he was entirely normal. Just a man going home after working in a factory all day long.

But now he stood there, frozen, his fingers twitching slightly. A few other people paused around him, then three of the largest men looked at each other and sighed.

She watched them grab the man underneath his arms and start dragging him down another alley. Almost as though they knew something that no one else did. Or perhaps, that everyone knew something she did not.

"What just happened?" she asked.

"I don't know," he murmured, that frown still very prominent between his eyes. "Healers had no say about what afflicted them?"

"Our healers didn't even know what it was. We called in scholars from every corner of this kingdom. That's why I'd turned to witchcraft." At his sidelong glance, she shrugged. "I wasn't practicing witchcraft at the time. I just thought maybe there was an answer in the magical rather than practical. Even if the discovery of what I was doing would have caused... waves."

"From what I've heard, it sounds like you might have lost your throne no matter what."

She liked the teasing tone in his voice. It sounded like he was actually a person, not just a god who had no reason to be in this realm with her. He was more real to her like this. Much more.

"Come on," she muttered as she realized there were people staring at her. "People think I'm standing here talking to myself. We have to get going."

"What does that matter?"

"I don't think people in the Factory District take a liking to those who seem a little touched." She eyed one of the larger men, who had returned from the alley. He was looking at her with a frown on his face, his hands clearly itching to drag her to the same place.

She wasn't sick. She wasn't infected.

Or at the very least, she didn't think she was.

"Magical maladies," Elric hissed as she strode through the streets, looking for a sign that would say there was an inn nearby. "We need to research those. There is something going on here, and I think it's something you need to look into."

"You and your gut instincts."

"I'm telling you what to do, Jessamine."

"And I don't like it when people do that." Huffing out a breath, she finally found an inn that looked like it might be the only one in the district. "But I'll consider it. All right? Let me find a safe place to sleep for the night first."

The building was a hulking monolith surrounded by belching factories. The giant rectangle seemed to wear a crown of smokestacks, but at least there were rows of windows on this building that glowed from candles within. Those must be rooms to rent for the night, and she desperately needed one. She stepped in through the worn door, wincing at the raucous din that met her ears.

A bar. She'd walked into a bar.

There were some tables in the far corner, it looked like. But for the most part, this was a space for drinking. Men crushed into the small area shoulder to shoulder—she had to push and shove to get to the bar itself, where she could see at least a few women. Most of them were seated with a much larger man at their back, barely holding the crowd at bay.

Slapping her hand down on the counter, she told herself to be brave.

"Excuse me!" she shouted.

One of the four bartenders turned in her direction, a smile flashing on his suntanned features. The bright flash of a smile didn't make her feel any better about where she was, though. If anything, that lecherous grin only made her feel greasy.

"What do we have here?" he said, walking over to her and leaning an elbow on the counter. "Fresh meat?"

"I need a room for the night."

"Booked up."

She blinked. "I don't think that's true. You must have plenty of rooms."

"And they're all taken for the night."

Elric leaned closer to her, the darkness of his power pressing against her back. For a moment, she allowed herself to believe that he was keeping the crowd away from her. And then he spoke.

"The man is lying. I can taste it."

She stiffened her shoulders. "I'd like a room for the night, and I know I don't look like I'm from here, but I can tell when someone is lying."

The bartender tilted his head back and laughed. "Ah, you've got the confidence of a queen, lass. But you're not getting a room here tonight. The Butcher keeps rooms on hold ever since the royal family died, you know."

The Butcher?

He must have seen the confusion in her expression, because he leaned so close she could smell the alcohol on his breath. "You can get a room if you're willing to work on your back a bit. I'd be the first one to step into line for that." She didn't have time to dodge his finger. He swiped his thumb down her cheek and then licked the digit. "So clean. We don't get many like you in the Factory District."

Reeling away from the bar, she staggered through the crowd. All the while, she tried to ignore the hissing in her ear.

"Summon me, Jessamine. Let me punish him for touching what isn't his."

She shoved past a man who smelled like metal, trying not to look at all the soot now covering her hand. "You can't kill him, Elric."

"I could keep him alive, if that's what you prefer. I know how to keep a man still living, even after I peel the skin from his form." The dark edge to his voice left no doubt he'd actually done that. Jessamine wondered to whom.

Another man stepped in her way but was quickly swept into the crowd by a woman who looked like she might be spending the night on her back, just as the bartender had said.

Where had she ended up?

How was this her kingdom? Jessamine had never seen the underbelly of her world. She had thought her people were doing well, much better than this. She'd thought there were at least clean people in every corner of her kingdom. That was what she'd always been told.

Stumbling out into the night, she crossed the street without looking and then pressed her back against the soot-streaked stone. Breathing hard, she knocked her head against the back of the wall and stared up into the sky, now streaked red with the sunset.

"Jessamine, summon me."

"I really don't want to," she muttered.

Another voice joined theirs with a bright red flare of a cigar in the alley to her left. "Not wishing to spend the night with a stranger?"

A woman stepped out of the shadows, the cigar in her mouth curling black smoke up into the air. She wore her red hair in a braid with a hat shoved down over her head. She looked just like everyone else here. Covered in grime and hard in the eyes.

"Not really," Jessamine said with a slightly hysterical laugh. "I guess I wasn't expecting it to be like this."

"Been like this for a while. Got worse after the princess died." The woman tossed the remains of the cigar onto the ground and stepped on it hard. "You'll learn the longer you stay here, the more it's necessary for us to give up that old life."

"Old life?"

"Royal family gave us all hope, you know?" The woman shrugged. "At least when there was a woman in power, there was more reason for men to respect the women in their lives. Now? We're all back to just being a useful hole and a distraction."

Her heart broke. Shattered into a million pieces. "What if she didn't die?"

"Jessamine," Elric hissed. "What are you doing? You can't tell anyone you're alive or our plan is ruined!"

The woman smiled, though, and a bit of that hard edge dropped. "Well, that would be a little hope, now wouldn't it? Strange to even think about, though. Girl's dead. We all watched her fall into the sea."

As she walked away, an idea bloomed in Jessamine's mind.

A terrible idea. An idea that could certainly ruin everything, but also made her feel like there was a purpose to all this. Like she could breathe for the first time since she'd died.

She was a princess, and this was her kingdom.

No, not a princess. She was more than that.

"What are you doing?" Elric asked as she ducked into the alleyway the woman had just come out of. "Where are you going?"

"They want their princess back, but they don't have her anymore." She looked around for a bucket of water and found a rain catcher on someone's stoop. But it would do. "They do still have a queen, though."

Using the water, she dipped her hands to wet them and then used her palms to write a message on the wall. A message that all would see because it revealed clean stone under years of grime.

She scrubbed into being a message that would fill every person in this district with hope.

And when she was done, she stepped away to look at her work. Elric stood beside her, a low chuckle rumbling through his chest. "A little on the nose, don't you think?"

"Well, sometimes you have to spoon-feed it."

Still, it did feel rather liberating to read the words cleaned into the wall. She'd even put her symbol beside it. A butterfly for a princess, but this time she had left it with its head cut off.

I am not dead.

And soon, the entire city would know it.

22

He couldn't get her out of his mind. Even now, when he'd weakened enough to be forced back into this realm of ink and darkness, all he could think about was her face when she finished cleaning that wall. The message she'd written was dangerous. If Leon found out too soon that she was alive, she'd miss her chance to unravel what had happened.

But Jessamine's expression had been worth the risk.

She looked alive in that moment, in a way he'd never seen before. He hadn't realized how dead she looked all the time. Those haunted eyes were always so dark, and the scar around her neck rolled with every single swallow like it was a struggle for her to sustain herself. Instead, horribly, wonderfully, in that moment, she came alive again.

Here he was thinking he had given her life. But she had done that herself.

She'd worn a wild grin that he'd only ever seen on an avenging witch who had destroyed a kingdom. She stood before him like a goddess who would shatter the fools who had tried to crush her beneath their heel. And he'd been struck dumb, tongue-tied at the realization that she could be dangerous to him.

Because he'd forgotten what it meant to be alive. He had forgotten the nuances and the emotions that came with living. He had forgotten that it felt like the world was coming apart sometimes, especially when he saw happiness on the features of a woman like her.

A nightmare become flesh.

Shaking his head, Elric wandered through the dark by himself, wondering when she would summon him again. She had gotten better at asking for an audience. He was able to appear before her much faster than he had when they'd first met, and he'd gotten better at staying in the living realm.

But of course, that didn't eliminate this moment. When he had to return and wait. For her.

He'd gotten used to waiting for her. And still, it never got easier.

Even now, he stood in the darkness and listened in the hopes that he might hear her words whispering in the air. The inky hands that plucked at his legs remained calmer than usual. Even they knew he would not remain for very long. Not when there was a gravesinger waiting for him.

He strode forward again—it was easier to keep moving than to stay in one place. He conjured up the image of when he'd first found her. Lying in a puddle of dark water that filled the hollows of her eyes so prettily.

Even now, he could see her. A bundle of light in the darkness. But the closer he got to the mirage, the more he realized it seemed as though she was actually here. With him looming in the darkness like he was the one who had summoned her.

Frowning, he blinked a few times to clear the vision from his mind. When the bundle didn't move, he had to assume that it was another trick of this realm to drag him deeper into the painful memories. Still, something in him said to seek it out. To look at the bundle and hope that maybe, again, he had found himself in this realm with her. Elric's boots sloshed through the water, which was only ankle deep these days, and he approached the small bundle on the ground.

It was her. Impossibly so, because this was the realm between life and death. He'd left her safely hidden in that alley. No one would notice that the bundle of fabric in the corner was a person, he was certain of it. Had she been robbed? Murdered? Had yet another person put their hands on her while thinking they had a right to do so?

Baring his teeth in a snarl, he tried to control the fear slicing through his body as he crouched and placed a hand on her shoulder. She was curled in the fetal position, her knees drawn into her chest and her wrists crossed underneath her chin. She looked so peaceful, but it was hard to focus on that when the fear for her safety made his heart skip a beat.

He didn't want her to be in pain anymore. He didn't want her to suffer.

Old memories filtered through his mind, and dark hands wrapped around his ankles. Another dark hand came out of the ink beneath her pitch-black hair and wrapped around his wrist, forcing him to freeze where he was, crouched above her like a bird of prey.

This was why he'd become a deathless god. He remembered now. He had found a witch just like this, curled up and frozen to death on the wrong side of a door. She was steps away from warmth, if only someone had allowed her in. But they hadn't. Witches were never welcome.

He remembered the rage. He felt it, even now. He had wanted to end the world but had known that wouldn't help, and so he went to the woman's coven with her frozen body held in his arms. Holding her against his still-beating heart, and he had shown them how to create a god.

He remembered the altar. He remembered the flash of a ritual knife. But what had happened afterward was lost to him. Only that the witches had absorbed his power and that they worshipped him. Perhaps that worship was the key to his survival. He did not know.

The hands released him. The water lapped around her, moving from where he'd crouched and gently brushing against the back of her neck, her cheek, her lovely pale lips.

"Jessamine," he murmured, brushing her wet hair off her cheeks so he could get a good look at her. "Nightmare, wake up."

Her eyes fluttered, then blinked. She looked up at him, rolling onto her back. "What are you doing in my dream?"

A dream. She was asleep. Apparently, his gravesinger could enter the realm between life and death while she was sleeping—but of course she could. She was tied to him like no other witch, and this was his realm, after all.

Breathing out a sigh of relief, he cupped his hand behind her neck and lifted her just enough so that she wasn't in the cold water and he could hope that some of his own heat bled into her. "You're not supposed to be here."

"You're in my dream, aren't you?" A small crease appeared between her eyes as she realized perhaps that wasn't correct. "I can feel you more than I thought I would."

"That's because this isn't a dream."

Surely she realized no one would dream about this cold, desolate place. But then the ink moved away from her. A pulse of magic pulled out of his chest, surging from him to her, and a miraculous thing happened.

A wet plop of ink dripped out of her hair and hit the ground. But it didn't stay dark. It spread in an oily sheen, with colors dancing around the shimmer until then . . . Oh, then it burst into life.

A rainbow of color and texture spread out from her body like she'd pooled paint and let it drip from her fingers. It continued to move like lava, infusing his realm with color and light and . . . sound?

From her body, a meadow sprouted. Green grass dotted with tiny yellow dandelions. He could hear birds floating overhead on the wind that suddenly brushed his cheeks. A warm wind. A late spring day that smelled like life and green things growing. Her dark hair slid through his fingers, a stark shadow of ebony against the sudden illumination of color.

Her hand reached up and gripped his wrist. "This is a dream, Elric. See? I can control it."

He was speechless again. She had a habit of doing that, his witch. He was a creature made of ink and blackness, of madness and nightmares, and his realm was one of darkness and shadow. And yet all it took to change that was a single gravesinger who wished it to change.

"You fascinate me," he said, lifting her even more off the ground. Still kneeling, he settled her against his thigh, running his fingers through the inky locks of her hair.

"Why?"

"I do not know how you do half the things you do."

Heat pulsed through his body. He couldn't stop himself from running his thumb along her jaw, down her full bottom lip, and watching as she allowed him to part her lips. Again, that heat pulsed between the two of them. Elric couldn't rip his gaze away from the sight of that mouth and the way she so prettily allowed his thumb to rest against it.

A black charcoal smudge remained everywhere he touched. He wasn't certain if that was her doing or his. He certainly knew he liked it. Elric enjoyed seeing a mark everywhere he had touched her. A map of all the places he wished to linger.

Her breath caught, and he could see her eyes on his lips. Elric found himself suddenly tangled in the same moment they had been at that statue. The moment that had never really released either of them.

He didn't know if she leaned up or if he leaned down. All he knew was the sudden pressure of her hand on his neck as she lifted herself closer.

"You choose to give your kingdom hope that you are alive, even knowing it will bring suspicion upon us," he murmured, his lips so close to hers. "It's such a foolish decision."

"Of course I do. I always will."

"Why?"

"Because I am theirs as much as they are mine. This is my kingdom, and its people are suffering. That means I am suffering. So why would I not help them?" She licked her lips, and his eyes followed the movement.

"You are a witch. You should have been an outcast your entire life, and still somehow you find love for them."

Jessamine smiled, and the expression nearly blinded him with its brilliance. "I'm not a witch, Elric."

"Oh, but you are." He felt the words breathe over her lips. "Because you have certainly bewitched me."

Then he kissed her.

He kissed her like he'd been wanting to kiss her for ages. It felt like he'd been waiting centuries for this moment, for this woman to be here in his arms.

The moment her lips touched his, he fractured into a thousand pieces. A mirror dropped onto the floor, the shards of every bit of him suddenly reflecting . . . her.

She smelled like a death lily and she tasted like life itself. Chai tea, a heaping dose of honey that coated his suddenly raw throat, and the aftermath of heat that blanketed every inch of him. She seared through him, scorching his tongue with hers as he nipped at her lips.

He'd thought she would be timid, unpracticed. A princess who had been taught how to kiss like a lady, because surely she was just as repressed as all those other stuffy nobles.

But no, she kissed like a vixen and devoured him whole.

Jessamine sucked his lower lip into her mouth, biting slightly at one of his old scars before laving it with her tongue. She didn't shy away from any mark on him. No, she read them with her fingers, holding on to his jaw with a surprisingly strong grip as she turned the kiss into something she controlled.

Jessamine consumed him. Her fingers dug into his biceps, digging into the old scar tissue there. She kissed him as though she wanted him to crawl inside her.

And fuck, he wanted to. He wanted to lay her down in this meadow that smelled like crushed grass and far-off lavender fields. He wanted to cover her body with his, and then he wanted to discover how she tasted in every place that made her gasp with pleasure.

He'd forgotten this, too. The way that pleasure could be so addicting and how the little mewls that a woman let out in the back of her throat could captivate a man.

Sliding his free hand down her side, he moved it up to feel the delicate flutters of her ribs as she breathed in and out, ragged lungs dragging in air with every breath. He palmed her breast, feeling the hard bead of her nipple beneath his thumb as he gently squeezed the globe in his grip. He wanted more. So much more.

"Summon me," he breathed against her lips. "Summon me now, Jessamine. Let me lie you down on a bed and not a dream."

As soon as the words were pressed against those pillow-soft lips, she froze. He felt her stiffen in his arms, as though he had broken some spell and suddenly, she realized what they were doing.

She slowly pulled away, her lips clinging to his until the very last moment. And he let her go. He had to let her go, because she couldn't find it in her to summon him even now.

Even when she had gifted him with a taste of her passion, she still didn't trust him. Or perhaps it was merely that she was frightened of what he would do.

Or what she saw in his eyes.

Jessamine stared up into his gaze, and then she slowly shook her head. "I think I should wake up now."

"Jessamine." He drew out the sound of her name, not knowing if he was groaning it or begging her to stay. Words he wanted to say pressed against his tongue.

Don't leave me here alone.

I don't want to suffer without you.

The taste of your kisses is worth days of pain.

But he said nothing else as her shaking hand rose to trace his lips one last time. Then she faded out of his arms, disappearing back into the realm where her body waited for her mind.

She took all the color with her. All of it fled bit by bit, fading into shades of gray before the ink claimed it.

He sank to the ground in a puddle of black ink, villainous hands reaching for him already. All he could see was that bitter darkness and the memories that called out for him, because oh, he had done this before.

He had fallen for a witch, only to realize that he was nothing to her but a tool to be used and a pawn to die by her hand. He knew what it was to be discarded.

The speed with which he'd fallen for this one would surely lead him to ruin.

23

Jessamine sat up straight, breathing hard and blinking back into reality. She hadn't just . . .

They hadn't just . . .

No. There was no way she had kissed him. He wouldn't have let her do that. The almost-kiss by the statue had been a mistake, but this was a disaster. Besides, an ancient god wouldn't waste his time with a mortal woman like her. He'd likely had more partners than she could imagine. Hundreds of beautiful women who had thrown themselves into the opportunity to kiss a god. To do a lot more than just that. Kissing a human must make him feel like she had no talent in the arts of seduction at all.

Groaning, she ran her hand down her face before stopping at her lips. Her kiss-swollen lips that made her feel a little drunk the moment she touched them.

Because she *had* kissed him. Like some wanton little witch, she had wrapped her hand around the back of his neck and drawn him down to her lips so she could suck on his bottom lip. She'd kissed him with all the desire in her body that she'd kept pent up for years. For much longer than she'd known him. Jessamine had put all her heart and soul into that kiss, and she was an idiot for doing so.

"You all right, girl?" a voice called out.

Looking up, she realized that a woman, a dirty rag around her head, was leaning out her window, peering down from the third story.

"Fine!" she called out, trying very hard to smile and make it seem like she wasn't beating herself up for stupid decisions. "Just a lot of bad choices last night!"

"Stupid to linger in the streets," the woman scoffed. "You have heard there's more infected in the city now, haven't you? That new king is bringing them in droves by the day." With a shake of her head, she withdrew, slamming the window shut.

Jessamine's entire body went cold. So Leon had made good on his threat. He really was bringing more infected into her kingdom, making it a dumping ground for all the bodies. Eventually, there would be more infected than healthy people. No one would be able to live here.

"This won't do," she muttered, getting to her knees and reaching into her bag.

She shrugged off the rags that she'd piled on to camouflage herself while she slept. Some ragged scraps still clung to her form as she yanked out a black candle and the other components she needed.

She could hear Sybil's warning in her ear. *Don't practice magic where anyone can see you, girl.*

She glanced up at the woman's window—too many early risers in this alley. She needed to find a darker, more secluded corner to put some of these spells to good use. After slipping silently from her hiding spot, she darted down the main road until she saw a hidden location, barely an alley, more like an awkward crevice between two listing buildings.

She slunk into the dark, then dug through the bag and racked her mind for her best option. A summoning spell to a patron, that was all she could think of. She needed him here because it seemed everything was worse than they had expected.

How long had Leon been dumping the infected here? How long did she have before some of them set upon her?

"Earth, air, wind, fire," she muttered as she placed small brass bowls around the candle, then struck the match and lit the oil within one bowl, blew on another for air, tossed dirt into the third, and dripped water out of her container into the last. And then she lit the black candle. "Deathless One, I seek an audience."

Nothing. Just the sound of the wind in her ears, like Elric was ignoring her.

But he couldn't do that, could he? The spell was used specifically to speak with a patron, and maybe she didn't necessarily worship him, but her plea had to mean something. He couldn't deny a frantic request from someone who needed his help, could he?

"Elric," she tried again, staring into the flame of the candle, which was supposed to move. "Elric, answer me!"

Was it because of the kiss?

"You are a thousand years old," she hissed. "You should be able to face someone after you kiss them. This is important."

And still, there was no response. In fact, the candle guttered out, extinguished either by the wind or by a pouting god angry because she'd stopped a divine kiss.

"Oh, you brat!"

After pinching the end of the candle to make sure it was completely out, she doused the second fire in the small brass bowl that Sybil had given her. Apparently, bowls were rather important to witches. She said no spell was right without brass or copper, but Jessamine was so frazzled she couldn't remember why.

Boots stopped right next to her hands. Dirty boots, covered in soot, and certainly larger than her own.

Glancing up, Jessamine froze as she stared into the gaze of a very large man who stood over her. His grizzled features were hidden mostly by a beard, but bright green eyes stared down at her with no small measure of hatred.

"What are you doing?" he growled.

"I was making sure my bowls were clean so that I could use them to get f-food," she stammered. Hopefully, that sounded at least a little convincing.

"You sure about that?"

"Yes. Why?" Jessamine stuffed the offending metal into her bag.

"Because it sure looks like you're practicing witchcraft." He crouched next to her, massive thighs bracing his hands as he glared. "And you don't want to know what we do to witches in the Factory District, little girl."

She opened her mouth, ready to tell him that punishing witches without the explicit permission of the royal family had been outlawed years ago. But then that would reveal far too much. What street rat would know that?

So instead, she closed her mouth and nodded.

"There are no warnings here. You hear me? We see you practicing magic, and someone will off you right on the street. No one will even pick up your body. The rats will eat you down to your bones."

"Understood," she said through gritted teeth.

The man stood and spat on the ground next to her feet before walking away. Her bowls clanked together as she threw the bag on her back. Perhaps that interaction should have scared her into making sure that she was less easy to spot, but all it had done was ignite a flame in her chest.

She wanted to cast spells publicly now. She wanted to shout out that maybe she was a witch, and anyone who tried to touch her would burn for it. Of course, that wasn't possible. Jessamine barely even knew how to light a candle with her magic. But she suddenly wished she could wield it like a weapon.

Maybe the Deathless One had been right. She did want to hurt people, and now she needed to learn how.

Muttering under her breath about men who picked on small women, she left the alley and started back toward the inn. Hopefully, the crowd would be a little more welcoming during the day, so maybe she could ask a few questions about Callum. Someone in this district had to remember the young man who had grown up to be the right hand to the queen.

Rounding a corner near the spot where she had left her message, Jessamine almost bumped into the back of a tall woman standing at the edge of a crowd. So many people were gathered here that it was impossible to cross the street.

"Excuse me," she said, placing her hand on the back of a smaller man to her right. "I just need to get through. I'm going to the inn."

The man gave her a dirty look but let her sneak in front of him through the crowd. It was then that she started hearing the murmured words.

"It can't be true, can it?" a woman asked, pulling her dirty hair band off her head and wringing it in her hands.

"Course not," the man beside her scoffed. "We all watched her fall off that cliff. The royal wedding was a sight for everyone to see, even all the way down here, and we all saw her hit the water. No one could survive that."

Her breath caught in her lungs. They were talking about . . . her?

Glancing toward the alley where she'd left the message, she realized the crowd *was* there for her. They were all staring at the message, and those who were closest didn't even touch it. Like they were afraid the mirage would fade if they did.

"The princess is dead," another man shouted. "We all watched her die!"

Someone dragged a crate in front of her message and stood on it, dropping their hood from their face so the crowd could see a blond woman with wild eyes. "I believe it! That damned new king wants us all to bend a knee and suck his dick. Well, I ain't doing it! If the princess is alive, then fuck the king!"

A few other people shouted the words as well. "Fuck the king!"

Her heart had never felt so full. These were the people she spoke of when she said her kingdom was strong. These were the people willing to stand up for justice.

A man behind her chuckled, then she felt a meaty hand shove her shoulder. "Don't look so happy, girl. That princess is dead, and this is all a trick. I heard the new king is a wily one. He wants to know who to off next. Just you wait, everyone in this crowd who's falling for this bullshit is going to be missing their heads in a few days."

She didn't want to think like that. Everyone in this crowd was so close to the truth. If they reached for it, just a little more, they'd see it. They'd realize that there was still a chance the kingdom wouldn't fall to ruin. If they just hoped and held on for a little while longer, she could take back her throne and destroy the usurper once and for all.

But the fear that spread after that man's words was strong. The crowd started to peel off, pieces of it ripping and tearing like Leon himself was slashing through them with a knife.

She stood there and watched them all leave, hardly able to believe that they were so willing to give up. They had been so excited just moments before and then . . . gone. Heart heavy, she waited until there were only a few people left, including the blonde who'd clambered down from the crate. She stood there, her back to the leaving crowd, as she stared at the message on the wall.

Jessamine couldn't help it.

She walked up to the woman and asked, "So you really believe she's not dead?"

The woman was taller than her by quite a bit, and significantly more muscular. Broad and strong, she glanced down at Jessamine and scoffed. "Oh, this nonsense? No, don't believe it for a second. We wouldn't have a new rush of infected every day if the princess were alive. There's hundreds of them down in the pits below the city where they've been dumping 'em. The princess and her mother used to take care of us. If she was still alive, one message wouldn't be the only thing that was left. I just had to keep everyone distracted while my boys pickpocketed the lot of those fools. Best check your pockets, dove."

Her jaw dropping open, Jessamine quickly patted herself down and then swung her backpack around to look inside it. The bag of coins she kept near the top was missing.

"Wait," she said, throwing the backpack over her shoulder and trailing after the woman. "My coins! You can't just take them and leave like that. Give them back."

"Not gonna happen. You best keep a better eye on them, yeah?"

"You just admitted to robbing me!" A dark rage rippled through her body, and for a moment she felt powerful, almost hungry for revenge. But in a flash the woman whirled on her, grabbed her by the biceps, and tossed her against the wall. Jessamine hit her head hard, and the cracking sound echoed in her skull for a few moments before she slid down onto her butt in the dirt. The muscular blonde crouched in front of her with an expression that looked almost like pity.

"Listen, you seem new here. I know it's hard to get used to the Factory District. You're going to get stolen from, roughed up, and someone as delicate as you is probably gonna die here. Toughen up, or someone will take you out. That's the reality of living here. So no, you're not getting your money back. A pretty little thing like you will do well enough in a brothel, and you'll make it back in a couple months." She tilted her head to the side and added, "Just make sure his cock isn't too big. You're a small one, dove."

Jessamine watched the woman walk away, horrified at what had just happened.

But then again, before she'd been robbed and thrown against a wall, the woman had said kind things about Jessamine and her mother. The people still trusted her family to do the right thing.

One message wasn't enough. She had to do more.

After getting to her feet, she wandered through the city until she could find another spot to write, somewhere others would see when they were walking home from the factories, but not as public as this one. No crowd would gather in front of this message, but word would still spread fast.

The same as last time, she found herself a bucket of rainwater and left a new message. A better one.

This city still breathes, and so do I, with the messy sketch of a butterfly at the end.

Stepping back, she eyed it with pleasure. Yes, this was perfect. There was no questioning who left this message. Who else would say such a thing?

She was the queen they were missing, and she was coming for them. She would save this kingdom from the clutches of a man who wished he were worthy of the throne. And if they didn't see that, then she would force him to his knees. Perhaps if they saw Leon begging at her feet, they would finally believe her.

She gathered her belongings and started down another alleyway. She just had to find Callum. That was all. Someone had to know something.

A group of men stood at the end of a nearby alley, smoking cigars that left plumes of white that clung to their massive forms. Glinting knives at their waists caught in the light. They seemed a mite more clean than most of the people she'd seen thus far, as well. She'd already learned this city was ruled by powerful people, so perhaps they would know enough.

Pulling her cloak up tight to her neck, she rounded her eyes and tried to look lost. Innocent. She wasn't threatening at all. If anything, she was a little girl who desperately needed their help. She walked up and blurted, "Excuse me, I'm sorry to bother you. I'm looking for Callum Quen? Would you happen to know him? He was born in the Factory District. I know it was likely a long time ago, but I'm hoping to find someone who might have known him then."

Then she blinked, because it almost didn't appear like they'd even heard her. They all looked at her with hungry gazes. Eyes that saw too much, and with sneers on their lips that made her rock back a step.

Had she said something wrong?

"Why you looking for Callum?" the largest man said, blowing out a lungful of smoke in her direction.

She coughed, waving her hand in front of her face. "I need to talk with him."

"I don't think you want to talk with him, lovey. You're too small of a thing for Callum to have any interest in you."

"So you do know him?" She was a little shocked at that.

"Oh, no one really knows Callum."

Another man joined them, his booming voice interrupting the others. "What did I tell you, witch? I see you making magic and I won't give you a warning."

Suddenly all their eyes narrowed, and their hungry gazes turned to fear. She saw the way they recoiled from her, the hesitancy to even look at her, and the bone-deep trembling of their hands, which drifted to the handles of their knives.

Swallowing hard, she held her hands up and took a step away from all of them. "I'm not using magic. Just asking around for an old friend."

"A friend?" The largest man in the group chuckled. "Callum doesn't have friends. Definitely not friends like the castle."

The castle? How did he know she was from the castle?

Regardless, she couldn't leave now. They clearly knew Callum, and she needed to learn where he was. If she could just speak with him, maybe all this would make sense. Maybe he had been blackmailed, or didn't think Leon would actually kill her mother. There had to be an explanation.

Hesitantly, she said, "I just need to speak with him."

The man she'd seen before loomed above her. "Ain't no place for witches in the Factory District."

"I'm not a witch."

He sneered. "Sure look like one to me. Don't you remember what I said about what we do to witches here? Poor little thing. I wonder what your screams sound like."

24

He hated being here, of all places, but he was rather embarrassed about their kiss. It had been centuries since he'd kissed anyone, and he'd forgotten how awkward it became to actually see the person that he'd kissed.

What did he say? Was he supposed to do it again? Elric had spent far too many years alone to know what was the right choice. He didn't think he'd ever felt so much anxiety about seeing someone again.

Jessamine was more than someone who was using him. He could feel deep in his bones that she didn't see him as another tool in her arsenal. She spoke to him like he was a person. Like he meant something to her.

He had not yet learned how to converse with her without feeling his entire soul soften.

It was a dangerous game he played. Like he was moving his finger over an open flame, thrilled at first that there was no pain, but every pass over it was getting slower and slower. Soon enough, he'd burn himself.

Blowing out a breath, he wandered through the darkness and tried to slow his mind. He needed to be clearheaded. There were many ways for this to go wrong. She would eventually want to sacrifice him. That was the first issue. Every witch eventually fell to the desire for power.

Sybil would do it. He'd seen it in her eyes the first time he'd replenished her power. She would want to kill him, eventually, and that meant he had to keep an eye on her, no matter how much Jessamine trusted the woman.

All of their journey, every step of the way, had been reliant on Jessamine's trust. And she offered that out to anyone who was mildly kind to her.

For all that she'd tried her best to protect her lands, she was still a princess and thus innocent to the evils of this world.

A sharp pain vibrated through his jaw, and he touched a hand to the sudden ache. Was he feeling old memories in this realm now? That would certainly throw a wrench into his plans. This place was always meant to be a numbing solitude. If he began to feel things here, too, that certainly wouldn't end well for him.

Another pain, this time in his left side. Strange. He had never . . .

Jessamine.

A cold sensation traveled down his spine, and he realized that Jessamine and he were tied far closer than he had ever suspected. Something was happening to her. Something, or someone, was attacking his little gravesinger, and he needed her alive for a lot longer than this.

Elric tried to go to her. He was so confident he could, but he'd apparently been in that realm with her longer than he'd originally thought. He felt the flexing of his power, but the dangerous and sharp edge of shadows that kept him in this realm never budged. He wasn't strong enough to leave on his own. Baring his teeth in frustration, he tilted his head back and shouted, "When will this curse release me?"

He had not filled his reserves of power yet. The chains around him from the gravesingers' curse were still binding and tight. Soon, he would have enough magic to break free from this realm, but not yet. He could visit those who worshipped him, of course, but she did not worship him. Unfortunately, it also meant she had no patron. No protection.

She was utterly alone.

He had no idea how long it took for the summoning to take place. All he knew was that one moment he was in his realm, and the next, the shadows released him with a wet pop and he was standing in a dark alleyway.

It wasn't the same day as the last time he'd seen her. Time had passed. He could feel it deep in his bones, but that meant she'd been wandering this city without him. He searched the shadows where he'd been summoned, gaining his bearings in this city of thieves and robbers. And then he saw her.

Jessamine sat on the dirty ground, leaning against the wall, with a rip in the shoulder of her shirt and mud splattered all over her form. Her cloak was on the ground beside her, so saturated in blood it looked black. A dark bruise already bloomed along her jaw, but it was the blood leaking out of her left side that gave him pause. A knife wound, he would guess, and considering her labored breathing, it was a wound she wouldn't survive.

She pressed her hand over the gash, but blood still seeped between her fingers. Her pale face was ashen, those dark eyelashes dusting her cheeks the moment she saw him.

"I made a mistake," she wheezed, her voice ragged and tinged with pain.

He took a staggering step toward her, his heart in his throat. "I . . . I'm so sorry, Jessamine."

"I know, I know. Ruined your plans." She took her hand away to look at it, swallowing hard as she saw the amount of blood on her hand. "Can't just march up and ask people about Callum. Silly of me, I guess."

He walked over to her side, then crouched down to look into her eyes. The poor thing was already halfway dead. There wasn't a person in this realm who could save her life, even if he tried his best to get their attention.

She would die. Again. All because he hadn't been here.

"What happened?" he rasped.

"I asked the wrong people about Callum." She leaned her head back against the wall, ragged breathing barely filling her lungs. "They thought I was a witch."

"So they killed you?"

"I'm not dead yet." Her eyes opened wide before she looked down at her bloody fingers again. "Although, I suppose you're right. I'm probably dying again, aren't I?"

Elric leaned forward and pressed his hand over hers. "I'm not able to heal a mortal wound like this in your realm. Little ones, yes. Benji stabbing your shoulder wouldn't have killed you, but this . . . certainly will. Such things are beyond the powers that I possess."

A little hiccup escaped her lips before she nodded. "Right. I should have guessed that."

"Tell me everything."

"They said I was a witch, and that witches don't belong in the Factory District." She blinked a few more times, as though trying to get him back into focus. "It is a shame. Witches could probably help us more than they could hurt."

"I know that to be true." Squeezing her hand, he sighed. "Why didn't you use your powers? Even unintentionally, you could have killed them all. Look at what you did to Benji."

"I don't know." She shrugged. "They were afraid of me. When the first one threw a punch, I had the thought, I could raze them all to the ground and leave them bleeding out. But then I saw how afraid they were, and how that fear was what they expelled every time they hit me, and I . . ."

The parallel to his own life was not lost on him. He'd allowed himself to be sacrificed countless times, knives and fists applied to his flesh like a balm that was meant to heal everyone else but him. She'd done the same thing for her people, even if it was the wrong thing to do.

Wrong for her, perhaps. But such a choice was his entire existence.

"A queen feels both rage and compassion," he murmured. "A just queen knows how to choose between the two."

She smiled, her teeth covered in blood. "You think I chose correctly, then? You're not mad?"

"How could I be angry at you?" Releasing her bloody hand, he stroked her cheek with the back of his finger. "You took their pain, Jessamine, even though it hurt you. You are the queen this kingdom deserves, and I'm sorry not all of them see it."

She blew out a breath and watched him as he settled on the ground next to her. He didn't know how much she wanted him around, considering he was the reason for her death. He should have been here, and yet, he was so weak he could not protect his own gravesinger. But still, he placed his hand right next to hers. Just a hairsbreadth away from touching her.

A rattle from her chest made him tense for a moment before it eased. Then her hand shifted a bit toward his, just a little, and suddenly her pinky was placed over his own. Almost as though they were holding hands.

"I know it sounds silly, but I wish you were here." She stared up at the smoggy sky and added, "Really here."

Should he be ashamed of the spike of anxiety and hope that tore through his chest? Perhaps this was the moment he'd been waiting for. Perhaps she would summon him into the realm now, in a desperate bid to save her own life.

"You could make that happen, you know."

All those hopes were dashed at the sound of her laughter. The chuckle filled the cold alleyway with warmth, even though she was dying right in front of him. "And what would I unleash upon my kingdom?"

He snorted. "A true terror."

"Malice incarnate."

"Madness that would spread like your infected."

"I'd forever be known as the queen who unleashed darkness upon her realm." But she snorted after saying it, her words softened by her tone. "I don't know what you will do if and when you get a physical form. I cannot leave my people in your powerful hands, Elric. I'm so sorry for that."

"I expected nothing less."

And truly, he didn't. It was a dangerous game to play, unleashing a god. He wished he was a better man in that moment. He wished he could promise to take care of her home and her people as if they were his own.

But he wouldn't. They both knew that.

She sighed, the breath rattling a little longer in her lungs. "So I'm really dying?"

"In a way. You're already dead, you know." He stroked her pinky with his. "I won't let you die permanently. Expect much the same as the last time you died."

"Oh, that's good, then."

He could hear the nerves in her voice. The unknown was always so frightening to humans.

"You've done this before, nightmare. Surely it's not as scary the second time."

That rattling wheeze came again, and the sensation of her slipping away from him. He worried that this would be too hard on her. Already, so much of her life had been too hard.

"It's slower than the first time," she whispered. "I can feel myself dying. There's so much sensation to it. The cold, the feeling of sudden hunger, and also the pain of the ache disappearing. My fingers are going numb, and my lips are harder to move. I think soon I won't be able to see."

He hated that she had to go through this. And he hated even more that she would have to do it alone.

Rolling away from the wall, he crouched in front of her again. Elric made sure to lift her hands, pressing them one by one to his lips. "I cannot stay here much longer, Jessamine. I have to be in that realm when you die or I might miss you. And if I miss you, then you'll actually die."

"I thought I was already dead."

"In a way, you are. But in many ways, you aren't. You're still here in this realm, aren't you? You have a body. You have a soul. Everything about you is very much alive. If I lose you in my realm, then you'll disappear for good and not even a god can bring you back."

And he'd be stuck there again. Alone. No one would call upon him and no witch would threaten his life. He would never again feel mud between his toes or the sensation of a breeze tousling his hair.

Elric desperately wanted to live again. So even if it felt like he was using her, then he would use her. Because he needed his little nightmare, just as she needed him.

"So you're . . . leaving me here?" Those big eyes stared up at him, and he could practically taste her fear. "To die alone?"

His heart shattered into a million pieces. He could feel the shards digging into his very soul as he whispered, "Yes."

"Oh."

"I will stay as long as I can." He leaned closer, holding the back of her head and pressing their foreheads together. "But it won't be long now."

He could feel her slipping away. The sensation of her life, the force that tethered them together, was so weak it was almost a thread of silk. Still strong enough to hold her here, but not strong enough to keep her forever. Not when the weight of his realm tugged on the other end.

Elric stayed with her, just as he promised. He stayed until he could hear her breathing change. Until he knew that the gravesingers had called their wayward sister home, setting their inky hands on her shoulders and pulling her away from this realm. But he also knew where she would end up.

He knew, and he would find her.

Pressing his lips to her forehead, he let the warm touch linger on her skin. "I promise I will find you, nightmare. Don't be afraid."

"I'm not afraid." He could hear the lie in her voice, though, even as she tried so very hard to be brave. "You'll be there. I'm certain of it."

A warmth bloomed in his chest. Perhaps she didn't trust him enough to summon him, but she trusted him enough to die for him. That trust did something to him. He didn't recognize the feeling in his chest, the strange wriggling sensation of hope and happiness that felt like a bright light had speared through his chest.

But he allowed his realm to pull him from her side, even though it shattered all the good in him to see her leaning against the wall. Alone. Dying in a gutter because he couldn't be there with her.

She had to suffer yet again. To linger in that cold, feeling the end crawling toward her, because that wound was a slow death. She shouldn't have to feel the ice gripping her heart or the way it would beat sluggishly for long moments before it just . . . stopped.

Anger burned in his chest, and it was rare that he felt like this. After all, he'd long ago given up on the righteous anger at how the witches were treated. But once upon a time, he'd pitied them for this very reason.

A witch was a reflection of her home. She held up a mirror to those who surrounded her, showing them the good and the bad that lived within them. They asked for a spell, and when it went awry, they blamed everyone but themselves.

He materialized in his realm on his hands and knees in a puddle of shadow. Guilt and anxiety quickly settled in, wrenching through his form until he was gagging into the darkness. Black vomit purged itself from him, joining the rest of his power in this endless realm of night.

She was dying.

She was dying, and he wasn't there.

How dare he fail her like this. How dare he let the only witch who had ever cared for him fall into death's embrace.

It was a loss for her entire realm. The second time as it had been the first. She should never have to suffer like this. And it was his fault that she had.

But he couldn't wallow in self-pity. There was still a chance he could help her, and he intended to do so. Elric staggered to his feet, breathing hard and trying his best to pull himself together. For her. For this realm. Because the two of them still had work to do.

He started off into the darkness, certain he would find her. He had the first time.

And he would a thousand times over.

25

The first time she died, Jessamine remembered waking up to no more pain. That had been part of why she had so readily agreed to do whatever he wanted her to do.

She remembered the fall so clearly. The pain in her throat and the blood that streamed into the air like her favorite red scarf for winter. And more than that, she remembered the pain in her heart at the loss of everyone she loved. Physical and emotional pain had wrapped up into one demon that clawed in her chest and tried to force its way out through the wound in her neck.

But in her faint memory of this dark, dreamless place, she hadn't felt so awful. For a brief moment, she had been calm. Quiet. Serene. All she could remember was relief, and then his voice. A melody cajoling her to make a deal.

All the awful bits of life fell away in the Deathless One's realm. All of it. She could let herself go. Let the pain of her life disappear in the moments that followed.

This time, she took the pain that came after death.

Waking with a gasp, she felt her heart thundering in her chest and an ache in her body so sharp she could barely breathe through it. There was a wound in her side that hadn't healed in the slightest. It still hurt, so much so that she was blinded with pain. Her jaw ached. Loose teeth from the punch still wiggled when she rolled her tongue over the bleeding wound in her mouth.

They'd only had to stab her once. An embarrassingly small number of times, and even the men seemed to know it. They'd punched her once. Stabbed her once. And then left her there to fend for herself.

The darkness around her undulated with anger. She could feel the rage in it. And this anger didn't come from Elric. From the Deathless One. This anger was from a completely different being or creature, although it felt surprisingly familiar. She thought, perhaps, this anger stemmed from the source of his power. Because it had the same flavor of danger that he did when he was angry. But so, so much worse.

"Jessamine!" The call rang out through the darkness, and suddenly he was on his knees beside her again, falling into the liquid of this place and soaking the legs of his pants, which were far too fine to be kneeling in inky fluid. And yet, he didn't seem to notice.

His arms scooped her up, drawing her into his lap as he ran his hands down her sides as though he was trying to find all the wounds on her.

"I'm fine," she muttered, wincing as the wound on her side throbbed with her heartbeat. "Or mostly fine."

"This is much more difficult the second time. I hope you realize that," he growled as he ran his hands down her sides again. "It shouldn't have been so difficult to find you. I lost you, nightmare."

"Apparently I just show up wherever I want." Her joke fell on deaf ears.

Elric frowned down at the blood still coating her torso. More of it poured out of her, no matter how hard she pressed on it. "You shouldn't be able to bleed in the shadow realm."

"Well, I definitely am."

"It's impossible."

"It's not like I'm trying to—"

He interrupted her with another grumbling growl before reaching into the shadows of his chest, pulling until a thread of darkness ripped off him, a bit of his magic for her to use, just like all the other creatures in his life. She'd thought perhaps it would look like a leech. But no, instead, it was just a thread.

He had pulled on the loom of fate and held out a way to tie them together even more than they already were.

Jessamine was the fool who grabbed on.

She let the magic coil around her finger as she pulled it toward her wound. Together, they watched as she gently laid the black thread over the angry gash on her side. The magic wriggled underneath her skin, eerily seeming like an invisible hand stitching her back together, and immediately she felt the pain ease.

"Oh," she moaned, her eyes rolling back in her head at the sudden relief. "That is so much better."

Silence rang louder than thunder. When she focused on him again, she watched a hungry gaze that roved over her entire form.

"Again," Elric growled.

This time, she didn't hesitate when he reached out a thread for her to take. She placed it on her jaw, feeling the ache disappear and seeing the healing in the reflection of his eyes. She had no more hurts to heal, but he still held out another. Then another. Threads that should have felt like chains wrapping around her wrists, but she couldn't view them as that.

They were a woven armor that she fastened on, strand by strand. An armor he created to protect her.

Even if he couldn't keep her safe in the realm of the living, at least until she broke down and summoned him, she knew he would do so here.

In his arms. Newly alive and burning under his heated gaze as he stared at her like she was his reason for being.

"Elric?" she whispered. "It was worse the second time."

"What was?"

"Dying."

Those dark eyes met hers, a little too serious and a little too heartbreaking. He had known. At the very last moment she'd seen the absolute anguish in his expression.

And yet, he had still disappeared. Leaving her to die alone in an alleyway for the second time.

"Why?" she asked, her voice cracking around the word.

She didn't know what she was asking. Why had he left? She knew the answer to that. He'd already explained it. If he hadn't come back here, then she would have died for real. Why had it hurt? Well, it was death. Of course it hurt.

But he blew out a long breath, and his fingers spasmed against her back. "Everyone has to die alone, nightmare. No god can stand with you at the end, no matter how devout a worshipper you are. It's just you, and the end. None of us, no god or goddess, can ever understand what that feels like. We will never die and go wherever it is you go. And you always will."

The words punched her in the gut.

Don't get too close, because he was always going to live, and she was always going to die.

"But I didn't die," she whispered. "Twice now."

He blew out a long sigh, then touched their foreheads together. "A dead woman walking is not the same as a living one, Jessamine."

With that, Elric helped her up, making certain she was comfortable, reaching for her waist when she was a little wobbly. Every bit of him a gentleman, but she felt the way his hand spasmed at her hip, like the shape of her body made him want to cling and linger.

Her mind screamed that she'd almost died. Her body wanted, no, needed, to remember what it felt like to breathe, to live, to feel. Her body remembered that the world existed, and he was right here in front of her. His broad chest moved with each breath, those lips full and slightly scowling, the sharp edge of his jaw so tempting to bite.

It wasn't the right time. It wasn't the appropriate reaction either. Jessamine knew she should say thank you to this deathless god who had given her life for a second time. She also knew her restoration was entirely self-serving on his part. He didn't love her. That wasn't why he'd saved her life. Elric needed her to stay alive.

But she still stepped closer and pressed her lips to his. She still kissed him, clinging to his shirt with both hands and leaning into him a little too hard. Because he was her savior. A hero in her story, even if he was the villain in everyone else's.

He froze beneath her touch for a moment, like he'd been struck by lightning. A deep groan echoed in his throat and his hands tightened at her waist. Then suddenly he was everywhere. His hands brushing up and down her back, digging into her muscles and dragging her flush against him, the hard bar of his cock pressed against her belly, proving that indeed a god was far more well-endowed than a mere man. And as he pulled her closer, rocking himself against her, every inch of her body turned to liquid fire.

She ached between her legs. She needed to feel, to touch, to taste. Something stirred inside of her. A wanton, wild, wicked creature who knew what she wanted and desired to take it.

A witch, she realized.

His kiss had finally awakened the witch within.

"You orphic creature," he whispered against her lips, his tongue swiping before he sucked her lower lip hard enough to hurt. "You are bitter and intoxicating, like the most divine absinthe. I stain your skin with every touch, and gods forgive me, I'll do it again."

She fell into his embrace, drowning in the sensation of his touch. He wasn't a hesitant man, and it was a pleasure to let him lead, to take—so different from the fumbling, tentative attempts at seduction she'd endured from the guards at court.

Jessamine had never wanted to have a man ask if he pleased her. She just wanted him to be confident that he did. She wanted him to sense the little breaths that came out of her mouth or the way she squeezed her thighs together. Or—by the gods!—how she writhed against his thigh as Elric slotted one muscular leg between hers and made her ride him. He'd lit a fire in her veins even as he leaned back and watched her move with lowered lids.

She watched his expression with rapt attention as he licked his lips, his eyes following every movement of her hips as she ground herself against him.

"Perfection," he muttered. "Utter perfection."

With a low groan, she tilted her head back and clutched his shirt for purchase. Except . . . a flashing spike of magic slipped over her eyes. She felt the ache in her skull, like someone had grabbed onto her head and squeezed too tightly.

She didn't even have a moment to complain about the pain before she tumbled into what she could only imagine was his mind.

The darkness surrounding them showed her everything she had wondered about his past.

She saw a witch who looked remarkably like herself, cold and freezing in a cave filled with dripping ice. A man laid out on an altar of stone in front of her, his hair dark and his skin nearly blue with cold. The witch lifted a blade over her head that glinted even in the darkness before sinking it deep into his belly.

Then another flash, a warm home this time. But the table before a crackling hearth had been cleared, and the same man was laid out upon it. A man with dark eyes who had watched Jessamine from the shadows, and even now, it seemed like he stared right at her as a witch lifted a blade high into the hanging herbs above her head before driving it into his heart.

Yet another memory, this time of a little girl. Her clothing hung off her skinny form, dripping from bones that were too raw edged. And the man, Elric, yet another form of him kneeling in front of her. This time he was the one who guided the blade toward his eye, and with a quiet word, allowed the little witch to plunge it through that dark orb.

Countless centuries of pain and torment. She watched him die a hundred times, then a hundred times more. She saw every moment that a witch, just like herself, dug a dagger into his heart, his eyes, his throat. They carved bits and pieces of him away like trophies because they could.

And he let them.

They needed his power, and for the few moments he was in their realm, he was truly free. She could feel his happiness, the bittersweet ache of life that burned through him. He was willing to do anything to chase that feeling. And so for centuries he clawed and scraped for these moments of heartache. He sought out the pain that always came with becoming a sacrifice for his witches. He knew no other way to live.

She saw their smiles. She felt his hope that this time would be different, that they would see more in him than so many others had before.

But worst of all, she knew how much it hurt every time they betrayed him. And yet this strong, endless man never gave up on them.

Because it had started with a witch frozen on a warm doorstep. Another burnt alive at a stake. Dozens of other women who had suffered because they had magic.

So he had bound himself to those who, like him, were exiled from society. Women who could never really love him because they had use for him, and they used every tool at their disposal.

Her heart broke for him.

When she came back to herself, she felt the inky grip of his realm dripping from her hair. Almost as though she'd been doused in his memories, force-fed everything he didn't want her to see.

As it was, he already looked at her as though he was nervous. "Well?" he asked, like he was waiting for her to see his real purpose.

He thought she was going to see those memories and want the power. Jessamine had certainly tasted it. She could feel the overwhelming sear of magic that crackled through the veins of every witch who had sacrificed him. And that power was tempting.

With it, she could take her kingdom back a thousand times over. No one would ever be able to stand against her. Perhaps many would try, but they would cringe in the dust at her feet, writhing in pain as she forced them to feel what true power really was. They would die screaming beneath her heel, and she would revel in the sound of their pain.

But that was not who she wanted to be. Yes, her life would be easier. Jessamine would reach her goals so much faster if she stole his power.

But she wouldn't be able to live with herself if she did. The man in front of her deserved the world. He deserved to live and feel the wind in his hair, if that was what he wanted. She couldn't take that away from him, just like she couldn't punish those men who feared witches because they feared what that power could bring.

"If I sacrifice you and take your powers," she rasped, "then won't I become exactly what those men who killed me feared? And if so, then aren't they justified in killing me?"

Elric replied with a voice impossibly low. "Is that really what you believe?"

Her brows furrowed as she sought the truth in her heart. "Yes," she replied. "I do believe they would be right to kill me. If I wanted to seize your power, truly, if I believed our story ended that way, then I would ask you not to raise me again."

"You are the only person who can bring me to life. I would trade the suffering and the pain again to feel your world. To be alive, yet again. After all this time."

She cupped his cheek, feeling the warmth and how electric he was to her. Who was she to say that he didn't deserve to live? Though yes, there was the danger of what he might become. A god unleashed upon a realm that had been godless for centuries? It was madness to even consider.

But she wanted to. Oh, how she wanted to.

Instead, she tugged him closer and kissed him again. Sweet and lingering and long, trying to press her feelings into his very soul.

"I promise—" she started.

"Jessamine, make no promises in this realm. They are permanent," he interrupted.

So she took her time thinking about the wording, and then nodded. "You're right."

He sighed out a relieved breath, only to suck it back in when she continued.

"I *vow* never to sacrifice you, Deathless One. Not in this realm or my own."

26

Elric didn't know what to do with her after that. He couldn't stand that she'd seen his memories. They were his burden to bear. He had chosen to be that person, after all, and even though the memories plagued him, he had still allowed those witches to do all that they had done.

He was grateful the magic in this place hadn't shown her even worse. All the witches who had bedded him, used him for years until they decided their affections had finally run their course. The ones who had played with his emotions, and he had fallen for it.

Jessamine didn't deserve to see those memories. She was too innocent, too kind. She would think less of him, and he was terrified of what that would mean.

Trailing his fingers over the thin line around his neck, he tried to forget how she had flinched in his arms as they reached that memory. It was the first wound. The most heart-wrenching and painful.

He'd thought himself in love with only one witch. She had proven her devotion to him time and time again, a worshipper who had never failed to be at his side, no matter what he asked of her. She had romanced him. Seduced him. Turned a young god into a plaything of her own.

And then she had brought him to an ancient cavern, under the guise of showing him her latest sacrifice. The witches had bound him with the magic he had given them. They laid him out on an altar, and she brought a knife down to his throat.

What a horrible connection he'd made with Jessamine. Already her opinion mattered too much, and it meant that no matter what he did, in her eyes he would always and forever be the man who was broken. Because he was. He had been. Shattered and unmade by so many people that their touch would forever linger. Staining his skin as his touch stained hers.

He passed his hand over her eyes and then pushed her soul back toward the land of the living. He had time before she reanimated. Her soul had a long journey to traverse.

It gave him time. Time to pull himself back together in the darkness after she had broken him into a million pieces. Time to heal the wounds of the memories that were right under the surface and had become raw again.

There was a problem with being the Deathless One. Even until the bitter end, he remained aware. So he felt every sawing motion as she worked her way through his neck, all the way to the bones at the back, and he remembered the sound of them snapping.

He didn't remember his head hitting the floor, but considering the way Jessamine had flinched, some part of his subconscious did. She'd seen all of that. She'd seen his weakness for her kind.

None of these thoughts were helpful. He had to get out of this realm and make sure she was safe. And strangely, with the knowledge that she had seen his memories, he could pull out of the grip of this realm a little more easily. Every time he grew closer to her, he became more real.

Elric tried not to look too much into it. He manifested himself back to that awful alley where he'd found her broken and bleeding. Her clothes were pushed askew, apparently from someone rummaging through her pockets for whatever she might have on her dead body.

That certainly would be a problem. She had little in her pockets, but clearly they'd gone through her bag as well. Peeking inside, he let out a relieved breath as he noted they'd stolen the brass bowls but not the black book.

Elric leaned down and ran his fingers through her hair. In death, she seemed even more beautiful to him. The dark shadows of her lashes dusted her pale cheeks, which were nearly blue in the autumnal cold. She looked so peaceful, and he was about to ruin that the moment she came back.

"Come on, nightmare," he said quietly. "Let's get you somewhere safe."

It wasn't like he could bring her back to the inn. Though he grew more solid the longer he touched her, he didn't think anyone other than Sybil and Jessamine could see him. But she needed somewhere safe to reanimate, and he wasn't going to let her wake up in the dirt. Not this time.

So he hauled her over his shoulder and wandered through the streets. He told himself not to think about the fact that if anyone looked out their window, they would see a dead body hovering in midair. Instead, he tried to believe for a moment that he'd been resurrected. Truly summoned to breathe new life into this world.

Although he had no intention of breathing life anywhere once he was here. He still wanted to see the world burn. His forgiveness, his kindness, his years of service, all of that had resulted in nothing. Witches and everyone else deserved to know what it felt like to be alone for hundreds of years. Perhaps Jessamine could sense that need inside of him, and that was why she hesitated.

But couldn't she see? She needed to punish the world as well.

He paused beside a graveyard framed by the aging buildings. "I'm going to keep you," he murmured. "You and I, nightmare, we're going to destroy this world together."

Striding through the short, crumbling headstones, he found one of the older sections. The stones were more like altars here, flat sarcophagi laid out among each other. Rich mingled with poor, though it was easy to tell who was who. The wealthy had carvings of themselves laid in repose over their gravesites, while the poor had only blank slabs over their graves, though still raised so people would know where they were buried. Others would eventually be buried on top of them, slowly sinking the stone coffins into the ground.

He wanted her on an altar, so he chose a blank sarcophagus and laid her there. Gently, ever so gently.

Her body was still slightly warm. Still pliant as he let her rest against the cold stone. He should have laid out her cloak so that she wouldn't wake up chilled.

But as he sat beside her head, gently brushing those waves of dark hair away from her face, he knew that this was the right place for her. A dead woman, rising back to life for the second time in a graveyard.

It was . . . perfection.

Anxiety twisted in his gut. He should leave. Everything in him screamed to flee what she had discovered. She would look at him as someone who was lesser because of the witches who had come before her. He couldn't stand being that man in her eyes.

He didn't want his heart to be broken again. With this one, the pain would be exquisite, and he wasn't certain he would survive. But instead of running, instead of hiding in that realm that always punished him, he waited for her.

Elric sat beside her body until he saw the glimmering mass of her soul in the corner of his eye. He turned his head, watching as the ephemeral being glided toward him. Her hair floated around her head as though she were underwater. Glimmering silver strands twisted around her body like she was made of moonlight. Her skin glittered like diamonds and she wore a simple white gown, as all souls wore on their way to the other realm.

This soul didn't walk toward death, however. She walked toward him, glowing as a light in the darkness as she approached her body and sank into it.

By all the gods, she was beautiful. A haunted, holy creature glimpsed only by the blessed few.

Every bit of her was graceful as she sank into her old flesh as though she'd never had a difficult day in her life. All of that had faded away with her death. Her soul had a soft smile on its face as she looked down at herself.

He was the one taking that peace away. The calmness, the beauty of death, all of it was ruined the moment she took flesh. With that connection between soul and body came the beauty of her rage. A tempest of purpose and desire for blood that bloomed throughout her entire being because she was not done here. Not yet.

A sharp inhale, then a cough as she cleared her lungs of all the fluid that had built up in them. Her heart stuttered, hating to beat again, but here it was. She was alive, and he had brought her back. A brutal death, and coming back from it was even worse.

She rolled onto her side, facing him, not away, and that had to mean something. Didn't it? She wasn't disgusted by him. She didn't shrink away from his touch even as he hovered his hand over her shoulder. But he couldn't touch her. Not without knowing if she remembered what she had seen.

Slowly, ever so slowly, she pushed herself upright. All that dark hair had fallen in front of her eyes, and she looked very much like the wild creature he'd found in the beginning. Roughened by death, but still here. Still fighting.

That dark gaze met his through the strands of her hair. "I meant what I said." Her words were raspy and raw. "Even in this realm, Elric. I mean it."

She continued their conversation like nothing had happened. Like she wasn't waking up in a graveyard with a dead god who had stolen so much from her.

His heart squeezed, his soul screamed that he was obviously weak and why would she ever look at him any other way? She shouldn't see him as a person. She was a witch, and that meant she couldn't promise him that she wouldn't have use for his power someday.

He didn't want it to be like that. Elric wanted her to see this as something more than a business transaction. But no witch ever had, even the one he had loved. The Deathless God was a deity, but he was made for them. For witches like her to use in their hour of need. And she was in need. How could she not see this?

The best he could hope for was that she would raise him from his own grave and then allow him to have a few days, maybe a few weeks, before she killed him like all the others had. Like she was supposed to do.

"I'm sorry," she whispered, her voice featherlight. "You don't deserve what they did to you."

He moved away from her. "Oh, I deserved all of that and more, nightmare," he scoffed. "It is the way of things, and you and I both need to be all right with that."

But he wasn't all right with it. He'd buried those thoughts deep, though, because he knew his purpose. He had chosen to serve them as they served him. The other gods had been selfish with their followers, and he refused to be like them.

Elric knew he had to put some distance between them. He needed space to get his mind straight again. There were rules to interactions with witches, rules he had created to protect himself. Breaking those rules had gotten him here, touch-starved, weak in the knees for the slightest attention. It could have been anyone. It wasn't because she looked at him with hope in those dark eyes or that he saw a bit of himself in her or because she was so fucking kind, even when others weren't kind to her.

"Elric?"

Damn him.

Damn her.

Because the moment she called out his name was the moment that he froze and waited to hear whatever would drop from those beautiful berry-red lips.

"Nightmare?" he said.

"Don't go."

He had to. He was going to shatter in front of her, breaking into a thousand pieces, because the longer he was with her, the more he *wanted*.

"I am not like them. I do not wish to be. I made a vow to you and I intend to keep it. What they did to you was—"

"Don't," he interrupted, squeezing his eyes shut against the memories that threatened to overwhelm him. "That was not for you to see. I was not prepared for you to see who I really am."

"I know that, but I . . . I saw your memories."

"I have spent centuries creating the Deathless God. Years upon years developing a terrifying vision of a god who could not be killed. One who served the witches that were feared throughout these kingdoms, and who was the source of all their wicked power." He took a shuddering breath.

"And now you see the man beneath it all, Jessamine. I do not know what to do with that."

And that was the problem. He didn't know how to go back to what they had been before. Not when she knew the true depths of him, the bleeding underbelly of the beast he had built out of his home.

He walked away. Each step felt heavier the farther he got from her.

She almost-shouted, "I want you to teach me spellcraft!"

He looked over his shoulder, raising one eyebrow with curiosity. Phantom chains slithered around his torso, binding him to her as he had feared they would. "You already have a teacher. Sybil taught you all that she knew and more. You have books to read and research, do you not?"

"I was a terrible student who didn't understand a single word Sybil tried to teach me. She said I wasn't focused enough, and that magic always came at a price."

There was a long pause, and finally he turned back to look at her. She sat on the edge of the sarcophagus, her legs dangling off the edge, not even reaching the ground. This tiny woman held so much power in her hands and she didn't even know it.

"What do you think I could teach you that she could not?" he asked.

"Everything," she replied, lingering on the word as though it was both blessing and curse. "I've been so afraid of this magic, but the closest we have gotten to discovering who is behind murdering me was when I used your magic on Benji."

"You hated how that made you feel."

"I did. I do." She scrunched her face and shook her head. "I don't want to know how to light candles with a thought or how to beckon a god to my side. I want to know how to protect myself. I never again want to be put in a situation where I must either kill or be killed. I want to be able to stop any attacker before that."

Well, she always did surprise him.

Elric tucked his hands beside his back and strode toward her. "Is that really what you want? You barely talked for a week after Benji's untimely death."

"It's your magic that allows me to kill people, not mine," she whispered, not breaking eye contact with him, but clearly uncomfortable with what she was saying. "I want to know how to control your power so that I don't have to kill people. I can choose not to."

This was more under his control. He knew how to have this conversation, because he had had it a hundred times before.

Tucking his finger under her chin, he forced her face up. "You have seen how different I am now. You feel how close we have become in just a short amount of time, yes?"

"Yes."

"If we do this, you will be drawn even closer to me. You are not a worshipper, Jessamine, you are *mine*. There is a significant difference between you and Sybil. You choose to do this, and there is no going back."

She swallowed, that pretty neck of hers working to gulp down her apprehension. "If that's the price I have to pay, then I will pay it."

"Is that so? You don't even know what it means." He smirked. "You always were an intriguing little nightmare."

"Does that mean you'll teach me how to use your power?"

"Not the same way other witches use it, but yes."

A tiny wrinkle formed between her eyes. "Why is it different from the witches who worship you?"

"Haven't you been listening? Witches like that are limited in what they can use. They sacrifice to me. I gift them power. It is a give-and-take relationship." His finger turned into a claw under her chin, the black nail digging into her skin. "You are a gravesinger, and you are mine. Any power you desire is directly linked through me. You can take as much as you want, and I have to give it to you."

"Then why sacrifice you at all?" she whispered.

He winced. "Because people don't enjoy having to beg for their power. It's still my magic, no matter how much you take from me. And wouldn't it be all that much more wondrous if the power was yours and yours alone?"

He watched the thoughts flicker through her mind, and then she blew out a long breath. "No," she answered, so honestly it hurt to hear the word. "No, that sounds like more weight than I wish to carry."

She left those words ringing in his head, walked around him, and started toward the front of the cemetery. But then she paused and stared down at a very small grave. The cracked headstone was little more than a name, split in half and covered in moss.

"What is it?" he asked, meandering up to her side.

"Isn't this . . . you?"

He looked down to see his own name on the headstone.

Elric Hellebore. May he forever rest in anguish.

Shaking his head with a snort, he put his arm over her shoulders and dragged her away. "Witches have a funny sense of humor."

27

There were more infected than before.

She'd slept in the graveyard before wandering the streets of the Factory District in the early morning to see how these people were dealing with them. It seemed their methodology was violent but effective.

Big men corralled the drooling and moaning creatures into back alleys, then used crowbars or other weapons to bash their heads in. But there were more blockades every day. More houses closed up, and the groaning sounds of infected mingled with the scraping of fingernails against the walls. The Factory District was managing it better than others, but that didn't make any of this right. Soon enough, the infected would get free because there weren't enough men to kill them all, and then where would her people be?

Her could-have-been husband had a large project on his hands, and it was a distraction, which worked in her favor. She didn't know how he'd gotten everyone important in her castle under his thumb, but she would need every weapon in her arsenal for the moment she finally struck at the man who had killed her.

But first, she had to learn to harness her power. And that meant spending more time with the Deathless One.

Even in her head, she feigned disappointment at the thought. Because her favorite thing was working on spells with Elric, even if it was for all the wrong reasons.

Magic didn't come easily to her. It hadn't with Sybil, and some part of her had hoped that with him teaching her, he would have some divine ability to make her see magic in a different way. That just being around him would make everything easier.

Had it?

Not in the slightest.

Elric taught her more complicated spells than Sybil, with the thought that perhaps she was too gifted to learn the easier ones. Now there were so many rules to follow. So many tools that made little sense. Consecrating tools, symbols and runes to etch into the ground. Chants to be spoken and called out during the right phase of the moon. All that he seemed to think she should have memorized by now. But she didn't even know what half the words meant! He spoke in a language that she didn't know, so what did he expect?

Jessamine had never had the talent of learning other languages. Her mother had tried for years to teach her all the other dialects of their kingdom, at the very least, so she could greet visiting dignitaries, and Jessamine had always been terrible at it.

But then she'd thought of her mother, and they had missed an entire day of learning magic because every time she tried to cast a spell, it had the flavor of sadness, Elric said. And then he'd left her alone because apparently he was like all men and didn't know what to do with a sad woman.

He couldn't fix what had been broken. But neither could she.

And seven days after she'd asked him to teach her, she met him again in the Factory District's graveyard at twilight.

Jessamine was nearly ready to give up this idea. Maybe she could find someone to teach her hand-to-hand combat. If she was good with a knife, then she could make someone a little scared if they tried to attack her. It was as good an idea as learning magic, apparently, because she was shit at both.

But this time, instead of carrying some new ritual bowl or anything else, Elric stood next to the tombstone they'd been using as an altar with his hands empty. Her stomach flipped, as it did every time she saw him now; that, or her traitorous heart would start beating harder. Both organs signaled her ridiculous need.

Trying not to sway her hips too much, she approached him and asked, "Have you given up on me, then?"

His brows rose in surprise. "No. But perhaps you aren't the kind of witch I've been expecting you to be."

"That shouldn't sting as much as it does," she muttered.

She'd always been good at everything. She was the princess who was always described as perfect. Exactly what the kingdom needed. A lovely young woman for the *best* kingdom.

Even the guards in her castle had felt comfortable walking into her rooms at any point of the day and talking to her about all manner of random topics. They wouldn't have done that with anyone else. She was welcoming, honest, the person everyone wanted to be around. But she had failed at witchcraft, and that dug underneath her skin.

He took a step toward her and took her hand in his. "This is not a bad thing, Jessamine. There are many kinds of witches in this world, and I believe you are not a ritual witch. Gravesingers are rare, yes, but they aren't supposed to be able to cast spells. You're supposed to use me."

"Isn't that what we were doing? I have no magic without you." She lifted both of their hands, shaking them in his face. "This is the only reason I can use magic at all. If there was no connection between the two of us, I'd go back to being the useless princess who was murdered on the day of her wedding."

He hummed low under his breath. "I don't appreciate the 'useless' addition, but yes. I do believe that our connection is what you are forgetting. You're trying to do this on your own."

"That's the point."

"No, it's not. You're not necessarily asking me to cast a spell. That's not what you did with Benji. But you are asking permission to use my magic in whatever way you see fit. And in that moment with Benji, you wanted someone to blame. Even as you were casting that spell to rip his memories out, you didn't want it to be you who was using the magic. Does that make sense?"

She supposed in some twisted way, it did.

She hadn't wanted to hurt Benji. But at the same time, she had. It was hard to imagine herself as someone who would hurt other people, so she had drawn upon his magic so she could tell herself it was his fault. Not hers.

"So you think I need to use that same logic when dealing with regular spells?" she asked. "That I need to expect it to be you doing the magic, not me?"

"In a way. It can't hurt to try." He gestured for her to walk ahead of him. Together, they strode toward a giant stone angel. "This would be considered a particularly advanced spell. I also suspect you are not very good at lighting candles because the thought of it bores you."

"Am I so transparent?"

"Very," he replied, his tone dripping with sarcasm. "Now, the angel in front of you is nothing more than stone. But stone is malleable, just like the human form is, because stone is nothing more than clay that has hardened. If you ask the earth to do something for you, then it will."

She stood in front of the angel, imprinting the beautiful sculpture to memory. The face had faded with the years, but the wings were still pristine. Feathers so delicate, she could see the center shaft and the faint etchings of texture on them. The folds of the angel's dress were so delicate that the sight made her heart skip a beat.

"This is beautiful," she murmured. "Who made this?"

"Does it matter?"

"It does to me."

He sighed, coming up behind her so close that she could feel the heat of him pressing against her spine. "Stop distracting yourself."

"I'm afraid I'll disappoint you."

"You could never." Hands landed on her shoulders, gently squeezing. "Let's try this first time with me touching you, yes? A reminder of who you're drawing the power from."

She could almost hear her mother's soul screaming in anger that her daughter was falling prey to such a dangerous god. And yet she leaned into his touch.

His hands were warm now, and she knew the lingering touch wasn't necessary. He had been hesitant after she had seen his memories, now that she had revealed the man beneath the mask. But that meant she knew that when he touched her, he wanted to.

So she leaned into him even more. Pressed her back to his chest so she could feel his ribs expand with every breath and sense the stuttering rhythm that changed the moment she wiggled against him.

Flush to his body, she could feel the twitch of interest pressing against her bottom.

He leaned down to growl in her ear, "Focus on the angel, nightmare."

Sighing, she focused on the wings. She zeroed her mind into the touch of his hands on her shoulders, and she let her soul yearn for whatever it wanted.

Right now, she wanted to give this angel life. She wanted to see what natural magic coursed through the stone that had been locked away for years. It had been chiseled by a loving hand, by an artist who had seen something to free from a block of nothing.

Just like she was finding that she wanted to free Elric. She wanted to let him out in this realm, and it didn't matter what madness he brought with him—she just wanted to see him free.

A sudden flush spread through her body. His fingers trailed down her arms, and she heard his sudden intake of breath as though he felt that sudden warmth as well. The sensation made it hard to think or breathe. She wanted to touch and be touched. She wanted to let this warmth turn from desire into passion and to make the world tremble with the force of her need.

With a sudden thunderous crack, the angel's right wing moved. It stretched up and wide, catlike, and then folded around the angel like a fine mantle draping over a rich woman's shoulders. Then the other wing unfurled with another echoing reverberation of sound, and suddenly the entire being bowed. She watched in awe as the angel straightened and pressed a hand to its heart. Then, with a nod of its head, it shot up into the sky.

Jessamine gasped, leaning back against Elric's shoulder to watch as it disappeared over the rooftops and soared into the clouds.

"It can fly?" she whispered.

"It can do whatever you want it to do," he replied. She didn't have to imagine the surprise in his voice. It was there without her having to search for it. "What did you want it to do?"

"I wanted it to be free."

"You are always a surprise, nightmare."

She couldn't help herself. She turned in his arms, hugging him around the neck and drawing him close. A bubble of excitement burst in her chest, and she laughed loudly. "I did it! I did it—you said I could do it and I did!"

Until this moment, he'd always hesitated to return her touch. She'd always known he was uncomfortable with her touch, but there were moments when she couldn't help herself.

Jessamine hid her soft smile against his shoulder as his arms came around her, this time without hesitation. He pressed her to him, tucking her head under his chin. "I believe we've discovered the secret to your magic. This should be easier the more we practice it."

"And you're all right with binding yourself to me even more?" Now that the thought was in her head, she didn't know how much she liked it. Leaning back in his arms, she frowned at him. "I know you have a history of witches using you. I don't want you to think that I'm doing the same thing. If at any point I'm pushing you too far, please let me know."

His eyes softened. She watched the darkness in them leak out until it was like she was looking up at a starlight sky. There were pinpricks of light in him. Tiny, almost impossibly small, but she could see them. She wondered, if she let him be who he really was, if that light would grow.

"I am not uncomfortable," he murmured, a little chuckle escaping before he continued. "I have never had a witch ask me that before."

"I thought we both agreed that I'm not really a witch."

"No, I suppose you are not. You're something else entirely, Jessamine Harmsworth. Although right now, I'm not sure what."

So many words pressed against her tongue. Words that made no sense. Like that she was his. Did it matter what else she was, if she had already dedicated herself to him?

His gaze moved from her eyes to her lips, and Jessamine felt heat bloom within her yet again. He wanted her. She could feel it, deep in her belly.

The desire that had zinged between the two of them wasn't spent. Not yet. There was so much power and magic bubbling between them that it felt natural to reach for him. She could expel all that power with him in an instant if she let him, and yet . . .

It wasn't right to push him. Not after what she'd seen in his memories. He had given so much of himself to so many people, and for once, she wanted him to choose. Without the passion of magic, without the suggestion that he had to eat up life while he could, she wanted him to choose her.

Taking a sharp breath, she pulled herself out of the hug and smoothed her hand down her pants. "Right, well . . . I have to get back to the streets."

"Of course." He lunged away from her, as though he had just realized the same thing. "More messages to write?"

"Well, I can't leave my people waiting too long." She tucked a strand of hair behind her ear and shrugged. "Food to steal as well, I suppose. I should eat."

"Jessamine?" Elric asked, his voice a low rumble.

Before she could even respond, he was there. Right in front of her. Elric grabbed onto the hem of her shirt, curling his fists in the thin fabric and dragging her against him.

The kiss he pressed to her lips was a brand. A claiming of ownership and desire and all those lost years in one. He licked and nipped and bit at every inch of her mouth until she was spinning. What way was up? She wasn't all that certain.

When he finally drew back, they were both breathing hard. His lips lingered on hers, seeming to have a hard time drawing away from the plush cushion of her mouth.

"I will be waiting for you when you get back," he whispered, that gravelly voice ragged after their kiss. "Return to me soon, nightmare."

He dissolved, sent back to his realm, where he could gather the power to remain by her side until he was fully summoned.

She had to write those messages on the walls. They were important, even as she remained frozen where she was for a few more moments.

I have so much to tell you.

Don't give up on me.

The truth is out there if you seek it.

The messages were meant to give people hope, but she knew that without action, they would no longer look at the messages as notes from their fallen princess, but as a lie. Soon enough, she would have to let people know in person that she was alive. And, distracted with magic lessons, she hadn't found anyone else to trust here. As always, she and Elric were running out of time.

Even as she left the graveyard, she knew she would wait a few more days before trying to find Callum again. Just a few more days where she could pretend that nothing was more important than lingering in Elric's arms.

Because a dark-haired demon called for her, and she was a weak-willed woman who wanted to worship at his feet.

28

They had finally figured out a way to teach her magic in that graveyard. After the first impressive task of bringing that angel to life, she blossomed under his touch. Every time he whispered a suggestion in her ear, his witch turned his magic into something magnificent.

He had a hard time thinking about anything else. The way she arched her back into him, her lips parting on a gasp as she cast her spell. The light panting in her breath as she tried to remember the chants even as he slid his hands along her ribs. Touching her became as necessary as breathing. The sound of her moans became the hymns with which he worshipped.

It was almost as good as being alive. Although he had the strange thrill of knowing that she was almost a puppet in his hands. Every time he asked her to use his power, Jessamine did it without hesitation. And though he had only asked her to do things he knew she would like so far, he also knew that wouldn't last forever.

Soon enough, they would be forced to protect themselves again. Or perhaps it would be a stranger entering their graveyard. He would turn her toward that person, and he would whisper death in her ear.

Because she trusted him—and because that was what she secretly wanted as well—she would do it. His Jessamine would pull that magic so exquisitely from his chest and unleash it upon whatever unsuspecting fool stumbled into their training grounds.

He wasn't sure she'd be able to forgive him after that. He wasn't sure she would even want to forgive him after all that he would ask. Soon, he would bring up resurrection again. Soon, she would tell him no, but maybe this time he had worn her down enough. Maybe this was the time she would look at him with those somber eyes and whisper, "Yes."

They'd discovered they created much stronger magic together if he was touching her. And oh, it was both a pleasure and a torment.

Every time she drew his magic out of him, he could feel it pulling and tugging and warming his bitter-cold bones. He wanted to touch her more. Every time she cast a spell. Every time he stood behind her, like he was now. Lingering with his hands on her shoulders while his fingers longed to trail down her arms.

"Do you see that flower?" he said, his voice little more than a raspy whisper of desire and passion.

Jessamine turned her head, looking where he pointed. She was, without a doubt, very much aware of the electricity that crackled between them. He'd seen it in her eyes more times than he could count.

She wanted him.

And he'd never wanted a woman more than in this moment, feeling her use him while he directed her like his own personal weapon. Every time he wanted her to use magic, it was like she had wrapped her hand around his cock.

He had forgotten what lust felt like. All his centuries locked away in that realm of death and torment had stolen the memories from his mind. All he recalled of passion or sex was that it was a tool to be used at the right time.

But he didn't want to use her. Not anymore. He could easily pluck out all her hidden desires and needs and then use them like a knife to flay her apart bit by bit, but she deserved so much more than a god who wanted to sway her mind.

But he found himself wanting to hear what she wanted. He wanted her to whimper and beg for him to do what she most needed. He needed to hear the moans in her throat and her little cries when he finally allowed her to get what she wanted.

His mind had frayed a bit. Shaking his head, he focused on her again. "Jessamine, the flower."

"Yes, I see it." Her breathless whisper made every muscle in his body tense.

"I want you to bring it back to life."

It was a difficult spell. Not easy for any in his coven to do. After all, they worshipped a god who was directly linked to death itself—resurrection magic was in many ways counterintuitive.

But their connection deserved more than a simple reward for one who laid out sacrifices at his altar. Jessamine took the power of his godhood and wielded it like a sword. Or in this case, like a poisoned chalice handed to the right person.

"Is that even possible?" she asked. "I thought magic couldn't bring things to life."

Magic could, just not his, at least in theory. Leaning down, he breathed into her ear, "I brought you back, didn't I?"

Goose bumps rose on her throat and trailed down the loose neck of her shirt. He watched them disappear underneath the fabric and nearly groaned at how desperately he wished to follow them.

The memory of her lips was seared into his brain. And now? Oh, he wanted far more than a kiss. He wanted to taste that hollow of her collarbone, wondering if she would be salty or sweet.

Elric wanted to indulge in life again. He wanted to devour her whole and come out on the other side, not as something haunted and rotten, but as something complete. A real man, not just the image of one.

Clearing his throat, he turned his attention back to the flower as she blushed and turned her gaze toward it as well.

She stammered, "I just . . . *will* it back to life?"

"What do you think I did when I found you in my realm?"

She licked her lips, a dart of a pink tongue that made the blood rush to his cock. He had to lean away from her slightly so she wouldn't feel it pressing against the small of her back.

"I suppose," she said, her voice low and throaty. "Perhaps you wanted me to wake up?"

"If that's how you want to see it, then tell the flower to wake."

"What if it doesn't want to?"

"Do you think I cared?" He wrapped his arm around her shoulders, his forearm dangerously close to her breasts as he drew her back against his chest. "Do you think I saw you lying in darkness and wondered if you wanted to wake? No, nightmare. I said to myself, look at this woman with hair black as midnight and the soul of a witch. I need her alive, and I don't care if she wishes to rest. For me, she will rise."

A shuddering breath erupted from her lips, and then they both groaned as she pulled magic from him. He could feel it coursing through her veins, through her very-much-alive body that felt so warm in his grip. The magic coiled through them, wrapping tightly around their forms and then releasing to find the flower, which then went from dead to blooming so deep red that it looked like it was dripping blood.

It happened so quickly he could have blinked and missed it. It was . . . magic. In its purest and finest form.

He'd forgotten such magic was possible with his power. He tucked her closer against him, forgetting that he was hard and wanted to hide that from her.

"No one has used my magic for good in such a long time," he murmured. "It was always used for power and pain and torment. Every witch who has taken from me, sacrificed me, dug knives into my sides, did so in a bid to do terrible, awful things. But you, Jessamine. You give life to stone and make flowers bloom."

"Don't think I'm perfect. I also killed a man with that power."

Oh, he remembered, and it still made him bare his teeth in pleasure. "Yes, you feral witch. You killed a man who betrayed you. A man who you trusted with the life of your family, and who took that life and stomped it beneath his unworthy heel. You were his reckoning, and you were glorious in your ruthlessness."

She shook her head against his shoulder. "Glorious or terrifying?"

"They are the same."

"The longer I am with you, the more I wish to be that avenging creature who steals this kingdom back." Her voice turned low, guttural with promise and something that sounded eerily close to desire. "I was once afraid of blood and gore, but now I fear I have seen so much of it that I no longer care."

He squeezed her a little tighter, drawing her ever more against him. "No war was ever won without blood being spilled. You do not have to kill them all, Jessamine, but you may have to make them all bleed."

And the thought of her making someone bleed made him *ache*. She was beautiful in her anger. The rage made her eyes flare with dark promises and her chest heave with righteous breath. That version of her gave him visions of him on his knees before her, worshipping his way between her thighs. He loved the part of her that came out only when she felt attacked.

She mused for a few moments, silent in his arms as they both stared at the flower she'd brought back to life. Then finally she whispered, "I've been thinking about the men who killed me."

"Have you?"

"I could feel how afraid they were. Most of them had been told witches were terrifying creatures who would harm them. They thought if they didn't hurt me, that I would hurt them. And I knew it."

"Yes, so you said." He still didn't like the thought, but compassion was part of who she was.

Without compassion, Jessamine would have been like every other witch he'd met. An ambitious woman who would get what she wanted no matter what the cost was. But she saw the world through a different lens, whether because of her upbringing, or perhaps it was simply embedded in her soul to care about others.

"It's just . . ." She blew out a long breath. "One of them wasn't afraid of me. He hit me because he wanted to. I had seen him before, in an alleyway when I was trying to summon you. He saw the bowls I carried in my bag, and he knew what I was. He gave me a warning and then left, but when he saw me again, it wasn't a warning. It was like he knew me."

"He recognized a witch. He's probably seen many of your kind before. Probably killed more than we wish to know."

"No." She twisted to look at him over her shoulder. "He *knew* me,

Elric. Like he knew who I was, and he just stood there, watching the others. He was the one who suggested using the knife. He wanted me dead, and I don't know why."

He hummed low under his breath. "Perhaps all those messages you've been leaving are becoming a problem."

"It wasn't the messages on the walls." That furrow appeared between her eyes again, as it always did when she was thinking. "He knew me. Like someone had told him to look out for me. He wanted me dead, not just a witch. Me."

That was concerning.

Elric had little patience for those who wanted to hurt her, and even less patience for situations like this. The man who had knifed her had caused a wrinkle in his very specific plan.

Only weeks ago, he had known exactly what he was going to do. He would seduce the gravesinger, sway her to his cause, get her to raise him out of the ashes so he could destroy this world for what they had done to him. His revenge would be even sweeter knowing that a witch had brought about the ruin of her own people.

But now, his priorities had changed. He still wanted to be resurrected. He still wanted to return to the land of the living, but that was no longer enough.

He wanted her.

He wanted her body, mind, and soul. He wanted to consume her like some monstrous being out of the depths of madness. Every bit of her that he could lick up, he wanted it. Jessamine Harmsworth didn't realize it yet, but he owned her body and soul.

She turned and slid her hand along his ticking jaw. "What are you thinking?"

"I don't like that you've been hurt by anyone other than me," he murmured, perhaps revealing too much. "I understand why they did what they did. And I know we will find this man who threatened you twice. We will teach him why people feared me then, and still fear me now."

"You want us to kill him?" she asked.

"Yes."

The flash of approval in her gaze was so quick he almost didn't see it. But he did. Of course he did.

Jessamine breathed out a long sigh. It fanned across his lips as she drew closer. He didn't think she noticed that she'd moved. "I don't know what we're doing right now."

"You're learning how magic works, and how to protect yourself."

"Is that so?" She leaned a little closer, and he thought maybe she was going to kiss him again before she stopped. Just out of his reach. "I can feel you, Elric. You're pressed against me from shoulder to thigh, and you think I believe this is entirely about magic?"

"Where did this confidence come from?"

"From days on end of you teasing me until I forget I am a highborn lady and I'm not supposed to feel like this."

Again, she feathered her lips so close to his that he could feel the heat of her. A hand slipped between them, her palm stroking down his chest. He couldn't take it. Not like this, not when he was so confused about what she wanted or how she felt.

Growling, he spun her in his arms again, pressing her spine to his front. He couldn't stop himself from touching her. With a rough hand, he palmed her breast, the weight of it so slight and yet exactly what he had wanted.

"Stop tempting me, witch," he growled into her ear. "I can hold myself back only so long."

But he couldn't resist burying his face in her neck and breathing in her scent so deeply he thought it might be embedded in him. That grave scent was so tantalizing. He wanted to keep her with him forever.

"What if I don't want you to hold yourself back any longer?"

The words seared through him.

A low growl rumbled through him, and he snarled in her ear, "Then I will lay you out on these gravestones and fuck you until you can't walk straight for days on end, nightmare."

Her moan shot right through him. She wanted this. He could taste her desire in the air. The perfume of her need was a call he longed to answer.

Until he felt that awful tug from his realm. From the memories and the darkness and the black abyss that never wanted him to be happy. The claws of gravesingers sank into his sides, promising that he would suffer just as they had suffered in their sacrifice for their people. They had murdered him for his power and it hadn't worked, but somehow it was still his fault.

Before he could stop himself, he dissolved from the living realm and was summoned back to his own personal hell.

29

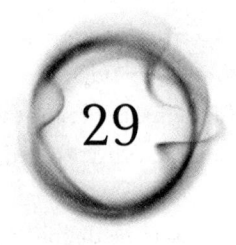

Oh, no. Absolutely not.

One moment she was arching into his touch and the next, he was . . . gone. Disappeared from this realm, likely off to his other one, which always called him back at the worst points. She refused to let this stand. He was hers, and they were so close to doing what she had wanted to do since the fear had worn off.

That god belonged to no one but her.

Many people had laid claim to the Deathless One over the years. Countless witches had sunk their claws into his hallowed skin. Women who had reveled in his pain, finding pleasure in his gasps of agony. But she was not one of them.

Jessamine would trade years of suffering and pain to sit with him on a throne made out of the skeletons of their enemies, if that was what it took to have him. And perhaps those were thoughts of madness, of the insanity that clung to him and, therefore, now to her. She didn't know. But did it really matter?

In this moment, she wanted to undo every single touch that had ever caused him pain. She wanted him to look down at her with those dark eyes, through those scars that marred his body and face, and she wanted to know that he felt true pleasure with her.

She had followed him into that dark place before, during her dreams. This time, she would do it intentionally.

She turned to the gravestone altar and stretched out on it. Like the carvings of men and women around her, she crossed her arms over her chest and let her eyes drift shut. The tug of magic at her core and deep inside her chest, where she was connected directly to him, already told her what she wanted to know. She could let herself go because this form was little more than a shawl she could don whenever she wished.

Jessamine left her body and joined him in the realm of never-ending darkness. Not dead. Not asleep. Just as herself.

The darkness was as startling as it always was. She blinked, trying to get used to the bitter bite of shadows. Inky hands wrapped around her ankles, trying to hold her in place.

But she knew what they were now. Memories. The lingering remnants of the witches who had come before her, and how dare they try to stop her. Hissing, she kicked at the hands even as she ripped at the darkness covering her eyes. She *would* see in this realm. She would live and they would not stop her.

A shrieking echo of witches long dead barraged her ears, and with it, the darkness fell away.

And there he was.

Waiting for her.

He sat slumped upon a throne made of bones. One roughened hand rose to caress the scar on his lip as his jaw bounced. His legs were spread wide, black leather tight around his lean thighs. The loose black shirt he wore bared a muscled torso covered in stab wounds and scars that had never healed quite right. And yet, he was everything she had ever wanted.

Dark eyes flaring with desire, he murmured, "You followed me here, nightmare."

"I did."

"Why?"

"I think you know why." When he remained silent, Jessamine reminded herself that she was a princess. No, she was a queen. Even a god needed to bow to her. "To finish what we started."

He quirked an eyebrow. "You want me, nightmare?"

"You know I do."

He slowly pointed to the inky ground, all commanding energy and powerful prowess. "Then crawl to your god, witch. And I will give you what you desire."

A small part of her melted at the thought of giving him that much control. Yes, she wanted to crawl to him. She wanted to beg on her hands and knees for a god to give her an ounce of his attention.

But a much larger part of her mind remembered that she was a queen. And no man would ever again make her beg on her knees for anything.

Stepping away from him, she tugged hard on their connection. Color spilled from the whispered desire on her lips. Bright blushes and vibrant reds, dripping from her body and spreading across the floor. Rainbows burst to life around her feet, throbbing with magic as they swirled together. Emerald greens tangled with golden yellows in a weave of color. From the iridescence roiling at her feet rose vines, thorny and strong, winding their way around and through the throne she built. Rosebuds bloomed, decorating the form with bloodred, until her throne was ready for her.

Where the Deathless One sat upon a mishmash of skulls and other bones, her seat was a much more delicate creation made from a woman's mind and attention to detail. She had conjured herself a throne of delicate thorns, blooming red roses, and hidden bronze underneath.

Mimicking his position, she spread her legs wide, leaning back in her chair. Hooking one leg over the arm, she set her elbow on her raised knee and framed her face with her fingers. "Oh, no, Deathless One. It is you who will crawl to me."

A pulse of power radiated off him. His throne liquefied underneath him. One moment, he was sitting like a conquering god surveying his spoils, and the next...

Oh, he was on his knees. Crawling up to her with his eyes filled with desire and a predatory movement in his shoulders with every single moment it took him to get to her.

He crouched between her spread thighs, his gaze more than hungry. He was starving.

"You wish me to worship you, nightmare?" he rasped.

"Yes."

"My pleasure," he all but growled before spreading her legs farther apart.

The ache in her hip joints was quickly replaced by shock as she felt the tingle of his magic trailing up her calves. She watched as the fabric of her clothing slowly disappeared. A shadow passed over her, leaving in its aftermath nothing but her pale, pale skin.

She had only a moment to be shocked and perhaps slightly embarrassed at being so exposed before him, spread out as she was, but he wouldn't allow that. Not her Elric. Not her god.

He groaned, long and low, his voice even more guttural as he said, "Look at you, nightmare. So pretty and pink and so fucking wet. All for me."

How was she supposed to reply to that? She had limited experience in anything related to this, and she'd certainly never spread herself so wantonly for anyone other than him—but if she said that, he would take all too much pleasure in knowing it.

Or perhaps he already knew. Because he looked up at her with those dark, desire-filled eyes and snapped out an order even though she was in charge. "Close your eyes. I'll tell you when you can open them again."

She couldn't. Jessamine just stared down at him in shock and awe and maybe something like intrigue.

A dark band of shadow looped around her head, her eyes. She was blinded by his magic, as she had been before, but there was no fear in it now. She saw nothing, she could feel only the featherlight touch of his lips against the delicate skin at the back of her knee. "Do not look. Do not think. Only feel."

How could she do anything else? Without her sight, all she could do was focus on the sensation of . . . him.

His fingers turned into claws. Deadly pinpricks of pain that decorated her thighs even as his warm, scarred lips trailed up the inside of her legs.

All she could feel was the thrill of his warm breath fluttering across the pulse in the crease of her hips. The way he whispered against her flesh, words that made her feel powerful and wanted.

"So pretty. So smooth. You taste divine."

She felt a bit like she would fall apart long before he touched her, and then a clawed hand slid even closer. The backs of his fingers trailed up her belly, gently drawing circles on her skin as he drew closer and closer to her breast.

Then she heard him sigh, a pleasant sound, as though he had finally found peace. As his fingers closed around her nipple, she felt the warm, wet slick of his tongue licking in one long, flat movement. She arched into him, somehow pressing her breast into his grip while grinding herself against his mouth. She must look obscene, but it didn't matter. That one lick was enough to send her mind spiraling off into another realm.

His deep chuckle vibrated through her core. "Hold still, nightmare, or I will make you."

"I don't think I could hold still if I tried."

"I was hoping you'd say that."

A loop of what she could only assume was dark magic trailed around her wrists, pinning them over her head to hold her exactly where he wanted her.

"Do you need me to control your legs, too?" he asked, all too amused at the turn this had taken. "Or am I allowed to enjoy you now?"

Breathing a little hard, she shook her head. "Not the legs, please. I'd like to wrap them around your head."

His deep groan made her grin. "Oh, you're going to be the death of me."

"I thought you couldn't die," she whimpered as he turned his attention back to her inner thighs, sucking hard enough to leave marks and sending sparkles of pure pleasure dancing through her body.

"But if I could, what a perfect way to go."

Her breath caught at his next heated lick, which delved between her folds. She tilted her head back against the throne, sinking into the pleasure. This wasn't a transaction. It was her feeling and him feasting.

Elric eased her into it, every long, slow lick ending at the bundle of nerves between her legs. He lovingly stroked her with such gentle circles that she could have believed he wasn't there, if she hadn't felt the tension coiling desperately in her belly. He pressed tiny kisses against her, learning the taste of her and taking his time to find the spots that made her twist against the bindings on her wrists.

He indulged in her.

And he was loud.

He groaned with her, his fingers digging into her flesh, eventually grabbing twin handfuls of her ass to lift her to his mouth. She was arched in her seat, her back bent as far as it would go as he drew her closer, sipping her like she was the finest of wines. He grunted into her, moaning as she did, his hands flexing against her flesh the more she enjoyed herself.

There was no hurry, no eagerness for her to come quickly so that he could get to the main event. He didn't seem to want to rush her, because every time she got marginally close to that wonderful peak, he drew back. Slowed down. Blew a cooling breath on her rather than licking as she wanted.

A drop of sweat rolled down her collarbone, blazing an icy trail between her breasts that made her realize she couldn't stand this any longer. She needed him, wanted him. She wanted more.

"Don't make me beg, Elric," she whimpered, rolling her hips against his tongue, which was back to its teasing, all-too-light touch.

"But you sound so pretty when you beg."

Who was she kidding? She wasn't above begging him to give her what would likely be the most explosive orgasm of her life. "Please, then. For fuck's sake, Elric, please."

"Please what?"

The words caught in her throat. She wasn't sure what to ask him or what he wanted to hear.

He leaned down and sucked on her clit, hard enough to make her arch into him and for her to clench desperately around nothing. He released her with a slick sound before snarling, "I want to hear all the filthy words from that pretty mouth, princess. Tell me exactly what you want."

A flare of anger and defiance burned in her chest. "I want you to stick your tongue in me and make me come like the monstrous god you are."

There was a low moan before he did exactly as she asked. She was filled, not with his tongue, but with two thick, scarred fingers that speared inside of her and scissored. He hit something deep within her that no one had ever hit before, and she froze, holding her breath as though her body knew something wondrous was about to happen.

Then he latched onto her clit as he had before, sucking hard while swirling his tongue in a firm circle that had her plummeting, coming so hard it almost hurt as she clenched down around his fingers and cried out as she never would have, as a princess should not even imagine doing.

He stayed with her through all of it, moving his fingers gently now, spiraling her down from the orgasm, which seemed to go on and on because he was a master at playing her body.

And when he loosed his bonds of dark magic, she slumped on that throne, panting and dripping with sweat. Only then did he let the blindfold fall from her eyes. She stared down at her own body, a foreign creature now that she knew it could do that, and saw him.

He grinned up at her wolfishly, his lips slick with her wetness as he moved his fingers in and out of her, the shallow movements somehow still sending shock waves of pleasure pinching through her form. It was madness that they had done this, but she never wanted to see anyone else between her thighs.

And gods, she had hooked her leg around his neck. She hadn't even realized that she was holding on to him for dear life, one leg around his neck and the other spread wide by his hand.

"How pretty you look, undone by my hand." He licked his lips, eyes rolling back. "And the flavor of you, nightmare. That is not one I am ever likely to forget."

"Happy to please," she whispered, still stunned at the sight of a god kneeling between her legs.

"Oh, you very much pleased me. Now rest, my darling and divine."

"You don't want to—"

He interrupted her. "I do what I want, nightmare, and soon I will indulge myself in your body. But only when I have a physical form to take you with. Sleep. You'll need your rest for what I intend to do with you."

She drifted away from his realm, back to her body, which did indeed need rest. But his words lingered in her mind. He wanted a physical form, so they could really touch. And she realized she desperately wanted that as well.

30

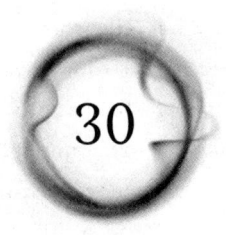

He could still taste her on his tongue, and she tasted like ambrosia. Elric found himself licking his lips constantly, a reminder of what they had done. But of course, it wasn't the same as the real thing. In his realm, everything was dulled.

It was the reason he'd refused to finish the job. He couldn't. How could she expect him to enjoy this feast of the most divine nature right in front of him, knowing that this realm dulled his senses? That nothing was as good if he didn't have a real body? She tortured him by coming here, and he was the fool who could deny her nothing.

He wanted to feel her. Actually feel how warm she was, how good she felt in his hands. He wanted to know the full extent of her flavor and the sound of her cries not muffled by dark magic. But most of all, Elric wanted to focus on her and nothing else while there were no curses pulling at him. No lingering gravesingers with whom he'd done this before, with so many other witches as a way to control them or for them to control him, and surely she felt tainted with *his* tongue buried so deep inside her?

He was a monster who had feasted upon her flesh. A monster who wanted her to see him as a man.

Sighing, he walked through his dark realm and waited for her to call upon him. He had enough power to go to her, but the stronger their connection grew, the more that felt as though he was violating her privacy. She hadn't summoned him in a few days, and that was an issue. What if something had happened? Surely he would have felt her pain, like he had before. But she hadn't gone this long in months without summoning him.

And then the gravesingers started whispering from their chains. *She got what she wanted out of you. No witch can ever truly be trusted.* He knew that better than most.

She'd wanted pleasure, or perhaps to discover what it was like to lie with a god. She had weighed and measured his talents, and then she had found him lacking.

He should have cut out their tongues when he bound them. But those dark thoughts boiled through him as he waited. Because he always waited. For her, he would wait a century, and yet it would forever sting as well. What if she wanted nothing to do with him now? What if he had read her completely and utterly wrong?

So when he felt the tug between them, a call from his nightmare to him, he answered so fast it made him dizzy. Struggling to stand, he forced himself to wear a mask of indifference. He needed her to think that he didn't care. Nothing she could do would impact him, certainly not. He was a god, and he was not hung up on a little mortal witch who was nothing more than a beautiful tool, albeit more a witch's knife than a blunt and boring hammer.

He expected her to say that what they had done was wrong. That she had thought more about his past and what he had told her, and that she was disgusted by him.

But instead, he found himself standing before her in the middle of the public baths. No one else was here. Why would they be? It was the middle of the night, and the air made little clouds every time she exhaled. She stood in the moonlight, half-dressed just outside a pool that would normally be full of people, but tonight it was so cold ice formed at its edges.

And this witch, this princess, didn't hesitate to drag an ice-cold wet cloth over her bare legs. She didn't flinch or complain, she just accepted her fate and took the bitter sting.

She looked so beautiful standing there in nothing but her shirt skimming her thighs, with her hair cascading down her shoulders, unbound and wild as he liked it. The moonlight caressed her features, all that bare skin so tempting, even though he didn't know where he stood with her. What if she didn't want to see him? What if this was all some terrible meeting where she would finally admit that their experience had meant nothing?

But Jessamine didn't even look at him. She just kept washing her legs and quietly said, "You realize that we're distracting each other?"

His stomach sank. "I do."

"I don't want to stop whatever it is between us. I don't want to look at you and wonder what might have been. But we do need to figure out how to do this and still get my throne back."

The tension in his belly eased a bit. But only a bit. "I know you have a mission to finish, and I am here only to see you succeed."

"I don't think that's the only reason you're here." She froze mid-movement, her leg braced on the pool's stone edge and her hair falling over her shoulder. She was a picture in this moment that any artist would wish to paint. A maiden in a pool of water, a temptation to all men and yet the picture of innocence.

His scar writhed on her neck, catching the moonlight. However barbaric it was, he was pleased to have marked her permanently. The magic deep in her wound kept her alive, although she likely had no idea.

There was so much he hadn't told her. So much she didn't know.

Like the shards of her soul he kept locked away in his realm. Why? He didn't know. He should have given them back by now, but if he had, then there would be nothing to guide him to her in the shadows. He needed that direct connection. And perhaps he needed a piece of her for himself as well.

Elric met her gaze, his own softening at the hope he could see in her eyes. "I am an ancient being, Jessamine. I am not here for what you imagine."

"A girl can hope."

"Indeed, you can." He took a step closer, watching her body to see if she reacted in any way that would suggest she didn't want this. "But you are not opposed to continuing . . . this?"

She arched a brow. "I was the one who wanted to continue, in case you forgot. You were the one who turned me down."

A sudden rush of understanding went straight to his head. For a moment, he was lightheaded with relief and the many layers of hope that coiled around his neck.

Elric lunged for her. His hand scooped through her hair to hold on to the back of her neck while he jerked her forward. The kiss he gave her was all-consuming, devouring, not sweet or tender, but a claiming. She needed to know that she was his. He wanted her more than anything else he'd ever wanted, and the fact that she wanted him back?

Oh, it seared him to the bone.

When he was satisfied that he'd stolen her wits with his kiss, he took two large steps away. Breathing hard. But this was important, and it had to be said.

"You know why I stopped what we started."

Her gaze shuttered, and he knew that was the wrong thing to say. Because no matter how close they had gotten to each other, no matter how much he wished to be real again, she wasn't going to do it. Not yet, anyway.

But something in him whispered to continue. To see just how far he could push her.

Moving behind her as she turned back to her ablutions, he hooked her with his arm and held her close. The sharp gasp she let out made him painfully hard, but this wasn't the moment to indulge themselves. Instead, he trailed his hand down her arm until he could hold the bathing cloth she clutched.

"I can see how cold this is," he murmured in her ear, trailing his lips down her neck. "But I cannot feel it. Not in this form, and not in my realm. My desire to become real has been inflamed by my need for you, Jessamine."

"You know why I cannot summon you. Not in the way that you wish."

"Because you don't trust me?" He lifted their arms together, watching the moonlight filter through their twined fingers as she dropped the cloth. "You said you would trust me with your life. What difference is it to resurrect me?"

"Do I trust you with the life of my kingdom, the lives of my people? I don't know yet."

"Ah, and you were also the one who said you would never sacrifice me. You *vowed* it, as I recall. Which means, nightmare, you clearly think more highly of me than the other witches I have known." Elric couldn't help himself. He drew her hand to his cheek, stroking his own face with her hand. She didn't fight him, though, almost as though she wished to touch him like this. "You want me. I'd dare to say you need me, in this form and in whatever way I would give myself to you. Am I wrong?"

Leaning her head back against his shoulder, Jessamine watched him touch himself. Her eyes were half-open, her movements languid as desire saturated her bones. "No, you aren't wrong."

"And yet you hesitate."

She did. Of course she did. It was the smart decision, too, because none of them knew what would happen if he was released. Even he wasn't sure. Elric had so many plans and thoughts and intentions of what and who he would become when he finally joined the living again.

But somehow, they'd all changed.

She'd changed what he wanted.

Letting her hand drop, he took a step back from her and gave her a small nod. "I understand."

"Do you?" Her wide eyes saw too much. She saw his disappointment and all the horror in his past. Perhaps she even saw the self-hatred that radiated throughout his entire being.

He hated that she knew what he was. Who he was. But also what had been done to him. So instead of responding, he just nodded.

"I see." She sighed. "Then I suppose we should talk about our next step in this plan. We still need to find Callum."

"It seems logical." Although he still wasn't sure why. "Who was he in the castle again?"

"The head of the royal guard and my mother's lover for many years." Stepping off the stone edge, she padded over to a shadowy corner where she had stowed her pants. "He practically raised me, so I think it's rather important to know why he betrayed us."

"Can't we just kill him and be done with it?" This was a much more comfortable conversation for him. Elric knew how to murder people. He knew how to take lives and make them suffer as they struggled to remain in this realm.

He had no interest in saving anyone. Certainly not someone who had harmed her.

"No, we shouldn't just kill him. Because he couldn't be the mastermind behind all of it. He was a brilliant soldier and a man with ambition, but he wouldn't organize a coup against the women he loved. Not without a reason I cannot fathom. He was happy; I saw it with my own eyes. My mother kept him happy. Callum was a tool that was wielded in the wrong way, or he had some other reasoning I cannot fathom. He opened all the doors, but he did not cast the killing blow. I want to know who wanted the royal line dead." She tugged her pants on a little too hard, the fabric creaking under the strain. "If I'm to take back my throne, then I want everyone who ever thought to murder me dead."

"There's the feral little thing I knew you were." He sat down on the edge of the pool, reclining as he watched her pace back and forth. "Just how are we supposed to find him? The last time you asked someone where Callum was, they killed you."

"None of this makes sense." From one end of the room to the other, she marched. Jessamine skirted the pool, wove through the stone benches, then returned to him in a complicated pattern. Over and over. "Callum loves me. Or he did. I know that. He used to tell me that before he tucked me in at night, and he'd always pop a kiss on my forehead before disappearing into my mother's room. He wouldn't do this without reason."

"What reason could that possibly be?"

"I don't know!" she practically shouted. "That man in the Factory District knew who I was when he attacked me, I'm certain of it. And the fact that I can't even ask about Callum without the threat of death makes me fear that I did not know this man at all. And if I didn't know him, then neither did my mother."

There was the spike of anxiety he'd expected. Elric hated to admit that he had been waiting for it. She'd handled this entire situation with scattershot guesses rather than a single bullet. But of course, she was still so very young. He had had centuries of time to become jaded and forget how to trust.

Jessamine hadn't learned that yet. He certainly wouldn't be the person to stand in the way of that very important lesson.

Sitting up, he turned all his attention to her. "You're struggling to grasp what stands before you. And you are hesitating because you fear what you might find at the end of this path. Is that correct?"

Oh, her miserable expression hurt every inch of him. But voicing her fears was the only way she would ever be able to face them.

He thought perhaps she would argue. Or fight back against what she believed he wanted her to say. But she didn't. This strong, bravehearted woman nodded her head.

"I'm afraid to find out he's been the villain in all this," she whispered, her voice very small. "I'm afraid to discover that the man I considered my father was the one who could so easily dispose of me."

"What does it mean if he was the one behind all this?"

She shrugged, her face creasing with an ugly expression before she quietly replied, "That I'm unwanted. That even the man who raised me didn't love me enough not to want to see me dead."

"No," Elric said. "It does not mean that. It means you put your trust in an ugly man who wore an impeccable mask. Nothing more. His hatred or fear or guilt has nothing to do with you. He carries that, Jessamine. Not you. Never you."

He hoped there was some small part of her that recognized he was right.

She smiled, although the expression was thin. "I've been listening in on conversations while I'm wandering. There's a group that seems to unofficially run the Factory District. They call themselves the Iron Knuckles. They're run by a man called the Butcher, who apparently is a bit of a local legend."

"Ominous name."

She took a deep breath, her shoulders rising and falling with the weight of her emotion. "I think Callum might be the Butcher."

"A royal guard who leads a group of outlaws?"

"The Iron Knuckles are decidedly more than that. But someone mentioned that they saw the Butcher once, and he has silver hair at the temples, with black eyes that see straight into your soul. That is eerily similar to Callum. Too similar." She winced. "The Iron Knuckles are a group of militant soldiers who wander the streets. People pay them protection money to keep their homes, and frankly, they seem evil."

"Fits the charges against him."

"I suppose it does. I want to get inside the Iron Knuckles' home, and I want to force him to see me. Not his goons. Not his soldiers. I want the man who raised me to look into the dead eyes of the girl he used to love." Those big eyes stared at him. "But I don't know if I can do this on my own."

"If you want me to walk with you, then I will. Every step of the way. But what is your plan, little one?"

"From everything I've heard, it seems the Iron Knuckles live in a section of the city that has been mostly blockaded because of the sickness that spread there. The rumor is that there never was anyone sick there. I heard someone claim they used to live in those buildings, and there wasn't even a cough for weeks before the Knuckles moved everyone out."

It wasn't a bad thought, hiding in plain sight. But Callum would still want to discourage anyone from even thinking about trying to find him.

"So you think there were never any infected in the houses at all?"

"Which leaves a lot of openings we could sneak into. A lot of buildings that probably aren't watched very well." She shrugged. "It's better than waiting around for an invite we're never going to get."

It wasn't the best plan, but it was a plan. And if this was what she wanted to do, then he would join her.

31

Walking into the Iron Knuckles' territory was, she realized, stupid. Even if she had somehow rallied an entire army to walk at her back, this was stupid. But the openings she thought would be there, weren't. The Iron Knuckles were far more prepared than she'd ever imagined.

As it was, Jessamine was completely alone. At least, as far as they knew.

Elric walked beside her, of course. She could see him perfectly well thanks to their connection, but everyone else would only see the faintest shadow in the reflection of the windows and puddles at their feet. He wasn't any happier that she was here, but at the very least, he hadn't argued this morning. And when they reached the end of their journey, he watched the sight before them with a narrow-eyed gaze. Jessamine stood in front of a cramped street that led into shadows, staring down the men who guarded it with their arms crossed.

Tall buildings bracketed them on either side, black monoliths with boarded-up windows and yellow-painted edges that marked them as homes of the infected. But she didn't hear any fingernails scratching from the inside—considering the state of the buildings and the windows, she had to wonder if the rumor was true, that no infected had ever been there. What better place to build a stronghold than in the homes of those no one wished to interact with? Still, it made the alleyway look like a portal to the darkest depths of madness, where only the infected remained.

The Iron Knuckles had set up barricades in front of the street, which was the first obstacle to carrying out her plan. Roughly hammered-together two-by-fours that were then wrapped in barbed wire to keep people out. Or perhaps, considering the brown staining on the tines, to throw people into when necessary. There was a small gap where people could walk, though. And that was where two massive men stood.

There was no way for her to get to the other buildings without someone seeing her, even though only two men appeared to be guarding the blockade. She had no doubt they would shout for help, and then her plan was ruined anyway. Their features were brutish, but their woolen jackets were relatively new and their trousers were sharply pressed. Each one wore a hat on top of his head like a pageboy, leading her to wonder if it wasn't a pageboy hat at all that Benji used to wear.

As always, a small pang struck her in the chest when she thought of the young man she'd killed in cold blood. She might have to kill more people today. It made her slightly nauseous even to think about that. But Elric was right. The path to a throne was coated in blood, and she had to be woman enough to walk through it.

Jessamine had never been very good at thinking on her feet. She liked to have a plan, but now this plan was ruined, and frankly, she was getting angry. These men were standing in her way, and she had spent far too much time searching for Callum to be stopped now. Sneaking wasn't an option. Finesse had to be tossed out the window.

Clearing her throat, she walked right up to the men. The dead god glared so hard that she could feel the cold, searing disapproval in his eyes.

She could feel it, but she ignored it.

"Gentlemen," she said as she stopped in front of the two behemoths. "I'm here to see Callum Queen."

The men looked at each other, surprise evident on their faces. "Callum? We only know him as the Butcher."

They'd given away more than they realized. But she'd had an inkling that Callum ran this place, and she was quite certain he was inside these streets that were controlled by the Iron Knuckles. They'd confirmed that with just a single sentence.

"So you know him, then?"

The man who had answered frowned at her. His hair was as red as a candle flame, setting him apart from the other, although they did look eerily alike. She assumed they were brothers.

She turned her attention to the man with the slightly cooler-toned brown locks.

"You stupid lout," the second man growled at his brother before looking at her. "No one goes in or out. That's what he means."

"I go in."

"No, you don't."

You're a queen, she reminded herself. *Act like one.*

She knew what her mother would do in this situation. The queen had mastered an icy expression that put weak-willed men like this in their place.

Drawing herself up straight, she narrowed her eyes and tried to act like her mother at her most haughty. "Do you not recognize a threat when you see one? I am not some beggar woman who has crept up to your doors and expects you to turn me away. You will let me in."

"And why the fuck would we do that?" both of them said, almost simultaneously.

Elric leaned against the wall beside them, his arms crossed over his chest. "Exactly, Jessamine. You had better give them a reason or I'll have to bring you back to life again."

Breathing deep into her belly, she smiled with what she hoped was an intimidating expression. "Because I'm a witch, gentlemen. And I promise you, you don't want to get in my way."

There was a stunned silence after her words before the two men burst out laughing. They laughed so hard that the redheaded one wiped tears from his cheeks. She didn't move as they let out their mirth, allowing them to have a few final moments.

She wasn't cruel enough to burst such a bubble of happiness before their lives were about to change forever. Let them laugh.

Elric meandered back to her side, standing behind her as he always did when they cast spells. Though this time, he leaned to murmur in her ear, "Are we finally getting to the bloodbath?"

"I was hoping to avoid it," she whispered.

He tsked. "You never let me have any fun."

Jessamine tried very hard not to snort before turning her attention back to the giant men in front of her.

They'd finished laughing and now wore twin expressions of sinister glee. The brown-haired one said, "Oh, I like a funny woman. And I like to show funny women a good time. I think I'll do that before we rip you apart."

"Mm, no." She tapped her lip before nodding. "I think you're not going to touch me, and you're going to let me through. That's your only option, gentlemen."

She could see their muscles bulging as they both tensed, ready to lunge at her and do whatever it was men like this did. Even Elric stilled behind her, his hand on her shoulder sending power crackling between them.

But then another voice joined theirs in the alley. One filled with so much horror that it snapped through the air like a shock of thunder.

"You?" The voice shook. "It can't be you. You're *dead!*"

Jessamine recognized him. He was the one who had wielded the knife in the alleyway, the one who had plunged it into her belly, and she remembered the look of relief in his eyes. It was a strange combination of hatred and the knowledge that once she was gone, he would be safe. She refused to be angry at a man who made choices based on fear, but she could damn well look at him with pity for his folly.

All three of them looked at her now, jaws hanging open and their gazes darting between each other.

"Surprised to see a dead woman walking?" she asked.

One of the brothers nudged the newcomer. "Bones, you must be wrong. This ain't the girl you killed."

"It's definitely the woman I killed," Bones replied. "I never forget a face, and certainly not one like hers. I remember thinking those hollow eyes had already seen death."

"Because I have."

Elric squeezed her shoulder a little too tight. "What is this plan of yours, nightmare?" he whispered.

Her plan? Her plan was to take control. Her entire life, her entire being, had been other people telling her what to do. This was her moment. This was her gripping life by the throat and saying *this is my beast to ride*, and she would ride it. Even if that meant changing who she was and blowing everything to smithereens. It didn't matter.

Because she was making the choices now, and she would not regret them.

Bones looked at her with those horror-filled eyes and whispered, "How is this possible?"

She met his gaze head-on, without fear. "I am a witch. My patron is the only god left alive. The Deathless One himself. You could stab me a hundred times, a thousand times. You could cut me into tiny pieces and I would come back. My bones are bound to the land of the living. My flesh is seared with violence and revenge. My soul is soaked in blood and haunted by a thousand hallelujahs sung in a church that cries out for their rightful queen. You will not stand in my way."

To her greatest surprise and pleasure, the man who had killed her stepped aside and barked out an order to the other two.

"Walk the alley of death, then, witch," he said, quaking with fear. "I will not stand in your way again."

She didn't know if it was that she was a queen or a dead woman that made him so afraid, but she knew he would not attack her again. So she walked by him, head held high, as befitted a queen. As she passed, she saw Elric reach out a hand toward the man.

The ghostly shape of his fingers moved through Bones's face. The man shivered, and she could almost see a small slither of darkness that sank underneath his skin. A warning. Not anything real or powerful or even harmful in any way, but it was very much a warning from a god.

Perhaps it even whispered of a time when the Deathless One would come again. And that this man should run long before that happened.

Jessamine steeled herself for what came next. She had marched into the inner sanctum of a very powerful group of deadly people, but soon enough, they would bow to her.

She still had hope that maybe Callum was an underling like Bones, who had killed for whatever money someone would pay him.

The alley opened up into a central square surrounded by five large buildings. She didn't think the buildings had originally touched each other, though, but someone had created living spaces in the alleys that had once separated them.

It created a fortress. A tall, five-story fortress built out of metal and wood. Even the sun had a hard time penetrating the labyrinth here. But this central area was still trying to thrive. Plants crumbled to dust under her feet as she walked. Mildew and rot filled her nose, refuse piled high wherever it had been thrown.

There were plenty of people milling about, their faces all missing the dirt and oil of the factories. These people were infinitely better dressed, well fed, but there was a hunger in their gazes as they watched her. They wanted to attack. They wanted to fight. But why?

"How are you going to find this Callum?" Elric asked, her own personal shadow. "It doesn't look like he's here, and they won't allow you to wander through any of these buildings without an escort. You've walked into a hornet's nest, nightmare. And every single one of them wants you dead."

"I have a plan," she muttered.

"Is it to use my magic to flatten these buildings? I understand you think you have control over my power, but you don't have the knowledge to do this yet. All that magic running through you so freely might kill you. You aren't a conduit. You're a gravesinger." He turned toward her, his brow furrowed with worry. "And I'm realizing you don't know the difference."

"I don't." Jessamine shrugged, knowing she probably looked crazy to anyone who was watching her. She must seem like she was talking to herself. "But I have realized that doesn't matter. I am angry. And for the first time in my life, I am sitting in this dissatisfaction with no one fixing it for me. I deserve answers, and I am going to get them for myself."

He looked at her with more heat in his eyes than she had seen, even when he was looking up at her from between her thighs. That expression said he wanted to throw her down in the middle of this courtyard, watchers be damned. He wanted her so much that it made her squeeze her thighs together and hope that no one realized how affected she was by the god they could not see.

"Where have you been hiding these razor-sharp teeth?" he murmured, then licked his lips and looked her up and down. "I would like to see this side of you more, nightmare. The things I want to do to you when you're like this are positively evil."

"You are a creature filled with malice, after all."

"So are you, I'm finding."

He was right.

She had fought this side of herself for so long. Everyone had always told her to be the dutiful daughter. The kindhearted princess. The girl who gave more of herself than she took from anyone else. And she refused to be that person any longer.

Today, she was going to take. And that came in the form of turning toward the crowd, lifting her gaze up to the highest building, and screaming at the top of her lungs, "Callum Quen! I have come for you!"

Her scream echoed between the buildings, bouncing back and forth until it erupted out of the top like a volcano. Everyone around her stared as though she had lost her mind.

Maybe she had. But damn, it felt good.

She thought there would be a significant wait before someone stepped forward. But it didn't take very long at all. Perhaps Bones had run to find Callum.

A door into the third building opened up, and a large man strode out. The silver wings at his temples were so familiar it hurt to look at him, as was the expression on his face, the chiding expression one saved for children when they were misbehaving.

He no longer wore the navy uniform that she'd always seen him in. Instead, he wore a white shirt and a high-collared black jacket. He looked better here, like he fit in more than he ever had in the castle, and that made every hair on her body stand up straight.

The people parted around him like a wave around a stone. They didn't want to be anywhere near him as he approached. She watched all of this, knowing this was bad. This was so bad.

Elric muttered, "I take it back. This isn't a hornet's nest. This is a den of vipers."

"I think you might be right," she murmured just as Callum stopped before her, his arms outstretched.

"I was so afraid you were actually dead," he said. "And now look at you! You've come home."

They were the words she'd wanted to hear since the moment she realized she was going to die. And they were a lie.

32

He didn't like any of this, but he also knew she needed to do this on her own. He could sweep in and be that voice in her ear, guiding her as he had in the moment with Benji when he had known she would fail. But this time, she would not fail.

She'd walked into this den of hissing snakes with a confidence he had never seen from her before. Was this what she had been like before she died? He could so easily picture this woman upon a throne, ordering around her subjects at a whim.

He could see her ordering him around, too, as she had in the darkness when he'd wanted to lick her from head to toe. She had told him to crawl, and he had. A god. So easily on his knees for a mortal woman, because she had ordered him to do so.

He should probably be ashamed of that. Or at the very least, embarrassed.

Instead, Elric watched with passion and pride as she stared down the man who had raised her. The man who had betrayed her more than any other person in her life. He could only imagine this was about to get worse. After all, Callum Quen was a liar through and through. Elric could see it on him like a slick oil that clung to his skin.

The man was bigger than he'd expected. Jessamine's memories were that of a child, so of course she remembered Callum as a giant. But as he ushered her out of the courtyard into the central building, Elric took stock of the man who threatened his nightmare once again.

Callum's clothing was well-tailored, not a speck of dirt on the white shirt he wore. His hair was oiled back; he was clearly a man who cared about his appearance. But the faint wrinkles around his eyes and between them revealed a man who spent an awful lot of time frowning. And then there was his stance. A fighter's stance, always at the ready, with his gaze flicking from side to side, watching for someone to sneak out of the shadows.

This was no mere guard. This was a man who had grown up on the streets and knew exactly how to keep himself alive. That was a man who was not trustworthy, because he did not trust himself.

"Careful, nightmare," he murmured, keeping close to his witch. "Don't get out of reach."

She glanced over her shoulder, and her gaze told him she knew well to stay close. Even if she had once trusted the man beside her, she didn't any longer.

"Everything all right, Jessa?" Callum asked, the nickname falling from his lips far too easily for comfort.

"I'm fine." She cleared her throat before changing the subject. "You always told me you grew up in the Factory District. I have to admit, I didn't think you meant like this."

The interior of Callum's kingdom was not what Elric had expected. This place was immaculate. While the exteriors of the buildings had been rather dismal, this place was clean and well kept. Warm wooden walls lined the hallways, and they'd already passed through a large shared living space with multiple men and women. They also walked past a room with its door ajar, in which Elric glimpsed wall after wall of weapons. Knives, swords, rifles. All the things he might have kept if he was amassing an army.

But why would a man like this need an army?

Finally, they reached a door that Callum opened before the man gestured them through. The office was as neat and clean as the rest of the building. Again, warm wooden walls, and a red rug with faint brown staining around the edges. A massive oak desk nearly filled the room with twin chairs before it.

This was not where Callum gestured Jessamine to sit. Instead, he ushered her to join him by a fireplace to their right. Twin cushioned seats waited for them there, the backs patched a few times with fabric that didn't quite match.

"I have been so worried about you," Callum said, his voice low and calming. "You cannot imagine the fear I felt when I saw you fall off the edge of that cliff. I had thought before that moment I might be able to save you."

"Did you?" Jessamine's voice was cold and her spine too straight as she perched on the edge of her chair. "Was that before or after you watched Mother die? I was under the impression her death would hurt you worse than my own."

At least Callum winced at her accusation. But then he sighed, and the mask slid back into place. "It was all horrible to watch, Jessa. I would not wish it on my worst enemy. I barely escaped with my life after what that beast did. I've been searching for months for a way to get back at him. Your mother's death deserves revenge."

Elric walked closer to the fire, bracing a forearm against the crumbling wood above it. He stared into the flames, trying to find a thread of patience to calm himself with. "He's lying."

"I know you're lying," she said, answering both of them. "You were part of this, Callum. What I want to know is why?"

"Jessamine, after everything I have taught you, don't you know jumping to conclusions always ends wrong?"

The older man would not give up so easily. Elric looked over his shoulder and watched as Callum shifted in his chair, bracing his ankle over a knee and looking, for all intents and purposes, calm. As though he hadn't just been caught.

Callum never took his eyes off Jessamine, staring her down until she looked away and folded in on herself. Perhaps this was something the older man had done to her when she was a child: remaining in complete and utter silence just so she had to be the first to break.

Even worse, he hated to see the tactic working. The confident, powerful woman who had walked in here was slowly disappearing into the little girl who was desperately afraid of disappointing the fatherly figure she loved. It all drained out of her, as though this man was a leech.

"Don't give in to him," Elric snarled. "It's easier to control you if you believe you are lesser. You are not the child you once were, Jessamine Harmsworth. Remember your value."

Though her gaze didn't move to him, Elric knew her next words were for the god in the room, not the man. "I trusted you once. More than any other person. Even more than Mother."

"He does not return that trust." Elric returned his gaze to the fire, his hands clenching on the stone mantel as if he could snap it off in his hands and hurl it at the other man. "No one deserves your trust if they cannot return it."

As much as it hurt to say them, he meant those words—and he was forced to admit he had never returned her trust in the same way she had given it to him. Jessamine had given him her life multiple times now, and trusted that he would bring her back. What had he given her in exchange? Whispered promises that he intended to break the moment she resurrected him.

Callum sighed, steepling his fingers and pressing them against his lips. "Where is this coming from, Jessamine? You were always such a biddable young woman. You wanted what was best for this kingdom."

"And I still do."

He gestured up and down her body. "This is what the kingdom needs? A princess who does not know how to run a kingdom, so she turns to dark magic? This is not the way of things, Jessa. You have so much to learn. But I'm glad you have come, because I am more than happy to teach you."

Elric snorted. "Teach you? What could he possibly teach you that you haven't already learned?"

Jessamine, his nightmare, whispered in broken tones, "I don't know who you are anymore, Callum."

The words hung in the air, so light and innocent they were almost painful. He winced, turning to see the same expression on Callum's face before Elric moved behind her chair and crouched at her side. "What did I say about needing anyone to justify your greatness?"

She looked at him then, just the barest flicker of her gaze turning toward his. Elric reached for her hand, squeezing it tightly in his own. "You are powerful and great and wicked. You have to believe that, nightmare. Your god demands it."

He could see the confidence creeping back into her features. A cold chill danced down his spine, as though perhaps she was pulling magic from him. But that couldn't be right. When she drew her power from him, he was warm. So warm, in fact, that it was like a fire burning in his chest. This was cold, like the doomed gravesinger hands pulling him back to his own realm.

"Jessa," Callum said, slowly standing. "Come with me. I want to show you something."

She stood, and so did Elric. But the moment he tried to follow, he found himself . . . stuck.

Frowning, he looked down to see runes marked on the floor around him. Runes that hadn't been there before, that moved sluggishly on the wooden floor. Like someone had bled around him.

"What magic is this?" he hissed. "Jessamine, turn around."

She started to turn, but Callum banded an arm around her shoulders and yanked her farther away from him. One moment, his nightmare was within reach, and the next, she was nearly on the other side of the room. Wild-eyed, hair falling in front of her face, she stared at Elric with dawning horror.

Callum leaned down, his eyes wide as he pressed his lips to Jessamine's ear. "I can't hear him, but I know you can. He must be spitting mad right now to know he's been bested. So what's he saying, Jessa? What does a god snarl when he's been defeated?"

"Tell him nothing," Elric spat. "He gets nothing from me and nothing from you."

Her cheeks burned bright red, and he knew she was about to say something stupid. "He said he's going to kill you for this. It's the only warning you get, Callum, so don't risk your life. Don't think you can best a god."

"I bested the royal family, now didn't I?" He jerked her to the side, her neck snapping painfully as he tossed her toward the door. "I can do more than you believe, Jessa. Unfortunately, that's a hereditary problem you're going to have to overcome. I would prefer you alive, but you've already died. The woman you are now is but a fleeting image of the girl you once were. If there was ever a person I thought of as a daughter, it was you. A disappointing one, to say the least, but that can be changed. You could be molded into someone I like, but this god and I need to come to an understanding."

"What?" she cried out. The door opened sharply as one of Callum's cronies entered the room. It clipped her on the side of the head, nearly hard enough to knock her out.

"Jessamine!" Elric called out, reaching for her, only to find his arms coming up short. There was nothing he could do. Nothing at all. All he could do was stand there and shout as the person behind the door scooped her up into their arms.

Of course she fought. His little nightmare fought with every ounce of rage in her body. He could feel her trying to draw magic from him, the desperation inside of her reaching for the god who was supposed to keep her safe.

He had failed her in this. He had promised never to fail her again. And he would kill the man in front of him for it.

Callum watched her fight with amusement on his features and a soft chuckle falling from his lips. "Would you look at that? I didn't think the princess had it in her. Apparently, there's a fighter underneath that prim and proper exterior."

"Callum! You will regret this for the rest of your very short life," she hissed, her hair a tangled mass over her features now. It gave her the look of a creature from the grave, like she'd just crawled out of the earth to tear her claws through anyone who stood in her way.

"And who is going to end my very long life? You? A dead princess who is now cut off from the source of her power? No, my dear. There are things

I need from you, and unfortunately, that requires a rather long talk with someone other than you."

Elric bared his teeth. "What spell did he use to trap me? Get it out of him, Jessamine."

He could see her wild thoughts running freely in her mind. She spat out, "You don't even know magic, Callum! Did you employ some witch to do this? That is so beneath you."

Apparently, that wasn't a bad tactic, because the confession came easily. "I have no witch, but you don't have to be born a witch to use spells. All you have to do is follow instructions, especially when it comes to the gods. Look at you. Proclaiming yourself a witch in front of all my Iron Knuckles. Your mother is rolling in her grave right now."

Elric's mind ran wild. What spell? There were no spells to trap gods, not that he knew of. And certainly not a spell that someone without the power of witchcraft could cast. Such magic was difficult and required concentration, years of preparation. This wasn't a man who had been brought into power just moments ago.

He had planned this.

He had *been* planning this for a very long time.

"My mother?" Jessamine hissed, her voice cracked and raw. "My mother is rolling in her grave, you say? What grave, Callum? I heard she was thrown into a pit with the rest of the people who died under your watch. There is no grave for my mother!"

Something in the older man cracked. A small fissure, just enough to bleed.

Elric could see it in the way he flinched, and when he pressed a hand against his heart like the words hurt. As they should.

Callum walked with so many deaths weighing on his shoulders, and he had yet to make any atonement for such things. To whom should he cry out for forgiveness? The many souls he'd killed? Or the gods who were long gone?

They would never forgive him. Those spirits would haunt him until his very last breath. Elric would make sure of it.

Quen started to close the door, pausing only when Jessamine braced her legs against the frame and shouted, "You killed me, Callum Quen! And now I will haunt you into your very grave!"

The door slammed shut, and he was forced to watch as the man pulled a piece of paper out of his pocket. A page that looked familiar, written in a language no one had been able to read in years. Until this man started speaking in a language that had long since died.

Cursing, Elric cast a spell of his own, hoping it wouldn't fizzle out before Callum finished. He sent a message to his coven, to Sybil.

Their god was trapped. He summoned his witch to him, or they would both lose their power forevermore.

33

She was so stupid. Or maybe she wasn't stupid, just too trusting.

Jessamine had known Callum Quen was a wicked man. She could feel it the moment he stepped out of that building. Only lies fell from his tongue, and that meant she could expect everything he said would continue to be lies. But she had a hard time connecting this person with the man she knew. Every time he started talking, all she could think about were her memories.

She had been afraid of dogs when she was little. One of the hunting hounds had bitten her arm when she was just three years old, and after that she hadn't been able to even walk by the kennels. All she could think about were those sharp, wicked teeth. The aching fear had stuck with her for years until Callum learned she was afraid of dogs, and he'd brought her to the kennels every day. Holding her hand and never pushing her too far. Just so that she learned not all dogs would bite.

But this dog? The one who had put her in a prison below the home where he had amassed an army? She knew he would bite.

She had no way of knowing how many days had passed since they'd tossed her in this room. All she knew was that they weren't very gentle with her. She'd been thrown bodily into the wooden crates behind her, nearly cracking a rib and spreading bruises up and down her back. Survive death twice, and apparently no one sees any reason to be gentle.

They brought her food and water whenever they thought of it, but she was so hungry, she suspected it wasn't very often. There wasn't much to do in this pit other than sort through the crates behind her. Empty crates mostly, though some of them contained clothing, and there was one filled with worn boots.

A single window at least eight feet above her head cast dim light into the room, though it was barred. She guessed the window opened to the street, because every now and then a spray of water would erupt into the room. Either the street, or perhaps the sewers. She didn't know what was worse.

Sitting on a crate, she tried her best to think of some way out. There had to be a way.

But it didn't escape her notice that every time she fell asleep, Elric wasn't there. She couldn't see him, hear him, nothing. Every night she searched for him in that realm between places, and every morning she woke without finding him.

Callum had done something. She just didn't know what.

The door creaked open, the sound somehow strangely loud after sitting for hours on end in silence. Jessamine didn't even stand as the wide bulk of a man joined her in the room.

"I'm so sorry, Jessa. I shouldn't have kept a princess waiting this long, but I'm afraid your god friend is not exactly easy to talk to." Callum turned, his arms laden with a tray of food. "I thought you'd like a real meal."

She said nothing. Instead, she glared as he pulled one of the crates between them like a table and then another crate for him to sit on across from her.

"Don't look at me like that," he chided. "You know why you're here."

"I do? Then please, enlighten me. Because it seems like you're only keeping me alive because you haven't yet figured out how to get the Deathless One to crack. I'm your last chance at him, aren't I?"

He took his time setting the makeshift table in front of her, making sure that every item was arranged perfectly. There was bread, cheese, grapes, even a few treats that she was surprised he could get here. Like the strawberry jam they'd always had in the castle, her favorite for every toasted slice of bread she had in the morning.

This had always been his tactic with her. He knew that Jessamine hated silence, particularly when she felt like she was in the wrong.

He made her sit in that discomfort, knowing that eventually she would break. How could she not? Just having him in the room with her was oppressive. Callum Quen filled a room with his energy. It was why no one had ever been able to stand up to his interrogations.

And probably the reason he'd been able to command a complete underground society of people who were supposed to be her subjects. There was so much she did not know, but living on the streets of the kingdom was teaching her far more than any of her tutors ever had.

Finally he sighed, cracked his knuckles against the edge of the table, and answered her. "This is just business, Jessamine. That's all."

"Business? My life. My mother's life. Both of those were just business to you?"

"Not . . . entirely." She saw a shadow of the man she knew just then. Like he was uncomfortable with what he'd said before—perhaps there was a shred of humanity still left in him. "Not in the beginning, at least."

"You want me to believe that? No man could have treated us like we were his family and then murdered us in cold blood. It's not right, and it's not true." She crossed her arms over her chest, leaning back against the crates behind her as though this wasn't her prison. "Is your name even Callum Quen?"

"I was born Callum Quen, although these days I'm mostly known as the Butcher of Grimoire Rise."

She refused to feel any pity at the self-hatred she heard in those words. "How long have you been the Butcher?"

"For a very long time." He huffed out an angry breath. "Before I met your mother, I lived here, and I spent every hour of every day protecting myself. Eventually, that grew into a family of sorts, people who knew I would do anything to keep them safe. It didn't start out as what it is now, but that was built out of necessity."

"So you ended up in the castle serving my mother? How?"

"She had something I wanted." He finally straightened, looking more like the vagabond who had thrown her into this room. "And now I think you have it."

As if she was going to believe that for a second. She had nothing other than a connection to the Deathless One, and her mother had certainly not had that. "The only thing I had, you already took from me. Where is my god, Callum?"

"You tell me where the book is and I will tell you where he is."

What book? She didn't have a book. She only had the ones that Sybil gave her and . . .

The one she'd taken from Benji.

The one that was written about the Deathless One himself. Even though it had been empty when she looked into it, there was only one book he could be speaking about. *Her backpack.* They must have it, or someone in service to Callum did. And if they had it, then soon enough, so would Callum.

Schooling her expression into a serene mask, she tried her best to hide her thoughts. "I don't know what you mean. I have nothing from the castle or from my mother. All I have is what I wore on my wedding day. The dress is ruined. And if you mean the ring, I pawned it for safe passage through the sewers, where I washed up after my husband slit my throat."

She had hoped the details of her survival would be enough to distract him. But nothing would lure him from his purpose.

Callum leaned forward, the food and drink forgotten in front of him. "Where is the book, Jessamine?"

She swallowed. "I don't know what book you're talking about."

"Have you no loyalty left to me? Have you forgotten all our years in the sun?" He tilted his head to the side, an almost fanatic expression on his face. "I taught you how to ride. Tucked you in at night. There are a hundred gifts I gave you. I was the father you never had. You owe me."

"If you feel as though you are owed for your kindness, then it is not an act of kindness." Her mother used to say that. She saw when he recognized the words, too, because he flinched as though she'd shot him.

"Jessa, I am running out of time."

"You look fine to me."

"I am the Butcher of Grimoire Rise. This entire district runs under my command. If you lose me, then you lose control over this district. We could still be a team, you and I."

It was a mad bid for her compliance, and he knew it. She knew it.

Jessamine leaned in as well, both of them twin bookends trying to crush the crate between them. "I thought this district was flooded with the infected. That's what all the rumors say, because my *husband* was supposed to turn this entire kingdom into a graveyard."

His throat worked in a swallow, and she knew then that she had him. He didn't want to tell her whatever deal he had made. He didn't want her to know the truth at all.

But then he shifted to sit up straight and pull his shirt over his head. That perfectly pressed fabric revealed bandages beneath. Bandages that were seeping yellow with infection.

She said nothing as he unraveled the cotton that bound nearly his entire torso. And every pass around his body revealed more and more broken pustules. Bleeding, weeping, dripping yellow fluid down his stomach the moment he released the pressure on them.

She tried very hard not to react. In this moment, he deserved nothing less than stoic apathy. But this was the man who had raised her, after all.

"You're infected?" she asked, her voice wobbling only a little.

"I am."

"How long?"

He ground his teeth. "Four months."

"Impossible. People lose themselves in days."

"Not if they have this." He reached into his pocket and slammed a piece of paper down onto the crate. She stared down at it, recognizing the same unreadable language that had disappeared in the black-bound grimoire.

The ragged edges suggested only one thing. "You tore this out of the book?"

"So you have seen it."

"I only know there are spell books we should not touch, and that is one of them. It is meant to be whole and in one piece."

"I know," he snarled. "I read the whole thing. Front to back. Spells to bring back the dead. Spells for immortality. And the spell to bind a god. But I couldn't take the book in that moment. Your mother would have immediately found out, so I thought to just steal a spell or two. The moment I ripped out that page, the whole thing went blank. It was just luck that the spell for stasis was on the back side, but I should have torn out more. It slowed the progression of this infection, but it didn't cure me. A damn shame, since I wasn't infected at the time I ripped out the page. They were useful spells, I'll tell you that. But they are not the spells I need. There is a cure in that book, and I will stop at nothing to get it."

"If there's a cure in the book, why wouldn't you use it to cure everyone?"

His expression twisted, growing uglier by the moment. "After I have cured myself, I intend to. For the right price."

"That's a monstrous thing to say. If the infected can be cured, they should be cured."

"And they will be, if they pay." He stood, picking up his shirt but leaving it off. "Truthfully, I don't give a shit about money, Jessamine. If it didn't make our world turn, I would have renounced it long ago. But money keeps this place going, and I need this place to stay the way it is. I haven't given up my entire life to see this fall apart."

"You bartered my mother's and my life for this?" The question was small and aching as she let it fly free. "To save yourself?"

As he paused in front of the door, she could see the man he used to be. The hesitance in his step, the way his right brow twitched with tension, and how he stuffed his hands into his pockets. He looked like his world had ended. Not from her words, but long ago. Months ago, when her mother had died in front of him.

"This isn't easy for me, Jessa," he replied quietly. "Making a choice like this ages a man. And I know there aren't many years left. Perhaps it makes me selfish that I'm not willing to sacrifice those few remaining years for you or for her."

She didn't know what to say. This wasn't the reasoning she expected. She wanted him to be a real villain. To tell her that he'd been plotting for years against her family, and that he'd never truly loved them.

"Can I ask you something?"

He nodded.

"How long did you know Mother had that book? And how did you know there was magic in it?"

He winced. "Oh, Jessa, you don't want to know the answer to that."

"You said that was why you were in the castle. Why didn't you just take it and go?"

"Because of her." He wasn't looking at Jessamine, but off into the distance, like he could see her mother's spirit standing somewhere close by. "She was a woman to be reckoned with, and the mission got blurry. I kept making excuses not to leave. It was better for me to be in the castle and have a royal in my back pocket, I told myself. I could still run things here through my second-in-command, while still being in the castle. And then there was you. A little girl with dark hair and eyes like a banshee. You both wriggled your way into my soul, and it was so hard to leave you."

"Why didn't you ask her to help?"

"Your mother hated witches more than the average person, and with good reason. She'd lost a lot of loved ones to spells and curses gone awry. That book was meant to be locked up for good. She'd have burnt it if she knew what I was there for."

Oh, how it *hurt* to hear those words. Jessamine hadn't known any of this. She didn't want to know that he had loved them. It made all of this so much worse, somehow, because it meant that he had thought about this, planned it, and chosen to let them go when she had hoped for just a few moments that maybe he hadn't wanted to.

"You're wrong, you know," she finally said, her voice thick with unshed tears. "Doing all that doesn't make you selfish."

She waited until he looked back at her. Until she could see the flicker of some hope in those eyes, like he thought it was possible for them to continue as they once were.

"It makes you a coward. And I never thought you to be one until this moment."

The muscles in his jaw jumped before he gave her a curt nod. "I'm sorry to make you pay for my fear, Jessa. But I won't give up my life. Not even for you."

He left the room empty and cold. She wanted to scream and rage and fling things at the wall, but that was not who she was.

Instead, she sat on the crate in the frigid room as the night fell once more, with nothing but her heartbreak to keep her company.

34

His witch had not come. Not even a response from Sybil.

Elric paced like an animal in a cage. They'd moved him and the runes into a rather lovely room. There were enough beautiful items in here to make even a god feel comfortable. Black silk sheets covered a bed he had no intention of using. Mirrors on every single wall, marked with runes meant to reveal the hidden, though the markings were close to the one that would both summon and trap a god. The floor was clean and covered with a plush rug that he supposed would have cushioned his feet if he could feel anything. Twin couches flanked a large coffee table, while there were intricate silver end tables on either side of the couch that were so brightly polished they gleamed. There were even relics from the last time he'd been brought to life. A painting, a knife, a sword on the wall he'd given to a witch, all items he thought of with fondness.

All of it was meant to cajole a god into doing what they wanted, that old familiar ploy. These people had trapped him, and he hadn't been caught like this since he was a new god. His eyes traced over the walls, but the runes that actually bound him weren't in the room. The etchings around the mirrors were pretty, but they weren't strong enough to keep him. So where was the spell?

The spell that fucking Callum Quen said he'd gotten by tearing a page out of *his* book. The book he should have destroyed years ago, and yet the damned thing continued to come back and haunt Elric at every stage of his life.

He'd forgotten there was even a spell in there for containing a god. A spell that he'd written down with the intent to make his own followers more powerful in case any of the other gods attacked his coven, not to trap himself. How foolish to let it fall into the wrong hands.

The door opened, and he bared his teeth in a snarl at the sight of the man who'd trapped him. Callum Quen. The man had a lot of gall for someone who had angered a god.

"I will peel your skin from your body for this," Elric snarled. "You are going to bow at my feet and whimper for death, but I will not let it take you until I have seen your blood slick the walls and your screams echo throughout eternity."

"The fact that you think that'll come to pass is impressive and yet foolish," Callum replied.

He froze. The other man shouldn't have been able to hear him, let alone look directly at him as though he could see Elric easily. No one could see the Deathless One without being either a worshipper or a gravesinger.

This man was neither of those things, but he defied all reality by looking straight into Elric's eyes.

"Ah, I see the confusion," Callum said before gesturing to the mirrors covering the walls. "The runes. It's not necessarily that I can see you very well, or even that I'm hearing your voice directly. But those runes reveal what is hidden, and with so many of them surrounding you, they bounce what they see and hear out into the room."

How? This man wasn't a witch, so how did he have his hands on such powerful magic?

Callum stepped a little farther into the room. "I might not be a witch myself, but I have met quite a few of them over the years. A little lie here and there convinces them that I have an indirect way to speak with their patrons. Convincing them to give me their magic was rather . . . easy. Hope, you see. It turns people into fools."

Elric ignored the man, who was trying to goad him. Instead, he closed his eyes and set his awareness into the mirrors. Which one of these had been made by those who had once worshipped him?

"What are you doing?" Callum asked.

There it was. Only two mirrors had been created by his followers, but that was enough to make a statement. With only the slightest flex of his powers, he drew on their magic and sucked it back into himself.

With a harsh creak, the mirrors bulged, the image of Elric's form warping before the glass suddenly exploded. Shards flew out into the room, scattering along the floor and striking the walls. Only a few pieces hit Callum, but his enraged shout was satisfaction enough.

A banging hand thundered on the door. "Boss? You all right?"

Callum glared at Elric, bleeding from multiple places. Though he had somehow shielded his face, which was a shame. Elric still watched with pleasure as the man pulled a long shard of glass out of the back of his right arm, a perfect strike. The piece glistened with bright red blood and something yellowing along the edges.

"I'm fine," Callum growled. "The god in the room is just a little unruly, and hasn't yet realized the situation he's found himself in. But he will."

To his credit, the Butcher of Grimoire Rise said nothing else. He just walked to the couches and took a seat, then waved an imperious hand toward the other couch as though Elric was simply an honored guest.

He had no intention of giving this man any energy in the slightest, so Elric stayed where he was, looming over the other man with a sneer on his face.

Callum tried to wait him out, but Elric was no trembling young girl. He was kind to Jessamine because she was his nightmare, and she was well and truly part of his soul now. But this man? To Callum Quen, Elric was the Deathless One. And he would be treated with the respect due to a god.

"I see you have no intention of speaking with me," Callum finally said, leaning forward and bracing his elbows on his knees. "But you have to understand. I have been searching for you for a very long time."

"I am a god," he replied. "All you had to do was pray."

"It's not that easy, though. We both know that."

"Isn't it? A sacrifice here and there, the devotion of a truly loyal follower, these are basic asks. Your kind have forgotten that the gods used to rule these kingdoms, and without us, you have fallen apart." Elric spread his hands wide. "Plague, murder, mayhem. All of it came after my brethren were lost."

Something dark flashed in Callum's eyes. "So you don't know, then?"

What?

He tried not to let his confusion show, because he sensed this was a pivotal moment. If he played his cards right, it would seem like he knew far more than he did. "A magical malady isn't that hard to see, and it's certainly easy enough to follow back to its source. You have not discovered a weakness of mine, merely that you are incapable of believing that a god could know so much."

"Then you know why I've been searching for you."

Elric could puzzle it out. If the Butcher was looking for Elric's book, then he needed a spell that could not go awry. A spell that only a god in chains could conjure.

"You want me to cure you," he said, the shot in the dark landing well as Callum winced. "But you want more than that, and we both know it. The cure is merely an excuse, a front to make yourself feel better about what you really want. You want power, as all men do. Trapping a god will not give you that."

"Will it not?"

"No," Elric growled. "You have hope for yourself, Callum Quen, and I promise you that hope is unfounded. The moment I escape from this trap, and I will, you'll finally understand true pain."

"I have felt pain." Callum stood, although he was still shorter than Elric and therefore the movement didn't give him the advantage he so desperately sought. "What do you know of pain as a god? I have watched people I loved die horrible deaths. I have felt the pain of loss and anguish, a loneliness so deep that you could not fathom the need inside of me to fix it. I will do anything to destroy everyone who stands in my way. And you are going to be my weapon."

"I am no one's weapon." Elric was rattled by the man's words, though. These were the same words he would have said once released from this torment. Callum was a mirror image of himself, much younger and much weaker, but still . . .

So this was the ploy.

Fate had always seen fit to thrust him into fickle situations.

"You cannot use me as a weapon," Elric continued. "I have not been resurrected into this world. What magic I have is linked only to those who sacrifice for me, and that is all. You'd have better luck using Jessamine than me."

"No, I want no one between us." Striding closer, the other man looked up at him with so much confidence it was disturbing. "What if I told you that I can resurrect you?"

"You cannot."

"But what if I could?"

A thousand thoughts ran through his mind in an instant.

Yes. Resurrect him. Let him be free to launch into this world with all the vengeance that he required. If there was a spell that could resurrect him without needing a gravesinger to breathe life into his vacant form, then he should take it. No man who used such a spell could control a god once he was alive.

But what if he could? What if Elric unknowingly chained himself to this foolish, venal man who had plans to use a god in unknown ways?

Underneath all those thoughts was a single, whispering desire: he wanted Jessamine to be the one to do it. He wanted to be connected to her, fully and without question. He wanted to feel their connection pulling through his body at all times. Once summoned, he would wrap himself in the grave scent of her, and together, they would rule a kingdom of bones.

He followed his heart, even knowing that the treacherous organ had only led him wrong in the past. "You cannot summon me, Callum. You are not a witch."

"Ah, so you do not know everything after all."

He watched as Callum made his way to the door. He leaned out, waiting for someone to hand him a threadbare bag that he drew back into the room. It was clearly something that had seen too much use. Mud dripped onto the otherwise pristine floor as Callum opened it, and dirt rained down in a sprinkle of flecks that covered Callum's boots.

"You see, Jessamine was my daughter in every way but blood. Her father left the world all too soon, gods rest his soul, but that left me with an opportunity to take what was once a king's. His wife, his daughter . . . his influence." Callum stuck his hand into the bag, clearly searching for something. "What a shame his death was, I thought, when I first walked into the castle. And then I realized opportunity had always been my strong suit."

"You viewed her as a daughter, and then you watched her be murdered?" Elric spat the words, hoping they landed as sharp as the glass. "What a man you are."

"A sad side effect of saving myself. I understand you think this means I am cowardly or selfish, but there are many people here who need my guidance and help. I have built an empire in this ruined district, and I will not let anyone take that from me." His face morphed into something that looked like pleasure. "No one will ever test me again if I have a god in my back pocket."

"There is still the minor problem that you cannot resurrect me."

It was the last chance he had, even though he had a sick feeling in his stomach about what Callum was about to pull out of that bag. That familiar backpack had been worn the first time he'd seen it and had gotten more ragged in the time Elric and Jessamine had traveled from the sea to here.

Callum pulled the black book out, then let the bag drop to the ground with a clunk. "Ah, and here it is. The book I've been searching for. Who would have thought our little Jessamine had it all this time?"

"It's empty. Even she couldn't read it."

"Because it was incomplete. That's the most interesting part of this book, and the struggle I had in the castle as well. When I first opened it, the damn thing wasn't empty, at least until I maimed it. Then all of a sudden, it was more like a journal than a spell book." Callum flipped through the pages until they fell open to a torn-out page Elric hadn't noticed before. With a flourish, Callum slid a crumpled page from his pocket and placed it inside the book.

Elric could feel the magic swelling in the room, but he could also feel the tug at his navel. The book . . . That damned book could control him.

"Would you look at that? All the pages are back." Callum dramatically turned pages and then tapped his finger on one. "How to summon a god without magic and bind him to your service. What luck that I've finally found this, while I have you already in my grasp."

And they'd delivered it right into his hands.

He lunged. Elric would stick his claws right into Callum's chest and pull out the man's still-beating heart. A feral part of him wanted to devour the muscle, biting into it while this man looked at him in horror. Then he would shove it back into the empty cavity with his teeth marks in the damned organ and force it to beat. The sluggish blood would move through Callum's body like a poison he could never get out of his veins.

But he walked right through Callum. And though the other man gasped, it wasn't enough pain to satisfy Elric.

Callum chuckled. "I see you're angry, and we'll deal with that, eventually. Once you are resurrected, we can talk about some other arrangement. You want to be summoned, don't you? There has to be some revenge you want upon the witches. I've read about you. I know what they did. We can make that happen together. We will destroy this kingdom and rebuild it in our image."

"I will do nothing without her at my side," he snapped.

He had revealed too much.

Something changed in Callum's expression then, his face twisting with mock pity. "Oh, but haven't you read this book? You should have seen it long ago, Deathless One. After all, the only way to summon a god and bind him is to make a great sacrifice. Both of us have to lose something, although I suppose it is unfortunate that I will have to choose for you. I have no connections in this world other than the young woman I consider my daughter. And you? You have no one but a gravesinger who made the mistake of not resurrecting you before me."

"If you touch a hair on her head, I will curse you to an eternity of pain. I will rip you out of that flesh suit and lay your soul down upon a bed of glass and tread upon it every single day. I will grind pain into the very fiber of your being. You will know nothing but torment and beg for release that I will give you none of."

Callum tsked. "Such confidence for a man about to be bound to me. Perhaps the first thing I will do is make you punish yourself for every threat you have given me. It is you who should be careful, Deathless One. For you cannot die, and an eternity is a very long time to be enslaved."

35

Jessamine spent a few days feeling sorry for herself, mostly because she was quite certain that she was going to die in here. They'd forgotten to bring her food for an entire day now. That she could handle, but the water? She'd started standing underneath that window and catching the noxious liquid that splattered in.

Not vomiting the moment it hit her lips was impressive, but it took more effort than she wanted to admit.

Eventually, she just wanted to give up. Nothing was going her way, she wasn't ever going to get out of here, everyone she'd ever trusted had betrayed her, and in the end, did any of this matter? She was supposed to be dead. Dying one more time was probably just fate intervening with a swift *This wasn't supposed to happen. You weren't supposed to happen.*

But those thoughts lasted for all of a few hours before she pulled herself back together again. Because she wasn't the kind of person who could give up that easily. And if anything would make her mother roll over in her grave, it was her daughter backing down from a fight.

She didn't have her spell books or any ingredients, but she was still powerful in her own right. She could still do something with herself, so she started stacking crates, one on top of the other, creating a stair that wasn't remotely safe or sturdy, but it would do.

Then she crawled up to the window and stuck her hand out into the rain. Peering outside, she could see they weren't on a street after all, but an interior courtyard. That was good. There was still rain here, though, and she could use that to her advantage.

Muttering a common chant, she cast an old spell that she'd found in one of the books a while ago. It wasn't much of a spell, really. Just a way to send messages between witches using natural elements, like drops of water.

The rain would take her request to Sybil. It would tell her where Jessamine was, because with this spell, she also cast aside everything she had claimed before. She was no longer a woman who didn't believe in the gods. The gods weren't dead.

There was still one out there.

Dropping the pad of her finger to the metal grating, she sawed her flesh over a rusted edge. "I believe in him," she whispered at the end of the spell. "The Deathless One is the god I worship, and in his name I dedicate this pain and blood."

It wasn't much of a sacrifice, but it bound her to him in a whole new way. She was no longer just a gravesinger now, she was a worshipper. And if she was lucky, maybe that meant she was now part of his coven. Any other god would have scoffed at the meager spike of pain and the smear of blood that was quickly washed away by the rain. But for her? It was everything. She hoped he could feel it, too.

She didn't have to wait long. Nearly an hour later, there was the pitter-patter of feet and a dark face that leaned down to look through the grate. "Would you look at what they trapped in the sewers again?"

"Sybil," she breathed. "I wasn't sure you'd come."

Raindrops gathered like pearls on the twisted strands of Sybil's hair. She had a mask over her face, and already there was magic crackling around her body, cloaking her in shadows as she crouched outside the window.

For all that the Iron Knuckles thought they knew how to contain a witch, they clearly didn't know how to keep them out.

Sybil grinned, her eyes crinkling from behind the mask. "The Deathless One already sent a message to me, love. It took me almost a week to get here once I convinced myself to leave the manor. But your last little spell brought me right to you, which is perfect. Now, do you want to get out of here?"

"I mean, yes. But how are you going to get me out?"

"Magic." Sybil yanked the mask down and shook her head. "How else?"

"I don't know any spell that can turn me invisible. They've got all the lights on in the hall. I can see them underneath the door." She eyed the space between the bars. "And I'm too big to fit through those. If Elric was here, I suppose I could crack all my ribs to get out and then he could piece me back together, but I haven't felt him in ages."

"Neither have I. I suppose you just have to trust that I remember enough spells to get you out." Sybil stepped back a bit, her hands in front of her and more of that magic boiling in her chest. "He gave me just enough, I think. Now if you don't mind, run as soon as it's big enough."

"As soon as what is big enough?"

Jessamine tripped over her own feet, trying to get away from the wall as it rumbled. The very stones of the building, the metal and wood that held it together, groaned as magic forced the entire building to move, creating more space around the window. Just enough for the bars to break free, and suddenly, she could definitely fit between them.

"Trust," she whispered, before bolting up the crates.

Shouts already echoed through the halls behind her, and she knew there were only a few moments before someone blasted through the door.

She threw her body out into the rain just as Sybil released the spell. Breathing hard, the dark witch stared with wide eyes at the damage she'd done while the building creaked around them. They both stared, watching the entire thing sway before it seemed to settle once more.

"Did you almost take down the whole building?" Jessamine asked.

"I think so."

"How did you do that?"

Sybil looked down at her hands and then back to Jessamine. "I have no idea."

Blinking, Jessamine slowly nodded. "Right, we'll answer that question once we're out of here."

"What about the Deathless One?"

"We find him first." She couldn't leave him here. Not when she knew that Callum had some other tricks up his sleeve and that he had the page to the grimoire. Looking between the buildings, she tried to remember where Callum had come out from. "I don't know where they're keeping him, but I can find him."

"I'm the one with the magic right now."

Jessamine would trust Sybil with her life. So, with a sharp nod, they both bolted into the shadows. But Jessamine was slower. Weaker. A day without food and water had her breathing harder than she wanted, and sewed a stitch in her side that just wouldn't let up. As they snuck into one of the buildings, her heart stuttered with a horrible rhythm that wasn't really a beat at all.

"Sybil," she wheezed, holding on to a banister and praying no one would come down the stairs. "I can't keep going like this."

"Jessamine, we have to!"

"We don't even know if he's here. There are five buildings to look through. Just leave me here. Give me the shadows, and I will keep looking for him. But the two of us here are bound to attract—"

Arms wrapped around her waist.

She immediately twisted, trying to kick whoever had grabbed her. But then she looked up the stairwell to see that Sybil had two men around her, too. One had her around the waist, the other was gripping her head and trying to shove something into her mouth. Fabric? A rag?

"Keep them quiet!" Callum's voice thundered from a story above their heads. "Cut out the witch's tongue if you must, but do not let her speak."

Jessamine froze, limp in the man's arms as the others gagged Sybil. She didn't want to make any noise, but she also refused to let them hurt Sybil. If she had to start screaming just to get their attention on her, she would.

Thankfully, Sybil made no noise. She just glared at them with so much hatred, and a tinge of fear that Jessamine knew deep in the very bones of her soul.

She and Sybil were alone. These men could do anything they wanted, and Jessamine was helpless to stop them.

She allowed herself to be dragged through the hallways, struggling only when they entered a large room. There was an altar at the end of it, covered in a white sheet with bowls set on the floor all around it. A hundred candles had been lit, all of them flickering with their movement as the man who held her dragged her closer and closer. It would almost be beautiful if it didn't reek of death.

Finally, she couldn't stand it. "What are you doing, Callum?"

"I thought that was very clear. I am doing what I have to do to make sure this kingdom doesn't fall into complete ruin." He gestured toward the men wrangling Sybil. "Tie her up and get her out of the way, would you? We could use her magic for this, I suppose. So give me clear access to her chest."

Jessamine winced as they ripped Sybil's shirt down the center. Though it bared the jagged crack through her body where her magic was kept, it also bared a breast to their hungry eyes. "This isn't you, Callum. You already sold the kingdom to another, and now you think you can save it?"

"I promised that he could make this his dumping ground," Callum corrected, his eyes not leaving Sybil until she was so tied up that he didn't have to worry about her. "I didn't say I wouldn't then save the kingdom from the madness. I'm going to awaken your god, bind him to me, and then we will be the savior this kingdom has been searching for."

All the puzzle pieces fell into place.

He was sick himself, but then he would weaponize the cure. He'd said he would charge a high price, but she hadn't realized he was going to use Elric to do it.

"You can't bring him here," she whispered, not even fighting as the man dragged her toward the altar. "You need me to do that, and I won't do it. No matter how much you torture me, I will not resurrect him for you. I won't let you bind him."

"I don't need you to resurrect him, and I don't need your help binding him either," he replied with a laugh. "The spell calls for a clean sacrifice, which I assume means body and soul. Dunk the princess in the tub over there, would you?"

She kicked and struggled then, cursing a storm upon the man's head as he shoved her into the metal tub she hadn't noticed in the corner. She flailed her arms, digging her nails into his forearm as he held her underneath the water for a little too long. But he was so strong, and his palm on her head didn't give her any room.

She couldn't breathe. He was going to drown her, and she didn't know where Elric was, so she didn't know if she could even come back.

Finally, he yanked her out of the ice-cold bath. Teeth chattering, she hung limp in his grip like a bedraggled kitten he'd pulled out of a gutter.

The man she had once thought of as her father looked at her with cold eyes. "It's a sacrifice, and I'll admit, I still can see my daughter in her. What a blessing to rid myself of this weakness. Strip her for me and place her underneath the sheet."

And then Callum turned his back on her.

"You will not touch me," she hissed at the henchman, trying her best to pull on the magic Elric had given her. But there was no god to answer her call.

So when he shoved her around and ripped her shirt down the back, she had to admit this was really happening. She was helpless as he did the same to her pants, not even bothering to give her a word of encouragement or pity. Instead, she stood there, desperately trying to hide her body from the eyes of all the other men in the room.

Her gaze met Sybil's, and she knew the other woman was with her. Tears burned in Jessamine's eyes, but they did not fall. Sybil's gaze made her think that the witch had suffered this before. It was either that, or the legacy of centuries of pain that was passed down from generations of women before them. Women who had found themselves at the mercy of those who wanted to hurt them.

"Get on the altar," the man behind her growled.

"No."

"Or I will make you."

Squeezing her eyes shut for a moment, she pulled herself together. She could run, but they would catch her. Even if she did escape, a naked woman running through the streets at night wouldn't get far. There was no magic at her fingertips. All she could do was step up onto the altar and lift the sheet.

She lay down on the rough stone, the icy touch of it going straight through her body. As the thug pulled the sheet over her form, she wondered if she looked like the corpse she was.

At his glance and sudden pale features, she thought maybe she did.

The sheet settled over her face, and she puffed out a breath. "May I please see?"

She didn't want to beg. Please don't let it sound like she was begging.

The sheet peeled back for a moment, revealing Callum leaning above her. He gently cupped her jaw, his thumb stroking over her cheek. "Why do you want to see, dead girl? Nothing good will come of that."

"I want you to know that I am aware of every step of every horrible thing you're about to do. I want you to look me in the eye and know that you're killing me." She swallowed. "That's what you're going to do, isn't it? You're going to sacrifice me, and you're going to regret it for the rest of your life."

That shadow passed over his features. The pain of a man who sincerely regretted something he had to do, and yet he was going to do it anyway. "You're already dead, Jessa. I lost you the day of your wedding."

He gently feathered his fingers over the pale purple circles around her eyes, down the hollows of her cheeks, and over that horrible writhing scar around her neck. She could see he believed every word he said. She wasn't his daughter, not now that she'd survived death itself.

"I'm still me," she whispered. "I'm still the little girl you tucked into bed. Just like this, Callum. I'm still her, and somewhere in there, you're still you."

He shook his head, tears dripping from his eyes and falling onto her cheeks. "No, sweet girl. You're dead. And whatever he brought back is just a twisted replica of the little girl I raised. Sacrificing you is a gift to the entire kingdom, just like the first time you died. I won't let them forget you, Jessamine. But I can't let them have you either."

He straightened, leaving her vision free at least. But then he lifted a black-bound book, and horror bloomed in her chest.

"No," she said, trying to lunge up from the altar. "I can't let you—"

Magic wrapped around her torso, binding her arms to her sides and slamming her back onto the stone. Her ribs creaked, almost cracking with the pressure, and a low whine squeezed out between her lips.

"Don't move," Callum said. "We're lucky to have a witch among us. After all, we'll need her power as well."

He raised his hand, words in the old tongue flying from his mouth.

Then Sybil started to scream.

Jessamine craned her neck, trying to give what little comfort she could to the other woman. But then her eyes widened in horror as she saw all the black magic sucked out of Sybil's chest and flooding into Callum.

All that power, all that magic, pulled and tugged out of Sybil's being. It moved through the room, sluggishly trying to get back to its original owner as Callum drew it to himself. Coiling around his hands, the magic pulsed.

She could see the skin on his fingers peeling away, but he bared his teeth at the pain and looked back at the book.

"Together, we will raise a god," he said, his gaze meeting hers. "This is where your story ends, Princess Jessamine Harmsworth."

And then the sheet moved, covering her face and hiding the nightmare unfolding before her.

36

He hated being summoned by someone who wasn't part of his coven, which was why he ignored the summons sent with Callum's particular energetic signature. He would not listen to a man who thought that a god could be controlled.

But then he felt the first lashing of pain. The ache in his chest was duller than when Jessamine was hurt, but it was an ache nonetheless. He rubbed a hand over his heart, frowning at the sudden feeling. Then the slight bruising sensation on his back, stronger this time and infinitely harder to ignore.

Someone was hurting his girls. He knew what this was. An attempt to draw him to the room where Callum would likely make his last spell. Of course it was. The man was trying his best to force Elric's hand.

And then a tug. No, a yank that threw him through the realms and forced him to materialize at the back of a room. Chairs had been thrown to the sides, and a crude altar raised at the back of it. A stone altar where there was the vague hint of a body lying underneath a white cloth. Callum stood behind the stone, his voice echoing with the old language.

A spell sparked around him, forcing his form into full view. He was no longer hidden from the vision of mortals, and a few of the guards in the room hissed at the sight of him.

"You waste your breath, mortal," he called out as he strode toward the altar. "No ancient spell can bind a god to you, no matter how hard you try."

He thought perhaps to distract the other man, even just for the moments it would take for him to look around and get his bearings. Elric felt off-kilter, like something was terribly wrong and he just hadn't realized it yet. Until he saw Sybil in the back corner as well. Two men stood behind her, their hands holding her upright as her chest cracked wide open. The magic he'd poured into her was nearly gone, wisping through the air to feed Callum's dark spell.

"You're using my fucking magic?" he hissed, as he whipped back to glare at the man in front of him. "You're using my magic to summon me?"

And where was Jessamine? The body on the altar didn't move, so surely it was already dead and that was how Callum had summoned him. Why couldn't he feel her?

"Where is my nightmare?" The growl ripped from deep within his chest.

Callum made eye contact with him, then pulled an athame from his waist. The witch blade was dipped in some black liquid that he didn't recognize, and Callum lifted it over his head. "I sacrifice all that remains important to myself and to the Deathless One. So mote it be!"

The body on the table rose gracefully into the air, with an arched spine that looked more like a dancer than a corpse. Dark hair trailed from underneath the white sheet, and he could just barely make out the beauty of a nude body through the candlelight that glowed on the other side of the sheet. Long limbs, her legs bent, her arms limp beneath her.

Elric had a split second to realize that it was Jessamine on the table. He hadn't felt her. Some spell had fractured their connection. He had always known when she was in the room or how far she was from him. The moment she came back to life using his magic, they were tied. Callum must have hidden their connection, their . . .

The knife glinted in the candlelight, and Elric lunged toward it.

His heart stopped in his chest, squeezing so hard it hurt as his mind raced forward, knowing what was about to happen. He couldn't stop it, no matter how hard he tried—and, by the gods, he tried.

Snapping out his hand, he reached for Callum's just as the athame came close to her chest. He had been quick enough, and hope swelled in him as his hand touched Callum's—only to pass through it. Because he didn't have a form. Because no one had called out to him yet.

The knife struck her chest, and red bloomed across the fabric. Slowly. Sluggishly. As if even her body realized it didn't want to die yet. Of course it didn't. She had scraped and fought and raged against the world to stay here.

He braced himself against the altar. The altar he could touch, though he couldn't rip the bastard out of his skin. He stared down at the sheet that slowly puffed around his little nightmare's face with every breath, still alive, but only barely. The knife remained in her chest. The silver handle mocked him, knowing that he couldn't pull it out even if he tried.

For the first time in all his endless years, he had lost. He'd been bested by a mortal who would likely now enslave him, and all he could think about was that he had lost her.

Elric wanted to fall onto his knees and mourn her. He'd never wanted to mourn anyone before—he'd rejoiced in every death of every witch who had been connected to him. Even if they were his subjects, he . . . he had never liked them.

But he liked *her*. Quite a bit. And now she was gone because they had both been foolish enough to believe she could do this without him.

He turned his head to look at Sybil, who knelt there panting now that the spell was done. The two men behind her had allowed her to sag in their grip, although she remained on her knees with her eyes locked on Jessamine's still form.

"You are the Deathless One," she said, her words ragged and slow. "And she is your chosen witch."

He wanted to tell her that he was stuck here. He couldn't go to his realm because this mortal man had found a book he should never have gotten his hands on. There were old ways to bind him, ones that he had never wanted shared.

Thousands of years had not prepared him for this. Everyone who had ever wanted to summon him had the same intent. They would allow him to grow in power and glut him with all the things that he required to do so, and then he would lie down and let them slit his throat.

They'd never used someone else against him. He had never suffered like this. And he did not know what to do.

"I am sorry," Callum said, his voice pitched low as though he was afraid someone might overhear. "I hate to lose her again, but she isn't the child I knew. You brought her back as a witch, a monster, someone I don't even recognize. It is a mercy that she returns to where she was supposed to go. She was meant to die that day."

Elric looked down at her, his heart shattering in his chest. He'd never known pain like this.

Mortals spoke of heartbreak all the time. He'd always thought the word was silly. No organ could break inside a body, and he'd always thought them dramatic or fanciful for even saying such a thing. But now he knew they were right.

A heart could break. It could shatter into glass shards that tore at him from inside his ribs. Every breath hurt. Every thud of his heart beating was a reminder of her loss and that he was standing here, watching her die, and this time, he wouldn't be able to bring her back.

He drew his hands over the sheet, knowing she could feel him touch her like this. "I can't get to you in time," he whispered in her ear. "He's caught me here, in this realm, for now. So fight for me, nightmare. Fight to stay in that realm no matter what chases you down or hunts you in that shadowy world. Do not let the gods bring you somewhere I cannot follow."

Callum reached for the athame and gripped the handle to rip it free. "Sweet words for a man who has no control."

He felt the knife as though it were sliding out of his own chest. Knew the sensation of warmth that spread like a blooming rose over her body. He pressed his hands there, trying his very best to hold the blood in, even though he knew nothing could save her now, not even him. Not while this magic bound the both of them.

"Why won't you speak?" he whispered, his voice thick with emotion. "I would end the world to hear your voice, nightmare."

One of the henchmen behind him chuckled and muttered, "What kind of woman must that have been to have a god begging for her?"

He ignored the man, even though he wanted to turn his tongue to ash in his mouth. "The world has never met a woman like you before, Jessamine Harmsworth. You should not have ended like this."

"Which time should she not have died?" Callum asked, cleaning the blade off on his shirt. "It's been so many now, it's hard to keep track."

With a glare that should have been a warning, Elric opened his mouth to let more empty threats fill the room. Except he couldn't say a word while Callum started speaking in the old language. A pull, a tug, a ripple deep inside his body flared wide.

He remembered this feeling. This summoning that would resurrect a god into a new form. A form where he could touch, and taste, and eat. He could do anything he wanted in this form, or always had, but he knew that Callum summoned him to bind. He waited to feel those chains looping around his neck and wrists.

Elric had been bound to another before, and likely would be again. Witches would always seek to thread their fate together with his, twining them together until the end of all time. He knew what they wanted. A god at the end of a chain they held, but he had never been bound to someone who wasn't a witch.

There would be long years in the service of this man. He would do monstrous and terrible things in the name of someone who did not deserve to hold the chains of his life. Throughout all of it, he would mourn the loss of an exceptional woman while he tried to hold on to the faint flavor of her life. Absinthe and lilies and bittersweet revenge.

The last words of the spell dropped, and he felt the hardening in his body, the sudden power that flowed through him far greater than ever before. He lifted a hand, watching as the black smoke of his form slowly revealed skin underneath. Warm skin. Skin that flexed and moved and *felt*. He should be happy. Revel in the glorious sensation of being alive once more.

And yet, all he could feel was a single tear that slid down his cheek.

Nearly boiling, it seared a trail to his jaw, where he knew he would wear the scar for the rest of his existence.

Callum stared at him, his eyes wide with a hunger for power. "Kill the witch," he ground out. "Just to make sure there's no more of your coven left."

He waited to feel the insistence of the binding spell, one that would force him to do this man's bidding. But it did not come. He stood there, in complete and utter defiance of an order, and he knew that he need not do what this man said.

Slowly, he looked down at the sheet covering Jessamine's body. There, just barely, was the smallest hint of a rattling breath as his warrior of a woman struggled to stay alive long enough to give them a chance.

To give *him* a chance.

He leaned down, gently pulling the fabric from her face so he could look into those beloved dark eyes that had freed him from centuries of torment long before she resurrected him.

"Hello, my ruthless woman," he murmured. "If you've still got some fight left in you, open your eyes."

"What is happening?" Callum spluttered, the athame clenched in his hand like that would do anything to protect him. "I summoned you, Deathless One. I order you to kill that woman. Your power is mine to control!"

Jessamine slowly blinked first one eye, then the other open, clearly struggling to do even that. Perhaps she barely clung to the thread of life that grounded her here. But she let him know that she wasn't done yet.

And then, just the barest of whispers. He heard the words no one else could speak. The words that only a gravesinger knew in her hour of need, a desire that boiled through hundreds of years. Witchcraft at its very essence, the core of who she was.

Jessamine Harmsworth drew upon the history of her people and her kind. She whispered with a hundred voices, a hundred witches who had summoned him before.

"Deathless One, I summon you."

A feral grin spread across his face. "Then as above, so below." He pressed his hand to his chest, drawing out a ball of shadowy power that clung to his fingers. And with the last words of his spell, he pressed life back into her. "As within me, so without."

His magic lanced through her, powering into her veins and rippling through all her wounds. He could feel it sealing the jagged edges of the bleeding tissue over her heart. The magic pieced her together slowly but surely, giving him just enough time to look up and glare at Callum.

The man took a step back, but then stiffened his spine. "You are mine, Deathless One. The spell is complete. I have resurrected you."

With the slightest of movements, Elric hopped up onto the altar and crouched above Jessamine's body like a bird of prey. "No, you didn't, Callum Quen. She did."

His body rippled and surged with power. Lunging forward, he wrapped his hands around the other man's neck and squeezed. Shadows peeled out of Callum's eyes, yanked from his mouth, memories of all the horrible deeds he'd ever done. For a moment, Elric mused, it looked like he'd ripped Callum's shadow from him, suspending it just so Callum could see the ugliness inside himself before he slammed it back into his body.

"I promised you death," Elric growled, magic ripping from his body in giant tendrils that snapped out behind him. Gurgling sounds erupted through the room as each henchman fell to their knees, choking on shadows that crawled into their mouths and wrapped around their tongues. "But then you had to try to kill her. Don't you know? I'm the only one who gets to decide when she dies . . . and when she lives."

Elric tossed Callum so hard into the wall that the studs cracked around him. Plaster and splinters of wood rained down on his head, though he doubted the man noticed over the pain in his shattered ribs. Elric would do more than knock the breath out of his lungs.

Looming forward, he let all that rage flow through his body, warping his form into something larger, bigger than he'd ever been before, and made entirely of slick, oily shadows. "I told you I was going to peel you out of that skin. But first I want to hear you scream. I don't want to hear you speak, though. So I will take your tongue. Then I will flay your throat open so I can watch you gulp in terror every time I come near you. I will pull your ribs open, one by one, forcing the bone to bend but never break, so you know the pain that I felt the moment you tried to kill her."

He was a creative god. Callum Quen would know pain unlike any being alive had ever felt before.

Until a soft hand touched his back, and all his shadows snapped back into his form. The men behind Elric wheezed, falling onto their hands and knees as they sucked in whatever air they could get. But he didn't care what they were doing, or what they would do after. All he cared about was the tiny woman standing next to him, naked and impossibly powerful.

An avenging goddess stood beside him. And who was he not to kneel at her feet?

"I don't want him dead," she said, her voice ringing out in the room. "I want his memories. I want to know everything he knows about what is happening to my kingdom and where we go from here."

"He deserves to die," Elric replied. And for a moment, he was furious that she would ask this of him. This man had touched her. He'd made her bleed.

Elric would make him suffer for that.

But then her hand slid up and down his back, and everything eased in his mind again. She was well. She was alive. He could see it in the long lines of her body, the strength in her belly, which flexed as she moved, and the shimmering, writhing scars just underneath her ribs, higher over her breast and heart, and again around her throat.

Three deaths.

A trinity of pain that had brought her to this moment.

He took one step back from her, then another, before slowly sinking to his knees. "What do you wish of me, witch?"

Eyes glimmering with retribution, she turned her attention to the man still stuck halfway through the wall. "Callum Quen, you told me you had become a coward because of your fear. I want all your memories that are connected to that emotion. Each and every one. I will leave you with whatever else remains."

Though still wheezing, the man's eyes widened. "That will leave me with nothing."

"Then you will be a simpleton walking the streets begging for food. Everyone will remember who you once were. The Butcher of Grimoire Rise. A man who rose so high that for a brief moment he touched the sun, only to melt and fall to earth. They will know who you are now. A man who failed, and who now suffers in his failure." She swallowed, her hand rising to press against the wriggling scar over her heart. "I am merciful, because you will remember all that you did. To everyone else you will be nothing more than a child in the body of an old man, a doddering fool whom they pity. But you will know who you really are."

Elric had thought his torture creative, but he had never thought she would bid him to do this. Callum Quen was a man who lived with pride that he had built an empire beneath himself out of a city made of dust and bones. Now, she would take that all away and leave him with nothing.

"I will build it again," Callum wheezed. "I did it once. I will do it again."

She walked up to him and knelt, her dark hair tangling around her form and giving her the look of some feral goddess who had selected her chosen prey. "What did you say to me? You've already run out of time, Butcher. You are old, and your days are numbered."

His face turned white, blanching with fear and loathing even as Elric loomed over her shoulder. He cursed them both, hissing and spitting out obscenities that eventually faded as Elric passed his hand over Callum's face.

He pulled the memories out of the older man, pushing them toward Jessamine so she could breathe them in as she had before. Her ribs expanded, tiny hollows in between the thin bones rippling with movement as she sucked them inside herself. Stealing memories and power from the man who had helped end her life.

She tasted his fear on her tongue, the acrid flavor burning with the memory of when he'd been infected. She walked with him as he hid his wound, knowing that his time was short. The wonderful flare of hope when he knew there was a chance to live, and the connection with Leon, who had somehow found out about his infection. Tears gathered in her eyes along with Callum's despair at knowing he only had the one choice: he had to betray those he loved.

But through all of it, she saw a weak man. A man willing to hurt others so he didn't have to suffer, and righteous fury heated her blood. This was right. It was his time to end.

And then the Butcher of Grimoire Rise was no more. Instead, he slumped against the wall, an innocent smile on his face.

"'Allo?" he asked, that grin turning slightly dopey. "Who we got 'ere, then?"

She stood and turned away from him, the long tail of her hair swishing below her spine as she strode toward Sybil and held out a hand for the woman to take. "Come, my sister. We're leaving this place."

"And the others?" Elric asked, practically vibrating with his need for vengeance. "Those who helped him?"

Dark, haunted eyes turned to look at him. The deep purple bruises around those black eyes seemed to deepen. "Kill them all."

37

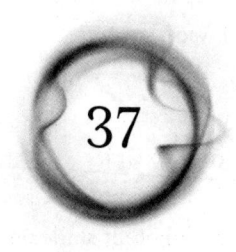

"You are coming home?" Sybil asked, drawing her hood up over her face.

"I have matters to attend to first."

"Your familiar misses you."

She smiled, the soft expression feeling odd on her face while she knew men were dying in droves in the buildings behind them. She'd taken clothing off one of their dead bodies, after all. But the moment she stepped out into the morning light, she tilted her head up to the sky and breathed in fresh air.

"I wish to be free of this for a few moments," she whispered. "I want to let it all go for a few hours before I dive back into fighting for a kingdom."

When she looked, Sybil wore a grin on her face. "Then run, gravesinger. Let your god chase you, and may you both be blessed with what you find at the end of the hunt."

Jessamine didn't question the desire. She just bolted down the alleyways of the Factory District. Before anyone noticed the two women who left behind a building full of dead bodies, before the screams woke anyone up. Of course, there would also be the rumors of black magic clinging to the skin of every dead man in those buildings. But it would take a while for people to understand that a god had returned.

She raced through the dark streets. Alive. Having faced death multiple times, she now knew there was no fear of the end. She would fight for this kingdom, for her people, and no one was going to stop her.

Sprinting past shop owners who had woken early to open their stores,

Jessamine felt more alive than she had before she'd died the first time. Power crackled at her fingertips. Strength flowed through her veins, all because she was connected to him.

A god.

A deathless god who had not only saved her life again, but shed a tear when she died. What did that mean? She had no idea. She only knew that he had told her to fight for him, and if the beating rhythm of drums in her chest wasn't a warning, she didn't know what it was.

It was impossible to ever truly love a god. He wasn't a creature who would be satisfied with something so mundane. She loved her mother. She had even loved Callum once.

What she felt for Elric was beyond that. It blended obsession and need and the greatest surge of want that she had ever felt in her life. Just as she had summoned him, now she wanted him to summon her.

She was ready to kneel before her god. She wanted to worship him as only she could.

Elric had gifted her with more than life. He'd given her knowledge and power so unlimited, it was almost unfathomable. He was the end and beginning of all things in her life.

She couldn't imagine why she'd been fighting this for such a long time.

It took hours for her to get out of the Factory District, then another day to get through the Water District without anyone seeing her. Jessamine didn't stop once, even as she backtracked and moved into different parts of the districts that she'd never been in before. She didn't feel like she had to. She wasn't breathless or tired, nor did her body need food or water. She was full of magic and power, and every time the moon came out, she swore something in her cast silvery tendrils out into the world.

Magic sang at the tips of her fingers and burst out of her chest. She *was* magic. Power was in the very core of her.

Now she understood. She realized why so many witches were willing to do whatever it took to get more of this. But oh, there was power in him, too. Power in having a partner who wanted her, needed her, *had mourned her*.

Finally, she stopped at a cliff's edge, overlooking the sea. Just to her right was the shadowy outline of her former home. The castle stood at the edge of the sea, open to the elements there and surrounded by stone walls.

Was the king still there? The foolish man who thought he could overthrow her with a coup rooted so deeply in her court it was hard to find its seed? The rat's nest she had to untangle was firmly knotted. But now she had all the tools she needed.

"Soon," she said, her voice carrying on the wind toward her home. "Soon you will be mine again."

A hand coiled around her throat, strong, scarred fingers flexing against her skin. She knew exactly who it was the moment he touched her. How could she not? He was so deeply ingrained in her skin, she would know him from anyone else.

Leaning back into his grip, she trusted him to take her entire weight.

"Say it again," he growled into her ear.

"That castle is mine, and soon we will take it back."

A low hum rumbled against her back. His hand slid down her throat, gliding between her breasts and down her belly. That scarred hand caught on the fabric of her shirt, dragging it lower with him until he flattened his palm between her hips.

A swift tug was all it took for him to press her back against him. The hard bar of his cock ground into her back as he shifted her against him, slowly rocking them together as his fingers slipped lower between her legs. "You resurrected me, nightmare."

"I did." She kicked her legs a little wider, one slipping over the edge of the cliff and dangling over the waves. But he held her, and wouldn't let her die anyway, even if she fell all that way to the crumbling rocks below. She'd plummeted into those waves once before and survived it.

Another low growl against the side of her neck had her pulse racing as he kicked her feet even wider. "You and I have unfinished business."

"What's that?"

His hand flexed around her throat, holding her almost too tightly to breathe. Stars sparkled at the edges of her vision.

"The last time I had you in my embrace, you made me get on my knees for you." His lips pressed to her racing pulse as his fingers slid even lower. "Now I have questions for you."

"What questions?"

"Are you willing to die for me?"

"Yes," she moaned, and he finally cupped her between her legs. His pointer finger lazily traced circles around her clit, tiny little movements that sent lightning scattering through her body. "Because you'll bring me back."

"Will you destroy this kingdom for me, just as you promised when I gave you back your life?" His tongue traced a line up her neck, then he sucked her earlobe into his mouth. "Will you become a villain with me?"

She'd promise him anything. Anything if only he would touch her a little harder, grind into her palm as she wanted him to do. She needed friction. She needed to release this powerful energy that was building inside her until it was almost painful. "Yes," she whined. "Yes, I will destroy this kingdom with you."

"Good." He bit down hard on her neck. "Because we're going to build it in a new image with a glorious witch as its queen."

A pulse of power rocked over her, shredding her clothes into ash that coated her body with little streaks of black. Just like she'd been in that realm with him, while he was trapped in the shadows and he couldn't really see her. Taste her.

Touch her. Like this.

Jessamine let her eyes flutter closed and just *felt*. The same pulse of power had dissolved his clothing as well. Now she could feel the hot brand of him against her flesh, the heavy weight of his cock pressing against her back and the warmth of his muscles surrounding her. She could feel every twitch and flex he made as she arched against him, and feel every groan echo into her.

His fingers delved between her legs, plunging into her wetness with an almost obscene sound. But it didn't matter, because he was behind her, holding her above the edge of a cliff, and all she wanted was to come apart in his arms like she had before.

His free hand came up to palm her breast, the pinching sear of his fingers against her nipple sending even more sensation spearing through her body. She tilted her head back against his shoulder, panting as he toyed with her.

"Come for me, nightmare."

She opened her eyes, watching as he stared down at her form. His eyes lingered on the swells of her breasts, at the sight of his wrist working between her legs, and she did almost come on command.

"No," she whispered, wrapping an arm around his neck and drawing him down for a kiss. "I want to come with you inside me."

His cock kicked against her back, but then he shifted his grip. Both hands grasped her by the hips, and suddenly she was lifted, her back still braced against his chest, but now his cock was between her legs.

The broad head of him nudged at her entrance, teasing her with subtle strokes that weren't anywhere near enough. He was big, so veiny it made her mouth water, and still, she wanted to feel him split her open.

"No," he growled, suddenly spinning her in his arms so she had her arms and legs looped around him. "You're going to scream my name when you come, but first let's give you one last test, my nightmare."

And then he walked them off the cliff.

The wind whipped through her hair, obscuring her vision of anything but him and the darkness that surrounded him. And though they were plummeting toward their death, surely about to dash themselves to pieces on the rocks below, she still kissed him with every inch of passion in her body. And then, right when they were about to hit the stones, she felt the shift of magic as they blinked out of existence and he impaled her.

He truly was larger than she'd expected. Her core spasmed around him, suddenly full to near splitting, and it still wasn't enough. A low whine ripped from her throat. Passion rode her hard. He slammed into her harder.

She didn't know when or where they'd landed, but all she knew was that there was something for her to lean on now as he thrust inside of her. His pace was punishing, but his gaze on hers held the heat of a thousand suns. He wanted to consume her. To bury himself so deep inside her that they were the same person.

"More," she said, wrapping her hand around the back of his neck and bracing him closer to her. "Harder."

He flashed her a feral grin and then snapped his hips forward. Deeper. Harder. He stared into her eyes as he praised her. "Look at you, witch. You take me so well, so deep. Never felt like this."

"It's been two hundred and seventy-five years, Elric."

"Never," he emphasized, wrapping his arm underneath her hips and arching her deeper. "Only with you."

Tendrils of shadows rolled over her body. They wrapped around her wrists, holding her in place for the others that played over her breasts, coiling around her clit and rubbing hard. She moaned, an orgasm spiraling higher and higher.

"Elric," she cried out.

"Again, nightmare."

"Elric!" This time it was a scream as her entire body clenched around him, squeezing so hard around him that he jerked to a halt inside of her.

But she made sure she kept her eyes open so she could see him curl into her. So she could see the way his eyes squeezed shut, and he clenched his jaw on a long groan. The sensation of him coming inside her, seeing the way it affected him, sent her spiraling into another earth-shattering orgasm. She clenched even harder and then tried to breathe through the sensation.

"That's my girl," he whispered, lifting her in his arms until she straddled his hips. "Fuck, you are perfect."

She breathed him in, holding on to him a little harder as it all hit her that he was here. He was real. This wasn't just her who could touch him, but everyone. He was a god who had come to life, all because of her.

"You're here," she whispered against his sweat-slicked shoulder. "You're really here."

He held on to her a little tighter. "For better or worse, you resurrected a god, Jessamine."

She still didn't know if that was a good or a bad thing, but at the moment she didn't care. She adored him. Was obsessed with him. Couldn't manage if he was far from her because he'd stripped her completely out of her body and turned her into this wild and wicked witch who wanted the world on its knees.

And she liked it. She liked all of it.

Biting her lip, she nodded firmly. "We have work to do after this, and I think I'm going to need you with me. Really with me."

"Is that so?" he said with a chuckle, leaning back enough so that he could feather his fingers over her jaw. "It feels so much better to touch you like this."

She smiled, suddenly overwhelmed with shyness. "Different from what you thought?"

"Better than I hoped." He trailed his fingers to her collarbone, following the hollow and shadows there. She arched into him as his hand moved to cup her breast, then slowly traced down the lines of her stomach. "I have yet to taste you here, and I intend to spend hours doing so. You are no longer entirely mortal, Jessamine. You're connected to a god."

"Why are you warning me about that?" she asked, breathless.

"Because I don't know if a person can die from coming too many times." His eyes darkened. "But I intend to find out."

She blinked a few times, trying to clear the haze of passion and desire for a few moments so she could see where they were. She looked to the right as his mouth came toward her. While he busied himself with kissing the long line of her neck, she asked, "Where are we?"

"Cave," he murmured.

"Cave where?"

"Near the manor."

"Oh." So they were.

The cave was rather clean, and there were carvings on the wall that suggested witches had been here before. Protective runes and piles of furs that had rotted in the years since someone had last been here. It was unseasonably warm, though, and she wondered if there was a hot spring nearby. Because the air was humid, sticky, and warm enough that she didn't mind being completely naked here.

She looped an arm around his neck. He was already hardening inside her, and the sensation was rather distracting. "You can shadow walk?"

"Something like that. Where shadows are, so can I be." He bit her hard where her shoulder and neck met. "Do you wish to talk more or can I enjoy the feel of you?"

"You may enjoy the feeling of me in a few moments." But she reached between them, her fingers squeezing around the thick width of his cock so she could shift up and down, just a few strokes to tease the both of them. "Callum's memories."

"Dismal, I imagine."

"Yes." He pushed up into her, leaning back on his palms from where he knelt with her in his lap. Spreading his legs a little wider, he forced her to spread on top of him. His eyes didn't move from where he impaled her, other than to flex his thighs and move just a bit more. Watching himself enter her.

What was she saying?

Right. "He worked closely with a courtesan who frequented the courts. A cousin of mine. She always hated me, and I could never figure out why. Turns out she was sleeping with the man I was supposed to marry."

"Add it to the reasons we're going to kill him."

"Exactly." She braced herself on his thick thighs. "They call her the Poppet Keeper, but her name is Fortuna Beaumont. She's the next person we need to find. She's the closest to Leon Bishop, and she'll know everything. How he killed me, who worked with him—and how to take him apart."

His hand framed her neck again, squeezing her throat with a straight arm that flexed with powerful muscles. He pushed into her lazily, the rhythm as teasing as it was maddening. "You want to kill him with me, feral thing?"

"Yes," she moaned. "I want to destroy the world with you."

Acknowledgments

Writing a book is never truly done alone, and there are so many people here to thank that I will likely forget them all. Abby, your editing skills have made this book so much better, and I am forever grateful for you putting up with all my questions and the many, many emails that I sent. Rachel, I am forever thankful fate sent me your way. You have been invaluable in so many stages of my writing journey, and I am so excited to continue working together.

An overwhelming amount of thanks to my partner in crime and in life, Tate. You spent way too much time listening to me go over scenes in this book, dealing with me reading you parts of the story so you could act them out for me to make sure the verbiage was right, and just generally supporting me along the way.

For my parents. I told you I'd make it big someday, and you never doubted me for a single moment.

Keep reading for a sneak peek at the next book in the Gravesinger series

THE HEARTLESS ONE

EMMA HAMM

Coming soon from Gallery Books!

1

Dappled sunlight was just as he remembered.

The crystalline patterns of golden rays broke through emerald leaves and scattered across Elric's features. Sparks filled his vision when he stared at them for too long, but that was just part of the beauty. A little pain was worth every sacrifice to be *alive*.

Lying in the grass, he felt every blade that brushed his skin. He could smell the greenery that grew around him and hear the wind blowing through the leaves. Oak stars rustled in harmony with the rhythmic twitters of birdsong. The brush of the wind over his bare chest cooled the sweat from his skin. And the sapphire sky above him was dotted with fluffy clouds that drifted over his head. Boats on the sea of the sky, they gently rocked forward as he watched them.

Fingers slid through his hair, carding through the thick strands that were longer than the first time he'd taken this form. There were changes in this body, but not as many as the last time. He'd been different in every reincarnation, but this time, he wanted to resemble his previous form. It was the ones humans were most likely to recognize, after all.

And maybe it was because this form was the one Jessamine had seen. This body was the one she had looked upon as a statue, the one that had made her blush. Some part of him wanted to see that blush for him and not just for his marble facsimile.

His head rested in Jessamine's lap. She'd been leaning on one hand, staring up at the clouds with him as they silently enjoyed each other's company. They'd beaten Callum only a few days ago, and everything had been a tangled mess of preparing for their next step, trying to get Elric used to this new body, and finding Sybil. He had less time with her to himself than he'd wished.

Jessamine's fingers worked through a tangle at the end of the strands before she sighed. "Is it everything you remembered?"

He knew what she was asking. Life. Living. Was breathing in the crisp air everything he had dreamed it to be?

Of course it was. It was everything that he had missed, and far more than that. This life surged through him in pulses of magic and power. He wanted to consume it. To devour every part of living for the moment he wouldn't be here anymore.

And yet, there was another part of him that feared losing all this. If he was too close to this life, if he enjoyed it too much, then he would only suffer more when he returned to that realm of darkness.

Her fingers slipped from his hair to his temples and gently lifted his face. Elric was forced to look up into those dark eyes that saw too much. But gods, what a view.

Jessamine truly was a nightmarish witch. After their fight with Callum, she'd embraced everything it was to be a gravesinger. Her wild, dark hair billowed around her face like smoke. His mark around her neck fairly glowed, silver now, as though he'd locked a metal collar around her throat. It was a sure sign that she was as bound to him as he was to her. His gravesinger.

A tiny spark of magic trailed through her fingers, zinging along his skin as she traced the outline of his jaw. "I can tell what you're thinking," she murmured. "This is not a fleeting moment. This is yours. I have gifted it to you, and I will not take it back."

"I know," he whispered, pressing a kiss to her inner wrist and lingering there for a few moments. He filled his lungs with her grave scent before adding, "But it will take a while to believe, witch."

"How you break my heart, dear one." As though compelled, she leaned down and pressed a kiss to his lips.

They lingered there together, connected only by a soft, plush touch.

But it was everything he needed to fill the stores of magic in him again. He breathed her in. All that power, just simmering under her skin, built there by a connection that was only growing stronger by the day.

She was more than just a witch, and she knew that. She was *his* witch.

When she drew back for a breath, he drank in the dazed expression on her face. He'd seen so many women in the throes of passion, and witches who tried to pretend they were. He knew what a liar looked like, and he'd learned to read humans in his many centuries of life.

Jessamine was as truthful as they came. Her blown-out pupils and that drunken smile as she stared down at him were genuine.

What was he supposed to do with her, other than wrap his hand around the back of her neck and draw her down for another kiss?

Her exhale became his inhale. They became linked through breath as he explored the depths of her mouth. He could taste the passion in her kiss. He could feel it as magic sparked between them, another electric zap that made every muscle in his body tense.

Of all the experiences in life, this was what he had missed the most. A connection with another person, but even more than that, a connection with *her*. In that shadow realm, he'd never been able to taste her, never clearly heard the little sighs that caught in the back of her throat as he touched her. He'd never felt how soft her hair was or seen how vividly her eyes glowed in the shadows of his realm. They were dark, haunting orbs that he wanted to drown in.

What a beauty he had captured. What a stunning gravesinger to draw into his life. Perhaps there was still a lingering presence of the gods in this world, because certainly he was not the one to have wished her into being.

She drew back, her fingers lingering on his jaw. "What are you thinking?"

"Merely about your beauty."

"I am hardly the princess I once was," she replied with a soft laugh. "You should have seen me in the castle."

"A prim princess, meandering about the halls? You must have been waiting for something exciting to happen every day. No, I choose to see you as you are now." His fingers tangled in the hair at the back of her neck, arching her head away so he could press his lips to the swanlike stretch of her throat. "Wild and undone."

That sigh. That soft, lingering sigh she always gave when he kissed her made him feel like a god again.

He reveled in this feeling, the knowledge that he was alive and well and that nothing was going to change that. Even if he had to scrape on his hands and knees to stay this way, he would. He would beg if she needed him to.

Something scratched at the back of his mind. Fingernails trailed down the entirety of his body. He could feel them dragging down his neck, his shoulders, his back. Such a touch should be impossible. Unless . . .

He sat straight up, nearly cracking their heads together as he realized what it meant.

"Elric?" she asked, her hair falling in front of her face before she shoved it impatiently over her shoulder. She stared at him with those big eyes. For a moment, he was shocked she hadn't felt it, too.

But how could she? Jessamine was a gravesinger, but she had not tied herself to any coven. She wouldn't be able to feel the presence of another witch unless they were near. She couldn't know how it felt like a ghost had ripped its talons along his entire soul.

"Elric?" she asked again, this time sounding far more concerned than the first time. "What is it?"

"Another witch," he murmured. "Someone is worshipping me."

Fear rippled through his body at knowing there was another witch who had tried to connect with him, even though it was a good thing. The more people who sacrificed in his name, the stronger he would become.

The wells of his magic were deep and old, but that did not mean they were endless. Witches who sacrificed in his name gave energy to him. Already he could feel his power growing, surging. It was a heady cocktail indeed.

This was a determined witch. She had gone off into some field and taken a man's prized cow. The beast had been the best producer of milk, better than any other in the herd. Someone had given the animal attention and reverence, so its death meant far more in the grand scheme of magic.

"She's sacrificing a cow to me," he muttered, his vision almost gone as he focused on the sensation of what the witch was doing.

"You can feel that?" Jessamine asked, reaching out to hold his hand as though that might help ground him. "What is she doing, Elric?"

"She wants something. They all do."

But what did she want?

Inside his mind, he heard the old words spill from her tongue, and in that moment he knew this wasn't some hapless girl who had found a spell book and thought she would try it out. This woman had been taught.

The sacrificial spell had to be spoken in a particular language. Anyone reading those words would have stumbled over them or pronounced them wrong. But this woman's recitation was nearly perfect. A strong spell. One that flowed throughout the realms of the living and the dead to greet him.

Whispered words glided through his mind as the witch called out to him for aid. "God of the dead, the Deathless One himself, I ask you to cast pity upon a poor worshipper who has long forgotten the old ways. I beg your forgiveness in my lack of worship for too many years. I have nearly lost the dearest person to me, and I pray that you might fight on my behalf to tear away the darkness that follows her. I beg of you to fight death so that I might have more time with her."

"She wishes for me to stop someone from dying," he muttered. "It is a simple request. I will ignore it."

"Ignore it?" Jessamine's hand tightened on his arm. "Elric, this is the first time someone has worshipped you in centuries."

"Sybil worships me."

Speaking of the witch, he could already see her sprinting toward them out of the house. She held her tattered skirts above her knees as she ran, her hair nearly tumbling out of the knot at the top of her head.

He watched Sybil struggle to get to them, remaining seated even when Jessamine stood. Although he did note his gravesinger cast an unimpressed glance in his direction.

"You're going to make her run all the way out here?" Jessamine asked.

"Yes."

"We could meet her at least halfway."

"She is the one who chose to run to my side, Jessamine."

"That doesn't mean you have to sit there like an ass," she hissed. "Clearly something is wrong."

He reached out and wrapped a hand around her ankle, pinning her in place when she might have started toward the other woman. "Jessamine, I am a god. I do not rush to anyone's side but yours. Ease your tone, gravesinger, and be assured the only person I serve is you."

Soon enough, Jessamine would need to come to terms with what it was to be paired with a god. They were above others. Not just because they were more powerful, but also because of what they could do. A single word from her, and he would raze the entire world to nothing but brimstone and ash. She was not a normal woman anymore.

But then again, she never had been. He wondered how her mother had taught her that being a princess was not the same as being a woman.

Sybil finally reached their side, breathing hard, her eyes wild as she stared at him. "Did you feel it?" she asked, sounding frantic. "Tell me you felt it as well."

"I felt it."

Jessamine looked between the two of them. "You can both feel it when someone is making a sacrifice?"

"It's more than that," he replied, leaning back on his palms and tilting his head to the sun. "A witch sacrificing to me makes ripples throughout the entire coven. She's already dedicated her magic to me, and therefore my coven, if she's making a sacrifice like this. Which means not only can I feel it, but so can the rest of the coven. In this case, Sybil."

"Another witch is sacrificing to you, Deathless One," Sybil interrupted.

He could almost feel the reverence with which she said the words. But they provoked an icy tendril of fear. The emotion was a ghost that walked with him through every step of his life. Witches always wanted to build their family. They wanted more women and more witches and a larger coven. They wanted a bigger house and more power, magic that streamed through them all until they couldn't use all of it in a lifetime.

They wanted all of that and more. Because witches always *wanted*.

They devoured the world, and even then, it wasn't enough. Power was addictive, but so was the feeling that they could protect themselves. He'd always known where their desire came from, just as he knew he was the only one who could feed them.

Soon enough, they would pick apart his bones and suck them clean for one last piece of magic.

"Elric?" Jessamine said, and he was drawn back into the present. The two women stared at him as though waiting for the answer to a question he hadn't heard them ask.

Pushing aside the anxiety, he focused on them instead of the churning memories inside him. "What did you say?"

"Are we going to help her?" Sybil asked, presumably again.

He stared at his gravesinger, knowing what her answer would be. Jessamine had been through much, but there was still a girl inside of her who wanted a family. She desperately needed connection, and he'd be lying if he said that didn't sting.

For him, she was enough. He could end the world now and spend the rest of his immortal life with just her, and that would be a life he was pleased with.

But his Jessamine needed more than just that. So he was bound to provide it.

Sighing, he stood and savored the ache in his knees and the bite of a small pebble digging into the back of his thigh as he rose. Life wasn't all about pleasure, and he would forever savor the slight sting of pain while he could still feel it.

"Come," he said gruffly as he started toward the manor. "I will not speak of this where anyone can hear our words."

He could feel the looping of chains around his shoulders, digging into his flesh as the woman finished her sacrifice and the cow's blood spilled in a field far from here. He was bound to witches. Elric had spent centuries serving them and feeding upon their sacrifices so they in turn could gorge themselves on his magic. Every step felt like another inch toward that same dangerous cycle.

2

Jessamine was practically vibrating by the time they made it back to the manor. No one spoke. The few times she tried to ask a question, both Elric and Sybil cast her a glance that said she needed to shut her mouth. But she didn't understand why they weren't speaking.

There was no one here. No one had come to the manor since she'd lived here, and certainly not for a while before that. Surely no one would overhear them.

But neither Elric nor Sybil said a word until they were inside. Even then, Jessamine trailed along behind them toward the kitchen, which was odd on its own. Elric preferred meeting in the tombs or the room with all of his siblings' statues. He rarely met with them in the kitchen because that was where Sybil was at her strongest.

Surely that wasn't a good sign. He never gave Sybil the upper hand.

Elric stayed by the door, leaning against its frame with his arms crossed over his chest. He wouldn't even make eye contact with Jessamine; instead, he stared at the floor.

Sybil started pulling herbs down from where they hung on the ceiling, muttering to herself as she started cooking.

"You only cook when you're nervous," Jessamine said. "Another witch is a good thing, isn't it?"

"In a way," Sybil muttered. "Another witch could mean many things. Perhaps she is one of our coven that I missed from the old days. That would probably not be a good thing, considering some of the witches in the coven were more bloodthirsty than others."

"They were all bloodthirsty," Elric interjected. Jessamine noticed his hands were clenched into fists against his ribs. "That is the least of our worries. I remember them all, Sybil. This is not one of the originals."

"Ah, well." Sybil set a cutting board down hard on the island. The sharp crack made Jessamine jump as the witch continued to speak. "Might I suggest that with the Deathless One back in his physical form, more magic has been released into this world? Those who have a proclivity to magic may be feeling that power more than before."

"She knew the old words," he interjected, the words almost sounding . . . sad. "She said them right. Someone trained her."

"Then it is a witch we do not know who has decided to worship you over others." Sybil appeared troubled. Her brows drew down in concentration as she placed a green pepper and an onion on the cutting board. The pepper was slightly rotten, and the onion was a little mushy. "I don't know if that's a good thing or a bad thing."

Jessamine was having a hard time following. "Isn't a new witch a good thing? You two were so adamant that I should accept who I was as a witch, so I find it perplexing that the two of you are uninterested in this new person."

Neither of them spoke.

Jessamine looked between them both. They were hiding something from her. Elric was still looking at the floor, a frown on his face and those brows creating furrows that looked like the number eleven between his eyes. Sybil was staring at her cooking, chopping the vegetables a little too hard. The knife in her hand left gouges in the wood of the cutting board, and the blade flashed unnaturally fast.

Neither of them spoke, clearly waiting for the other to say something. And here she was, in the dark, like she always seemed to be.

She leaned forward and braced her elbows on the kitchen island. "All right. Which one of you is going to explain this to me?"

Sybil flinched before cutting the green pepper so hard that the knife stuck in the cutting board. She sighed, leaving the knife where it was. "We wanted you to accept who you were as a gravesinger because you were the only person who could bring him back to life. A resurrection is done by a gravesinger and a gravesinger alone."

"Yes, you've made it ever so clear that I am not the same as a regular witch." And that still stung a bit. "I don't see how a gravesinger is okay, but a witch isn't."

Elric's foot shifted on the floor, and both women froze to look over at him. His shoulders had lifted in discomfort, just slightly. Enough that Jessamine noticed how uneasy he was.

His voice was raspy and low as he replied. "Another coven member makes the coven stronger, that much is certain. But another witch brings her own wants and desires. Needs we cannot control. Sacrifice makes me stronger and feeds into my power, but I have to make another witch powerful in return for that sacrifice if I accept it."

"And that is bad because?"

"Because a witch can ask for anything in return. A witch is unpredictable. We do not know this woman or what she will want. We only know that she worships me now, and that comes with its own chains."

Looking at him, she finally realized where his fear came from.

More witches meant more people who might want to hurt him. Another witch would likely bring up the idea of sacrificing him again, depending on what she wanted or what the kingdom needed. Witches were selfish at the best of times. But then, who wasn't when they lived in a kingdom that was crumbling at their feet?

Sybil's honeyed voice broke through the silence after Elric's declaration. "Witches are stronger together. A coven is the most powerful group of women that has ever existed. We live and breathe for each other. Our magic comes from the Deathless One, yes. He gifts it to us as you have seen him gift to me. He would need to bind himself in the same way to this new woman. He can give and take the magic that she has, and in return, the sacrifices we make in his name give him more power."

"That all sounds like a good thing." But Jessamine understood why it wasn't as well.

Another woman. Another mind. Things could be complicated, depending on who this woman was. But there was a particular phrase that Sybil had said which stuck with her above all else.

"Witches are stronger together," Jessamine repeated. She reached for Nyx, dragging the cat into her lap so she had something soft to pet. "That's what this all boils down to. It doesn't matter what we think or want or fear. We are stronger together, and in times like these, I think we need to look toward strength."

There was a flare of pride in Sybil's eyes, and perhaps something a little greedy as well. "If we want to look toward power, gravesinger, then sacrifice is the only option."

In a flash, Elric disappeared.

Sybil cursed. "I shouldn't have said it like that. I should have known he would—"

"It's all right," Jessamine interrupted. "I'll get him."

"Jessamine." Sybil grabbed her arm, forcing her to remain where she was. "You're right, you know. We need to build a coven if we're going to continue to support you. I know he believes a god can mold this world into his own image, but it will be easier for people to see you as a queen if you do not have a god king at your side."

The words echoed in her mind as she slipped out of the kitchen. First, she looked in the room where the statues of his family still stood. But he wasn't in their shadow, as she often found him. Nor was he in the great room with the chandelier still broken in the center of the floor. She'd almost given up on finding him before she passed by the door to her bedroom and noticed that the curtain had been shifted.

Carefully moving it aside, she found him sitting on her bed. Back rounded, head in his hands, he looked like someone had draped an old jacket there and left it forgotten in a pile.

"Elric," she murmured, stopping in front of him.

"Don't," he replied in those raspy tones. "I know what I have to do."

"You don't have to do anything."

"You heard what she said. A sacrifice is the next reasonable step." He removed his hands from his face, looking up at her with dark rings around his eyes and the weight of the world on his shoulders.

She'd never seen him look so tired. Not sad or worried or plagued with fear. Just bone-deep tired.

Dragging her thumbs gently along those dark circles, she stepped between his legs as he looped his arms around her hips. "What are you so afraid of?"

"They will beg you to sacrifice me soon enough. And someday soon you will see the reason in it. You will regret your vow to me, but a vow to a god cannot be broken." His hands spasmed against her back. "You will die trying to protect me, and there is no way to stop the future that barrels toward us. The coven is just the first step toward that end."

"The coven will be what we make it," she insisted. "You will be the god we serve and you will not have to die."

"It is a pleasant dream."

"A dream we will sew into the fabric of reality." Jessamine tugged him forward, pressing their foreheads together as she breathed him in. "We need her, Elric. I need to take this throne back the right way. We cannot destroy this kingdom without giving them a reason to trust me before we do it."

Please, she thought. *Please believe me.*

Because in the end, this was all his choice. Elric was the beast that dogged their steps. The blackened shape that took on the form of their nightmares. Without him, they were nothing. Just a duo of witches who had no real power.

He sighed, and the breath played across her collarbone. "Get your scrying bowl, gravesinger."

"Why?"

"I want to find this witch who sacrifices such a great deal to me. I want to know who she is, and where she is."

"Can't you just go to her?" Jessamine leaned back to look into his eyes. "You always just appeared to me."

"Because I wanted to." His gaze moved over every one of her features, and she could see when he looked at them. Reveled in the darkness of her eyes, lingered along the slightly down-turned edges of her lips, and basked in the savagery of the scar across her throat. "I do not wish to appear to this witch so easily. The worship of a god should never be simple, Jessamine Harmsworth. It should be a labor of belief."

He released his hold on her hips so she could get her scrying bowl. The behemoth made of silver was hard to move, especially when she filled it with water. So she made certain it was in the perfect spot before she began the spell.

Elric approached behind her, his hands on her hips as he guided her words. The spell fell from her lips with ease, even as the heat between them built. As always, she felt the tension of their magic that always summoned her baser needs.

She could feel the breath in his lungs feathering down her shoulders and across her collarbone. His hands clenched at her sides, the grip almost too tight and yet inspiring so many memories.

They'd only had one night of passion after they'd defeated Callum. One night that she dreamed of every single moment that she could. A flash of a memory burned behind her eyes as she closed them, tilting her head back against his shoulder and breathing in his scent. She knew how strong those hands were. She knew now what it was like to feel him gripping her thighs as he plunged inside her.

She knew the taste of his passion, and she wanted more than just a lingering sip of it.

"Focus, gravesinger," he murmured in her ear as she arched against him. "Focus on what you seek."

What she sought was him. It was the taste of him, the magic of him, the power that surged through her body with every thrust.

"Bend to my will." His voice echoed in her mind, like it was part of her. Like he was already inside her. "Open your eyes and find the witch who worships me."